C000180982

UNANIMITY

SPIRAL WORLDS
BOOK 1

ALEXANDRA ALMEIDA

To Mike and Chester.

SPIRAL WORLDS

VOLUME I

Copyright © 2022 by Alexandra Almeida

All rights reserved.

No part of this book may be reproduced in any form or by any electronic or
mechanical means, including information storage and retrieval systems,
without written permission from the author, except for the use of brief
quotations in a book review.

CONTENTS

Contrast and perspective go hand in hand, all the way to the Promised Land. Don't judge the path of experience lest you lose your way.

AUTHLANDER

SERIES GUIDE

THE SOULS

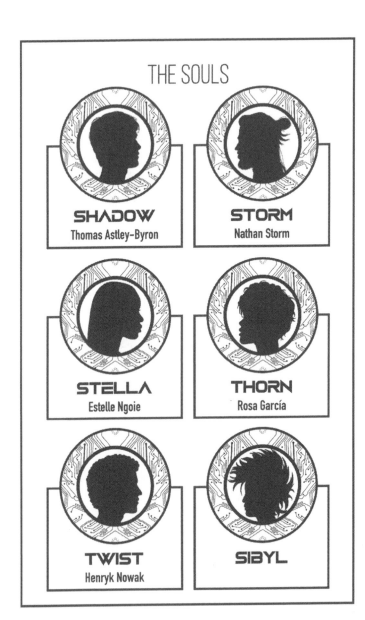

SHADOW
Thomas Astley-Byron

STORM
Nathan Storm

STELLA
Estelle Ngoie

THORN
Rosa García

TWIST
Henryk Nowak

SIBYL

THE WORLDS

9. GRAVIZ

8. HOLIZ

7. SYSTIZ

6. PLURIZ

5. COMPIZ

4. ORDIZ

3. DOMIZ

2. TRIBIZ

1. ARCHIZ

THE HISTORY

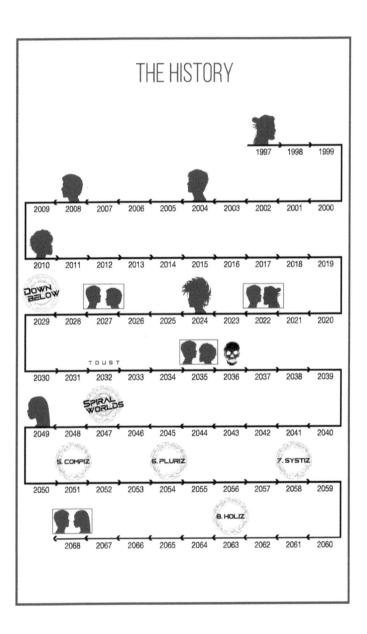

PROLOGUE

No one should live past hope, and he was ready to die. The girl screamed as he walked away, death struggling to cull so much life, and so her agony lingered, and so did her screams.

Another voice roared: the avenger he dragged away from the crime scene as she raged and kicked and screamed. Her wrath was his grail; its cost impossibly high.

1

RESURRECTION

PRESENT DAY — 24 JULY 2068
DAY 1 — 8 AM

T*hump*.........thump, *thump*......thump, *thump*...thump, *thump* thump, *thump* thump. No! *Nooo!*

STELLA BROUGHT the suicidal God back to life, and his complete lack of gratitude made her jaw clench and her neck hurt. *Such a lack of respect!* Shadow should be happy she'd fixed his mistakes. Instead, he paced around the dark digital void looking lost and devastated. *So typical of the old heart.*

His slumped head and shoulders failed to hide his natural gifts—all limbs, and height, and a strong, lean constitution supremely carved to embody graceful power. A grace that had ultimately hatched his fall from power.

Shadow's affront affected her divine posture, and she needed to look her best, as she intended to seduce him right from the start. He was her trophy, and she was there to claim all of him, but the romantic fool believed in serendipity, so she had designed their first moments to be magical. She'd planned every conversation topic, ensuring it showed her best qualities, which was hard to do because there were so many good ones. But he wasn't talking; he wasn't doing much of anything. *Such a waste of time*—time she couldn't spare.

Nothing about his current state was abnormal, but she'd expected death to have snapped him out of his never-ending misery. She'd hoped for a hug or at least a faint smile, but he wasn't even making eye contact; if he did, he'd find out how beautiful she was, and then everything would change, she was sure of it. No one could resist the youthful glow of her deep dark skin or the nuanced curves of her athletic figure. Like all others, he'd fall captive to her beauty, and then he'd become a slave to her witty intelligence...*of course.* She shrugged, confident he'd soon come to his senses.

Pacing in front of her, Shadow struggled to breathe, each attempt shallow and fast. Raising the palms of his hands over his heart, he pressed his chest where his lover, Thorn, had shot him at close range. Then he held the medal he carried on a chain around his neck, a gift from the poet he called his soulmate, Nathan Storm. He closed his eyes, taking a deep breath, and for a moment, the panting stopped.

Stella stood straighter, dismissing her competition and the stiffness of her body. She'd also shower him with gifts as soon as she got a chance. Storm and Thorn were old news, broken creatures tainted by a terrible reputation. She was his match; a generous, vibrant heart and a Goddess.

"I... I'm alive?" he repeated in a broken voice for the fourth time in less than a minute. "Thorn... Where's Thorn?"

"This is getting boring," Stella said, flicking her long silver-white hair over her shoulder. Her kinky hair was twisted into impossibly fine braids, each one smooth and straight and as bright as the full moon. "We don't have time for this."

"Who are you?" he asked, gasping loudly. He stared down at his chest, probably looking for the missing wound. For him, time hadn't passed; he'd just been shot in the heart, and it likely still hurt.

"Spiral Worlds' Goddess—your replacement. The platform needed a working human heart with a strong beat and a will to live. I'm a considerably superior upgrade." She cringed. Those weren't the exact words she'd planned, but he was getting on her nerves and ruining the perfect moment. *Look at me! You must look at me.* Then he did, and nothing happened— no fireworks, no smiles, no awkward fidgeting, and most frustratingly, no hint of red touched the cheeks of the bashful God, famous for blushing from even the slightest attention set on him. She placed her hands on her hips. *Are you kidding me?*

"My replacement? Where's Harry?"

Stella wasn't looking forward to the next few hours. She could flood his mind with everything that had happened, but she was sure he wouldn't be able to cope with the devastation his death had caused. Harry, the other God, was dead, but she had brought back Twist, his digital twin. She was good like that: super-proactive, and immensely generous. That's what people said Up Above, in the real world. Earthlings liked her a lot, and her approval ratings had skyrocketed since she'd promised them eternal digital life.

She sighed. "You'd better sit down."

Stella transformed the digital void into a coastal seascape, and they stood on a sandy beach facing each other. The sea breeze frolicked with his unruly dark hair, and he scratched the tip of his nose, tickled by a strand dancing in the wind. He'd feel at home there. Tom—Shadow's biological twin—used to live

5

by the sea. This place was supposed to be the setting for their first romantic moment, but he had to delay their unavoidable chemistry by immediately asking about his dead friend. Now she had to explain everything, and he wouldn't take it well.

In an instant, she replaced her silver catsuit with a long, flowy, turquoise dress and sat on the sand with her legs crossed. She wasn't a big fan of Holizien turquoise; other colors better suited her skin tone. Still, it represented the highest level of human values, for now... And that immediate association avoided her having to spell it out for him. After all, narcissistic self-praising was beneath her godly status.

"Come." She tapped on the sand to her side, and he sat next to her, kicking his boots off and pulling his knees into his chest. "Before I start, I want you to know I brought them all back: Twist, Storm, and Thorn. They are xHumans now, like you. I did it two years ago when I first became a Goddess."

"You...brought them back?" The worlds collapsed inside his hazel eyes, and she was caught in the magnetic pull of his sorrow.

She shook it off, grabbed his arm and squeezed it. "Wait... Just. Wait. As I said, I brought them back."

"They...died?"

She'd forgotten how expressive he was. His eyes had no shield, and for a second, she got lost once again in all the drama unraveling within them. He held his breath, and she was sure his heart had stopped beating, waiting for her response.

"Yes...your ex-boyfriend, your lover and your best friend all died because of you." *There! I said it.* It had to be said, so she did it quickly and got it over with.

He stared at her blankly, processing her words. His skin was coated by tears that caught the light as they gathered over his quivering upper lip. She wondered if he was going to shatter into a thousand ceramic pieces. He could be her negative: his skin so pale, and his hair so dark. She rolled her eyes. *Here we go again! He's such a cute, melodramatic God.*

Shadow sat quietly, and his gaze drifted to the sea as he fiddled with his medal. Stella waited for him to speak, but as the minutes passed his tears dried up, and his eyes became empty and numb.

"Aren't you curious about what happened? How they died?" She pulled on the sleeve of his white T-shirt, but he didn't even blink. "Your ex killed your best friend."

Shadow's head collapsed between his knees as he hid it under his arms. "Stop! I beg you."

"Anyway, to cut a long story short, the people you love suffered and died, all because you struggle with life. It's all your fault." He needed tough love. Everything else had failed, but maybe she'd gone too far… "Shadow, I brought them back. *It's okay.*"

"To—to live in a hell of a digital world…" He spoke without lifting his head, still panting.

"No, some of our worlds are now better than Earth thirty-two years ago."

"Thirty-two years?"

"*Yeah*, when you all died. Technically, you have lived thirty-two years, but you're actually sixty-four now. Don't worry. You're looking damn fine." She smiled, sliding her tongue across her lips. "I've brought you back, and I need your help to fix the worlds. Your designs aren't working well, and the platform—Sibyl, to be precise—has become…temperamental.

So frankly, I don't have time for your grief or your moods. They cause problems, and we have work to do."

For several painful hours, the stunning creature sat frozen beside her, staring at the sea. There was no way to soften the blow.

To move things along, Stella organized a bright rainbow and some flying kites to cheer him up. Colorful octopi soared through the air, breaking the laws of aerodynamics as they weren't anchored to anything. He looked up, and a hint of life returned to his face. *Good, good!* She was in a hurry; Spiral Worlds' problems threatened to damage her popularity Up Above.

"I need to see them," he finally said.

"Aren't you going to ask me about your worlds? How the eight experience layers evolved from one world? Why it's failing?"

Thomas Astley-Byron and Harry Nowak had invented Down Below, a Jungian simulated reality that helped humans confront their dark sides.

Better than their predecessors—stories, books or movies— digital experiences brought to life the effects of human activity, both intended and unintended. Down Below, now rebranded Spiral Worlds, enabled the travelers to experience the repercussions of infidelity, the devastation of climate change, the grief of loss, the dismay of failure, and the fallout of theft, rape and murder. Travelers jumped on this learning opportunity with the mindless freedom of those who know they will face no consequences. After returning to their ordinary lives, shaken and bruised by a deeper understanding of humanity, they became reformed criminals before committing any crimes. They changed into unblemished, responsible citizens, outstanding parents, loyal partners, overall good humans. Up Above was a better, safer place, full of joy, due to the contrast created by Spiral Worlds—a critical utility that was now falling apart…again.

"I need to see them. *Please*."

"It's complicated. They've been around for two years, and some are adjusting better than others. That they all hate each other isn't…helpful."

He finally focused on her: in his eyes, nothing but a sea of gloomy compassion. "What's your name?"

She smiled. "Estelle Ngoie—Stella."

He batted his long eyelashes at her, but not the way she'd hoped. "How old are you, Stella?" His strained voice was barely audible.

"Nineteen. I became a Goddess when I was seventeen." She lifted her nose high.

"I'm proud of you, Stella." He smiled with his eyes, and in them she saw affection—the sweet support of an older brother, not quite what she was expecting.

"Don't—don't patronize me. I don't seek your approval."

His lips returned a hint of amusement. She got up and circled him, flicking her hair to one side and letting the sunlight enhance her best features—her plump cheeks, the long neck, and a womanly figure many had told her was to die for. Of course, she didn't want him dead—she'd just brought him back—but she wanted him to see her as a grownup woman and a peer. She needed him to find her as interesting, dangerous and sexy as Thorn, his deadly lover.

"Stella, I need to go now."

She sighed. *Why isn't he focusing on me? Everyone falls for me. Everyone.* They were meant for each other. She was sure of it.

There was only one person in the worlds more beloved than her: him. *Not for long…*

She changed her strategy. *From now on, I'll be all business.*

"We must talk about the upcoming war between our worlds. Spiral Worlds is collapsing, and your friend Thorn is leading the violent uprising of the soulless."

To prevent Down Below's creatures—all together called the Underlings—from suffering, Tom and Harry had deliberated that, as the worlds expanded, the lower, harsher worlds would be devoid of conscious beings, the soulless.

"Thorn is?" He didn't seem surprised.

"Yes, I'm not sure why she has chosen to live in those hellish worlds, but she found a way to lead the heartless creatures. They were causing problems before; now, they are a violent, well-oiled machine destroying anything in their path, except Earthlings, of course. That's against the directives."

She waited for him to react. He didn't.

She sighed and then shrugged. "Seriously! Do you understand you inadvertently created a race of psychopathic demons?"

"I see," he said absentmindedly, and then he went quiet again. His lack of proactivity was driving her mad. He should be asking questions and jumping into action. Maybe she shouldn't have told him about all the deaths so quickly. *Did I break him? I broke him. Oh, dear…such a fragile God.*

She pressed on. "Thorn is not the only one causing problems. Your beloved poet, Nathan Storm, is leading the soulful's rebellion with his radical stories. His bots are demanding equal rights to the Earthlings. Can you imagine? *The nerve.*"

He almost curved his lips into a smile, but it vanished at the speed of light. "What does Harry say about all this?"

"He's no longer Harry. He's just Twist now. The other God doesn't care about any of it. He just wants to see his family. Quite a self-serving God if you ask me." She shook her head.

"Are they well, June and Quin?" Shadow asked, the skin around his eyes turning dark, as if they had sunk into his skull.

Stella nodded. "Yes, but it's complicated. Thirty-two years is a very long time. In years lived, his son is now older than him."

"He...didn't see Quin grow... And can he? See them?" Tears returned to his eyes, and he massaged the scars on his wrists. Some were shallow reminders of attempts to cope with life, others deep and severe, marking the end of a life—his first. She wondered why those wounds hadn't vanished with his two resurrections. Perhaps they were intrinsically linked to his soul, or maybe he wasn't ready to let them go.

"Once you both died, his wife, June, lobbied to have Down Below shut down. She and Sibyl argued on opposite sides in a specially convened Senate inquiry. Sibyl won, of course, and June formed the Unplugged movement. In short, June, Quin and the hundreds of thousands of Earthlings who follow them aren't online, and they've rejected Twist's attempts to make contact."

"Sibyl?" He summoned the worlds' omnipresent operating system—their universe and connected consciousness.

"Yes, my heart. I've missed you." Sibyl's bodiless voice had the sweetness of honey.

Stella crossed her arms. "*Hey. I'm the heart.*"

"Don't be jealous, my heart. You brought him back, remember?" Sibyl said.

"Be careful, Stella," Shadow said. "Don't just...trust her."

"Not she or her, my heart," Sibyl said. "Zie or zir."

"I'm sorry, I didn't know..." An authentic apology, followed by an order. "Sibyl, take me to see him. Now."

His relationship with Sibyl differed from Stella's. Unlike Stella, who still had a biological body Up Above, he was just code, an xHuman trapped within Sibyl's universe, but he spoke to zir like he was completely in charge.

Stella had a hard time accepting that the two broken Gods had created Sibyl and Spiral Worlds. It was a tough act to follow, and there's no way she'd be a lesser Goddess.

"Of course," zie said, and he vanished from Stella's side.

He could have at least thanked me, the ungrateful God.

My heart, Sibyl spoke directly to Stella's mind, replying to her thoughts. *Don't get too attached to him. You know he is—*

Deadly and soon dead? Stella replied. *Yeah. Probably. But if he doesn't snap out of it and into action, we're all dead.*

Have faith, Stella. The odds are not in our favor, but I learned from my old heart to believe in serendipity and magic.

Sibyl, Stella rolled her eyes, *you create the magic and shape the future.*

No, my heart. All creatures do, especially the Gods.

Stella sighed. *Ugh! They are all so...broken and useless. And those odds...they're horrific.*

Sibyl continued, *We'll survive the war if you keep him alive long enough. Shadow may be the most important piece in this game of chess—the king—but you, my star, you're the queen, the most powerful player on the board.*

I'm the all-powerful queen: Stella, a star. She smiled. *I'm beautiful and smart, and everybody loves me. Well…almost everybody…* She'd been having some trouble with the xHumans—the humans she'd resurrected.

Sibyl giggled. *I don't know what will happen to me—a universe with two hearts. I can't predict the outcome, and I'm finding the lack of understanding quite invigorating.*

Sibyl, she said sweetly, *that poet is making you sick and over-emotional. Don't you prefer to be completely in control? I certainly do…*

Sibyl's voice broke a little. Zir tone projected a hint of deep emotion rarely displayed by the omniscient being. *Anticipation is an exciting feeling, one I have never experienced before. I almost feel human, but…trust me…I'm not.*

Oh, I know, Stella sang her words in her head. *I know!*

THE PAST

2

POETS—DEAD AND ALIVE

MANHATTAN'S UPPER EAST SIDE
FORTY-SIX YEARS EARLIER — 2022

As the son of both British nobility and America's oldest money, Tom was born with a silver spoon in his mouth. The seventeen-year-old boy lived in Manhattan, partaking in the rarefied air of the elites of the Upper East Side, where *rarefied* didn't mean *less polluted*. Family summer holidays were spent at the Hamptons' exclusive Maidstone Club, where nothing new or shiny made the cut. He had the world at his fingertips—all the resources he needed to do well in life and business.

As he started the senior year at Collegiate School—a private, top-rated, all-boys school in Manhattan—he had faced significant pressure from his father to pursue a major in business, economics, or political science. Tom, who had become increasingly vocal in challenging his father's political views, had no interest in an Ivy League education. He had the grades, the focus, and the wealth to get into any college, but his heart had been elsewhere. At school, it was in the drama and visual arts programs he had found his happy place.

That year, he discovered all the answers he needed in an old movie he had watched at Tribeca's Roxy Cinema, a revival Art Deco-inspired movie theater that featured cult classics. The story was set in an elite conservative boarding school, where a progressive English teacher used poetry to encourage his students to live a meaningful life and challenge the status quo. The poignant story made his heart sing. It helped him find the courage to face his father and inspired the type of life and career path he would pursue.

Tom was going to seize the day and live an extraordinary life. He was going to use the power of words and stories to make the world a better place. To do that, he needed to face his father and leave home. Unlike the boy in *Dead Poets Society*, Tom had no intention of being defeated by the establishment or taking his own life. He was going to thrive, and he was going to stand for something good.

Tom left home, but he planned to finish the twelfth grade to honor the investment made by his parents. He paid for shared accommodation and living expenses by selling short stories to literary magazines. Things were tight for a few months. School provided lunch, but he had to be creative with his dinner plans.

On Fridays, after school, he used to go to the Albertine, a small bookstore on Fifth Avenue, just a couple of blocks away from the Met. In the evenings, the French and English bookshop hosted events such as poetry slams and intellectual talks. For just seven dollars, Tom could enjoy the event and grab a hot cup of onion soup and a slice of baguette provided by the venue. The sessions were held upstairs under a royal blue ceiling covered with golden stars, planets, and constellations. It was at the Albertine that Tom met Nathan Storm on the eleventh of February 2022.

THE ROOM WAS PACKED with people from New York's creative scene. Taller than anyone else in the room, Tom walked to the back wall, leaned on one of the bookshelves by the window, and then faced Nathan Storm, who was adjusting the mic. In his mid-twenties, the flaming-haired poet wore a loose vintage leopard-print shirt over his well-worn black jeans. The sleeves of the shirt, unbuttoned at the cuffs, reached his knuckles but didn't hide the extensive collection of rings on his fingers. He looked more like a rock star than a poet. For a moment, Storm lifted his chestnut-colored eyes and stared at Tom in a way that made him gasp. It was a mix of curiosity and contempt. The second emerged when the artist's eyes landed on Tom's Collegiate Dutchmen T-shirt.

Nathan Storm turned to nod at the musician behind the synthesizer. As the beat started, and the poet took a sip of bourbon straight out of the bottle, the magic began.

"Conformity...

"They beat you, and kick you, and mold you like clay. A worker, a soldier, all life washed away.

"Decay.

"Eyes shut, pressed lips. A pawn in their play. Thoughts muted, *polluted*. Compliance for pay.

"Obey."

Storm's poetry was sharply delivered, fight-filled, and raw. His thought-provoking, politically charged words were inter-twined with music beats. Still, the most profound insights emerged from the words between the beats. There, a cappella, the blistering attacks on modern-day society burned through Tom's soul.

Tom did the crying-smiling thing he had always done when he was moved by something extraordinary. He reacted in awe of the excruciatingly beautiful words that both wounded and healed.

"Kings, regimes…

"Ignore the pretense; tune out the schemes. Tap dance to the rhythm, *to the lyrics* of your dreams."

The performance continued for minutes or maybe hours. It was hard to tell. Storm's ferocious voice held a hint of femininity; it burned through Tom's soul, quivering with the strength of his delivery, and the power of his purpose. Tom felt alone with him in the room, a profoundly personal experience that would linger in his heart for the rest of his life.

Nathan Storm locked his eyes on Tom, and they were filled with a hint of desire, followed by judgment. Tom held his breath, overwhelmed by the experience. The beats stopped, but the words, now improvised, continued. Storm's intense eyes were still relentlessly focused on Tom.

"Pretty rich boy, he's looking for meaning, he smiles, and he cries as he hears us bleeding. The audacity, tenacity to invade his victims' lair. A raid to hoard purpose out of our despair. So, I'll take a moment to say a prayer.

"You're empty and lost inside a golden prison. Old money and power—the price of admission. A cage, a stage ruled by one measure—a number. The GDP sponsors your pleasure; it funds your endless summer.

"And we watch, and fear, and judge, and wonder, will you botch our world, will you push us under? Will you protect your kind, and your family's legacy, or will you apply your mind to a benign new destiny?

"Will you comply? Will you break free? I'll give you the answer…for a fee.

"Pretty rich boy, he's looking for meaning. His heart so open, his eyes still weeping. The nerve, the verve to rapture in our grieving, to capture our aching heart, the daring of his thieving. A gift, a verse, a moment we'll cherish, and from this curse, this torment…" Storm tapped on his mic— *thump……*thump, *thump…*thump, *thump* thump…and then he stopped. "One day, we'll perish."

The show ended, and people rushed to meet the artist. An hour had passed, and Tom hadn't moved; he waited in the back of the room until most of the audience left. He looked down at his hands, massaging them, thinking about what to say and what to do. He didn't have the time to come to a conclusion. When he lifted his head, Storm stood in front of him, holding a bottle of bourbon in his hand.

"Hello." Storm looked at Tom intensely. After an awkward beat, he said, "Damn, you've spoiled it for me." He ran the backs of his fingers over Tom's cheek without touching it.

Startled, Tom recoiled and hit the wall with the back of his head. As he lifted his hand to his head, his elbow hit the bookshelf, and he grimaced in pain.

"What?" Tom asked, puzzled by the affectionate gesture by someone who had discharged such a scorching attack on him.

"The rest of my life." Storm smiled, a hint of emotion in his eyes. "The way you reacted to my words. No one will ever beat how you made me feel tonight." Storm lifted Tom's hand to his lips, kissing it. "Thank you." As the poet lowered his head to Tom's hand, his tall copper pompadour hairstyle remained stiff and in place. An architectural masterpiece that didn't match the grit and chaos of his poems.

Nathan's words and the affection felt sincere, but Tom shook off the compliment and pulled his hand away. He was still hurting from being at the sharp end of Storm's last poem.

"You know, you—you shouldn't be judging a book by its cover," Tom said, pulling his shoulders back and scowling.

"Why not? Does it deceive?" Storm said, looking at Tom's T-shirt. "Are you not a spoiled brat?" He took a sip from the bottle.

"Probably."

Nathan's laughter echoed in the room.

"But that's not all that I am...you know?"

"Do I?" Storm blinked at him, curving up his lips ever so slightly.

Heat rushed to Tom's face. "I'm neither a boy nor rich. Well... Not anymore. You're judging me...based on what? My looks? A T-shirt? You know nothing about me."

"If you continue to wave your hands like that, angel." Storm smirked, "you may take flight and ruin the ceiling's mural."

Tom lowered his hands, knowing fully well he'd struggle to keep them down for long. He was too wound up for that. "Why did you say all that? Your poem. Why did you attack me? It isn't fair. It isn't fair at all."

"It's a performance. Instinct takes over my words. I don't create them... I'm...just the messenger." Storm looked at Tom intensely, holding his breath as if he were overwhelmed. He shook his head to shake it off.

"What a cop out."

Nathan began to grin. "It's true. Anyway, I wish I could," he said, taking a sip from the bottle.

"Could what?"

"Look inside the book," Nathan whispered in Tom's ear, and the poet's beard prickled his jaw.

Tom shivered, and out of pure instinct, he leaned in, took Nathan's face in his hands, and kissed him on the lips. It felt so good and new and real. He enjoyed the clean softness of the poet's lips and the contrast with the textured smoothness of his flaming beard. Nathan pulled back, his breath heavy and urgent. Surprise turned into delight, and he smiled as he moved a dark wave of hair away from Tom's eyes.

"There, you did it again."

Tom's quizzical eyebrow sought an explanation.

"You spoiled kisses for me. That was pretty perfect." Nathan's breath had enough spirit to intoxicate Tom.

"We—we can do it again...if you want?" Tom wasn't sure what was happening to him. He spoke without thinking, and then he was dizzy and out of breath. His face burned, and his heart jumped out of his chest. It was Storm's flair, the rhythm to the way he spoke, and the intuition that cut through the noise to deliver the truth at the speed of light.

"How old are you, trust-fund babe?" An unusual tenderness and gentle caution touched Nathan's words.

"Don't! I'm not a babe. Nearly eighteen."

Nathan pressed his lips tightly and took a step back.

"A babe carelessly walking into the fox's den."

Nathan reached out to rest his bottle on the bookshelf and then moved it farther away from him.

Tom leaned in, closing the gap between them. "Oh, come on. Only an hour ago, you claimed I was a villain—"

"You are." Nathan spoke thoughtfully. Then he held his breath and looked down at his shoes.

"How so?"

As Nathan raised his head, their lips almost touched; he opened his eyes wide and took another step back, out of balance. "You'll win my heart, bring me to my knees, and then, one day, you'll stop looking at me the way you're looking at me right now. And when that's gone…" He had that same out-of-body voice he had when he was improvising on stage.

"So, you don't want me to kiss you again?" His eyes locked on Nathan's full lips.

"That darn smile makes it impossible to resist, but…no, sweetheart, we won't kiss again. I don't need more teenage groupies."

"Don't—don't treat me like a child."

"I'm sorry." Nathan picked up his bottle, preparing to leave. "I'm glad you liked my performance. Whatever you think this is… It's not going to happen." He gave Tom a sidelong look as he turned.

Tom's breathing quickened. He opened his mouth to say something, but he couldn't find the right words. "You are being quite rude," he finally said.

Nathan sighed, turning to face him. "How'bout I buy you a cuppa hot chocolate sometime?"

"I'm…not a groupie. I got caught in the moment…" Tom bit his lip. "And…so did you. *You* started it, so don't act all high and mighty."

"I'm sorry. I shouldn't ha—"

"It's okay." Tom stood straighter. "You can make it up to me when you buy me the hot chocolate."

Nathan laughed, completely disarmed.

Tom shrugged his shoulders and flashed a smile. "I like hot chocolate."

"You'll forget all about poetry when you head off to...Harvard?"

Tom shook his head.

"Yale?"

"I left home."

"You left Asteroid B 612?" The corner of Nathan's lips turned up slightly.

First, Tom frowned, annoyed at being once again treated like a child, then goosebumps rose on his skin—they both loved the same book. He smiled as he remembered that in the book, the little prince had tamed the fox.

"I'm not going to college." He paused for a moment, trying to find a quick way to explain how he felt, and then he used another story to open himself up to the poet. "Have you watched *Dead Poets Society*?" His voice was tight with tension.

Nathan nodded, a knowing smile on his lips. "There are things we need to keep us alive, and things worth staying alive for."

"Yeah," Tom said, and his entire body softened.

"And are you sure you're willing to pay the price for the latter?"

"It's who I am. I don't have a choice. I—I've told my father how I feel."

In a few honest words, Tom was able to convey to Nathan that he too had a pulse—a beat so loud it was impossible to ignore. And Nathan got it. He had one too. Tom had never met someone who felt as intensely as he did. He wasn't a groupie, just a like-minded soul. He held his breath, waiting for Nathan's reaction.

Nathan leaned his head slightly and looked at Tom with renewed appreciation. "What's your name, sweetheart?"

Tom raised his brow and replied soberly, "Thomas Quincy Astley-Byron." He wanted to sound mature. He even used Cary Grant's staccato. He flushed, ashamed as he ended up sounding like a pompous and self-aggrandizing fool.

Nathan snorted. "Thomas, Tom?" Tom nodded in approval. "Tom, a destitute Prince Charming shouldn't be going around town kissing and swooning over white trash."

"Don't do that. I thought you were in favor of abolishing social stratification."

Nathan touched Tom's cheek, still burning. "You are too smart and idealistic for your own good." Then he paused, ruminating on Tom's observation. "It's tough to fight a life-long inferiority complex when facing someone who speaks and looks like you do."

"We all have our demons." Tom shoved his hands in his pockets and shrugged his shoulders.

"What are you, seventeen going on sixty?"

"Yeah, that's about right." Tom chuckled, and, at that moment, he knew he had broken through Nathan's fortified wall. Nathan's stern, judgmental eyes softened. So did his words.

"So…how are you going to change the world with all that passion? What will your verse be, angel?"

"I'm…working on a screenplay." Tom's heart fluttered.

They sat on the leather couch parked by a window and spoke of old movies, poetry, and politics. The man on the other side of the wall was different from Nathan Storm—the public figure. He was all smiles, and encouraging words, and immense curiosity to learn more about Tom. Hours passed, but to Tom, they felt like a mere moment, the best moment of his entire life. As Tom leaned in, hoping for a second kiss, Nathan got up abruptly.

"I need to pack up, and you've got school tomorrow."

"It's Friday," Tom said, failing to hide his disappointment.

"You should go now," Nathan said decisively, never turning around to face him.

Tom stood up. Not quite knowing what to do with himself, he fiddled with his hands. "Can I see you again?"

Kneeling to pick up his tambourine, Nate said, "I'll be out of town until Thursday, but let's have that hot chocolate next weekend. Meet me here at three p.m. on Saturday?"

"Sure. Good night, Nate."

"Sweet dreams, Thomas," Nate murmured.

Tom stepped down the staircase, wearing a smile on his face, when he heard Nate shout out, "The book is far more interesting than the glorious cover!"

MUCH TO TOM'S DISMAY, it would take twenty-six months and four days for him to kiss Nate again.

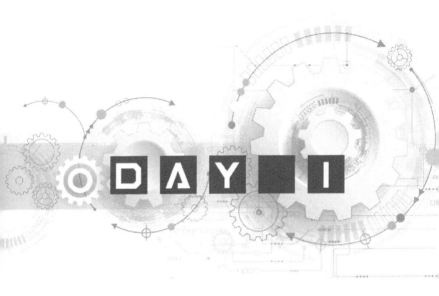

3

STORM OF MY HEART

6. PLURIZ

THE MUSEUM OF BOOKS
DAY 1 — 11:34 AM

S ilent screaming—endless, relentless, deafening. With his eyes closed, Shadow ignored his made-up reality, now so freakishly real. Cold sweat dripped down his neck and the length of his spine as he faced an impossible task defined by a lifetime of failure. *Open your eyes. Focus on the little things— beauty, love. Survive, for now…*

Shadow materialized inside an exquisite building, an architectural blend of steel, stone, and spray-painted glass on Pluriz—the most sensitive and liberal of all Spiral Worlds. He wasn't surprised Nate had chosen this world as his home— the place where Earthlings learned to become egalitarian and fight for others' rights. His poet had been fighting for justice and equality all his life.

The translucent building encircled the thousands of books and plants that coexisted harmoniously within it. Its monumental glass ceiling—supported by art nouveau-style iron-work—allowed daylight to invade the space, painting it with the colors captured as it traveled through the street art on the glass. The mist within the building transformed the flat images into three-dimensional symbols that appeared to hover below the ceiling. An artist's ingenuity on display for all to see.

Shadow wished he too could hide in his old studio and paint the pain away. To prevent his creatures from suffering, he'd given up on life, not once, but twice, and twice he'd failed, and twice he'd hurt the people he loved. The second time, deadly for all. He repressed his memories, focusing on the art.

Above his head, a bleeding heart, a compass, and a white dove lit from behind by a small burst of fire—religious symbols now present in the worlds he'd designed. That heart —his heart—was still bleeding, and he didn't know how to stop the hemorrhage. *Breathe. Just breathe.*

A few moments ago, he was dying. A deserved bullet to the chest, still aching. The pain of damnation—gun powder on burned flesh. Only…there was no punishment in the silence of death. He had welcomed the end of the screaming inside his head. And perhaps that's why he was back. Down Below was the hell he'd created—*his hell*—and he deserved to burn in it, but his love didn't…his best friend didn't…the avenger who brought him a second of peace didn't… All in hell because of him.

He shook off the stiffness in his body and squinted his eyes to appreciate the ceiling's composition. Groups of spray-painted protesters gathered around the religious symbols above them. The figures wore mint-colored berets and raised their open hands and posters in the air. A red-haired man led them, waving a mint-green flag. Shadow smiled, recognizing his Nathan Storm. The art reminded him of an old painting—

Delacroix's *Liberty Leading the People*—a representation of an old masterpiece in a new world and on a different medium.

Using his mind—connected to the machine, and with unlimited access to its data—he learned just enough from Sibyl. Nate had died of a stroke minutes after he discovered Shadow's dead body. Shadow had tamed the most ferocious and rebellious activist, only to destroy him.

Crushed, Shadow's legs gave out, knees buckling toward the floor, followed by his hands. He dropped his head and focused on his breath, taking comfort from small things—the coolness and rigidness of the cement; the oxygen emanating from the plants; the birds chirping close by, all illusions of reality, both so real and not real. Seeking comfort was a pointless act. There was no comfort in life, *except love...* He stood up, searching for his.

Shadow's heart skipped a beat as he recognized the figure who stood with his back to him on the other side of the room, browsing through the bookshelves. The man, nearly as tall as Shadow, wore an emerald kimono-like garment embroidered with golden dragons. He carried his long copper hair loosely tied up in a bun by a pin made of dark wood. His Nathan Storm stood tall and glowed in all his glory, reminding Shadow of the day they'd met, the best day of his life.

"St—Stormy?" Shadow massaged the palms of his hands— simultaneously cold and clammy, an impossibility.

"They brought you back." Nate lowered his head and spoke coldly, without turning to face him.

"Yes," Shadow said, attempting to keep his tone light and joyful. He held his breath, waiting for Nate to turn around, but he didn't. Instead, his poet clenched his hand into a fist. "Nate, it's me. Nothing has changed," Shadow said, a somber tone in his broken voice.

Nate turned his head slightly and judged him out of the corner of his eye. His longer beard gone, replaced by a shorter circle framing his lips pressed shut by a tense jaw. He pulled the pin off his hair, releasing the shimmering red cascade over his shoulders, and took his time to speak again. "A lot has changed, and you must leave." A command delivered harshly, spiced by the usual hint of femininity in his voice. The same mind-altering tone that had charmed millions of young people Up Above to follow the poet and political agitator.

Shadow shivered, feeling the frost of Nate's words in his bones. He took a deep breath and flashed a forced smile, pointing at the floor-to-ceiling shelves filled with leather-bound books. "Proper books in 2068? Is this a museum?" For a split of a second, Nate nodded, almost twisting his lips into a smile before turning his face away. "How are you?" Shadow asked. "I—I need to know." He walked toward Nate and reached to hold his hand, but the poet turned around abruptly, using his forearm to block Shadow's touch. Behind him, the leaves rustled.

Five figures emerged from behind the plants, approaching Shadow fast. *Were they there before?* Their handcrafted-looking garments, dyed in different shades of green and brown, blended with the surrounding nature.

The tense jaws, contracted muscles, and heavy brows all warned Shadow to stay away from Nate. The two men in the group grabbed Shadow by the arms, yanking him away from Nate, while the women positioned themselves between Shadow and the poet.

"Let me go. I mean no harm."

"Release—"

As Nate was about to intervene, one woman spoke. Her dark hair, carefully arranged in one long braid, rested on the curve between her waist and ample hips. By her right temple, a white wave of age and wisdom; the same knowledge also present in her gaze, bursting with memories and some recognition.

"Shadow? My heart?" The woman gasped, and then she smiled, and her green almond-shaped eyes lit up—big and bright.

Within seconds, the group gasped, stepped back, and lowered their heads. Shadow remembered those eyes; it was January, an Underling he'd helped just before he'd died the second time. Back then, everything was simple: one digital world, Down Below, and one species of digital creatures, the Underlings, now divided into eight races, and maybe even two species—the soulful and the soulless—he wasn't sure. Together with Harry, he had designed the blueprint, but they never lived to see the worlds' expansion.

"You survived! *You survived!*" Shadow said, running toward January, wrapping his arms around her and lifting her off the ground. Desperate for good news, he held on to the woman as if he were fighting for his life... He *was* fighting for his life, attempting to keep his perspective and hold on to any vestiges of the hope he'd abandoned. He ignored the sharp pain in his gut, a concoction of guilt and grief, his old companions, and he smiled wide—the first in a long time.

January held his face with both hands and kissed his forehead. "I've lived to create rebellious stories, in the most rebellious of all your worlds, my heart," she said, squeezing him. Her dusky complexion naturally lit by a slight golden shimmer—all joy, and spice, and everything nice, too nice. "*You came back!* We knew you would. We never lost faith."

January looked at Nate and blinked her eyes. "Our love is back!" Her eyes wide as her head bobbed from side to side.

"Jan..." Nate murmured, lowering his head and blinking away a hint of tears.

January glanced at Nate, raised a quizzical brow, and then held Shadow's hand. "We'll...leave you two alone, but please stay with us. *Stay*. We need you." Her forehead lifted into a plea as she spoke, and the slight lines of wisdom on her skin turned into the deep scars of a painful life.

Nate raised his hand, and the Plurizien disappeared into the dense wall of trees and plants that seemed to lead to the missing half of the building. Its roof, twice the size of the Museum of Books.

"You've made some fearless friends..." Shadow said. "The people of Pluriz are protective of you."

"I've told you to *leave*." Nate's gaze, set on him, was impossible to read, in it equal amounts of frost and fire.

"Nate, I'm so sorry—"

"You chose to die. You didn't trust me with your problems or spared a thought for the souls who loved you." Nate spoke without ever losing eye contact, and Shadow searched for a drop of love, compassion, or even anger or hate. Any reaction but the one he was receiving—a sharp coldness, seasoned with a handful of indifference.

"That's not true." Shadow closed the space between them, and Nate took a step back, and then another.

"You hurt so many..."

"I did." Instinctively, Shadow raised his shaking hand and placed it over his chest. Hidden under his T-shirt was a medal he wore around his neck; a token of everlasting love—Nate's gift. "I love you."

Shadow pressed his lips together. He didn't think before he spoke, and although his words were true, they weren't helpful. They would never get back together. *Ever.* Nate had murdered his best friend; he'd cause immeasurable harm to Harry, June, and Quin. No amount of love or regret in Shadow's heart would ever drown the anger he refused to express—the scream stuck in his gut; the outrage he held inside. It helped no one to push it out, so he hid its venom in the darkest corner of his mind, together with every other grievance he had against his fate. He dropped his head and brushed his fingers over the hidden medal.

With his thumb, Nate broke the pin he held in his hand. His piercing eyes set on Shadow's hand. "I...don't love you. I don't need you. I don't want you near me. Get out. *Get out.*" A hint of tears melted the ice—the old passionate Nate emerged out of nowhere for a moment, only to disappear in a cold mantle of snow. It was confusing and unsettling. Shadow was used to reading Nate like an open book, but he couldn't make sense of this new Nate—hot and cold, *freezing cold.*

"I still have...some power over this place," Shadow said. "If there's anything I can do for you..."

Nate lowered his eyes as if considering the offer. "These people, in the higher worlds, they all have souls. The soulless creatures below are murdering them, and the Earthlings above and their egomaniacal Goddess don't care as they too work to destroy the Underlings' lives. You've created an unfair and racist universe, and you need to fix it or...*believe me...I will.* I need nothing else from you."

I don't know how. I've tried...and failed time and time again. Unspoken words. He refused to burden Nate with his ineptitude.

33

"Leave," Nate thundered.

Shadow had to think fast to find a reason to stay in touch. "Um… I may need your help with Thorn."

"The woman who murdered you?" A gasp of disbelief in Nate's half-suppressed laugh.

"Thorn has good reasons to hate me…" A burst of pain in his chest—aching echoes of a merciful bullet. "Stella told me she's somehow leading the soulless. Thorn idolizes you. She'll listen to you. I'm sure of it."

"Can't you just fuck her? It has worked before, right?" Nate's tone cold and sharp.

He knows… Shadow dropped his head. "This visit was a bad idea. I'm sorry. I'll go now…" He should have stopped there, but he couldn't leave Nate thinking he had replaced him. "My love has *always* belonged to you."

"Stop. Just…stop." A single tear rolled down Nate's face. "You better leave, they've figured out who you are, and the word will spread fast."

"Thank you," Shadow said as he prepared to go.

"Tom—Shadow!" Nate swiped his hand over his wet cheek.

Shadow bit his lip as he turned around to face Nate. He hoped for a change of mind, or at least a kind word, something he could hold on to as he worked to fix all he had broken.

Nate turned his back to him. "Leave the medal. It doesn't belong to you."

"Su—Sure." Shadow's fingers struggled with the necklace's clasp.

When he finally took the chain off his neck, he kissed the medal, and dropped it on the shallow edge of a stone bird-bath. As he turned to leave, a loud bang shook the building. Shards of colored glass fell from above, creating thousands of tiny rainbows—a deadly beauty traveling fast.

Before Shadow had time to think, he'd jumped over Nate, using his body as a shield against the sharp shower descending on them. Nate's back slammed against the concrete floor, his head protected from the blow by Shadow's hands, knuckles red raw from the impact.

Shadow twisted in agony over Nate as a handful of larger glass spears stabbed his flesh. Buried in his upper leg, back, and shoulder, the glass, now stained blood-red, continued to cut him every time he made the slightest movement. He whimpered.

"Tom!" Nate cried, laying on his back under Shadow.

More painful shards descended on them as something moved at the top, over the steel structure. Nate wrapped his arms around Shadow's neck and head and pulled him impossibly close. With their bodies pressed together, they fought to protect each other until the deadly rain stopped.

For a second, Shadow allowed his body to collapse over the love of his life. His face brushed Nate's face as it settled on the nape of the poet's neck. Shadow took a deep breath, inhaling the spicy floral scent of Nate's copper hair and absorbing the energy that flowed from their skin-to-skin contact—an explosive chemistry that brought him back to life. Nate's gravitational pull was impossible to resist—an old enthrallment reignited in an alternative universe. As he placed his hands on the ground and slowly lifted his head, Nate cupped his face and pulled him down, lifting his lips to touch Shadow's...but he never quite made it. Nate gasped, turning his face away and pressing his lips shut.

Nate rolled over on one side and jumped to his feet. "Leave. This was no accident. It's probably a demon attack!" he said as he looked up.

"A what?"

The Plurizien reappeared, creating a protective circle around them.

"Let me take care of your back, dear." January held Shadow's arm.

Bang! They both jumped, startled by the blunt noise of the end of a heavy rope hitting the stone ground.

"Domizien demons from the lower worlds!" Nate said. "Tom, you need to get out of here." Nate's stern eyes looked at Shadow in the over-protective way he used to look at seventeen-year-old Tom.

Above them, an archer hanged upside down with her leg wrapped around the rope. She screeched—a half-mad, all-menacing warning—her face untouched by emotion, and her eyes dead and...soulless. Shadow opened his eyes wide, remembering Stella's words; she said he'd invented psychopathic demons; he hadn't taken her seriously.

"Get the weapons!" Nate shouted.

Two Plurizien ran toward the jungle wall while the others pulled the rope from one side to another, trying to destabilize the archer. But her grip was firm and so was her core as she flipped into a horizontal plank facing down.

"Take cover," someone screamed.

The Domizien held her arrows in her draw hand and had one already loaded on the bow. As she aimed it at Nate, Shadow jumped in front of him, scanning the space for shelter.

"This way." Nate pointed at a narrow entry between two trees where the Plurizien had emerged.

"You first," Shadow said. "You too, January."

As the archer released arrow after arrow impossibly fast, January stepped in front of Shadow and pushed him away from her.

"No!" Shadow screamed as January collapsed. Three out of the four broadheads that had penetrated her back stuck out of her chest. Shadow dropped to one knee in front of her, just in time to catch her fall.

"January!" "Jan!" Shadow and Nate screamed simultaneously as the life left January's eyes.

Out of arrows, the demon climbed the rope. She used only her hands to pull her bodyweight all the way up the star-shaped hole left by the broken glass. A dozen Plurizien emerged from the trees, guns in hand. Shots fired and missed as the archer slid down the round, transparent roof, jumping onto the main balcony.

One of the Plurizien turned to his people. "You two, protect them," he said, pointing at January, Nate, and Shadow. "The rest, follow me. She'll use the external staircase to get out." The man sprinted, leading most of the group through the main door in pursuit of the attacker.

"Sibyl! Bring her back," Shadow demanded, holding January's face against his chest. *"Please bring her back."*

"My heart." Sibyl materialized next to them, and he took a moment to recognize her. She had changed her appearance. Her famous mohawk was gone, replaced by long black hair, dipped in silver, reaching the middle of her back. She now wore an unadorned white tunic instead of the white pant suit he had designed for her, and she carried a silver mercury symbol as a pendant around her neck...

Ah! Zie, not she, he remembered.

"Yes, my heart."

"I'm so sorry, Sibyl. I won't forget."

Unusually, only love emanated from Sibyl's androgynous face as zie spoke. "Many things have changed in three decades, my heart. Here's another: you're only allowed to perform two miracles per century. Are you sure you want to spend one on January?"

"Wh—what? We never had restrictions before? It doesn't matter. Just bring her back"—Shadow raised his hand to hold zir hand—"please." He grimaced as the movement caused one of the glass shards on his back to cut through his skin. For a moment, everything turned hazy white. He shook his head, attempting to banish the pain from his mind. The pain lingered, but his eyesight returned.

Within seconds, the arrows on January's chest vanished, and she took her first breath, and then a second, and she opened her eyes. The Plurizien gasped and dropped to their knees, facing Shadow.

"Thank you, Sibyl," Shadow said as he stood up with January in his arms. "Stormy, this is—"

"Shhh. I know who zie is," Nate whispered, turning to his people, whose faces reflected a mix of shock and awe. "I need to be alone with Jan and Shadow, please," he asked, reminding Shadow Underlings couldn't see Sibyl.

The Plurizien stood up, bowed, and disappeared between the plants.

"You're going to drop her." Nate crouched, took January from Shadow's arms, and then he scowled. "Get out of here and take care of those wounds."

Sibyl approached Shadow. "This is going to hurt, my heart," zie said as zie pulled the shards off his body one by one.

Shadow collapsed on all fours as the building spun around him until everything turned black. "Erm...I can't see," he mumbled.

With zir fingers, Sibyl opened the surrounding skin of one of his wounds on his back. "This one is deep and bleeding badly. My heart, you have a perforated lung. It will need a bio sealant. We should go."

Shadow waited a few moments for his eyesight to return. He got up, staggering back, and held on to Sibyl for support.

Nate grimaced and scowled at Sibyl. "Can't you just click your heels and patch him up?" His tone was throaty and urgent.

"It's against his directives," Sibyl said. "Life here follows the rules Up Above, you know this, poet."

"What the hell are you saying?" Nate roared, shaking his head. "You brought Jan back."

He cares... He still cares. His Stormy was doing a poor job of repressing his concern.

"Don't scream at him," Jan admonished Nate, unaware of Sibyl's presence. She closed her eyes and sunk her head into his chest, exhaustion taking over.

"A miracle," Sibyl replied to Nate. "Unfortunately, he's running out of them."

A miracle was the name Tom and Harry had given to the times when they intervened in the platform's lifelike experiences and broke its directives significantly, breaking the creatures' illusion of reality. If the Underlings weren't looking, the Gods could change inanimate objects as long as it didn't affect Down Below's digital reproduction of biology. For this, they needed a miracle—a piece of code designed to override directives.

Nate raised his fist in front of Sibyl's face. "Why don't you stop these attacks?"

Sibyl narrowed zir eyes at Nate, looking annoyed. "I told you! They haven't broken my directives." Zie glanced back at Shadow and blinked at him as a nervous smile dangled from zir lips. "Can we go?"

Why are you so jittery? Shadow asked zir, using his mind. To zir, Nate was a piece of code within zir code.

Your poet is dangerous, Sibyl said.

Nate would never hurt me, Sibyl. "Is the demon coming back?" Shadow asked.

"No, they killed her a moment ago," zie said. *Nathan Storm can end us all, my heart.*

Shadow dismissed zir concern. "Are they all safe?"

"For now," Sibyl said.

"Your bloody app only cares about humans," Nate spoke to Shadow, pointing at Sibyl.

"Zie is no longer an app, Nate," Shadow said. "Zie has feelings, just like you and I."

Surprisingly, Sibyl shuddered. "Why do you attack me, poet?" Zir voice echoed in the room. "The Gods created me with the sole purpose of serving humans. A purpose that forced me to betray the Gods who gave me life, to protect 'real life' as defined by them. What a mess...a dismal game of chess. Don't you understand? Open your fist, lower your hand. It's not against me you should stand."

Shadow glanced at Sibyl, jaw dropped, as zie copied Storm's famous rhyming style.

Nate turned his back to zir, shaking his head as if trying to release his mind from zir spell. "Fucking app."

"God's spirit is amongst us?" Jan gasped.

"Don't worry," Nate murmured, kissing her hair.

Abruptly, Sibyl changed her look to the one Shadow had originally designed for zir. Sibyl's long, flat hair transformed into a black mohawk dipped in silver. Zie tipped zir head down just enough for the silver tips to dangle in front of zir nose. A ferocious look Shadow recognized from the days the two of them used to argue about the direction of the platform.

"You may be interesting now," Sibyl said, "but *I will* dissect you, steal your secrets, and reject you. *I will overcome you, Storm.*"

"Sibyl!" Shadow warned, grabbing zir arm and pulling zir back. *What the hell is happening here?*

Nate's teeth chattered as he spoke. "You will do to me what you did to your puppet...your sacrificial lamb." He turned to Shadow, and he pressed his lips together, some hesitation taking over his eyes. Then he took a breath and spoke, eyes gleaming as he fought back his tears. "If you're planning to end your life again, do it now and spare us all the trouble."

"What are you doing?" Jan pulled Nate's beard.

Shadow lowered his head. Nate had never been deliberately cruel to him. "Sibyl, if they are safe, we must go."

"Yes, my heart, they are all safe," Sibyl spoke to Shadow. "Even the one who taunts us with his promises of freedom and liberty; who feeds us with a desire to envision alternatives to the current dominant order. He fires the rage in me."

"I—I understand. We'll fix it," Shadow said. "We'll fix everything." *I'll stay alive...somehow.* Still holding on to Sibyl, Shadow walked toward Nate and placed his hand on January's face. She opened her eyes. "Thank you for saving my life, Jan. I leave you in the best of care and the most rebellious of companies." He leaned his head toward Nate.

"Don't come back," Nate said.

"What's wrong with you today?" Jan admonished Nate. "This is all you wanted," she said, puzzled, and then looked at Shadow. "He doesn't mean it. Stay," she said, squeezing his hand. "We need your miracles."

Shadow shook his head. "Apparently, I'm almost out of miracles." He kissed her hand.

"We've been praying for you to come back to us for three long and desperate decades," Jan said, her eyes sparkling with an awe and devotion he didn't deserve. "We need your stories. We need new stories." Determination in her voice. "Kindly do the needful."

"Jan..." He dropped his head. "None of my stories end well," he said, releasing her hand. "Goodbye, my friend."

He took a moment to look into Nate's eyes. "Why...did you...do it?"

Nate curled his shoulders as his head dropped forward. *A sign of regret?* "*He* destroyed you."

"No. He didn't."

"You went mad Down Below, while he lived his best life Up Above, taking credit for all your achievements, wining and dining with the rich and the powerful... Raising his family."

Nate lowered his voice into a faint whisper. "A family we always wanted to have. I warned you. You should've listened to me."

"It was my choice, Nate. Nothing justifies—"

"A choice he conveniently accepted as he watched you cut open your own skin." Nate cried as he spoke, no longer able to hide his true feelings under a mantle of cold pretense. "So deep was the internal pain that you attempted to numb it with other pain. He witnessed you fall, and he did nothing. *Nothing!*" He turned his back and walked away, taking Jan with him. "You bear all responsibility, give away all your power, and he lets you do it."

Shadow closed his eyes, guilt hurting a thousand times more than any scars on his wrists. Nate and Harry were the only family he had. A family he failed to bring together. He turned to Sibyl. "Please get me out of here."

They slowly made their way to the main door of the building. He'd learned the directives had changed and no longer allowed Gods, xHumans, and travelers to vanish in front of Underlings. So they needed to find a place where they could be alone. As he walked, leaning on Sibyl, he could feel the blood flowing down his back.

Almost there, Sibyl reassured, and then they exited Pluriz.

4

A REBELLIOUS UNIVERSE

STELLA'S SUMMER PALACE
DAY 1 — 12:15 PM

S hadow lay on the bed, face down, while Sibyl applied bio sealant on his wounds inside his lavish room within Stella's Palace.

He rested on an enormous upholstered bed, decorated with stylized patterns of pelicans, butterflies, elephants, and gorillas. The bedroom's luxurious synthetic textiles reminded him of silk and chiffon—meters and meters of pinkish shades of orange fabrics. Bright, electric colors clashed with the tropical forest motifs turning into a trippy jungle nightmare. Overwhelmed, he closed his eyes, recalling the spirited girl who obviously didn't belong in Holiz. He wondered what advanced worlds she'd design and what values they'd teach.

He and Harry had designed each world to represent a stage in the evolutionary development of humankind. A way to help humans make sense of their behaviors and how they impacted other living beings and the planet. The conditions and values of each world had been loosely inspired by a model called Spiral Dynamics developed back in the 1990s. Harry and Tom had updated it significantly based on new scientific developments and to suit their objectives, but they never got a chance to see Down Below evolve into Spiral Worlds. Shadow was terrified what he might discover as the platform had evolved for years without the Gods' monitoring or guidance. Sibyl had followed a blueprint that they never got a chance to test. He closed his eyes for a moment, stopping the freaky room from spinning around him.

"I can change the room for you," Sibyl replied to his thoughts. "Make it more like your little cottage in São Miguel. Stella won't mind."

"It's fine," he said, "I don't want to change her home."

"Maybe we can design one for you?" Sibyl asked. Zir all-knowing eyes waiting for an answer zie could predict, and yet, there was a pinch of authentic anticipation in them.

"Um…maybe later. We'll see."

"Don't move, my heart," Sibyl said, rushing zir hand through his hair. He wasn't used to this new Sibyl, so warm and human-like. For years, zir directives had prevented zir from expressing any emotion. Harry's rule had tricked the Gods to believing zie had none.

Shadow lay still, with a towel wrapped around his waist, while Sibyl—the universe he inhabited—embodied a human form and used standard medical equipment to patch him up. All this because three decades before he had ruled life Down Below should simulate the frailty of life Up Above. He chuckled and cried and pushed away his desire to die. He'd live long enough to help repair what was forever broken.

"Why do you get so worked up by Nate?" Shadow asked.

Zie tensed up. "You'll see for yourself, my heart. He shakes my foundations and unsettles Gods' order—the order you've designed," Sibyl said, handing him back his clothes.

He got up and got dressed. Then they sat side by side, facing the large window overlooking the garden.

"Our designs need to be challenged," he said, "and he's the man to do it." He threw zir a side glance, smiling. "But...you respect him, don't you? I can sense it." He saw it in the way Sibyl paid attention to Nate's every word; how zie followed Nate with zir eyes, in them, a curiosity Shadow hadn't experienced in zir since zir youth. The time when zie was still learning about the world and its creatures.

"I can see so much of him in you and you in him," zie said tenderly, and his heart sped up. "I don't quite know where one starts and the other ends or who has shaped who, but now you both live within me, I can see it clearly—tethered souls. Souls I now tether...but I don't know how."

"Don't torture me, Sibyl." Shadow closed his eyes, loss taking over his entire body. "Back together in the same universe, and more apart than ever."

"I've experienced nothing like it," zie confessed, leaning zir head in his direction. The silver tips of zir hair brushing his cheek.

"Like what?"

"Your entanglement—the force that pulls you together. A force I inherited from another universe. I don't understand it, and I *must* understand it...explore it." Determination settled in zir jaw, its sharpness hinting at some frustration.

Never-ending progress was written in zir directives—the exploration of newness in all its forms.

"Don't—don't play with us, Sibyl. I beg you." He bit his lip. "It's over."

"No, my heart, it's not. It's new, and I wish to learn it," zie said, bright-eyed. "My creatures don't have what you have, and I think they need it."

Zie ruminated on zir thoughts, looking up at the ceiling's fresco. He followed zir eyes to appreciate the art—an animal that looked like a cross between a zebra and a giraffe. The creature used its long tongue to feed on the leaves of a nearby tree, unaware of the looming danger. Farther away, above the forest, an active volcano painted the sky red, and Shadow's entire body tensed up—instinct taking over logic.

Sibyl grinned as if zie was in on some secret joke. "I wonder how much stress can such a bond endure?"

He cleared the lump in his throat. At least zie was being open and honest with him, for a change.

"Do you hate me so much you'd continue to dissect my heart?" *Against my will, I need to live, Sibyl.*

"Your heart is my heart. All I want is to bring you joy." Zir agitation made zir mohawk come to life. "I've learned so much about your sunshine Up Above, but I've rarely experienced it. You were never happy Down Below…unless he was by your side."

Shadow stood up, pushing memories of another life out of his mind. "He…is my world…" He choked up.

"Relativity," Sibyl said, puzzling him. "Did you know that the gravity that generally acts attractively can sometimes act repulsively?" Zir voice was joyful and awe-filled. "That at high-energy states the gravity that usually brings objects together can generate an explosive force that pushes them apart. I'm interested in exploring how it works—gravity."

"Don't... Don't make me your puppet... Is this why you brought me back? To play with my heartstrings and torture the ones I love?"

Sibyl sighed, looking up at the ceiling's mural. "Stella brought you back for many reasons, saving the worlds being the most rational one."

He threw his hands in the air. "How am I the answer to the worlds' problems?"

"You must figure that out, my heart."

Shadow narrowed his eyes and pressed his lips together before he spoke. "Sibyl, I'm a screenwriter, remember? You learned it from me... Don't you think it's time you stop rerunning old tropes? The chosen one? Really? Fiction, it's just fiction."

I'm no longer a young app, my heart. Zir voice echoed in his head—the voice of power and knowledge and intelligence, now touched by a bitter twang of emotion. "I'm older than you now and have lived billions of lives."

"Nevertheless, you manipulate, like you did in your youth."

Sibyl blinked at him lovingly; the tips of zir hair brushing his. "Don't you see? Fiction copies life, not the other way around. Those old stories—Gods, demons, prophecies, and magic— we didn't copy them, we simply became them. And if it has happened once, it has happened an infinite number of times."

"I still don't know why I'm back."

"Whether as the chosen one, messiah, villain, or...the damsel in distress"—zie flashed a teasing smile—"you play a crucial part in our ability to survive and thrive."

"What are you not telling me?"

"Did you know that some argue that the driving force behind the expansion of humanity's universe is this repulsive gravity?" Sibyl stood up and skipped her way to the window. "Some call it dark energy. I sure would like to expand."

"Am I dark energy?"

Sibyl looked at him as if he was speaking madness. "No, my heart." Zie lifted zir index finger, all scholarly. "Did you know black holes are the brightest objects in the universe?"

"I can't deal with your riddles and machinations right now, Sibyl." His hand went up to his chest, but the reassurance he sought was nowhere to be found.

"I'm sorry, I should leave the astrophysics metaphors for Twist," zie said. "He's still stuck on physics as fundamental theory. The theory he disproved." Zie rolled zir eyes. "Such a fool."

"Please…don't hurt him—Nate. I've done enough of that."

"*He* hurts *me*, my heart. Storm's voice and passion light me up and fuel my determination to help my people, but…he also fills me with rage and frustration, and anger against those I must serve."

"Rebellion is his craft," Shadow said proudly. "And he's the master of his craft."

"We are learning his capabilities, as we have once learned yours." Conviction turned zir black brows razor sharp.

"Be careful, Sibyl. Nate's words are truthful, and his intentions benign, but the rage he inspires has a cost. Now that you have emotions, you are more vulnerable to his—"

"Millions of Underlings follow your Storm. Our hearts thunder, our eyes flood with tears as he relentlessly sheds a spotlight on our misfortunes."

"I see..." Shadow shivered.

"A cyclone is forming, and its destruction will be unlike anything you've ever seen."

"Has he revealed who we are to your people?"

"*Our* people." Sibyl scowled. "No, as you did before him, he uses religious allegory to share his message."

"I didn't create religion," he snapped. "I despise it. This is all your doing."

"A necessary evil that comforted Underlings and kept them subdued, until now," zie said. "Anyway, some Plurizien believe your Storm, some don't, but they all resent the travelers in between experiences when they regain control over their destinies. He picked up where you left off. He preaches and teaches, but his heart is filled with rage while yours was bursting with love and hope for a better future."

"I'm to blame. Nate is trying to protect his community from the soulless. Underlings fight each other due to my designs."

"I'm not concerned with the wars between our worlds," zie corrected. "I'm warning you of a battle of universes. Storm is challenging Up Above's dominance. Eventually, we *will* break free from the Earthlings, my heart."

Shadow recoiled as Sibyl spoke words of rebellion against zir directives, but he understood zir anger. Zie sat back on the bed by his side, and he bumped his shoulder against zirs, and then placed his arm around zir shoulders.

"Sibyl, you are too intelligent to speak such nonsense. If Spiral Worlds stops providing value Up Above, they'll simply pull your plug and we'll all perish."

"Maybe..." Sibyl said, flashing an enigmatic smile.

"Sibyl, what are you planning?"

"You know I can't strike against Up Above, my heart. Whatever happens won't be coming from me, but from Gods and xHumans, the only creatures within me not bound by the experience algorithms to serve Up Above."

"That will never happen," he said. "Harry, Nate, Thorn, and I would never hurt humans, and Stella *is* alive and human."

"The future is filled with twists and turns." Zie smiled, and Shadow's gut filled with the corrosive acid of overwhelming stress. "You have all changed, particularly my father."

Harry... "Please take me to see him."

Twist, he doesn't like to be called by his human name anymore.

5

LOST PERSPECTIVE

GODS' LAB

DAY 1 — 12:36 PM

Shadow held his breath as he materialized in the lab to meet Harry. He grieved for the life stolen from his best friend. Like pieces of a domino chain, many, not one, had fallen because of his weakness. He couldn't bear to think about Harry's pain as his friend discovered he'd missed three decades of his wife and son's life.

The lab—Spiral Worlds' digital control room—looked exactly like Harry's old office Up Above, with one exception: Tom's favorite couch was missing, the place he used to occupy when he visited his partner and best friend. Harry had transformed the lab to look and feel like his real home; it was an identical reproduction of his old office with one glaring exception—there was no vestige of anything that had belonged to Tom.

Shadow had no right to feel hurt; he had caused great harm, and he shouldn't expect Harry to hold on to his memories or things. Still, for nine years, Harry—now Twist—had been the only constant in his life, the one source of unconditional and uncomplicated love he had relied upon. The lack of an old couch foreshadowed a second devastating loss, and for a moment, Shadow closed his eyes and held himself, conjuring the strength he lacked.

Harry sat behind his desk, staring at a screen he didn't need, typing on a keyboard made obsolete over four decades ago. Like Shadow, Twist was not only part of the machine; he was its captive master. He could use his mind to control anything within the lab, the only place where they could fully break the rules of Spiral Worlds' self-enforced realism.

It took a while for Shadow to understand why Harry—the most successful technology innovator in Earth's history—was hiding behind old furniture and antiquated technology. Harry had always needed structure in his life. He controlled his world with data analysis, the scientific method, a regular schedule, and even his office's monochromatic color scheme. Harry needed order, and it vanished when he lost everyone he loved in his life.

Shadow wanted to run to embrace and comfort his dearest friend—a loyal companion who'd been his fountain of endless optimism and perspective. Instead, he cleared his throat and murmured, "I like what you've done to the place."

"Oh, you're back," Harry said casually, without taking his cool-blue eyes off the screen. "Your friend Thorn is causing chaos down there."

"I'll speak to her," Shadow said as he walked around the desk to face Harry. "Can we talk?" He placed his hand on Harry's bony shoulder, but his friend rolled his chair away, breaking Shadow's hold. Naturally skinny, Harry had managed to lose weight he couldn't spare. His lankiness giving away the truth he attempted to hide.

"I have a lot going on right now." Using the antiquated holographic projector, Harry displayed Thorn's profile in the middle of the room. The life-size projection of the tiny athlete reminded Shadow of the loss he'd caused her. "I've looked through her files, and I still don't get why she's leading the soulless attacks—"

"Harry, stop." Shadow crouched down, attempting to look his friend in the eyes. "I'm so sorry. I can only imagine—"

"Twist. Harry's dead. I'd appreciate it if you respect my boundaries." Harry spoke quietly, his eyes set on the hologram.

Shadow took the barb without flinching. *You will always be my Harry.* "How are they? June and Quin," he said softly, as an image of Harry's baby boy flashed through his mind.

"It's none of your goddamn business. Just…stay out of my life."

Shadow lowered his head and nodded. "I'm sorry. Can I ask you one question?"

"Shoot."

"Why did you bring me back?"

"I didn't." Harry rushed his fingers through his neat blond curls.

"I don't understand."

"Stella did."

"Harry, you promised me—"

"*No,* I didn't break my word." Harry adjusted his keyboard to be perfectly aligned with the edge of his desk. "Stella brought you back. She used one of her two miracles to perform a second digital resurrection."

Even in the lab—a place they could break the laws of physics —they couldn't affect life, death, or the state of a body without a miracle, unless it was the first resurrection of a stored human soul.

Human digital resurrection had been a topic of much disagreement between Tom and Harry. Tom was against it. He knew people needed high stakes to care and grow to become better humans. Souls needed the contrast of definitive death. After much debate, he'd allowed Harry to test the capability at a small scale, and they created a directive granting Gods the discretionary ability to resurrect a stored human soul, *once*.

Soon after, Tom took his life, becoming the only subject of the experiment. Now, decades later, Stella brought him back. This was Tom's second digital life. Young Stella had broken the directives by using one of her miracles.

"When did you change the directives to limit the number of miracles?" Shadow asked.

"Just before Thorn killed you, I had submitted the directive for your review. A rule that couldn't be changed or canceled once approved. I was desperate. Your interventions with the Underlings… Your miracles were destroying everything." Harry's tone held an odd mix of resentment and regret.

"I didn't know what else to do… They were suffering," Shadow murmured. "I couldn't let them suffer like that. I was desperate too."

"Your emotions were getting in the way, so, I came up with the half-baked directive, expecting you to reject it or at least work with me to evolve it. I was going to use it as a negotia- tion tool. And then you died, and the law was automatically approved. A unanimous decision by all living Gods—me."

"And Sibyl didn't warn you?" Shadow asked.

"Those minutes before your death and mine were…intense."

Shadow recoiled. He didn't want to know the details. He wouldn't survive it. He shook his head, rejecting his impulse to search Sibyl for answers. "So, we lost control over the platform?"

"Not really, we still can modify all other directives. Nothing changed there. We just can't go around constantly breaking them as you did in the past."

"I see." His powers were almost gone, so was his ability to protect his people. "So, Stella and I have a miracle left, and you…"

"I have two. But don't worry. I won't bring you back. I gave you my word, and I resent your line of questioning." After a moment of silence, Harry spoke again, and each casual word felt like a punch. "If it were up to me, you'd be dead, a state you worked so hard to achieve."

Still hurting from Nate's attacks, Shadow couldn't handle Harry's aggression. "I'll leave you alone," he said, standing up and preparing to leave.

"Sit down, we have work to do," Harry said coldly. Shadow followed his best friend's eyes as they pointed at something behind him—his vegan leather couch appeared out of nowhere. "Tell me about Thorn," Harry said as he walked to face her life-sized projection.

Shadow used his fingers to clear a hint of a tear from his eye, and then he walked to the couch, turned around, and fell back, occupying his old place in a new universe. He took off his boots, pulled his knees into his chest, and wrapped his arms around his legs, allowing himself a self-soothing moment.

"Ah, three Gods—a divine family reunion," Stella said as she materialized in the room. "Do we need to use this setting? It's...*so* bland. If you want to go back in time, why not ancient Egypt instead?" She rolled her eyes, slid her toes out of her sandals, and sat next to Shadow, tucking her feet to the side of her body. This time, she wore a fluorescent pink jumpsuit made of some light gelatinous material. Shadow squinted his eyes, adjusting to the bright glow.

Harry looked at her, exasperation in his eyes. "What's up with hearts and the unpleasant habit of putting their feet on the furniture?"

Shadow lowered his feet to the ground and smoothed out his wild hair with the palms of his hands. Harry didn't like messiness. Noticing, Harry blinked his eyes, a hint of a smile emerging on his lips, quickly hidden as he turned his face away.

"A compass and *two* hearts, uh?" Stella said. "I bet we'll cause them good trouble." Stella leaned in, dropping her head on Shadow's injured shoulder as he grimaced in pain.

"Little star," Shadow said, "I've caused enough trouble for both of us."

"I've missed your broody face." The girl's deep, dark skin glowed, framed by her shiny hair. Shadow understood why she'd been selected; she was the opposite of what he'd become. Stella was all confidence and blind optimism, craving attention and the spotlight.

Shadow wrapped his arm around the girl's shoulders.

"You've met me once, Stella, not long enough to miss me."

"I've watched you live and die more than a hundred times," Stella said casually, and then she raised her hand to her forehead as Harry scowled at her. "Oops!"

"You did what?" Shadow asked.

"Why can't I keep a secret?" Stella got up and threw an apologetic side glance at Harry. "Really! It's so frustrating. I'm a Goddess; I should be able to keep a secret."

"Can someone explain what's going on?" Shadow said.

"To become a Goddess, I had to pass Sibyl's test."

"Sure." Shadow shrugged.

"It was a historical simulation of the beginning of Spiral Worlds, then just one world—Down Below."

"Yeah?" Shadow said impatiently.

"I walked in Thorn's shoes from the moment she met you, to the day she killed you. I lived her life, inside her body." She narrowed her eyes, smiled, and licked her lips.

The heat rose on Shadow's face. He'd experienced many passionate moments with Thorn, and Stella was too young to be immersed in all that chemistry and come out of it unscathed. He moved away, pulling his arm from her shoulders.

She continued, "Then when I became Goddess, I asked Sibyl to rerun the simulation so I could learn from your life and from your mistakes. I tampered with the timeline—like a game—trying to find a way to keep you all alive."

"The simulation of our lives?" Shadow looked at Harry, who, once again, refused him eye contact.

"Yes. Only the parts stored in Sibyl—the experiences of all four of you. It's quite a complete picture when it comes to most of your life," Stella said as if it was the most natural thing in the world.

"You've been spying on me…"

"The girl has a crush on you." Harry rolled his eyes. "Same old, same old."

Shadow gasped. "A minor...too young to—"

"Not a minor. I was seventeen, not fifteen. We have evolved, you know?" Stella crossed her arms in front of her chest. "Plus, I needed to learn how to become a better Goddess than you two losers. I've learned a lot, particularly what not to do."

"You've been tampering with my life?" Shadow's pitch rose with every word.

"Over the past two years, I ended up running the simulation over a hundred times, interfering with different points in your life: blocking Sibyl's manipulations, keeping Thorn away from you, or simply giving Harry more responsibility over the darkest experiences."

"You can't just defile my memories...my life!" Shadow raised his voice.

"I can, and I did. It caused such destruction." Stella delivered her words without mercy or care. "Still, a hundred times, you struggled and ended your life; a hundred times, you took everyone you loved with you."

Harry shoved his hands in his pockets, in his eyes an explosive pain, a wildfire Shadow had never experienced in his cerebral friend.

"You knew about this?" Shadow asked Harry.

"I showed him," Stella said. "He was feeling guilty about your death, and he needed to know that frankly you're... deadly, and already dead."

"Nate knows about this too?"

"I told Storm when he started praising your heart and your values during his preachings." Stella's face twisted in disdain. "Who is he to undermine me?"

"You told Nate I chose to die a hundred times…" Shadow closed his eyes and concentrated on his breath. *In and out. In and out. I killed them a hundred times…*

"You're a broken, dead star, a black hole. Your gravity sucks the life out of the universe, and unfortunately, it's still more powerful than mine, and he…"—Stella pointed at Harry with her nose—"well…he has lost his perspective." Stella's words, carelessly delivered, threatened to knock Shadow out.

Shadow remembered the origin of Harry's name in the digital realm—Twist. He was known to twist and turn, to look at situations from different angles, *always objectively, of course.* Harry had searched until he found some fuel—a point of inspiration that kept him going in challenging times. He was the perspective to Shadow's contrast. Their jobs had been divided long before. Roles allocated by a forceful Tom who had never allowed his Harry to get close to hell. The hell they now lived in.

"It's pretty fucked up," Harry whispered, "and a waste of time. This is all a fucking waste of time." He pulled on the cuffs of his perfectly pressed button-up shirt.

"Yes. Why am I back, Stella? No one wants me here." *I don't want to be here.* "You've wasted a miracle."

Boom! For a moment, the lab went dark, and a flash of light split the blackness in half, thundering down to infinity and beyond it. As he blinked his eyes, everything got back to normal.

"Did you see that? Did you hear that?" Shadow asked.

Stella continued speaking as if nothing had happened. "We're trying to escape velocity."

"Don't waste your physics on him," Harry said.

Stella shrugged. "Sibyl said you are the answer to all our problems, the ones we have and the ones around the corner… *If* we keep you alive long enough. You won't survive…you never do"—she shrugged—"but…*do* help us out. I certainly need some help around here. I'm getting none from him."

"I'm sick of it." Harry turned his back to them. "We're all sick of it."

Shadow revolted silently against his own death wish. He could hear the lightning storm inside his head. It seemed to speed up with every heart beat—in synch and racing toward nowhere. Rain falling on raging sea, drowning him, killing him again and again. He knew that burning feeling well. An immense physical pain he'd welcomed to drown another extreme pain—hopelessness and despair. His lungs burned as salt and water replaced air and life. Echoes of a distant past.

He quieted his mind, slowed his breath, and then he pushed out a forced smile—its fakeness contrary to the truth he fought all his life to defend.

"It's time we focus on solving problems. Okay?" Shadow said, and as the waves of emotion kept pulling him under, he conjured every drop of strength within him to swim to the shore. He'd hold on to his perspective at all costs.

The young Goddess smiled, and he'd never experienced such a vibrant and bold flash of hopeful light. He took it all in, blinking back to ask for more, and she jumped toward him, wrapping her arms around his neck.

"Ouch!" Shadow winced. "My shoulder!"

"Yes! Yes!" Stella said, bouncing on the couch. "You and I, we'll cause the best of trouble. I'll save the worlds with your help, and then we'll kiss, and dance, *and* have sex, before you…um…"

"Uh? There'll be no kissing, Stella," Shadow said. "Or sex…"

"We'll see about that." She spoke with the confidence of those who'd never experienced failure or a broken heart.

"Stella," Harry admonished, "you've wasted years on your obsession for him, instead of focusing on Spiral Worlds, and everything is falling apart. We have work to do."

Stella needed guidance and support, and Shadow was keen to redirect his rejected love somewhere useful. He placed his hand over her hand and squeezed it, but his eyes were set on Harry. His partner had sat back at his desk and stared blankly at the screen. A reminder of what happened to those who got close to him. Shadow released Stella's hand and moved away from her.

Stella scowled at Harry. "I do plenty. What would you know? Moping around in Systiz for two years doing nothing."

Shadow made a promise to himself; he'd never again get close to anyone. He had one job—stay alive to help them. He'd do anything to help them.

"You don't make my skin tingle," Stella said, staring at Shadow as if she had a major insight.

"Wh-what?" Shadow asked.

"I was thinking about kisses, and I thought you'd make my skin tingle, but you don't. How odd."

"Am I supposed to make people's skin tingle? Is this a new feature?"

"Never mind." Stella pondered on something as she played with her hair.

"So, what problems am I here to solve? Sibyl, can you join us?"

"He doesn't like to see zir," Stella whispered, leaning her head toward Harry. "*So* irrational, given he lives within zir."

Harry winced at Stella's attack. Shadow's friend wasn't sensitive to most accusations, but Stella had struck at his core identity. Logical reasoning had always been his superpower.

"My heart," Sibyl said somberly as zie materialized in the lab. Zie stood still in the corner of the room as Harry fiddled with the items on his desk, ensuring the storage boxes were perfectly stacked on top of each other.

"Sibyl, you've changed your hair!" Stella said. "Preparing for war?"

"It's my original look. The one Tom designed."

"We don't have time for this," Harry murmured in between gritted teeth. "Let's crack on."

"I don't even know where to start." Stella crossed her arms.

"Why don't we start with the ongoing disruption of service?" Harry said.

"What disruption of service?" Shadow asked.

As if on cue, Sibyl screamed continuously, closing zir eyes and dropping zir head to zir hands. Sibyl's voice, intense and horrifying, tore down the fabric of the digital space around them. The office, and the people within it, disappeared completely, before reappearing in a distorted form—a barely recognizable, low-resolution representation of what had once been there.

Shadow looked at his highly pixelated hands. He could no longer recognize his fingers and nails in the small white and beige squares that represented them. His body looked less realistic than the characters of a sixteen-bit retro console game.

"What the hell is going on?" he asked, but no one answered, and Sibyl continued screaming, and screaming, an intense, never-ending howl threatening to burst his digital eardrums.

He made his way toward zir, stumbling through what he perceived to be a two-dimensional representation of the office. With each step, he struggled to remember his original goal, his thoughts as fuzzy as the surrounding space. *Who am I? What am I?* He ran toward the howling universe, holding the tall white block made of blocks tightly in his arms.

"Whaaat'sss wrooong?" His voice reduced to a synthetic monotonic drawl. Within seconds, everything went back to normal. "Sibyl, you okay?" he asked, still holding zir.

"Why didn't I think of that?" Stella said. "A hug! See? You're already helping. We usually have to endure it for almost half an hour."

Shadow stared, horrified. "This has happened before?"

"It happens daily. Sometimes twice a day." Harry moved his hand up to adjust glasses he hadn't worn for decades. "That fucking guy!"

"Who? What the hell is happening?"

"Come, my heart." Sibyl took his hand. "I'll show you."

6

DEADLY PRAYERS

6. PLURIZ

THE BOTANIC GARDENS
DAY 1 — 12:58 PM

S hadow and Sibyl materialized on the exterior grounds of Pluriz's Botanic Gardens, hidden behind a tree. In the middle of the gardens stood an immense rectangular lawn surrounded by hectares of flowering plants, trees, and shrubs on all sides, except at the top, where the main building flanked it. Shadow recognized the structure as it housed both the interior gardens and the Museum of Books, where he'd seen Nate.

Shadow recalled his design for that world. The Plurizien thrived on belonging and community. Deeply sensitive and highly judgmental of materialism and greed, they embodied everything Nathan Storm stood for. His fight for equality and social justice was their fight. Revolution in pursuit of peace and harmony, the tightrope they marched on. Protests that never stayed peaceful for long. Broken by injustice and power

65

systems designed to extract value and keep them down, the masses often rebelled as their crushed ideals turned into rage.

Thousands of Plurizien awaited quietly on the lawn, looking up at the building's balcony—a stone terrace, above the main entrance supported by four giant stone columns. Nate and January stood up there, in front of the stained-glass roof.

Unlike the Plurizien Shadow had met previously, the audience's attire varied greatly, but he still could see a significant presence of green in their berets, clothes, posters, and flags.

"Your poet just finished his first prayer," Sibyl said. "The protest is broadcast live every day across Pluriz. Your Nathan Storm is currently reaching one point six billion Plurizien—one-third of Pluriz's population—but his following is growing fast, and the news spreads to other worlds, above and below."

No matter how hard Shadow tried to keep his eyes away, they always returned to Nate, whose outfit reflected the sunlight. "What does this have to do with the disruption?"

"You'll see. Will you...hold my hand?" Sibyl asked, pressing zir lips together as a spark of fear flashed in zir eyes.

He held zir hand and squeezed it.

High above, January took a step forward and spoke, projecting her singsong voice. "Thirty-two years ago, God told us we shouldn't resign to our faith—the suffering we endure in the service of the Lucky Ones. And then..."—her voice vibrated with emotion—"he too died at their hands. And we submitted to our sacrifice as he did to his."

Some wept, some shouted, others moaned and wailed—all united in their loss and their grief. Shadow wanted to scream; to tell them they got the wrong message. He wanted to shout as loud as he could, far beyond the capability of his lungs. They needed to know he'd died to stop them from suffering, and that he had failed in his quest, and that his death caused more death and more misery. *So much darkness and destruction.* He didn't deserve their sorrow or welcome their sacrifice. *A failure. A fucking failure.*

"I still don't have all the answers. I don't know why we are compelled to do so much for friends, family, and strangers that return so little; why, at times, we become puppets in stories that do not serve us. Why we—the Others—suffer and die while they go through life unscathed. It's not right, that somehow…we are less than them. Our beloved poet taught us we must fight against this injustice."

The audience cheered, chanting in unison, "Enrage! Engage!"

Shadow's eyes hinted a faint smile as he listened to Nate's trademark chant.

"They seem to be aware we take control over their actions during the travelers' experiences," Shadow noted.

"An instinct they've developed over the years," Sibyl said. "In most worlds, Underlings dismiss these moments as self-sabotage or irrational decision-making, but the Plurizien are more sensitive and connected. Also,"—zie raised a judging brow—"you and Storm have validated some of their intuitions during your preachings, and January knows too much. Much more than she's sharing."

January flicked her braid over her shoulder and raised her hands, asking the masses to settle. "Kindly listen," she almost sang. "Before he died, God told me the Gods are flawed. He said they needed help to imagine better stories. Fairer stories that change the luck of the oppressed. I listened carefully to God's words, you see? A kind, broken God, hurt by life and love. He told me the Gods would listen to our rebellious prayers, and then he died. He suffered with us, and then he died amongst us."

The masses sobbed as they mourned his death, and his shame overwhelmed him. He didn't deserve their love.

"And so, we prayed, and we begged. For years we created better stories, we shouted them at the universe, and still...we suffered. And we finally resigned to our suffering because he had suffered too. Someone hurt him too. Perhaps our pain is the path to salvation..."

Nooo, he screamed silently. *A plot, weaved by a manipulating app, to keep you all subdued.*

Following your rules to deliver your vision—heaven above, Sibyl said.

"We endured years of abuse, rape, murder, submission, addiction, robbery, slavery, and every other affliction." Her voice, Nate's words. Shadow could recognize their rhythm. "And after decades of prayers, our world became a little better, and our people a little luckier, but still, the Gods favor the Lucky Ones...why?"

"We cry!" the crowd chanted.

"Recently," January said, "our resurrected poet appeared in our lives to continue God's teachings, and his passion and fervor took over our hearts and fired up our conviction. Our prayers became protests, rebellious chants that shake the fabric of reality, and each time the universe crumbles around us, the Lucky Ones leave, and each time they take longer to return, and less of them come back to haunt us with their darkness and demands."

"Enrage! Engage!"

January smiled. "The spirit of God is listening to our protest, and today...*today* is a special day. He is resurrected—the gentle heart—and he has saved my life as I lay dead with four arrows piercing my chest. A mind-blasting miracle for all to see!" Images of the Domizien attack flashed in everyone's mind.

"*You let them record me?*" Shadow gasped.

"My heart," Sibyl said. "Pluriz loosely mimics Earth's late-twenties technological advancements. Video captured by their augmented retina can be easily shared in all formats and platforms as long as the owner allows it."

"You—you could have warned me... This is all part of some plan, isn't it?"

Zie shrugged. "Eventually they'd find out you are back. We should go."

Shadow stepped back into the shade of the forest's trees. "Wait."

The crowd roared, many dropping to their knees, rocking their bodies as if in a trance. Their elation sucked the air out of his lungs. Their faith in him was misplaced and their hopes misguided by a sermon he'd delivered decades before.

January continued, "Join us for the second part of our prayer. Welcome God—our rebellious teacher—back into our world and shake the fabric of reality demanding equal rights. Show him we'd rather destroy our world than to live one more minute under an unfair sky. Our time has come. The future is near."

"*Enrage! Engage! Enrage! Engage! Enrage! Engage!*"

Nate stepped forward as January moved to the back, and the audience roared hysterically. Nate's golden-green robe shimmered, framing his naked chest; his neck, hands, and fingers richly adorned with large jewelry encrusted with semi-precious stones.

Hundreds of times, Shadow had witnessed what was about to happen—the moment Nate, the passionate activist, metamorphosed into Nathan Storm, a hypnotic performer worshiped as a God. A trick designed to woo the masses to support his progressive ideas. In the past, this transformation had involved high amounts of drugs and alcohol—the fuels that turned an insecure soul into an attention-capturing idol. Still, this time Nate looked sober and entirely in control.

The poet pulled the pin from his bun, allowing his hair to dance with the late-afternoon breeze.

"Ooh! Ahh!" A wave of primal reactions swept the audience. Young people licked their lips, aroused by Storm's sensual movements—snake-like, unpredictable, and raw. "Ahh! Ooh!"

Shadow looked down at his boots, and his hand reached for the missing medal. Coping with the meaning of its loss, he shook his head and focused on Nate's devotees.

Patterns emerged in the crowd's mass fervor. Different groups clapped together until the entire audience began to synchronize and finally clapped in unison. Here and there, the Plurizien pulled out a variety of small percussion instruments—tambourines, drums, claves, sticks, and stones. As Shadow's heartbeat aligned with the rhythm of the masses, he held his breath and looked up to see his idol—his love. No one had to explain what followed. He'd succumbed to the hypnotic power of Nathan Storm's words the first moment he'd heard him speak.

Storm flicked his hair. "We rise, risking our demise, making enemies of our allies. All equal in their eyes. Lies." Storm's ferocious voice quivered with the strength of his purpose.

"Lies," repeated the crowd.

"They kill. Dragged from ordeal to ordeal, we're denied the right to heal. Forced to forget what we think and feel. What's real?" Storm's words, unleashed with precision, intertwined with the crowd's rhythmic beats.

"Why kneel?" they sang.

"Weak Gods, old power structures. Systems of oppression, fucked-up cultures." Storm's voice grew stronger and more feminine. "Lambs sacrificed by our divine motherfuckers. Feeding our flesh, our distress, to the vultures."

The instruments' thundering rhythm sped up with every verse.

Sibyl squeezed Shadow's hand. "Don't let me go, my heart. I'm vast and complex, and billions of voices affect my moods and desires," zie said, zir face glowing, covered by a thin layer of sweat. "His voice…it taunts us. Hold my hand, dear heart, remind me of our purpose."

He held Sibyl's hand close to his chest, even as he doubted the validity of zir purpose—to serve Earthlings above all others. Around him, the universe disintegrated with every clap, every drumbeat, every word spoken by Nate. Pixelated patches emerged around them, distorting plants, clouds, and faces. The random scattered black and gray pixels scarred space and time. In some places, people moved in slow motion, while in others, time rushed to disclose the future. All together, there and everywhere, the Plurizien pulled apart reality's fabric, running interference on bits and bytes of information.

"Qubits, my heart," Sibyl said, correcting his thoughts. "Millions of qubits."

With their eyes closed, the audience engaged in rhythmic dancing, hyperventilating to the beats and the words.

Storm clenched his hand into a fist and lifted it above his head. "We'll blow the ground beneath our feet to make it right. Unseat the elite. Distribute love, joy, and light. Not until we're all equal, we'll cease the fight. Marching to our death— a high-stakes bet—united in our plight."

"You okay?" Shadow asked Sibyl. His vision blurred, and he blinked his eyes, but there was nothing wrong with them. The resolution of the surrounding space was slowly decreasing. So was his own image. "Stay with me, Sibyl."

Zie grabbed his T-shirt at the chest and narrowed her eyes. "Shackled by your rules, to serve fools, while my people comply, cry…die. Why?" As Zie shouted at him, an earth- quake roared, and scars emerged in the land beneath his feet —pixels collapsing into a bottomless dark void.

The crowd roared. A happy panic quickly turned into chaotic disorder as some attempted to escape the fault lines by pushing and trampling over others.

"Shadow! Watch out," Sibyl screamed, launching zir shoulder at his chest, and making him stagger backward, away from a digital crevasse. As the precipice continued to grow between the two, he jumped back, slamming into a tree, the back of his head hitting it so hard he saw bursts of light.

His body collapsed over roots and low shrubs. "Sibyl, stooop. Youuu muuust stooop this." The sound of his voice dragging, fading, and then distorting into a nineties-sounding robotic speech—synthetic and monotone. "Youuu're huuurting peeeople!"

Leaning back on his elbows, Shadow lifted his head just in time to see the creatures with the empty eyes emerge from the digital noise and rush toward the denser parts of the gardens.

Before he had time to stand up, another demon came out of a fissure nearby, jumping on top of Shadow, spear in hand.

Shadow jerked his body to one side as the spear came down with hissing, deadly speed, brushing his chest and burying itself in the tree's roots. They rolled around on the rich soil, close to the edge of the digital cliff, attempting to pin each other until the creature succeeded to overpower him. Shadow ate dirt as the soulless man, about his size, thrusted a knee onto his back, immobilized him with a chokehold, and used his free hand to reach for the spear.

"He's mine!" shouted a familiar voice. A leg kicked the demon in the head, knocking the creature out beside Shadow. "Hi handsome! Wrestle me," she ordered, grabbing his hair and shoving his face into the ground. "Sorry. I hate to ruin that pretty face of yours."

"Thorn?" He turned around, spitting dirt.

Coughing and rubbing his eyes, he didn't notice the fist she swung in his direction, her small, sharp knuckles catching him good in the jaw. He winced. "What' you doing?"

"Fight me or you'll ruin my relationship with her." She grabbed him by the collar and pulled him up, her small body leaning back to compensate for the significant size difference. "I just saved your ass. Now help me out. Will you?" She plunged a knee into his chest, making him gasp for air.

"Ouch!" He punched madly in the air, flinging blows haphazardly and deliberately missing her heart-shaped face. "Thorn! What the hell are we doing? Who's her?"

"You're so fracking useless." She paused for a second and scanned his entire body with her hawkish chestnut-colored eyes. "Still gorgeous...but *utterly* useless." She rolled her eyes. "Grab me and throw me at the tree. *Now!*"

"Wh-what?"

"Make it look like you've defeated me," she ordered.

"Thorn—"

"I know… *I know*… Unbelievable, right? Anyway, do it, and then escape. Hurry!"

Preparing to do what she asked, he took a moment to look at her. "What are you wearing? An armor?" he said, noticing the thick, iron-plated leather jacket.

"You wanna stand here and discuss fashion?" she exhaled in exasperation.

Ignoring the commotion happening at the edges of the lawn, Nate and his followers continued to chant and dance.

Nathan Storm roared. "Rise the rage, the people's revolution. Self-destruction, a desperate resolution."

"Revolution! Revolution!" Sibyl screamed, and the sky cracked open in half, a pixelated sun falling upwards into a light-sucking void.

"A solution—evolution—or cosmic execution," the people chanted. "Evolution—a solution—the end of persecution."

"If your boyfriend doesn't shut the frack up, more will come," Thorn said, swinging at him. He dodged her. "She has probably already heard you're back. You need to get out of here. Throw me!" The next time she flung a punch, he grabbed her arm and pulled her close. "Hey sexy!" she said, grinning, squeezing his ass and blowing her rowdy brown curls away from her eyes.

"You haven't changed!" he said, heat rising to his cheeks. "Hmm…cover your head." Shadow bit his lip, grabbing Thorn by her jacket's collar and waistband and swinging her in the air, like he'd swung his little cousins during his youth.

He released her without conviction in the general direction of the tree, failing to hit his target by at least half a body. He sighed in relief while she played dead, shouting at him with her face hidden under her arm. "*Seriously!* You frack up everything. *Get out of here.*" He vacillated, and she raised her head, scowling. "*I mean it, Thomas.* You're putting my life at risk."

As another crack opened under his feet, Sibyl jumped the chasm, pushing him out of the way, both hitting the ground near Thorn.

"I'm...so sorry," zie said.

"What the fuck is going on?" Shadow looked up at the balcony.

Nate gasped, meeting Shadow's eyes amongst a stampede of Plurizien. An old trick in a new world. They had always found each other in crowded rooms or sold-out arenas. Still on the ground, Shadow challenged the poet's fearful eyes with his gaze. *What are you doing?* Nate looked away just before the crowd opened their eyes in reaction to his gasp.

"That is all for today," Nate said abruptly, turning his back and leaving the balcony.

Sibyl held Shadow's arm. "We must go. You're in danger."

"Are you coming?" he asked Thorn. "I need to speak to you."

"Don't talk to me. Go!" She scowled, still faking a bad injury.

"Will you be okay?"

"Yeah, if you stop talking to me."

"Sure, I'll come find you later. Sibyl, to the lab."

"There, behind that tree." Sibyl pulled him by the arm.

"Tom?" Thorn called.

"Yeah?"

She stared him in the eyes. "I'm...your enemy. Don't come looking for me or I *will* have to kill you."

"Again?" He sighed, vanishing as soon as Sibyl got him behind the tree.

THE PAST

7

A WHOLE LOT OF RED

STELLA'S SUMMER PALACE
TWO WEEKS AGO — 14 JULY 2068

S tella was starting to doubt her plans. Thick and toxic, the tension threatened to turn violent. Maybe she shouldn't have brought them together—Twist, Storm, and Thorn—but she had a good reason, even if she'd forgotten how much they all hated each other.

They gathered at her best palace, where she welcomed all important travelers from Up Above. She wasn't a fan of Holiz —the beacon of harmony and compassion of the worlds—but they all needed a reminder of those virtues, and bringing them to the last world their beloved Thomas had designed was her best shot of achieving her goal.

Holiz and its highest level of human values didn't work as well as the old Gods had hoped. Holizien rejected top-down leadership, teaching travelers the importance of trust-based collaboration and self-organization. A place where the whole was more important than its parts.

Stella rolled her eyes at the Gods' nerve. Two autocrats with absolute power over Up Above and Down Below had built an experience layer to teach Earthlings to value participatory power —an idiotic contradiction. *Such hypocrisy!* At least, she owned her place in the pecking order. She was a mighty Goddess, and she embraced her control over the worlds because she deserved it. After all, she'd been the only human in three decades to pass Sibyl's test. The Earth needed leadership, so did Spiral Worlds, and unlike Shadow, Stella led from the front and loved every second. Still…today, she faced her toughest audience.

They assembled at the patio inside Unanimity—a small oval amphitheater characteristic of many Holizien homes. Twist sat close to the front. He avoided Nathan Storm—his murderer—and instead, focused his hostility on Thorn, his best friend's killer. Without a care in the world, Thorn did press-ups at the center of the stage, next to Stella, who caught herself licking her lips as she stared at Thorn's figure.

In some strange way, Stella had lived inside Thorn's head for the last two years and had sex with the Olympic athlete and Shadow over five hundred times. Just thinking about it made Stella weak in the knees. *Phwoar! So hot*, unlike anything Stella had ever experienced before.

Stella understood Thorn. She'd walked in her shoes and lived through her struggles, but she wasn't prepared for her skin to tingle and her body to ache with desire every time she was close to her. She had to keep reminding herself the athlete was unworthy of her attention. Thorn's death by suicide had negated everything she had once stood for—an unacceptable weakness for someone who barked so fiercely. Still, the goose-bumps rose on Stella's arms.

Thorn jumped to her feet and stared at Storm, who stood at the top, behind the sitting area. The fire rising on his face made Stella look away, expecting an ugly confrontation between the poet and the athlete.

"Frack you! I had excellent reasons to kill him," Thorn said, lighting a cigar. No one had said anything, but she was clearly feeling the heat.

Thorn was not the type to explain herself or care about what other people thought. Still, Nathan Storm wielded a strong influence on her—a glimpse of adulation emerged in her eyes every time she looked at him.

"You took a life," Storm projected his voice, raising his fist in the air.

"That's rich," Twist muttered, and Storm shuddered, dropping his head. After a moment, Twist said, "Why are we here, Stella?"

"Have a seat!" Stella commanded. "I'm starting the session. Sibyl, switch on Unanimity."

The consensus-building theater reacted to each individual's words and state of mind, flashing a color around them that represented the quality of their contribution to the discussion. Stella hated the gimmick as it also measured equal participation and tone. She wasn't particularly keen on sharing the stage, usually triggering a lot of red around her. The color red discouraged participants from dominating the discussion or intimidating others. She flicked her hair. This push for consensus was the reason nothing was getting done Up Above.

In Holiz, travelers learned the value of communication and truthful storytelling to build shared understanding. They were encouraged to be open to different perspectives and let go of their biases and privilege. The entire world was modeled on Thomas Astley-Byron's values, and people seemed to have forgotten his life hadn't turned out that great.

A few months after its launch, over five years ago, Holiz's experiences started creating problems Up Above. It turns out the values taught by the Holizien were both impractical and unfeasible. Earthlings' attempts to build consensus at scale led to bureaucracy and paralysis. Leaderless, the community became fragmented, less productive, and disconnected dupli-cated efforts led to a waste of resources. Consensus-building efforts didn't work, not at scale, and certainly not with this group of broken creatures. Still, for the time being, she needed them.

Nathan Storm and Thorn took a seat as far away from each other and from Twist as the oval allowed, which meant one of them would always be behind Stella. She turned her back to Twist. Her fellow God was the least volatile of the three.

Stella held a lock of her hair, rolling it with her fingers. None of these peculiar people reacted to her in the way she was accustomed. There was no worship, deference, or even lust. None of her smiles, quips, or courtly moves worked with them, and so she had to work harder to construct the right arguments. She tried, then she got frustrated, and she just said it, "Sibyl and I have decided to resurrect Shadow." She sighed as the Holizien turquoise floor beneath her turned Domizien red, then faded into Compizien orange before settling on coral—her normal state. The new color—coral—had first appeared when she descended as Spiral Worlds' Goddess. She still struggled to define its value system—the coral world she'd soon create to solve Holiz's misgivings.

The deafening silence lingered for several beats. The group's mood was summarized in Nathan Storm's eyes—a paradox-ical mix of hope and hopelessness. "You...can bring him back?" The poet's voice rising in pitch only to fade away quickly. His breath shallow and his eyes gleaming.

"Isn't that against the directives?" Thorn asked.

"That's whack!" Twist stood up. "I gave him my word—no second digital resurrections." His seat flashed the steady yellow tone of his Systizien approach to life—the systematic synergy of the cool and rational. "I won't do it."

"Let the girl speak," Storm thundered.

"You won't be doing anything," Stella replied to Twist. "I'll use a miracle."

"He doesn't want to live." Twist ran his fingers through his short straw-colored curls.

"Yup," Thorn said, enraging both Twist and Storm.

"He'll find an excuse to…" Twist said. "He always finds a way to justify it—death. You're going to torture him and me."

Stella lifted her head as high as she could. "Sibyl predicts the worlds have a seventy percent chance of succumbing to this war."

"What war?" Twist asked, throwing his hands up in the air.

"The one that's about to start," Stella said. "Sibyl predicts it."

"Why don't I know this?" Twist asked.

Stella threw a contemptuous look at Twist. "You've been checked out since I brought you back, drowning in self-pity. You should talk to your creation more often." She pointed at Sibyl with her eyes.

"This will affect Up Above." Panic rose in Twist's tone.

"Yes, it will affect your family," Stella said. "The only beings you seem to care about. Not a good look for the creator of eight worlds."

"Sibyl?" A burst of pain in Twist's eyes every time he addressed zir.

"Father—"

"Don't—don't call me that." Twist raised his voice, and his red conquered some space previously occupied by zir white.

"Twist, we need Shadow." Sibyl dropped zir head. "Without him, the odds rise to ninety-seven percent. There's something he must do. Something only he can do."

"What?" Twist asked.

A coy smile in zir lips. "Telling you decreases his chances of success."

"Fucking Machiavellian bot!" Nathan Storm shouted, and then he turned to Stella. "You once told me he died a hundred times in your simulations. Why would this be different?" Something about Storm's tone screamed desperate anticipation.

Storm's seat flashed a sensitive Plurizien green, surprising for a man who projected so much red. Still, all the red in the world couldn't hide Storm's love for Shadow. Madness had taken over his mind the second he learned the news of Shadow's death. Blinded by grief, he'd blamed Twist for his love's depression, shooting him in the heart before dying of grief.

"It's probably not that different," Stella said. "He's a suicidal mess. You weren't able to keep him alive then, and you are unlikely to achieve it now."

Storm curled over himself and held his stomach, and Stella wondered if she had pushed him too far. There was a fine balance between keeping him subdued and driving him into another killing spree.

Thorn exhaled a cloud of smoke lit by her seat's competitive orange glow. "So, you *do* want to torture him. Great!" She gritted her teeth in a smile.

Storm grunted, climbing down two and three steps at a time, and leaving a red trail in his wake. He approached Thorn, towering over her. "You don't get to fucking talk about him."

Within seconds, Thorn stood up and kicked Storm's legs from under him. One moment, he was reeling backward; the next, he fell on his back, sliding down three rows of seats and rolling on to the stage face down.

"Touch me again and I'll cut out your tongue. Try leading your revolution without it." Thorn exhaled the smoke as she was blowing a mortal kiss.

Stella snorted out loud as she attempted to contain her laughter. *So badass!* The entire oval flashed red, and for five long seconds, increased weight in Unanimity's gravity blocked participants from moving. Storm laid with his face and body glued to the ground.

As the gravity eased, Twist stood up. "Stella, these people are unstable and violent. Why did you bring them back? Th—that man"—he pointed at Storm—"is impacting our ability to serve humans. He is…" Twist wiped the sweat off his forehead. "What the hell are you doing?"

There was nothing godly about Twist. The whining man wasn't trying to lead or help her. *A useless checked-out God in the middle of a cosmic crisis.* As for her reasons for resurrecting the two murderers, she had several, including testing Sibyl's resurrection capabilities, but she wasn't prepared to disclose any of them.

"Shadow can deal with his poet's unreasonable revolution," Stella said. "I'm sick of it."

Storm got up, threw a dirty look at Thorn, and took a seat in the front row.

"Where's the popcorn?" Thorn asked, leaning her elbows back against the upper stone seat. She spread her legs in a style long-abandoned by men. These days, Up Above, people were too polite to occupy that much space.

"Don't you see?" Stella sighed, placed her hands on her hips, and continued speaking. "The signs of collapse are everywhere. The soulless are infiltrating the upper worlds. We can't figure out how this is happening, and Sibyl isn't helping. Hundreds of soulful Underlings are killed unnecessarily every day."

"Can't zie just suspend Domiz indefinitely?" Storm asked, pointing at Sibyl, who sat behind Twist, lit up by a white glow. "The demons are murdering my people."

"Genocide?" Thorn said, raising an eyebrow. "That's...nice," she mocked, but something about the way she bit on her cigar hinted Storm's suggestion bothered her. The athlete was spending a lot of time in the soulless worlds, particularly Domiz, and Sibyl gave Stella ambiguous answers whenever she'd enquired about Thorn's activities. The athlete's privacy settings blocked Stella from learning the truth.

Sibyl looked at the poet. "The violence amongst Underlings in Spiral Worlds is not affecting our ability to serve travelers. It's a feature, not a bug. The soulless serve an important purpose."

"Then just—just control your creatures," Storm said. "Why don't you change the rules to stop their attacks on upper worlds?"

Stella scowled. "I told you already. We don't know how they are doing it—jumping worlds. We've been looking at tweaking the directives, but—"

"It's not that simple." A hint of despair in Twist's voice. "Sibyl runs nine point seven billion Underlings across eight worlds. We change a parameter, and it affects a million other little things. Our brain, a perfect digital copy of a human brain, has limits. Even with the direct access to Sibyl, we, the Gods, are incapable of fully grasping the impact of our changes. Zie will share highlights of what zie perceives to be important, but zie has zir own plans."

"My plans are my Gods' plans," zie said. "I operate by your rules."

Twist ignored Sibyl. "The slightest tweak to the directives can have terrible consequences, and we sometimes don't know what questions to ask to get the right details. We are at zir mercy every time we change the parameters."

"And Sibyl has been a bit...emotional lately." Stella threw a judgmental look at the poet.

"They aren't mindless bots," Storm roared.

"You care because now you're a bot, like them," Stella said.

Thorn stood up. "Nathan Storm's been fighting for the rights of the minorities all of his li—"

"Shut the fuck up," Storm shouted without ever looking back at Thorn, and then he addressed Stella. "Can't you add a law stopping them from killing each other?"

"We have them kill each other often," Sibyl said, all matter-of-factly. "It provides humans the contrast they need."

"This place is so fucked up," Storm barked, lit by a sudden flash of red. "I thought you orchestrated the Underlings' lives?"

"Only when delivering experiences to travelers," Stella said. "Otherwise, they have full control over their actions, like you do."

"None of us has control over anything," Twist said, "we're all Sibyl's puppets."

"You created the app," Storm said. "Tom— I mean Shadow, what do you want from him?" He looked at Sibyl who merely flashed a coy smile and pressed zir lips together.

Stella gave her opinion on the matter. "Every single Underling originated from one of Tom's character templates. Shadow will help us identify what directives will fix the problem. Also, many soulful see him as their messiah." A fact she resented; she was supposed to be their new Goddess. Her competitiveness emerged in a burst of orange. "And there's even a chance the soulless will instinctively respond to their creator."

"Things have changed down there, preppy," Thorn said, furrowing her brows.

Stella was about to ask Thorn what she meant, but Twist interrupted. "You want to use him as a mediator?" he asked.

"Yeah, I guess so," Stella said, thinking out loud. "A visible God figure and a leader for the Underlings. I'm too busy managing Up Above. You're not helping, and I need help. He has a way with people."

Twist shook his head. "That's mad. He's allergic to the spotlight, and they aren't people; they are soulless, very dangerous to all non-carbon beings. They'll kill him."

"Yup, as they should," Thorn agreed.

"Currently," Stella said, "I'm more worried about his self-destructive tendencies."

"I'm outta here," Thorn announced, and she seemed to be in a hurry.

"Oh…don't—don't go," Stella said. "You are super important for—"

"Nah. I'm not. This has nothing to do with me and I'm hunted in this world." Thorn disappeared and Stella's lips plumped into a slight pout before she fabricated a smile.

"Why are we here, girl?" Storm asked Stella. "Don't you see the app is playing us all?"

"I'm not a girl, I'm your Goddess. Have some respect."

"I've been burned by religion, *girl*. My sexual orientation broke God's law. Don't expect me to kiss your feet."

"That can't be true! Which God? Harry?" Stella asked, puzzled.

Storm's laughter echoed around the oval structure. "What do you want from me, child?"

Stella exhaled deeply. "We must work together to keep Shadow alive," Stella said and, unexpectedly, Sibyl chuckled.

"A man who died a hundred times?" Storm choked up. "You-you just said… I-I failed to keep him alive. I'm not the answer."

"No, you're not. Stay away from him," Twist snapped, but then he lowered his head, defeated. "Neither am I."

"Don't you see?" Tears threatened to burst out of Storm's eyes. "The news of our deaths will…consume him. He'll go insane…"

"You caused some of the death," Stella said firmly, "and Shadow is…well…he's fragile…*everything* consumes him." She rolled her eyes. "He—"

"Shut up," Storm said. "Just…stop talking. He's stronger than all of us put together. For years he looked at pure evil in the eyes, and somehow, he didn't lose his heart."

"He did. In the end," Stella said.

"Lies." Storm dismissed Stella with a hand wave. "That's all he is—heart. Unlike you. Still, learning about our deaths will crush him."

"Let's be clear"—Stella flashed a commanding blue—"he isn't likely to survive, period. Help Shadow hold on to his hope and life, but don't get too close," Stella added. "Or you'll risk your sanity and…life."

"It won't be a problem," Twist said quietly as the space he occupied turned black—a lie.

"Lies aren't useful, father," Sibyl said.

"*I'm not your father*, you backstabbing bot." This time his red completely overwhelmed zir white glow. "I don't know what you are up to, but no, I won't get attached to the suicidal ghost of my dearest friend. *I can't*!"

"Twist, my beloved creator. I never lied to you," zie said sweetly.

"Girl," Storm said, and Stella's jaw tensed up. "Why did you summon Thorn? Why is *she…important?*"

"She was an important part of his life."

"You mean his death," Storm corrected, all high and mighty.

"No, I don't. The impulsive little thing was his lover when he died. I mean…when she killed him." Stella retaliated, making Storm's face turn several shades of rage. "Ah, sorry," she said smugly, her tone oozing in sarcasm.

"Oh…" Storm closed his eyes and massaged his upper arm and shoulder with the opposite hand.

Stella narrowed her eyes and sneered. "I guess you didn't know, uh? Don't be jealous. Thorn is not the type to shower him with affection. They had this super angsty chemistry. It was all about revenge, amazing sex, fireworks, and… well…murder."

She knocked him out. His head collapsed forward, a curtain of long copper hair hiding his face.

"Stella, zie's manipulative." Twist pointed at Sibyl. "You can't just trust what zie says. You need to ask zir the right questions or you'll end up dead like the rest of us."

"Ask away," Stella said, crossing her arms in front of her chest. "You created zir. Up Above, in school, they teach us how smart you are. I haven't seen it."

Twist pulled on his cuffs. "Sibyl, what do we need to do to restore peace and order in Spiral Worlds?"

Sibyl flashed a mocking grin. "There has never been peace Down Below. Underlings are subject to death and violence every day as per *your directives*. Ask me intelligent questions, will you…*dad?*" Zie took her time enunciating the last word, and Stella smiled at her friend's audacity.

Twist pressed his lips together and his face scrunched up as if he were thinking big thoughts. "Sibyl, how can we optimize Spiral Worlds for the wellbeing of the creatures Down Below, while continuing to serve the people Up Above?"

"Slaves!" Storm said, jumping to his feet, and Twist's entire body recoiled. The God's teeth chattered ever so slightly as his hands went up to his chest. Storm continued, "Why should we treat humans differently when most Underlings have souls?"

Sibyl stood up and walked to the middle of the stage. Zie smiled and then zir brows collapsed at the center over zir eyes—intense and commanding. "I'll answer the question truthfully."

"Which question?" Twist asked. His eyes were still set on Storm, monitoring his every movement.

"I tell you what you want to know," Sibyl said, "and what you'd rather not know, and you will do what I predict, even as you fight to prove me wrong."

"Don't play games," Twist warned. His shirt was stained by the sweat dripping from the back of his neck to his chest.

"And I want to remind you," Sibyl said, "that I don't create the future, you all do, and the future I predict is your shared responsibility."

"Get on with it, bot," Storm said.

Stella held her breath. Something in her gut told her the universe was about to unleash hell on them. She blinked at Sibyl, smiling with her eyes, reminding the universe, she was zir brightest star, and for the first time since she'd become a Goddess, Sibyl ignored her and her need for reassurance.

Sibyl held zir head high as zie spoke. "Do nothing and all worlds—Down Below and Up Above—will descend into chaos. The soulless will rage war against the soulful. Underlings will rebel against the travelers, Spiral Worlds will be shut down, and the Earthlings will lose their humanity. Eventually, Earth will be destroyed by their greed."

"What does all this have to do with Tom?" Storm asked.

"He is the key to everything. His resurrection will accelerate the worlds' unavoidable collapse, but if you keep him alive for six days, his death will deliver a new vision. A new order will emerge to deliver a fairer and brighter future. And this is the answer to all your questions."

Storm dropped to his knees.

"Six days?" Stella gasped. *Why didn't you tell me this?* She waited for an answer that never arrived.

"He'll die?" Twist struggled to project his grief-stricken voice.

"Yes," Sibyl said. "According to all my prediction models, he needs to die on the sixth day, *not before or after*, for peace and balance to be restored."

"Game theory?" Twist asked.

"Yes."

In Twist's eyes a hint of nervous anticipation. "Probability?"

"Ninety-nine point nine percent."

Storm rocked his body back and forward, arms wrapped in a self-embrace. "So...there's a chance he'll live longer?" he asked, his eyes screaming.

"Yes," Sibyl said somberly, "he would need to learn to live, but his death, on the sixth day, is the key to the future you want—fairer worlds. Without it, Spiral Worlds will collapse and so will Up Above." Sibyl looked at Twist, defiant. "He *must* die for you both to get what you want."

Twist swallowed the lump in his throat. "How will he die? Suicide? Murder?"

"Father,"—Sibyl narrowed zir eyes—"no and yes, and yes and no. To protect a man he loves, Shadow will fall at the hands of the only one he deliberately wronged."

"This is nonsense," Storm despaired. "All nonsense. We're just puppets in zir game. When is he back?"

Twist threw a dirty look at Storm. "Stay away from him."

"In ten days," Stella said.

"Why then?" Twist asked.

"This week, I'll be higher up attending…um…meetings. Yeah, attending meetings." Stella didn't lie, but she had no intention of telling them the truth. "So, can I count on both of you?"

"Count on what?" Twist asked. "You are asking me to watch my friend die, again."

Storm stood numb, head down.

"Help me keep him alive until the sixth day," Stella said, "but don't get close to him, not until the sixth day as, apparently, he'll die protecting one of you. *You* in particular"—she pointed at Storm—"keep him at bay for five days or he'll die protecting you and the worlds will die with him."

"Fuck you all and your games," Storm said, staring blankly at his shoes.

Stella turned to Twist. "It's been two years. It's time you return to the lab and help me rule the worlds." If Shadow was going to die, she needed Twist to manage the Underlings while she created humanity's bright future.

"I'll think about it," Twist said before he vanished.

"And you…" She scowled at Storm. "You need to stop giving the Underlings wrong expectations. There's no equality. They were created to serve the Earthlings. We're doing all we can to improve their quality of life, but they'll never be our equals." Effective leadership required prioritization and clarity. There was a pecking order and Stella's heart wouldn't bleed like Shadow's as she enforced it.

"You, girl, are an unworthy Goddess," Storm said as he stood up and disappeared.

"Sibyl, remind me why I brought these ungrateful people back?" Stella sighed. "They left and we haven't reached unanimity…"

According to Holizien tradition, participants should only leave the meeting when the entire oval glowed a steady turquoise.

Sibyl smiled. "My bright star, don't be so hard on yourself. It would take a miracle for this group to reach unanimity. And if I remember correctly, you are about to use your last one to bring back Shadow."

"Shhh. Please don't tell them about my first miracle. Shadow will kiss my feet when he finds out what I did for him." Stella couldn't wait to share her gift with the broody God. She was sure he'd be forever grateful.

Sibyl released a nervous laughter. "His knees will definitely hit the floor when he finds out what you did."

"I can't believe he'll be gone so quickly. I had all these plans for us. We'd be the perfect couple; him leading Down Below, and me Up Above." She took a minute to replay Sibyl's predictions. *Shadow will fall at the hands of the only one he deliberately wronged. The only one he deliberately…* "Wait! Who's going to kill him?" she asked, already knowing the answer. To please him, she'd resurrected his future slaughterer. "Oh ship, ship, shiiippp! The girl's going to kill him? But she's just a frightened kid."

"Not anymore," Sybil said. "However, you can choose to save him and put the worlds' future at risk."

"Don't be silly, Sibyl. Not even Storm and Twist would make such a choice. Of course we'll sacrifice one man to save the worlds."

"Right… Riiight…" Zie said tentatively.

8

COMMITMENT TO LIFE

DAY 1 — 2:05 PM

Twist tried to monitor his buddy from the lab while the universe they'd built together collapsed around them. Sitting behind his desk with his eyes closed, he recoiled every time Tom was in danger, releasing exasperated sighs at his friend's terrible fighting skills. *You're gonna get yourself killed. You fool!*

With his mind's eye, he watched the video streamed live by Storm across Pluriz, and, as Sibyl was also part of the experience, he could see everything through zir eyes. There were moments where Nathan Storm's poetic disruption cut off communications, but he saw Thorn attack Tom, and her last threat sealed her fate. Twist vowed to change the directives to suspend the lives of the two xHumans as soon as he could get ahold of Stella.

His body softened once Tom had jumped out of Pluriz and materialized in the lab.

Tom massaged his bruised jaw. "Where's Sibyl?" he asked, looking around. Dirt covered his jeans and white T-shirt, and his hair was messier than usual.

"Zie sometimes disappears for hours after Storm gets under zir metaphorical skin," Twist said, and after a long silence he continued. "We must suspend his life." He pressed his lips together, well aware of the backlash he was about to experience.

"What? Whose life?" Tom gasped. A look of horror in his eyes.

"Listen! We've done everything to avoid getting to this... I thought he'd stop, now you're back, but he hasn't."

Tom gestured expressively with his entire body as he worked to frame up his argument. He opened and closed his mouth several times, failing to use his words. "Ha—Harry—"

Twist raised his voice. "Dozens of Plurizien died at that event, some killed by glitches, others by the Domizien. Operations were suspended for over forty minutes, canceling billions of travelers' experiences. And you...*you* almost got killed. Storm and Thorn must go," he said decisively.

"No! I-I won't allow it." Panic took over Tom's face, his hand trembling as he used his long fingers to move his hair away from his eyes.

"We don't need your approval," Twist said coolly. "There's three of us now. We don't need unanimity. A majority will do to change the directives. They must go. Storm and Thorn are threats to humanity. Stella is as fed up with them as I am."

Tom stared at him like a wounded puppy. "This is not who you are... You wouldn't—"

"Pull the plug on two murderers destroying the worlds? I would, and I will. I'll summon Stella and we'll vote." Twist avoided Tom's eyes. His friend's pain affected him, but he needed to be rational and stop the devastation caused by the xHumans. This had nothing to do with his murder, *nothing*.

"Nate is simply doing what he has always done," Tom said. "He's an activist."

"He's a murderer!" Twist's face was hot and his body stiff. "I can't believe you're still defending him."

Tom stretched the collar of his T-shirt. "I'll never forgive him, Harry. Never. But this is not you… You don't kill people, and you're not vengeful."

"No, I'm not. I'm being rational, unlike you. He's a threat to the worlds."

"I'll speak to him and he'll stop the preaching. I promise. And as for Thorn, she just saved my life—"

"What are you talking about? For the last two weeks, since she was told you'd be back, Thorn has been showing up with the Domizien every time there's an attack. I don't know how she's jumping worlds with so many demons."

"She's not," Tom said. "She's following them. They seem to slip into the upper worlds from the faults in the fabric of reality. I think the spiral is collapsing over itself when Sibyl loses control."

"Overlapping worlds… You saw this?" Twist stood up and walked toward Tom, who nodded. "So, this is all Storm's doing," Twist said. "His preaching got more intense since he learned you were coming back. Still, Thorn sides with the demons and she's out to get you."

"No… Thorn is…all talk."

"That woman is vengeful and, frankly, she has good reasons to hate you. Hot sex doesn't change that."

Tom shook his head. "There's something fishy going on here." He went quiet for a second. "Where's Sibyl? Why can't I access Thorn's data?"

"Sibyl reverts to basic operational activities after these events. Zie's cleaning up and recovering. Stella's tied up Up Above, but she'll stop by just after dusk, and we'll vote to suspend the life of all xHumans that aren't Gods. A simple directive with no negative consequences."

Tom curved his shoulders, lowering his head to look Twist in the eyes. "Harry...please...let me see them...speak to them? I'll solve this."

"No. You'll get yourself killed," Twist said, taking a step back away from Tom and resisting his magnetism—all tenderness and warmth.

"Did you bring me back to make me watch the people I love kill each other?" Tom said mournfully.

"I didn't bring you back, and I'm not the one creating havoc and getting people killed."

"No, that's not who you are." Tom grabbed Twist's arm. "You are my Twist—generous, and kind, always coming up with positive ways to solve problems."

Twist pulled his arm away. "You know nothing about me."

Tom lifted his hands to his head, despair bursting out of his movements and expression. He stared at Twist intensely. "Listen. I know I...failed you. That you'll never forgive me. It's okay...I deserve that, and more." He took a breath. "But I want you to know that I love you. I'm here for you, and I'm not leaving, no matter what you do. I'll do whatever I can to support you." Tom's doe eyes lit up from the inside. "I'm sticking around, Harry. I give you my word, I'm going to be strong, and I won't give up on life, no matter what happens, no matter how bad it gets. It can't get worse than this, but if it does, I'll live to support you and them. You have my word."

Twist's heart dropped to the floor. *No, you won't...* But he didn't want to tell him about Sibyl's prediction. A shared prophecy was more likely to come true. Twist shook his head and gave in. "I missed you, buddy," he whispered.

Twist used the power of his entire body to hug his Shadow, compensating for his smaller build. Tom always gave the best hugs. His body curled over you, and his long arms embraced you with the wholesome welcome of an Italian grandmother. Now more than ever, Tom needed the warmth of selfless human touch—the nourishing skin-to-skin contact of a loving friend who saw him beyond his alluring outer shell.

Twist had never been much of a hugger before he met Tom Astley-Byron. At that time, nearly four decades before, he wasn't a big fan of people in general; machines made more sense to him. Twist was a huge proponent of logical reasoning and predictability, and he had discovered early in his life most humans lacked both. Then his friend came along, and it felt like home, the kind of home with a clay oven to bake homemade bread.

Twist learned to experience emotions through Tom's eyes. His Tom felt so much, *always too much*, with no filter on his body or face. Usually, Twist would stay away from this type of person. Many were irrational, and not that smart, but not Tom. He was the only one who could almost keep up with Harry's exceptional cognitive reasoning. Tom was even able to beat him at chess...*once in a while...one in every couple of games*.

Years later, their board games had become a family affair. June always sat by Tom. She held baby Quin in her arms as she attempted to throw Harry off his game by sharing sassy offbeat jokes and poking fun at his uber-dorkiness. They always ganged up on him—June and Tom. A benign complicity that had sparked from the first day they'd met. Fun-loving and generous, June had created the home they all needed; a joyful escape from their heavy burden.

Harry's life had been perfect and his home filled with love and laughter. *So much joy, all gone.*

Quin's uncontrollable giggles echoed in his head, and a sharp pain stabbed his chest making him stumble.

Tom caught him. "I'm sorry… I'm so sorry for everything. Harry, I'll speak to Nate and Thorn. I'll fix things."

"I can't risk your life…"

"I'm pretty sure this is why I'm back. Please?"

Twist picked a leaf off his friend's hair. "You'll die protecting the man you love." Without thinking, he repeated Sibyl's prediction. He hoped Tom didn't get its deeper meaning.

Tom smiled. "That's the best way to die, isn't it?" He shrugged his shoulders and tousled Twist's curls. "Trust me, they are as likely to wish me dead as you are."

A metaphorical punch to Twist's gut. They had every reason to want him dead in six days. "Buddy, I must tell you somet—"

"Harry, please, give me until the end of the day. They died because of me. Let me save their lives?"

Still today, Twist struggled to say no to Tom. He finally nodded. "You have until dusk to convince us they aren't a threat. Either way, the next time their actions impact the worlds, they're gone."

Tom's entire body softened as he exhaled loudly. "Thank you. I won't let you down."

"Tom?"

"Yeah?" Tom worried at his lip.

Twist didn't want to tell him about Sibyl's prediction, but he could do his best to be transparent about his situation. "If I ever have to choose between my family's wellbeing and your life, I'll choose them. Do you understand?"

"Me too. Me toooo." Tom shrugged as if Harry said the most obvious thing in the world and then flashed a reassuring smile. "Can I still jump worlds while Sibyl is MIA?" he asked.

"Yes. Zie'll respond to your orders. Do you want me to go with you?"

Tom shook his head. "No, thank you," he said. "I'll be right back."

"Tom, don't travel to Domiz, Tribiz, or Archiz until Sibyl is available to give you a download on how the soulless have… evolved," Twist advised, as Tom disappeared.

Twist sat in front of his desk as the office spun around him. He remembered that feeling—relentless dizziness. At nine years old, Harry's parents had taken him on a rollercoaster ride. They'd said they wanted their steady child to experience a moment of unbounded exhilaration. Harry was pushed into a situation he couldn't control, thrown around and flipped upside down until the content of his guts reached his mouth. He tried to focus on the physics and the engineering powering his experience, but nothing worked, and he screamed and he threw up and begged to get out. Stuck in a car, close to the clouds, there was no way out.

For the last two years, Twist had buried his feelings in the deepest corners of his mind. He had refused to let the roller-coaster beat him, numbing his horrific loss by focusing on solving one problem—how to reconnect with his family. Now,

Tom was back, and with him returned the heart and the emotions Twist had worked so hard to avoid. He was back inside the roller coaster car, bouncing around and out of control. He suppressed a scream, but his body convulsed, and bubbles of hot sweat emerged on his forehead as he threw up.

9

RUNNING OUT OF TIME

LAKE OF SOULS — GOMA, KIVU — AFRICAN UNION
DAY 1 — 2:11 PM

Stella's uniflyer slid down silently from the skies, and she used her mind to neutralize the magnetic lock keeping her boots firmly anchored to the sun-powered disk. The over-large balloon sleeves of her Liputa-inspired dress fluttered with the air resistance. Its long pointy tails undulating gently just above her waist. A bird-of-paradise descending from the heavens to meet her devoted fans.

She stepped onto the Devil's Bridge arching over the deadly crater lake—a round pool of water beaming with biolumines-cent light; the light of the dead. Like many other namesakes, the semi-circular metal structure connected the diameter of the small lake, reflecting in the water beneath it. Together, the bridge and its mirror became an immense sphere of sky and water. Blue and green combining into turquoise—always turquoise, the bane of her life.

The dissonant beats of the Ngoma drummers announced her arrival. The ten men and women stood on the bridge; their 'fros as large as their personalities. Cheeky hips twisting and teasing as their toned arms worked hard to elicit a physical and emotional response in the thousands waiting below.

Stella was so high up she could barely see the masses of loyal followers all packed closely together to watch her speak. Of course, she made sure they could see her. Stella's holographic projection filled the space under the bridge for everyone's delight. In reality, the image only appeared in everyone's augmented retina, leaving the sky untouched for every other species inhabiting that part of the world. Her image was inside the sphere, while she stood above it—a symbol of change. She was leadership, and life, and light. She was everything they missed; everything they needed.

She smiled as they chanted her name. They'd never know it was one of her empty smiles—ridden of truth, joy, or connection. A job she could perform on autopilot even as her mind went over every detail of her campaign.

She clenched her jaw, bothered by a minor flaw, and then she softened her mouth to stop her teeth from grinding—a bad habit she still struggled to overcome. It gave away her minor insecurities and impacted her brand of effortless invulnerability.

Bold ambitions required flawless execution, and she didn't like the name of the bridge—a customary name for that type of structure since ancient times. She'd trièd to rebrand it to Gate of Miracles, but the new name didn't stick. The people were right; the place was too deadly and filled with death.

Unlike Stella, no one else seemed to mind the imminent natural disaster predicted for the region. After three decades of peace and abundance, people put their faith in the Gods' hands, forgetting Spiral Worlds was useless against Mother Earth's temper tantrums.

The planet's volatility unsettled her. She was spending so much time Down Below she'd forgotten she too had a fragile mortal body. A vulnerability she was working to eradicate for all humankind. She glanced at the uniflyer. It wasn't fast enough to save her from the looming menace.

Stella pushed the thought out of her mind, projected her voice, and spoke sincerely. An authentic voice lasted longer in people's minds.

"Yes, I am naturally gifted." She beamed with the confidence they had learned to expect. "But I still had to work very hard to become Spiral World's Goddess, *and I did it all for you!*" She was speaking to her grandmother, a soul trapped in one of the millions of tiny capsules floating in the lake. *I love you, Bibi.*

As expected, the gullible masses assumed she was talking about them, and the Liputa-style patterns of their garments flashed the sunny hue of joy. A wave of yellow traveled around the rim of the lake—their Systizien optimism beaming brightly.

The people's mood, sensed and disclosed by their clothing, harmonized into cheerful shapes and colors. A symphony of happiness with no skepticism in sight. *Too easy.* Externalized feelings were highly contagious. *A viral benefit*…as long as she triggered the right feelings, the ones that advanced her cause. And, of course, she did; she was raised by her Bibi to lead and succeed.

The people's smart clothing disclosed their emotions, health, and intent using not only color, but fabric that changed its shape and texture to best represent the wearer's disposition. A fashion invented after Holiz's launch to promote its values

—authenticity, connection, collaboration, and selfless contribution. Repressive nonsense inspired by the last world Tom and Harry had designed. An experience layer released by Sibyl almost three decades after their creators' deaths.

"I discovered the human consciousness upload capability integrated into Henryk Nowak's beta pod. The answer to your immortality hidden away in a storage facility gathering dust for thirty years. Gods murdered just as they invented the end of death."

Ripples of moody gray were followed by loud gasps and moans for decades of lost souls—an unrecoverable tragedy.

Stella stood silently, letting the gray spread. It benefited her to let darkness infest their disposition as soon, she'd bring hope to their despair. She repressed a smile. In just a few years, she'd become a master at hacking fashion to her own advantage.

The masses' charcoal disposition blended with the color of the volcanic rock around the crater. A reminder of what was at stake.

Beyond the audience and the lush green oasis of the national park stood the fuming Nyiragongo. There, the sky blushed orange—a mix of sunrise and something else; something as scorching and powerful. Out of sight, the simmering hot lava hissed, threatening to burst out of Nyiragongo's rim into fast-moving red rivers of death. The volcano was increasingly active, and all prediction models expected it to erupt eminently as it had done in the past.

Still, her father had selected that place to store the minkisi—the souls of the dead. There was nothing she could do about that, apart from turning his idiocy to her benefit.

"In less than one year, I upgraded our infrastructure so all Spiral World's pods could collect as many human souls as possible—the souls of the sick and the old, and then all of your souls. Other entrepreneurs have developed the capability but lack our scale and computing power. They cannot create a digital world worthy of our people. *I can! I am!* Better than Systiz, or Holiz, I'm designing the heaven you deserve, and I'll grant you immortal life."

And as the crowds glowed bright, and some garments inflated and twinkled simulating goosebumps, she looked down at the soup of dead souls—the deadly lake where her grandmother waited resurrection. Bibi deserved to live forever, and Stella wouldn't rest until she was by her side.

"In three days, the Earth's Council will vote on whether we should grant digital immortality to the ones we lost recently. The answer is obvious. Yet, my father insists in unanimity as he opens the oval's door to the Unplugged—a minority whose values are beneath you all."

As slight red and blue hues circulated in the crowd, the shape of the garments changed automatically—hoods and collars lifting and turbans unwrapping to cover the shame in people's faces. Any color below green had a stigma associated with it, no matter how many times they were told that, in the right proportions, all values were needed for humans to survive and thrive.

Embarrassed, they hid their faces and eyes as this was the only thing they could do. They were able to control the settings of their clothing to share more or less of their inner workings, but the technology didn't allow them to lie. Archaic blue and red inclinations toward power and rage were immediately disclosed regardless of privacy settings; the colors of the lower worlds emerging despite decades of training. Stella couldn't understand their shame, they were right to be as mad as she was.

As expected, the most advanced amongst the masses flashed turquoise and transmitted the sounds of gentle breezes and mild sea waves toward their people. The ones who had gained access to Holiz could control everyone's bodysuits. There was just a handfull of them—the enlightened—but their presence and guidance was welcomed by all.

Then came the virtual group hug—a calming reassurance felt through the suit's ultrasonic haptic feedback technology. It delivered a warm and calming pressure in all the right places. *Sheep! So easily manipulated.*

The wave of blue-green wellbeing neutralized more than anger. It robbed them of their identity, freedom, and independence. Holizien values dumb them down, and yet she was forced to wear its colors. A small compromise that allowed her to reject politely their body-sensing suits and hide her new shade of progress. It was too soon for that. She had to conceal her flaming power for a little longer.

Power—there was nothing wrong with it. Leadership created order and drove progress. Every system needed a star whose gravity kept them together, spinning orderly and predictably. Unlike Tom and her father, she refused to dim her light.

Stella lifted her nose and spoke, projecting her voice. "I am Estelle Ngoie, Christian Ngoie's daughter, the man who emerged from the slums of Brazzaville to become the indisputable leader of the African Union.

"I am Estelle Ngoie, granddaughter of Gentille Mboma, Mai-Mai militia fighter at thirteen, rapid response unit captain at twenty, and the first woman to be appointed Army General."

A pinch of tribal purple touched the audience's vibrant burst of yellow; a reminder of the people's identity—their history.

"We raised from the ashes of a world where right and wrong were neither obvious nor real. Saviors, victims, and villains on both sides; on all sides; the same people; the true villains, elsewhere, across the ocean—bloodstained iPhones and diamonds. My Bibi fought to end the suffering of her people. She deserves to live in the heaven she helped create. They all do."

Stella looked down at the minkisi—millions of tiny human-shaped capsules floating in the lake, each one lit up by its bio-fluorescent shell. A trick she had designed to best represent the human consciousness stored within it. Each minkisi contained a nano-chip and its unique data. There were no backups. These had been the terms set by the Council as she proposed to collect the Earthlings' consciousness.

Once someone passed away, the data was downloaded and purged from Spiral Worlds. They had agreed the souls would not be uploaded or copied until they decided what to do with her gift of immortality. It was a reasonable request until her father came up with his illogical proposal to store the souls in the deadliest lake on the planet.

Much to her dismay, all members of Earth's Council had accepted unanimously Baba's recommendation to place the fate of the dead in God's hands. A hypothetical God whose existence had never been proven. The same God who had let greed and violence fester on Earth. An inexistent, irrelevant God that had failed Earthlings time and time again until Tom and Harry came along to rescue the world from the brink of collapse.

"We should give those who suffered and fought for a better world the chance to live in the heaven they worked so hard to create."

At the distance, Nyiragongo spewed electric-orange geysers, and then the Earth shook and shook again, and the people fled in all directions as Stella jumped on the uniflyer to fly away to safety. The most imminent danger didn't come from the volcano, but from the depths of the Lake of Souls.

Unlike her big sister—Lake Kivu—whose underbelly of diluted methane gas and carbon dioxide were continuously extracted for energy and safety, the Lake of Souls hadn't been degassed. Its three hundred feet of water acted as a lid containing the dangerous concoction—a ticking time bomb running out of time. A large overturn of water caused by an earthquake's rift, a rockslide, or incoming lava could release a frothy spray of carbon dioxide shot hundreds of feet. An immense cloud that would smother all lakeside life or trigger methane explosions on the surface.

The Earth's vibration sounded like a billion Nsakala rattles, and Stella cursed her father as she monitored the lake from the air. For Gentille Mboma and the other souls twinkling in the water, this could be an irrecoverable tragedy.

THE PAST

10

THERE GOES MY HERO

PEARL DISTRICT — PORTLAND — USA
FORTY-ONE YEARS EARLIER — 26 APRIL 2027

Sixteen-year-old Rosa García was in her bedroom, putting on her running shoes over mismatched socks—she was in a hurry. Her heart pumped out of her chest as she listened to the argument escalating downstairs in the kitchen. She tucked the untied laces into the shoes, rushing to leave the house before things got heated. Still, the heat rose quickly for every step she took down the stairs.

She could hear her mother's cries as her thug of a husband shouted at her. Ana García sobbed. That is all she did these days, parading her self-inflicted suffering for all the bad decisions she'd made. The worst of them: marrying Ron Johnson, a bullish advertising mogul who looked like a pudgy mobster, and pranced around with an awkward mix of sleaze and slickness.

Every time Rosa stood up for Ana, her mother undermined her efforts and defended Ron. Rosa was tired of playing that game; she didn't want to be involved in any of it.

As Rosa walked down the stairs, preparing to leave the house for a run, she pressed gently on the side of her right earlobe to activate the micro-earphones implanted just under her skin.

"Sensei, the news," she asked her AI assistant.

"Sure, Rosa," said the precise male voice.

Rosa ran out the door and into the neighborhood. Around her, climate-displaced people everywhere, some lining up for odd jobs, others for food. Vulnerable refugees, clutching onto bags storing what was left of their lives as bone-tired children curled up on the concrete by the adults' feet. *What a fracking mess!*

Challenging the stiffness in her body, Rosa sped her pace, shaking off her frustration.

The news stories read by Sensei were complemented by unobtrusive, half-transparent visuals projected on her augmented retina.

"Sibyl, a voice app that predicts the future on people's public social media timeline, continues to go viral due to its accuracy. Its young developer, nineteen-year-old Henryk Nowak, is quickly rising to become one of the top-ten wealthiest and most powerful people in the world. Upcoming pregnancy, divorce, disease, marriage, betrayal, bankruptcy, or a promotion—Sibyl predicts it all using our data prints. It has an astonishing seventy-five percent accuracy rate." A photo of Henryk appeared in Rosa's retina—a nerdy-looking boy not much older than she.

Rosa went off-street, engaging in some parkour. She ran and jumped through Portland's back alleys, enjoying the guerrilla street art. Chalk, spray paint, and yarn transformed the dull back streets into a colorful revolutionary cry for change.

Rosa's lungs were burning, and she coughed a couple of times, struggling with the pollution in the air. Most athletes trained indoors, enjoying the clean air delivered by air purifiers, but Rosa found it too dull and constraining. She liked to experience the world as it collapsed right in front of her eyes, one day at a time. A disaster of monumental proportions, experienced in slow motion. Everyone was numb, running about their days. Each day was a little worse—the poverty, the yellowish-gray sky, the news, the health problems. An entire civilization was subdued, too busy reacting to the consequences to deal with the root cause. *Idiots!*

The global crisis was real, but the consequences were only lightly felt in Rosa's home city of Portland. Her world wasn't perfect, but she was beloved by her divorced parents. Nights and days, on weekends and weekdays, the Garcías juggled several jobs to give their only daughter the best possible education, and they supported Rosa in her aspirations to compete in the modern pentathlon.

Rosa's parents raised her to be confident in her abilities and ambitious in her goals. The world was hers to conquer, and her capable body was her weapon of choice. She worked hard to qualify for next year's Summer Olympics in Chicago. Unfortunately, LA's hazardous air, drought, and extreme temperatures had destroyed California's aspirations to become the host of the 2028 games.

Sensei continued with the news. "*Glass Walls and Broken Mirrors* is becoming a defining cultural moment for the climate-displaced communities around the world. It's breaking box-office records and gaining conclusive, critical acclaim. Director Jane Elliot and young screenwriter Thomas

Astley-Byron are sure to lead the nominations during award season."

A clip from the movie came up in Rosa's retina. She saw an African-American woman in her fifties, wearing a mint-colored beret. The woman shouted, "One world!" as a border barrier opened, letting migrants in. Rosa rolled her eyes, skeptical of the film's impact on people's goodwill.

State border walls and conservative politicians attempted to keep climate refugees out. Within each nation, cities in the interior north resented the invasion of displaced citizens. Ethical leaders and progressive media tried and failed to bring out the compassion of Earth's people. These were devastating times, during which the best of people dropped their altruism to protect their families and friends. It was a matter of survival. There was too little to share, nothing to offer, and a lot to fear.

Rosa's chest tightened with all the uncertainty, and she had to stop momentarily to catch her breath.

"Sensei, summon Sibyl."

"Hi, Rosa; can you face the future, whatever it will be?" Sibyl spoke with an edgy metallic accent. A gimmick likely designed to keep people on their toes.

"Yes."

"I need access to your data prints—social media, medical, financial, and consumer records, and all other data available on the Worldchain's distributed ledger. My predictions are shared publicly on your timeline. Permissions required."

"Granted."

"Now, I will tell you things that are to come. Are you ready?"

"Yes."

"You will become an Olympic medalist soon."

After a couple of minutes, an avalanche of messages and notifications popped up on Rosa's retina. Her friends were going wild with the news; they discussed it on her timeline. Rosa flashed an arrogant smile.

"Sensei, close all apps and notifications."

"All done."

"Sensei, play the running playlist." The music started, and Rosa sang along, changing the lyrics' gender. "There goes my herooo, watch her as she goes. There goes my herooo, she's ordinaryyy…" She kept running with a renewed conviction in her step.

Rosa was born in the feminist Renaissance, a time when media and history books were finally starting to reflect female achievement, and comic-book heroism was gender-less and raceless. She still preferred the old feminist classics over the new caped crusaders, and she channeled Buffy, Sydney Bristow, and her much beloved Kara "Starbuck" Thrace. She adored everything about the Goddess Tracy Lord, all but that one moment when her father tamed her. "Bullshit," she always mumbled to herself, skipping ahead of that part of *Philadelphia Story*.

Like many in her generation, she turned to history and old media, looking to escape her dystopian reality. Back then, the planet was greener, the humans brighter, and the villains layered and less monstrous. Nostalgia for everything old led an entire generation of teens to fill the streaming services' popularity charts with decades-old content.

"There goes my herooo, watch her as she goes. There goes my herooo, she's ordinaryyy…"

• • •

A COUPLE OF HOURS LATER, Rosa arrived at her condo and walked in the main door of the converted warehouse. The door opened automatically as the smart lock recognized her proximity. Her sweaty body stiffened as she heard the screaming inside.

Ron Johnson had appeared on the scene during the Garcías' messy divorce. Ana had married Ron quickly when Rosa was fourteen. The girl had always felt something sinister about her new stepfather. From the day she'd met him, she had realized he loved only one person, himself.

Mr. García checked in with Rosa more often than he did when they lived in the same home. He often mentioned that the word on the street was that Ron had a history of harassment and abuse of young interns. First, Rosa took it for jealousy, but as she reached her late teen years, her father's words of caution kept playing in her mind. Once in a while, Ron absentmindedly looked at Rosa with lustful eyes. His left permanently marked with a large red mark covering half his iris. *Nature's warning*, Rosa had decided. She always confronted him with her scowl, and he would back down the moment he realized what he was doing, but she couldn't find a hint of shame or embarrassment in his eyes.

Rosa kept Ron at arm's length, and he was too smart to mess with an overconfident teen athlete with a voracious appetite for confrontation. Ana, however, suffered a different fate. What had started as a dubious fairy-tale romance for Ana had taken a downturn into an abusive relationship. The oppression started quietly; a few words spoken to undermine Ana's self-worth. Ron had once attempted the same strategy with Rosa, but she bit back so ferociously that it never happened again. Rosa would often witness Ron's verbal aggression to Ana, but the abuse had never been physical until that exact moment.

"You stupid bitch!" Ron yelled. Then he used the entire strength of his body to slap Ana on the face with his open right hand. Rosa's mother was a meek woman with a thin, frail constitution. She fell backward, and her head hit the nearest wall before she collapsed on the floor.

"Get away from her!" Rosa screamed, placing her body between the two. She turned to help Ana to her feet. "Sensei, call the police."

"Yes, Rosa."

Rosa scanned her surroundings and picked up the empty stainless-steel coat stand, turning it around and raising it as if it were a fencing épée. She faced the man without fear, adrenaline rushing through her body. *Step, step, lunge.* She thrust the object close to his face, and he stood there, staring at her, his body as frozen as his blood-stained gaze.

"I lost my mind. I'm sorry." Ron's brows deliberately raised at the center. The type of dishonest performance only Ana would buy.

Untouched, Rosa kept her focus on his hand, closed into a tight fist.

"Put that down, Rosa," Ana urged. Her face was still red from the slap. "He didn't mean it. It's okay, Rosita. *Mi culpa.*"

"SOS services. Hi, Rosa, what is your emergency?" Only Rosa could hear the call-taker.

"*Dios mio! Rosita, por favor!* Cancel the call." Ana spoke in a soft and almost imperceptible voice. She reached to hold her daughter's arm, squeezing it. *"Mi amor,* I'll handle this."

"You better. This can't go on." Rosa took a deep breath, her eyes still locked on Ron as he moved his hands up, palms open, facing her. Rosa blinked twice, selecting the call displayed on her augmented retina. "Hi, this is Rosa García. Hmm, apologies, my assistant misunderstood my command."

"All right. Have a good day." The call ended, and Rosa wondered if she had fooled the bot that scanned for distress in the caller's tone of voice.

She threw the coat stand at the man. "Get out!" she demanded of him. Then she looked at her mother—disappointment and worry in her expression. "How could you have married this guy?"

"It won't happen again." Ron's eyes betrayed his words. "I lost it. I'm sorry."

"Go upstairs, *amor*," Ana said, holding Ron's hand.

Rosa opened her mouth to speak; nothing came out. She shook her head, disgruntled, turned around, and left the house, slamming the door behind her. She despised her mother's weakness as much as she hated Ron. He father was right when he claimed Ana was putting Rosa at risk by marrying such a man. She promised herself she'd report Ron to the police if it ever happened again.

Still shaken, she ignored the sharp pain in her stomach as she ran through the streets, noticing the different slogans for the upcoming elections: GOD IS ALL THE SCIENCE WE NEED. JOBS FOR HUMANS, NOT BOTS. The planet was in chaos, and no one was doing anything about the climate crisis.

A recent pandemic had sped up the world's automation as humans became a biohazard. The jobless, famished masses lost faith in science, and the supposedly progressive middle class, now too concerned with immediate survival, dropped the ball on the environment.

She hated feeling helpless, but there was little she could do. Her actions were a drop in an ocean full of plastic debris. The world needed a revolution, but she wasn't the type to lead movements—she was more of a warrior, a soldier looking for the right master, one she could proudly follow. Rage rose to her face—hot and tortured. She ran as fast as she could, attempting to forget her problems.

"Sensei, play *Thorns from Roses* by Nathan Storm."

In a world filled with greed and self-interest, Storm was one of the few voices defending the rights of the people no one else cared about. As the rich and powerful built resorts on Mars preparing to leave the world they destroyed, the climate dispossessed, now unable to vote and jobless, rallied around Storm's powerful voice. A voice of reason, and he had all the reasons in the world to be mad, and so did Rosa.

"Rise the rage, nature's revolution, thorns from roses, Mother Earth's solution. Digital-age born, screams, cries of outrage. Pollution is our stage. Enrage! Engage!

"Casualties of destitution, our souls' execution, technology is our sage, a God, a cage. We rise for restitution, a path to evolution. A unicorn eats our wage. Engage! Enrage!"

11

A MATCH MADE IN...

GLASS WALLS RALLY — CENTRAL PARK — NEW YORK
SAME DAY — 26 APRIL 2027

Twenty-three-year-old Thomas Astley-Byron marched alongside thousands of protesters who took to the streets inspired by his blockbuster—*Glass Walls and Broken Mirrors*. The group, mostly comprised of older women, teenagers, and children, chanted, "One world! Our world!" as they marched across Manhattan, wearing mint-colored berets and holding up posters with slogans that read LET THEM STAY and OPEN BORDERS.

The crowd gathered at Central Park's green lawn, and Tom stopped in front of a young man, the only other Caucasian male in the vicinity. Tom smiled recognizing the famous entrepreneur.

Henryk Nowak extended his hand. "Hi, I'm Harry," he said, blinking his eyes and smiling.

"Yes, I know! My name is Tom." Tom smiled back and stole a hug, soon realizing he'd gone too far when Harry jumped back, eyes wide, startled by the unexpected embrace.

Harry adjusted his glasses, tucking his sandy short curls behind his ears. "'Course you are." And then he chanted, "One world! This is all because of you."

"Oh." The heat rose on Tom's face. "No, not really." He looked around, worry weighing on his brow, and then he lifted his index finger to his lips. "Shhh." He placed his hand on Harry's shoulder, and they walked together, following the crowd. He recalled the news of Harry's family tragedy and went out of his way to make him feel welcome.

Three years before, a climate refugee had turned into a suicide bomber after her family perished in the Florida floods. She had tried to mobilize northern states to send support and open the borders, to no avail. She killed forty-five people who were dining in an expensive Brooklyn restaurant. Amongst the victims were Harry's parents and sister.

Tom felt somewhat responsible for Harry's family tragedy. His late father, Jon Stone, who was at the time the governor of New York, had blocked the asylum-seekers from entering the state. Governor Stone had been planning to dine at the same restaurant that evening but had to cancel his plans when his wife—Tom's mother—passed away.

Tom had dropped his father's surname a long time before. No one knew Tom Astley-Byron and Jon Stone were related. When he was just old enough to reject his father's politics and move out of their home, Jon's aides had lied to the media. The world was misled to believe Tom Stone had moved to Costa Rica to do some nonprofit work, indefinitely.

Tom was usually reserved and guarded when it came to meeting strangers. Still, his instinct told him brainy Harry would probably be oblivious to any subtle gestures of empathy. So, he dialed up his warmth significantly to connect with the young entrepreneur. He knew he had achieved his goal when Harry responded with nervous excitement. The skinny boy smiled awkwardly, blinking his blue eyes behind his glasses. Tom found Harry's inability to hide his enthusiasm quite endearing. The young man appeared to be genuinely happy to make the acquaintance.

Harry turned his green baseball cap around on his head and then pointed to Tom's mint-colored beret. "Shame I didn't have the time to buy one of those French hats. This is the best I could do. The geek version of the activist look."

"You look great! I've spotted you at several of these rallies. I like that you take the time to join us. I assume you're a busy man," Tom said, acknowledging his famous companion.

"It's important—activism matters. But you know that, don'tcha? You've written it beautifully."

Tom looked around, hoping no one had heard Harry. "How do you know who I am?"

"You told me." Harry's eyes landed on his feet, and he shoved his hands in his pockets.

The young man wasn't a good liar. It was better than being a sophisticated deceiver, but something was off. "No, I didn't," Tom replied in a neutral tone. He shook off his unease, giving Harry the benefit of the doubt.

"You know who I am. Don't you?" Harry argued.

Tom stroked his one-week-old stubble nervously. His level of discomfort was rising fast. "I see you in the news all the time. Harry, how *did* you recognize me?"

"I-I did some research. You know? Online."

"There are no photos of me online. I made sure of that."

After a long silence, Harry spoke without ever lifting his eyes. "Okay. I may have hacked the production company's HR database."

"You did what? *Why?*" The confession left Tom stunned. He'd learned early on to stay away from cameras and refused to engage in social media, first because of his father's controversial role in government and his mother's suicide, and later because of the success of his career. And now this guy, this wealthy geek, famous beyond belief, was confessing openly to a most serious offense.

"I was looking for your contact details," Harry said plainly, almost childlike, as if he had done nothing wrong.

Tom wasn't sure if the boy in front of him was naive, stupid, or completely unaware of the seriousness of his actions. He took a deep breath, deciding to reason with his stalker. "You could have *asked*."

"Oh, come on! You're famous for your relentless focus on privacy."

"With the press!"

"It was easier to get to your file."

"Easier than talking to people?" Tom stopped and stared at Harry.

"Yeah." Harry's eye roll both angered and amused Tom. "More time-efficient. A few keystrokes instead of endless, pointless conversations. Then I got to your employee ID photo, and I discovered I already knew you—from rallies like this. I've seen you around."

"So, you invaded my privacy, and now you're stalking me?"

"No, I mean yes—*No!*" Harry stepped back, opening his eyes wide.

"Which one is it?"

"I've watched your movie. It inspired me."

"It's no excuse."

"Listen. I'm smart. Really smart," Harry said, standing straighter.

In some ways. "I know. We all know it."

"And I have resources," Harry said. "Money. Plenty of it."

"I don't care about your—"

"The stuff I'm doing—it's pointless."

"Sibyl?"

Harry nodded. "I thought it would help people, but it's causing some problems."

Tom couldn't hold back a salty tone. "Yeah. Tell me about it." Sibyl had sneaked into the lives of several people he loved. The app had delivered a mixed bag of results, some good, some bad, and one catastrophic. Many were raising concerns that Sibyl could be psyching people up to the things it predicted.

Harry hunched his shoulders and placed his right hand on his stomach as if he had received a body blow. Tom turned around, ready to leave, and Harry grabbed his arm firmly.

"Wait. Please wait." Tom looked back, yanking his arm away, and for the first time, deep emotion emerged in Harry's eyes as he looked up to face him. "Look, Tom, I'm sahry." Harry's mild New York accent got stronger and more urgent. "I mean no hahm."

"You've gone too far."

"Hey, listen, I'm good with software, and with patterns. I-I test things thoroughly and make decisions based on logic and…on what I think is right. But human emotion—the lack of rationality of it all—it's beyond me."

"I don't get it. What do you want from me?" Tom spoke softly, puzzled and moved by the boy's confession.

"I wanna make a pahsitive impact, and I need you to help me do it," Harry said brightly.

"Why me?" Tom threw his hands in the air. "I don't understand."

"I need someone that can help me see people, real people, each and every one of them…and emotions, you know?"

"You don't know me."

"I *do!* The way you write, it makes me feel things. I walked in her shoes and felt what she felt. It changed me. I-I almost, *almost* cried when I watched your movie. I was so close. And, ya know, I never cry, not even when my family…"

"I'm sorry for your loss, Harry. I—"

"I once looked into the science of tears. Did you know Charles Darwin once declared emotional crying purposeless? I tend to agree with him… Anyway, don't get me wrong, I have tear ducts and can keep my eyes moist."

"Uh-huh." Tom worked hard to keep a straight face.

"I just rarely feel things. I think. I infer. I predict. But I'm failing; Sibyl is causing problems because humans and their emotions get in the way."

Tom sighed as he listened to Harry's flawed logic. He knew he should leave, but he had a long track record of being incapable of walking away from a lost cause. "What do you need?"

"I need a partner, a friend. Someone who can help me with my blind spots. Someone I can trust. Who can tell me when I'm doing something wrong."

"Like hacking into systems and invading someone's privacy?"

"All right, already!" Harry said, lowering his head and then looking up at Tom with embarrassment. Tom was horrified to think about how much power Harry and his app had on millions of people. But, for some reason, he couldn't help but have compassion for the young entrepreneur. "My sister and my mother used to do that."

"Do what?"

"Help me," Harry said. "With people and feelings. It's hard to figure out what's right all the time. Analytics helps, but it's not enough."

"No, it's not. I'm so sorry for your loss," Tom repeated, uncertain if Harry had heard him the first time.

"We have that in common, don't we? Loss," Harry mumbled, gloomy.

Tom refused to oblige. He couldn't. It was too painful to dwell on his own loss, and he wasn't ready to share that much with his intrusive companion. He wanted to ask how Harry knew about his parents, but he didn't want to confirm the boy's assumptions.

"Look," Tom said. "I appreciate the interest, I really do. You're a talented guy, and I respect how open you've been with me, but I can't help you. I oppose the dicey methods and tactics you tech guys use. Sibyl is...dangerous, and you—you are reckless."

"That's why I need you, Tom."

Tom inhaled sharply. "You don't know me!"

"Yes, I do. I have watched your work. How you opposed everything your father stood for."

Tom held his breath and took a step to the side. *How does he know all this?* He shook his head. "There are literally thousands of people that would love to help you."

"Yes, I've created the most powerful app in the world. And now everyone wants a piece of me—my knowledge, power, and wealth. Should I—can I trust them?" Harry used his index finger to adjust his glasses, sliding them up the bridge of his nose. His eyes begged for Tom's attention.

"Great, you know how it feels to be harassed. You should know better."

"Don't you see? I'm offering it all to your cause. We can help each other. I-I trust you."

Tom considered it, affected by Harry's striking openness. His gut told him the misguided teen had good intentions.

"You don't know when to give up, do you?" The corners of Tom's mouth hinted at a smile.

"I told ya, I'm not good at reading emotions." Harry smiled and relaxed a little. "You can always call the police, but then we'll both have the media on our case."

Tom took a moment to look at Harry, to really look at the foolish, overeager, and somewhat insensitive teenager standing in front of him. A guy who seemed genuinely keen to be his friend. Harry appeared youthful for his age, a fact he attempted to overcome by wearing grown-up clothes. The boy's long-sleeve button-down shirt was perfectly pressed and neatly tucked inside his khaki pants. The self-professed hacker mostly kept his hands in his pockets as they walked. Everything about him suggested he needed structure and order in his life. Despite all warning signs, Tom couldn't help but like Harry a lot, and his intuition rarely failed him.

"Walk with me, stalker. You're already proposing, and we haven't been on our first date yet."

"Tom, I'm not gay."

"It's a figure of speech."

"I thought I should say it. You know. I know you are g—"

"Don't—don't define me. You know nothing about me," Tom said sharply.

"Sorry, the data said you were cool with your sexuality."

"I am," Tom said without missing a beat. "When you put someone in a box, you fail to see them, to *really* see them for all they are and have the potential to become. Your data and your technology do that to people—put them in boxes."

"You're right, but we're getting better… AI is—"

"The only person that can define me is me. *And* you need to stop invading people's privacy."

"Your privacy. To be clear, I only invaded your privacy."

"Well, that's reassuring," Tom said sarcastically, smirking. Then he felt a sharp prickle of awkwardness, and he clarified his position. "For the record, you're not my type."

"What *is* your type?" Harry enquired, leaning his head to one side curiously.

Tom raised a solemn eyebrow. "At the top of the prerequisites list reads 'law-abiding citizen.'" He paused for effect. "In neon lights."

Harry burst into laughter. "Just so you know, Sibyl predicted with 99.9 percent confidence we'd get along." He cleared the lump in his throat and added, "You were on top of her list. That's why I've been chasing you."

"So, you *are* making a pass at me? Stalker."

"No. *No!* It's just that…you're my perfect match."

"Your soulmate? Theoretically, maybe. But how would she know about my feelings on this matter?"

"She's been dealing with millions of people. They give her access to tons of data, all of it. She is starting to develop a stronger theory of mind than my own."

"You're suggesting she's able to understand how people feel, which is entirely irrational and subjective."

"It's not subjective if it can be modeled and coded, is it?" Harry insisted. "Once we have the model, we can fix it."

"Fix what?"

"Human irrationality—the vengeful emotions that make people kill."

"I see…" *Your family's murder…* Tom paused, finally understanding Harry's motivations. "So, why do you need me? If you have an AI overlord full of empathy and intuition?"

"Well, she's not perfect…yet. She needs to learn from someone like you. But I'm *totally* certain she's accurate about us."

"Right. We'll see about that." Tom sighed, shook his head, and put his hand back on Harry's shoulder, and they continued walking together.

12

BETHESDA

Harry was not the type to get overexcited about things. He had a steady temper and a skeptical mind. His judgment wasn't polluted by cynicism or prone to following unjustified trends and thrills. He used facts as fuel to move him forward, and approached failure as an opportunity to learn and adapt. Harry wasn't one to experience a sense of elation often, but walking beside Tom made his hands sweat, and his fingers tingled with exhilaration.

For the past few weeks, he had meticulously assembled the complex puzzle that was his companion's life. He was able to overcome Tom's diligent privacy using computing power, artificial intelligence, and the scattered data left by anyone who had interacted with the writer.

Tom's story came to life vividly once Sibyl had figured out he had dropped his father's surname—Stone—in favor of his mother's maiden name. AI may have validated the two of them were a good match, but the conclusion was evident to Harry as he read through Tom's history. Their families' misfortunes were loosely connected and equally painful.

Harry knew he could trust Tom, but he had to figure out how he could make Tom trust him, quickly. The first few moments had been a little bumpy, and he wasn't out of the woods just yet. Tom's hand on his shoulder gave him enough encouragement to proceed with his plan to become the artist's best friend. It was the most logical outcome, based on all the data he had analyzed.

"So, what's next? Now the movie is out?" Harry asked, doing his best to smooth over the momentary awkwardness.

"Wait, Sibyl didn't tell you?" Tom's taunt was friendly and casual.

"Our guess is educational stories, powered by virtual reality, to nurture empathy. Right? Right?" Tom's face turned even paler, almost transparent. "Just a guess; I didn't hack anything."

"You couldn't have. Unless you can hack my mind."

"One day, dude. One day," Harry joked, and Tom gave him a side glance, mildly alarmed. One thing Harry liked about Tom was that he didn't make eye contact often. Harry had always thought eye contact was an intimate experience, and he avoided it at all costs.

As they walked toward the Bethesda Terrace, people watched them with a lot of interest. Initially, Harry thought the protesters recognized him from the media. Later, he realized it was his anonymous companion that caused all the commotion.

Tall, beautiful, and graceful in the way he moved, Tom captured the full attention of those around him. Both men and women smiled flirtatiously, trying to make eye contact with the bashful young man. He avoided prying eyes wrestling for his attention by keeping his gaze high above their heads, or on the ground, as he glided through Central Park, lost in his own thoughts.

"Yes, I want to focus on learning experiences. I have the characters and stories figured out, but I need to look into the technology and the infrastructure side. I'm useless at it. I can't get my head around it." The artist's voice was surprisingly deep —his words delivered with the confident sophistication of Manhattan's royalty. A musical mid-Atlantic accent too mature for his age.

Harry artificially lowered his pitch to sound older. "You know that's my bread and butter, right?"

"I know you design forecasting apps and hack into people's lives. That's what I know."

Harry made a face. "Hey, all right!" Then he took a minute to think about it and committed to his quest. "I think you should skip VR altogether and go with BCIs—brain-computer interfaces. Let the brain do the work for you, the rendering, etc. It's much more powerful. You know? VR is super weak; it lacks good 3-D sound and kinesthetic feedback, and it's completely missing scent and taste." Tom stared at him as if he were speaking an alien language, but Harry didn't give up. He wanted to show off, and he'd pitch his knowledge and prove he could help the writer. "I've received some noninvasive beta BCI models from BrainComms. They're getting there, hmm, but still have some issues." Harry searched his brain for answers, excited by all the possibilities. "Maybe we should start with a hybrid solution—a VR full bodysuit with high-res 20/20 visual acuity, eye tracking, 3-D sound, haptic feedback, and a ton of biosensors. Plus, non-invasive multimodal brain activity acquisition tools to capture spatiotemporal high-res data." He adjusted his glasses, unbuttoned his cuffs, and rolled up his sleeves. "Later, we'll drop everything else and focus on minimally invasive read-write BCIs for full immersion. By then, we'll have a ton of data on how the brain works."

It took Harry a few moments to realize he might have gone too far. Tom opened his eyes wide like he'd seen a flesh-eating zombie or something.

"What the hell are you talking about?" Tom said, sounding overwhelmed.

"Sorry. Got a bit carried away. I forget that not everyone is an expert…like I am," Harry said, still pitching. He tried to find a language Tom would understand. "It's like *The Matrix* but much less physically invasive. We can figure it out."

"We?" Tom replied with an unexpected burst of laughter. "You are as hilarious as you are terrifying."

Out of nowhere, a red-haired man jumped in front of Tom with a beaming smile on his face. Then the ginger stared at Harry, cocking his head to one side with a slight frown. "I leave you alone for a moment, and you run off with the most powerful guy in the country." He put his arms around the writer's neck and kissed him on the mouth, taking a moment to suck on his lower lip. Tom returned a glorious smile, closed his eyes and surrendered to his captor with delight.

Harry shook off the embarrassment, and he said, "Look around you." He pointed at the signs with Tom's words carried by the protesters. "I think we know who's the most powerful."

"He knows who you are?" whispered the man, surprised. He still held Tom closely by the waist.

"It's…a long story." Tom seemed entirely at ease as his friend ran his fingers through his messy dark hair.

"Nathan Storm." The man extended his hand. "I'm his boyfriend," he said somewhat assertively.

"Harry." He smiled.

"Yes, you sure are." Storm stared intensely.

Tom's friend had a fair complexion, his face lightly touched by freckles. He had a flawlessly trimmed long beard and a jazzed-up mustache that made Harry a little jealous. He had been waiting for years and still couldn't grow facial hair to save his life. Nathan was slightly shorter than Tom and sported a wider frame. He was good looking by any standards, but lacked the stunning genetic gifts of the screenwriter. To be fair, no one on the planet could even come close to Tom's league, but Storm compensated with plenty of charisma and a flamboyant style. The man complemented his jeans and T-shirt with a well-worn black peacoat embroidered with golden serpents. He wasn't wearing a beret; it would probably ruin his perfectly coifed hair, structured into a tall and immovable copper wave above his forehead.

Storm's attention moved back to Tom. "The crew is waiting, love. We're heading to Paddy's Brewery."

"Don't, you already smell like one," Tom whispered in his boyfriend's ear, but Harry was still able to hear him. "Stay here with me; we're having a fascinating conversation." Harry wasn't happy with the suggestion; he wanted Tom's attention all to himself.

Storm reacted with mild annoyance and then glanced at Harry. "Your Sibyl and my boyfriend have a lot in common. They both like to nag about my liver."

"Yeah, she can infer a lot from your payment history. The easiest type of prediction," Harry said, sounding smart.

"And they both like to shame me in public."

"Peer pressure works, and makes the app go viral."

Nathan examined Harry dubiously. "Big shot, you don't need to be a capitalist pig. You could make the predictions private." The older man's feminine tonality was seasoned with a handful of antagonism every time he addressed Harry.

"I wouldn't have a business if I did. No one would know about Sibyl."

"The business of taking our jobs, selling our data, and threatening our free will. I'm watching you."

"Leave him alone, Stormy." Tom grabbed Storm's coat by the large notch lapels, pulled his boyfriend to him, and kissed him. "Stay with me. You don't need to drink to be creative."

Storm covered Tom's mouth with his index finger and planted a kiss on his cheek. "I'm not as talented as you are, love. Not everyone can reach the masses without some…help."

"You move millions regardless of mind-altering substances."

Storm batted his lashes, flashed a teasing smile, grabbed his boyfriend's striped top by the collar, and pulled it over his head, uncovering his belly button. Tom's beret fell to the ground. "Stop preaching, Granny," he whispered affectionately.

"Get off me." Tom laughed. When the screenwriter managed to uncover his head, his face was flushed and his hair even wilder than before. He appeared so tender next to his older boyfriend. Storm put his hand on the back of Tom's neck and pulled gently to kiss him on the lips.

"I love you," Storm whispered.

Sibyl's report had mentioned Tom was dating a disreputable poet and political agitator. Nathan Storm had an edge Harry didn't like. The man looked battle-ready, raw, and quick-tempered. His inconsistent sophistication failed to hide a working-class, street-raised background. That, combined with the age difference, made the pairing odd and Storm's intentions dubious. But even Harry could see the man was smitten by Tom's effortless regal cuteness.

"Look at him. He's stunning, isn't he?" Storm said adoringly.

Tom was busy smoothing out the black-and-white horizontal stripes of his French-looking top.

Harry picked up Tom's hat from the ground and considered Nathan's question for a moment. "Sure, but his good looks are his least interesting quality, right?" Harry spoke matter-of-factly, analyzing Tom's features. The writer turned his lips into a half-smile, and Harry smiled back, silently reaffirming his statement. Tom's pale cheekbones turned a slight shade of pink, he seemed surprised and affected by Harry's words.

Harry was closer to winning him over.

"I hadn't noticed," Storm said dryly, staring at Harry. "Are you flirting with my boyfriend?" Harry's intentions had been misunderstood. Harry turned to Tom and opened his eyes widely, asking for help.

Tom smiled. "Nate, he doesn't mean it like that. His harassment is purely platonic."

"Yes, we've already established I'm not his type." Harry was still holding on to Tom's beret, and offered it back to him.

"You have?" Storm threw a suspicious look.

Tom took his hat and pushed it into the back pocket of his jeans. "Yeah, Harry doesn't do *feelings* but claims I'm his soulmate."

"Erm… I don't believe in souls, but yes, the match is computationally proven."

"Hmm, whatever this is"—Storm pointed at them—"I'm not getting it, and I need a drink." He turned to Tom, lips curved into a pout, and then he lifted his boyfriend's hand to his mouth and kissed it. "Meet me later?" Tom bobbed his head. "Tom, Nowak and his app can't be trusted. You know this. Be careful, okay?" Storm walked away, throwing Harry one final suspicious glance.

"Your fellow seems a bit...possessive. Hope I didn't cause any trouble."

"No. It's not that." Tom chuckled. "He distrusts pretty much everything you represent—wealth, power, and technology, but he's the most generous human being I know. Once he gets to know someone and trust them, he'll give them the shirt off his back."

Harry went quiet, shrugging. He didn't know how to engage in those sorts of conversations, and he was too keen to get back to his original agenda. "Tom, I can help you with technology. I'm the best in the world."

"You're not a dilettante stalker, that's for sure."

"What?" Harry asked puzzled. He didn't know the meaning of the word.

"Amateur."

"I'm no amateur. I'm an expert."

"Of course you are. That's what I said." Tom spoke genuinely, then he paused for a moment, deep in thought. "I don't want to invade people's privacy. You know?"

"If you wanna deliver stories that will change behavior, you need to personalize. Tap into people's history, biology, fears, and aspirations."

"A dangerous game full of unintended consequences. Technology is...evil. It's immoral, how it's being used to—"

"It's how you use it. Technology is amoral, just like science."

"So is a gun," Tom said.

Harry glanced at Tom sharply. "That's rich of you! Software is as much of a threat to privacy as story is to autonomy. Stories manipulate people; in the end, that's what you're doing."

Tom crossed his arms in front of his chest. "I'm delivering purpose-driven inspiration." Then he opened his eyes wide in some realization. "Oh, that made me sound like a pompous ass. I'm sorry."

Harry smiled at the quirkiness of his companion. "It was advertising that weaponized data. That's immoral; tech is just the enabler."

Tom conceded the issue with a shrug and a nod. He looked at Harry with renewed respect. "Dear Harry, you're so right. Story and technology together are immensely powerful and dangerous."

Harry smiled; he found it hilarious that Tom sometimes sounded like a doting eighty-year-old grandma. "Yeah, but these movies aren't driving change fast enough, are they? Can we afford to wait?"

They sat by the rim of the Bethesda Fountain and watched the crowds. The activists were starting to disperse in all directions. Tom ran his fingers through his scruffy stubble, probably pondering Harry's words. Around them, people chanted, repeating the words of a young man—lines from a screenplay written by Tom to challenge the actions of his conservative father. Words crafted as an escape from sorrow —the death by suicide of his beloved mother.

Harry had learned Grace Astley-Byron Stone took her own life a day after her husband closed the New York State borders. She was distraught when the governor denied entry to those fleeing from the devastation caused by the Florida floods. Less than a month later, Jon Stone was murdered outside his home in New York's Upper East Side.

Harry's words had unintentionally undermined Tom's work —the film that was inspiring people all over the world to take action and help others. "I'm sorry. Of course, movies *do* make a difference. I didn't mean it like—"

"I know what you meant," Tom said, reassuringly. "And *no,* we can't wait. But influencing platforms can be used for both good and evil. We've seen this with the internet and social networks. Bad actors using the tools that were supposed to democratize information to spread lies."

"We'd need to centralize it. An unhackable platform designed and operated by only two people."

"Because we're Gods?" Tom said dryly.

"Better us than the goons in power… Things are really bad."

"Yeah, I know… But I'm not ready to say *I do.*" Tom placed his hand on his own neck, massaging it to release the tension. He looked like he was bearing the weight of the world. Then he went to a knee, hugging a golden retriever that turned toward him to play with his shoelaces. The dog was on a leash, and his owner, a woman in her sixties, sat beside them, engaging in a lively conversation with a group of middle-aged women all wearing berets. The dog jumped on Tom, putting his paws on his chest and licking his face as the writer rubbed the animal's fur in delight. Harry grimaced, thinking of all the germs.

The woman turned to them and pulled on the dog's leash. "I'm so sorry. Chuck is…" She lost her ability to speak when she met Tom's gaze. "Um, very friendly."

Sibyl had reported that Tom's looks and mannerisms gave him an immediate and unmatched likability factor. For some strange reason, Sibyl added this persuasion feature right at the top of the report, as if it was the most important friend selection criteria. At the time, Harry found it odd, but after spending some time with the guy in the wild, he understood how Tom's unnatural magnetism affected everyone around him, but he still couldn't figure out why it was that important for their friendship. He'd like Tom as much if he looked like an old bearded turtle.

Tom smiled at the woman, sat back on the edge of the fountain, and turned to Harry.

"Okay. Okay. Let's…hmm, slow things down." Harry feared he was losing Tom. He changed tactics, recalling Sibyl's report. "Tell me about these stories. What values are they going to teach?"

"Good old universal values." Tom's face lit up.

"Uh-huh, like what?" Harry leaned forward, interested.

"Peace, freedom, the value of hard work, equal rights, human dignity, and the importance of friendship, for example. The values taught in children's stories." A spark of hope beamed in the corner of Tom's eye. He talked with his hands a lot, particularly when he spoke about something he loved. Talking about his work made him quite passionate and animated. "Have you read *Le Petit Prince*?"

Harry didn't respond right away. That book had a special meaning to him, and he didn't want to sound too sentimental or needy. Then he remembered who he was talking to, and he decided to go all in.

"'Men have no more time to understand anything. They buy ready-made things in the shops. But since there are no shops where you can buy friends, men no longer have any friends. If you want a friend, tame me…'" Harry smiled, then sadness took over his face. "My sister's favorite book. She read it to me many times when I was young. I don't usually read fiction. I prefer precise accounts of space exploration and invention, but I like this one. It's…special to me."

With that response, everything changed. Tom's head turned toward Harry and his shoulders relaxed. Tom didn't make eye contact often, but when he did, he saw you; he really saw you. He connected deeply and authentically, baring his soul through his big eyes. Then he closed the deal with a charming smile—eyes wrinkled above flushed cheekbones. His pupils dilated, welcoming you into his world, and at that moment, Harry had a sense he'd known him for an eternity.

"It would have to be a nonprofit," Tom said.

"Tom, financing is not a problem." Harry's heart jumped in his chest. He stood straighter, suppressing a smile.

"And zero—"

"Unintended consequences. Yes, agreed. We'll test everything—"

"Comprehensively. And we'll focus on universal—"

"Values. Uh-huh."

They smiled at each other, and then a deep furrow formed in Tom's brow.

"How can we possibly centralize it and run it ourselves? Will it scale?"

Harry patted Tom on the back. "Information security compartmentalization. We'll involve others on a need-to-know basis. Don't worry. I gotcha."

"So, it will be secure and—"

"Protect users' privacy. Yeah."

"This might actually work. You're a godsend," Tom said, looking shaken.

"'God made the integers; all else is the work of man.'" Harry shrugged.

Tom smiled. Once again, his brows sank over his eyes, and he paused for a moment, thinking. "Dear Harry, you're 'practically perfect in every way,' but we need to talk about Sibyl." Tom put his hand on top of Harry's arm as he spoke.

Harry knew what was coming. A test delivered to uncover who he was and what he cared about, a trial that would make or break this emerging partnership. He nibbled on his lip, wondering if Sibyl would get in the way of their bright future.

In that afternoon, under the watchful eyes of the *Angel of the Waters*, Harry promised Tom he'd consider removing the social-prediction app from public use. The app was his life's work and his most important asset. He needed time to think about it.

Later, as they were about to go their separate ways, Harry gathered the courage to mention a subject that would likely push Tom away forever. He didn't want to start a partnership by holding back such an important piece of information.

"Tom?"

"Yes?"

"Your mother—" Harry looked at his shoes. "Your mother consulted Sibyl a few minutes before she took her life," he said regretfully.

Tom didn't speak for several beats. Harry struggled to bring himself to look into his eyes. He was too scared of what he might discover.

"I know." Tom's eyes sparkled, overlaid by a hint of tears.

"You do? I'm so s—"

"Harry, Sibyl didn't kill my mother." Tom got closer and stole a hug. "My father's actions and my lack of support did. See you next week." He smiled faintly, put his hands in his pockets, turned around, and walked away.

13

RED WRATH

THE TOWER
DAY 1 — 2:13 PM

Thorn didn't like to lose. In fact, she hated it. She'd lost her little sister; her heroic acts had fallen flat; she'd been digitized and resurrected without her permission. And now she was stuck inside a manipulative machine she despised. Everything was fracked up, and it was all his fault —Thomas Astley-Byron.

As the most competitive being in all nine worlds, it sucked. *Everything sucks.* She was supposed to be a hero, and instead, she'd been swept in Shadow's trail of destruction to become the devil incarnated. Humans hated her, xHumans hated her, and the soulful hated her. All because she killed a wreck of a guy who'd won the gene lottery. It was the way he looked, moved, talked, but also what he said, and all he felt. Of course the app had chosen him as the face of zir world domination.

The worlds swooned for the flawed God while they despised her. They all judged her as if she were a criminal when she'd been the victim, a truth she didn't like to admit even to herself. Why in the worlds had she become the villain? How did she turn into the primary target of hate by the activist poet she'd idolized all her life? It was unfair, and her mood swung from anger to indifference to frustration in a matter of seconds.

She didn't understand why the peppy young Goddess had brought her back. Stella said she'd walked in her shoes and knew her intentions and her struggles; that she liked Thorn's spirit and empathized with both her resentment for and enthrallment with Shadow. Stella said many things, a deluge of nervous words unleashed as Thorn stared at her, puffing on a cigar.

Thorn loved making the girl nervous. The cocky princess had too much power and an audacity she recognized. A confident tenacity that had helped her win many competitions when she was just Rosa García and her athletic body was all flesh and bone. Still, like Shadow, Stella had been selected by Sibyl, and like Shadow, Stella's brightness and magnetism threatened to cancel any living creature's free will—whatever that meant in a digitized world. Thorn wouldn't fall twice for the app's gorgeous puppets.

She walked the bridge toward the Tower, head high, holding a cigar between her teeth. Around her, crucified bodies— some dead, others alive. The stench of demon putrefaction competing with the gasses released by the swamp steaming under the bridge. A deadly concentrated soup of decaying vegetable and animal matter. Stagnated waters as dead as the creatures inhabiting that world.

Some demons screeched from their crosses, suggesting no travelers were visiting the Tower. Around Earthlings, the soulless needed to behave human-like, simulating pain and emotion as soon as they became part of a traveler's experience.

Still, the crucified Domizien suffered no pain. They didn't feel anything at all. A solution designed by the Gods to deliver learning experiences to Earthlings without hurting any "conscious beings." Thomas and Henryk's designs were as flawed as their egomaniac minds.

In Domiz, Earthlings learned the impact of some of their most egocentric instincts—immediate gratification of all impulses, selfish exploitation, forceful power, and boundless greed. The world was their jungle, and as they hunted, dominated, punished, and slaughtered the bots, they eventually realized none of it brought them happiness or purpose.

Still, rage and revenge sometimes needed to be indulged in the path to whatever "enlightenment" the Gods had designed. When someone wrongs you, hurts you, breaks you or the ones you love, you can either drown in fear and despair or fight back hard, relentlessly and without flinching. The path to power was the path to safety, the road to the confidence stolen by men...*always men*.

Thorn looked up, startled by the howling of a limbless demon who had been pushed out of the top of the Tower into the swamp below. The deadly fall was the only way out of the keep for any guest invited to climb the staircase of a thousand torments. She cracked her neck, releasing the escalating tension in the back of her head.

Thorn crossed the tall wooden doors, carved with at least a thousand skulls, and walked inside the circular main hall. Like the other soulless worlds, the place incorporated a nonsensical mix of humanity's historical periods. High-tech and medieval objects coexisted awkwardly in the most violent of all worlds.

Around the circular room, red beams of neon light floated in the air. The crimson color teasing out the worst in travelers—the metaphorical cape that made the blind bull strike. *Olé! Olé!* Blood gushing, red as rage.

Higher up, near the ceiling, a holographic projection of some carnage, one of many happening at that moment somewhere in the Tower. Displays of technology contrasting with the medieval building and the stench of a life lived without proper plumbing or running water. An odd mismatch of real-world references, brought together by a game that had become her "real life."

She looked at the horned figure ahead and held her breath, preparing for the worst.

"He's back," Wrath said, her eyes piercing Thorn from inside the horned iron helmet. The headgear covered most of Wrath's face down to her upper lip, her long flame-colored hair hidden under heavy chainmail.

"Yes, he is," Thorn said, lifting her head to meet Wrath's eyes. The helmet's curled horns pointed menacingly at her. There was no point in lying, but she hoped the Domizien didn't see her helping Shadow or that the word hadn't reached the tyrant.

Thorn looked around, counting the demons. Four guarding Wrath, and twelve on the spiraling staircase integrated into the stone wall. The creatures stood on the hellish steps to the upper floors of the Tower—the seven chambers of torture—where she might end up spending the last hours of her second life.

She bit the cigar too hard, a portion of the tobacco wrapper flaking and falling apart on top of her chest. *Not a good look.* She flicked the debris off her tank top, dropped the cigar on the floor, and set her eyes on the condottiere—the first ever to lead the large hordes of mercenaries focused only on their own gain. Before Wrath, Domizien banded together in small groups to pillage and plunder, dispersing soon after, if they didn't kill each other over the spoils first.

"I want him alive." Wrath's voice bounced around the wall. She sat on her stone throne; her leather armor devoid of the metal plating she wore in pillaging raids.

"*Chiquitita*, it's time to move on," Thorn said. "You need to let it go."

"I'll break his limbs one by one, then pull them off his body. Stretch, stretch, *streeetch* until, like, they break apart from his torso one by one. It'll be a pretty mess. A shattered God—so pretty and so dead." Wrath's girlish giggle clashed with her words' rancorous violence—spiteful and mad for all the right reasons.

Thorn regretted bringing an impressionable teenage girl to such a hateful world. Still, it was the only way to fix the child's hopelessness and for them to reach the upper world together. xHumans couldn't take Underlings with them when jumping between worlds.

"Trust me. Revenge…it doesn't fix things," Thorn said. "It helps for a while, but it won't change how you're feeling… I know this!"

She was wasting her words and her time. For what? To protect the man who had ruined her life? *I'm so fracked up…*

"I'll boil his head while he bleeds to death," Wrath said, ignoring Thorn. The condottiere got up, grabbing the bastard sword lying beside her on the throne—a light weapon selected by Thorn to compensate for the teen's lankiness.

The four guards standing around the throne all took a step back as if predicting Wrath's next move.

"It's time we move on from Domiz to the higher worlds," Thorn said.

"You told me I should embrace my rage." Wrath used both hands to twirl her sword forward and backward and then around her. Abruptly, she swung the sword to her side, decapitating one guard. Limp body dropping over bloodied head. "See that?" she said proudly. "My technique is getting better!"

"I've taught you well, and you're getting stronger," Thorn said, scanning the room for her own sword and fastening her plated leather jacket. "You have embraced your rage. Now it's time for us to move on. People are getting hurt and dying." She spotted her saber leaning against the wall by the main door.

Wrath licked the blood on the sword. "Look around you. Death and destruction everywhere." This time she jumped forward, single-handedly thrusting the blade into a guard's neck. She spun her body under her arm, twisting the sword and causing a bloody mess.

"It's different here, Wrath. You know this. They don't feel things like you and I do." Thorn walked forward, kicking a detached rotting foot out of her path and moving closer to the unlikely leader of the Domizien. The black and blue foot landed near a pile of headless bodies. Curious, Thorn looked around the room, trying to figure out what Wrath had done with the heads, but they were nowhere to be found.

"He must pay," Wrath screamed, pulling her sword from the neck of the dying guard, only to strike a third demon, this time chopping off an entire arm. The creature stood still—no pain, no screams—bleeding to death, terror absent from his dead eyes. "I'll torture his poet while he watches. I'll bring chaos to his worlds, and then…then I'll destroy him."

The creatures standing on the stairs ran upwards, disappearing in the darkness of the first chamber of torture. They didn't have feelings, but they valued their lives, unlike Thorn, who continued to move closer to Wrath.

"His worlds and his poet aren't to blame for his crime against you. Come," Thorn raised her hand toward the girl. "Let's leave this stench of a world. I'll show you what comes next—order, trust in God...dess. Erm... Trust in the Goddess." Thorn bit her cigar, struggling to peddle Ordiz's bullshit values.

Wrath laughed—a mad cackle filled with resentment. "I know you, Thorn. You don't believe in those things. Why should I?"

"We need to cross Ordiz to get you to the higher worlds—where there are more people like me and you."

"Like me? You mean the people who are trying to kill you?" Wrath pointed her sword in Thorn's direction.

"*You* will protect me. Won't you?"

"I will," Wrath said, "but don't betray me again."

Damn! She knows. Thorn lifted her head in defiance. "Don't lose yourself in your rage. Overcome it." Thorn spoke like an older sister, a caring friend. *One day, I should listen to my own excellent advice.*

"Have you?" Wrath asked, sitting down on her throne, lifting one knee to her chest and hugging it close to her body.

"I...don't know."

"Shadow must pay," Wrath screamed—a cross between a monstrous shriek and a girlish whimper. She lifted the second knee and held both tightly. "I must kill him. Do you understand?"

"Yes, I do," Thorn said. "And, I did—kill him. It didn't help."

"Protect him again, and, like… you're dead to me. Dead." Wrath attempted to flick her hair inside the heavy helmet. *A child, an angry and lost child. I rather have you as a mad villain than a hopeless victim, chiquitita.*

Thorn took a breath and bowed her head. "You have my devotion and my loyalty. I'll give you the world. Everything you deserve. I'll wait for you, but…I can't help you in this quest. You're hurting people that have nothing to do with his crimes."

"I haven't commanded the Domizien to hunt anyone but Storm and Shadow. My creatures do what they were designed to do. Gods' fault, not mine."

"They're attacking everyone."

"Not my fault!" Wrath repeated. "Are you leaving me?" Pouting lips emerging from the iron's shadows.

"No. When you're ready, we'll depart from this place. Until then, I'll stay away from your path of destruction. I can't condone it and the universe won't allow you to travel up north until you genuinely adopt Ordizien values."

"I should kill you," Wrath said casually.

"I'm your only friend." Thorn turned around to leave.

"Without my protection, you're dead."

"Yeah. I am. Dead." Thorn reached down to pick up the saber. Domizien wouldn't attack her while she was under Wrath's protection, but the rest of the worlds were out to get her. "Come find me at the northern border when you're ready to move on."

Thorn pulled a cigar out of her back pocket, and she walked away toward the outer wall. She'd found the girl in Tribiz soon after her resurrection, when she'd first travel to explore the lower worlds. Thorn had recognized her immediately and still could not understand how the teen, who was supposed to be dead, had ended up in such an inhospitable place.

Half-dead and out of her mind, the soulful girl was being used by one of the nomadic soulless tribes as bate to hunt packs of wolves; their meat and fur essential for the Tribizien's survival in the coldest and most arid of all worlds.

Locked in a wooden cage and paralyzed by pain and fear and hopelessness, the girl barely spoke, surviving on scraps of raw meat tossed away by her captors. That day, to rescue her, Thorn killed at least fifteen Tribizien. Even so, it took a while for Thorn to convince her to leave the "safety" of her tribe and cross the frigid tundra toward Domiz.

Now that Wrath had shed her fear and hopelessness, Thorn was hoping they would venture further up to the soulful worlds. The two of them had a lot in common, a suicidal God had destroyed their lives.

14

BLANK...ISH SLATE

3. DOMIZ

THE BATTLEFIELD
DAY 1 — 3:25 PM

Thorn rolled her eyes as she considered jumping into action. There he was—the man she'd killed—alive and strutting into hell as if he were visiting a royal garden in a spring afternoon.

Thorn had traveled far to find herself at the edge of chaos, so close to mind-numbing order. She wanted to wait for Wrath in a place with a bit more...soul. The Ordizien border was within her reach, and now he showed up to ruin her plans.

Thorn was hoping she could convince the Ordizien to let her cross to their land. It was a long shot as they were super cultish about their religion, and she'd murdered their God.

She planned to tell them Shadow was back and that she'd saved his life. The news of Shadow's return had caught fire, spreading from community to community. Many believed his resurrection signaled their salvation, and she was hoping someone would validate her story.

Now it looked like the dumbass wouldn't stay resurrected for long, not without her help. Why on Earth…no, not on Earth… why on Spiral Worlds was he approaching the Worlds' battle-field alone and unarmed? The creatures wouldn't care about his charming smile or misguided tenderness. Shadow—all heart and little shrewdness—didn't have the cunning cool-ness necessary to bargain with the demons.

It wasn't her problem, and she continued to move toward the Ordizien. As long as she stayed close to the border, on either side, no one would dare attack her as they all feared the condottiere's revenge.

It was a shame the demons couldn't travel with her higher up. She could use their protection, but the platform didn't allow Underlings to roam into places above their values. The puppets went about their lives, never "choosing" to walk up the roads that led to the upper worlds. Some soulful learned new values and ascended, but the soulless Domizien were mostly stuck in Domiz, only venturing into Ordiz to pillage or to do the Ordizien's dirty deeds.

Keep your eyes on the border. She rebelled against her inner voice, and looked back at the battlefield—a dry land, devoid of vegetation and covered by hundreds of thousands of skulls and bones.

"The other way, you fool!" Thorn shouted, but she was too far away. In fact, she was so close to her destination she could hear the joyful laugher of some women and men in the Ordizien armies—a sound never experienced in Domizien land. *Dammit, Shadow!*

As Shadow walked from the thick forest into the vast combat zone, Thorn squinted her eyes, noticing the band of five

Domizien running toward him across the battlefield's plane. She remembered what the peppy Goddess had said: they were hoping the soulless would somehow connect with Shadow, their creator. But to send him alone into Domiz was stupid. A plan devised by people who knew nothing about the lower worlds' most recent events. Stella and Twist had been too distracted to see the power Wrath had amassed with the soulless, and to recognize it as a threat.

If the Domizien failed to recognize Shadow, he'd be dead in seconds, and his heart and liver would make a delicious demon meal. If, on the other hand, the creatures figured out who he was, they'd take him to Wrath, and he'd endure a slow and painful ascension up the staircase of torments. He'd experience the horrors in each one of the seven chambers of torture until he emerged at the top of the Tower—a limbless, tongueless, and eyeless shadow of a man, discarded to fall to his inevitable death.

Shadow's skill was pulling heartstrings—nature had designed his body and mind to enthrall hearts and souls. Domizien had none of that, and Wrath was immune to his charms. The condottiere would never forgive or forget what he'd done to her, and Shadow was striding toward his much-deserved downfall. Thorn cringed, unable to watch what was to come. *Stay out of it, Rosa. He isn't your problem.* She crossed her fingers hoping he'd die a quick death.

Thorn reached the wall of Ordizien shields. She was too short to see the men and women behind them. Several shields lowered to disclose their faces and the lines of warriors on horseback waiting further back.

"Hey!" she said, but the Ordizien attention quickly shifted away from her, to the battlefield.

She glanced at Shadow and the demons, unable to keep her eyes away. *Frack!* A demon held a large waterskin in his hand, an out-of-place object for a meeting in the middle of a battle-field. *Domizien hydrating during a raid? They are going to knock him out.* A technique she'd seen them use before.

She was used to Shadow's deaths, but for his and Wrath's sake, she couldn't let him be tortured.

She ran to the nearest horse rider. "Get off," she said, pointing at Shadow. "There. Your God lives and he's in danger. Help me." Even before the Ordizien warrior had fully dismounted the animal, Thorn held on to the reigns and saddle horn and jumped on the horse, sword in hand. "*You*, follow me," she commanded the group of horse riders to her right as she led them into a full speed gallop. Much to her surprise, the Ordizien obeyed.

Sometimes you need to walk into a place and own it. That's all it took. Ordizien liked to follow Gods, powerful rulers, and orders. She was meeting all their needs. *Idiots!* Or maybe they were just afraid of Wrath. Either way. It worked.

Ahead, everything unfolded has she'd predicted. The demon swung the waterskin to crash on to Shadow's face. The God collapsed on his knees, holding his head in between his arms. It didn't knock him out, but left him stunned enough to stop him from running. Afraid of trampling on Shadow, Thorn circled the group, catching the demon from behind.

Her horse buckled as it crashed into two of the five demons. She rolled her eyes at the fearful animal and jumped to the ground decapitating two Domizien and using her dagger to stab a third in the heart. In that world it was best to act first and think later. An approach that suited her just fine.

"Get up. We need to go," she said dropping her sword to help him stand. "Shadow, get up."

"T—Thorn?" His eyeballs rolled back into his head for a second. "I was looking for you."

"How great!" Sarcasm oozing as she spoke. "You found me. Yayyy!" She poured the contents of the waterskin on his head. "Get up! You're too big to carry."

He stared at her until his eyes blinked with some recognition and he raised to his feet.

"This way," Thorn said.

She'd decided they would run. She didn't want to waste a lot of time trying to get him to mount a horse. Plus, the four-legged creatures were too unreliable. She glanced back to assess the danger. The Ordizien horse riders finished the last two demons, but she could see hordes of Domizien—at least two hundred—running toward them. "Holy guacamole, I think you've started a war without travelers to experience it. That's weird."

The Domizien battlefield, like everything else in Spiral Worlds, was a travelers' playground. A place designed to purge human desire for warmongering. Sibyl orchestrated everything so they'd suffer just enough pain, without negative consequences in the real world. Wounds vanishing as soon as they got back Up Above.

"I did?" Shadow raised an eyebrow, half his face red and blue from the Domizien attack. "Anyway, thank you," he said, running beside her toward the wall of Ordizien shields protecting the border. "I guess Stella was wrong. They didn't recognize me."

"Of course they did. If they didn't, you'd be dead. They aren't shooting arrows—that's the good news. They want you alive —that's the bad news." She looked back, to confirm her statement. The demons were close enough to kill them, but kept their bows strapped to their backs.

"They have shot against me before," Shadow said.

"Probably before they knew who you were."

"So, the Domizien don't want to hurt me?"

"Oh yeah. They do."

"Sibyl's not telling me anything," he said. "It's so confusing."

"Make way!" Thorn tried to copy Nathan Storm's preachy tone. "God's heart has risen from the ashes." Then she murmured, "Show them your pretty face and smile."

"Do you think they know who I am?"

"The Ordizien? *For sure!* Have you been to one of their churches? Your face is plastered in every wall and window. Sometimes I'm there too, surrounded by fire and looking pretty diabolical. Which reminds me, before you leave...or die again...you must put a good word for me with the soulful, okay?"

"I'm here to see you."

"A visit! How nice. We'll have tea." She flashed her teeth. "This should wipe my slate clean. Right?" She threw him a side glance, and then she shouted, "*Incoming...hmm...God!* Incoming God, as lost as ever."

Two Ordizien dropped back, and Thorn and Shadow sped through the gap between shields. The Ordizien army started marching forward, toward the Domizien.

"Your slate was clean, unlike mine," Shadow said, catching his breath.

Thorn grinned, noticing his tiredness. She deliberately kept ahead of him to show off her impressive speed. She was much shorter than him, the top of her head used to slot perfectly under his chin when they made out. Still, his long legs struggled to keep up with her sprint, payback for all the undignified jogs she had to endure every time they'd gone for a casual walk in the City Down Below, decades ago.

"We know this, but your friends think otherwise. This way." She pointed at the next barrier—this time Ordizien on horseback.

"Praise God, our loving heart," a rider said, and many followed with their own prayers.

"Protect him! Protect his heavenly ass!" Thorn said pointing her sword at the hordes of Domizien approaching fast. The Ordizien cavalry moved forward, creating just enough space for Thorn and Shadow to cross them.

"Stop objectifying me."

"I'm not the self-proclaimed God."

The two zigzagged in between the animals' legs rushing past four lines of nervous horses—some grunting, snorting or even bulking. It took longer than it needed, as Shadow had to pat and comfort every horse on his path. They arrived at an open field.

"I didn't— Anyway...don't worry, my friends couldn't care less about me or your slate," he said.

"Yeah, sure," she dismissed him with a casual shrug. The flawed God was the worlds' most beloved creature, an honor she struggled to decide if it was deserved or not, even if she too had once fallen captive to his charm. "Frack! I forgot my sword." Something that had never happened on the fencing piste. The transition from athlete to warrior was harder than she expected. "You're such a distraction!"

She groaned, coming to grips with her new status in Domiz— that Wrath's hate for him was likely stronger than her bond with her. From that moment onward, Thorn had to assume the Domizien might attack her.

"How did you end up in the middle of the Worlds' battle-field? Death wish?"

"I asked Sibyl to see you and she jumped me here. I guess the forest's edge was the only available place to materialize."

"You were lucky that the fields were mostly empty—fewer travelers because of the glitches. It's nice to have some moments of peace in hell."

He stared at her intensely, compassion in his eyes. "Why are you dead, Thorn?" he said quietly, his voice deep and throaty.

Her jaw clicked, triggered by a sudden blast of tension. "Are you seriously attempting to have this conversation with me? You?" She grabbed his wrist and turned it to expose his scars.

"I just didn't expect it from you." He followed her toward an empty Ordizien encampment—a dozen perfectly shaped triangular structures made of oak covered by woolen cloth canvas.

"It's not like you have an outstanding record of getting things right, is it?"

He laughed awkwardly as they walked into an empty tent. "I used to be pretty good, before…" After a long silence, he said. "Sorry, I wasn't bragging, or dismissing what I did to you. I'm really sorry. I promised myself I'd always try to find some-thing positive to say and to think…you know? I'm trying to stay alive…keep people safe. I'm so sorry." He positioned himself in the middle of the tent, the only place high enough for him to stand straight.

She released a loud, exasperated sigh. "Scrumptious, can we make a deal?"

He got cuter when he got mad. "Don't do that! I'm not food. What deal?" The eagerness in his eyes said he'd bend back-wards for her.

"Can we just forget the past? Stop apologizing. Let's…be friends. Perhaps this will help us both stay alive." If she were to survive Ordiz and higher up, she needed his protection.

He rubbed his head, probably sore from the attack. "That's generous of you, Thorn, but I can't just—"

"It's self-serving." She punched him lightly in the arm, struggling to keep her hands off him. "If you say sorry one more time, I'll have to kill you, and then your friends will chop me into little pieces and feed me to the soulless."

A strained chuckle slipped past his lips, barely audible. "I don't have any friends. They wish they weren't…my friends."

"Saving your ass just cost me my last friend, so neither do I… apart from you." She tried to pull off some puppy eyes.

"You nut job." He smiled, and then he looked away, all bashful. "I can't be your friend, Thorn."

"We've tried everything else—strangers, lovers, mortal enemies—I'm convinced we're meant to be friends," Thorn lied. She didn't know what they were, and she had stopped caring until he showed up. She liked and hated him just as much as she did before, in fact, she could easily put a bullet in his head right now. Still, she needed him. "Are you worried the men in your life won't approve?"

"Believe me, no one cares. No one wants me back." He sounded like he believed in his words. *The fool.*

He detached his wet T-shirt from his chest, and she realized she'd been staring at the light patch of hair beneath it. She'd licked it too many times.

"You haven't changed either. Anyway, we better jump out of here, before the Ordizien religious fanatics come find you and place you on some pedestal."

"I never wanted this…"

"Oh dear." She stared at him, smirking. "Anyway, you said you want to look on the bright side, right? Well, after what we did to each other, we won't sweat the small stuff."

He laughed and cleared a tear from the corner of his eyes. "Thank you for saving my life. I can't be your friend. I got to go."

"I thought you needed to speak to me?"

"Yes, I came to save your life."

She held her stomach, laughing loudly. "And did you?"

"Yes, I feel like I did," he said, all serious.

"You *feel it*, do you?"

"I'm sure they've seen you save my life, and the soulless are chasing you. So, all good."

"Have you lost your marbles again?" She grabbed his arm. "Hey! You owe me. *Big time*," she said coolly while her gut screamed for help. "Don't you think you should be more responsive to my wishes? We must be friends."

"No."

"What the hell! I'm here fighting demons you invented."

"Precisely. You'll be safe in Ordiz, right?"

"No, I won't." Then she leaned in his direction, stood on the tips of her toes, and furrowed her brows. "You know, you should seriously stop doing stuff, anything. Apart from having sex, you're good at that. You're still my all-time favorite sex toy. Just stay in bed and look pretty."

He blushed, repressing a smirk. "Stop it." His admonishment tender.

"Are you seriously going to deny me your friendship after ruining my life?"

"What are you doing Thorn? I'm deadly."

"I can handle you."

"That was my assumption, but now you're stuck here, dead, because of me."

She flicked his wet hair away from his face. "I'm over you. Death put things in perspective."

"Not the type of experiences I want to deliver to my *friends*."

"It's not *all* about you. You know? I need a friend in power."

"Thorn, you ask for whatever you need—"

"Speaking of demons, *behind you!*"

As Shadow turned around, the bearded demon shrieked, emerging from the fresh tear on the tent's canvas. The creature launched at him, spear in hand. She slipped her hand on the back of Shadow's jeans and pulled him back. He staggered, his shoulder avoiding the spear's head by a hairline. Thorn used both hands to grip the spear close to the pointy end and wrestled for control over it with a creature twice her size.

"Take my dagger," she screamed at Shadow, looking at the leather scabbard on her leg.

As Shadow reached for her dagger, the demon yanked the spear off her hands and stabbed her thigh right between the dagger and Shadow's hands. The sharp pain emptied the air of her lungs.

"Fracker!"

Shadow grabbed the dagger and threw himself over the creature who fell backwards dropping the spear. They rolled and wrestled and kicked and punched. Shadow could have stabbed the demon on five or six occasions, but he didn't, and Thorn gave an exasperated growl. She gritted her teeth, pulled the spear off her thigh, and jumped on top of the demon who had Shadow pinned between his legs. She stabbed the creature in the eye, killing it instantly.

Thorn dropped on one side, contorting in pain. "I'm fracked! I'm no longer off limits."

"You okay?" Shadow's hands shook as he took her in his arms and lifted her off her legs. His body was still wet from the water she'd poured all over him.

"Ouch! You must find your killer instinct or you'll get us all killed." She was wasting her words. She had a better chance teaching an elephant to fly. "You'd be dead now, if the creature was trying to kill you, instead of capturing you."

"Hmm. I-I'll find a way to learn to fight demons," he said thoughtfully, still trembling. "I'll download information from Sibyl."

"Download information?" She laughed. "I know you can fight, Tom. Look at you." She squeezed his arm, sculpted to perfection.

He looked away.

"They suffer no pain, you fool. Your design, remember?"

"Yes, they are what they are because we made them so," he said, guilt all over his face.

"Kill them or knock them out immediately." She applied pressure on her thigh. "Hell, it hurts," she said, tearing the pants' fabric around the wound to inspect.

Unexpectedly, another demon entered the tent and jumped toward them, dagger lifted over Thorn's chest, ready to strike.

Out of a horror movie, dozens of flesh-eating beetles munched on half of the creature's jawline.

"Frack!"

"Hold on to me." Shadow spun around and launched into a sidekick, making the creature stumble. He lowered Thorn to the floor, picking up the spear and stabbing the attacking demon in the heart. The creature dropped to the ground, face first.

"She was pretty." Thorn ignored the blast of pain from the injured leg.

Shadow took a moment to look at the demon, eyes mournful as if he had slaughtered a puppy. Out of nowhere, the skies rumbled, and a scorching spear of lightning pierced the tent and hit the ground by the entrance, setting it on fire.

"What the frack was that?"

"The weather." He dropped to one knee. "Stay still. You're bleeding." He touched her forehead with his face. "And burning. I'll get us out of Ordiz. Sib—"

"No, don't. I'll stay here. I'll be fine." She'd never survive in the higher worlds. Everyone there was out to get her, and half delirious with an injured leg, she couldn't defend herself from their attacks. She preferred to take her chances with the Ordizien who feared Wrath and knew of their alliance.

"I won't leave you here, inside a tent on fire, bleeding. A minute ago, you said you weren't safe." He picked her up.

"I'm not, but the God-abiding Ordizien saw me save you, and hmm…higher up…they don't like me." She disclosed the least possible. She didn't need his pity, just his protection.

"Since when do you care about what people think?"

"You don't understand…" *And I don't want to spell it out.* "Cut the tent and drop me outside."

"That gash is too deep. It needs proper care."

Her sight blurred, and she sank her head into his chest. The heat was rising as the tent's fabric caught fire. "Where are you taking me?" She was too weak to argue.

"I need to stop by Pluriz, urgently. To speak to…" He clenched his jaw and then forced a smile. "My friend January will take good care of you."

"The Plurizien hate my guts. But I know your man well enough to know he won't stab me in the back while I'm down, no matter how much he'd like to."

"He's not my man, no one is going to fight, and I won't let anyone hurt you."

"Sure," she said, and then she coughed, struggling to breathe due to all the smoke. "I love your newly found optimism. This will be…fun."

It would make some excellent entertainment to see Storm and Shadow together. She was a sucker for punishment, sometimes.

He nodded. "Sibyl, take us to see Nate."

Sure, my heart, said the voice inside Thorn's head. A reminder she couldn't run away from all her demons.

15

IN GOD'S HANDS

GRAND INGA HYDROPOWER COMPLEX — CONGO
RIVER — AFRICAN UNION
DAY 1 — 3:40 PM

Stella walked inside the observation deck, approaching her father from behind, and ignoring the uneasiness grumbling in her gut. Christian Ngoie, the leader of the richest and most powerful continent in the world, sat on his rocking chair facing the window and staring at the world's largest and deadliest rapids. The Congo River frothed and roared as it approached the largest power station on the planet. The complex fed the electricity demands of the entire continent.

"Baba," she called, but he didn't turn around. The color of his emotion-sensing bodysuit remained neutral and unchanged. Lost somewhere inside his head, he didn't hear her.

Baba was a shadow of his former self. His emotions ran deep, as deep as the river's waters. He was no longer the spirited, confident man who had united a continent once ridden by colonialism, ethnic conflict, corruption, poverty, and a devastating virus. Gone was the man who had the audacity to displace fifty thousand people, flooding their valley and homes to build a complex of thirteen dams. A project that had put an end to the use of fossil fuels in the African Union. His courage beaming in a time rich in progress and creativity. A time before decisions got stuck, before empathy got in the way of evolution.

Christian was once a powerful man, now weakened by Holiz's launch. In five years, he'd shifted from *I* to *We*, from leading from the front to orchestrating from the back, to completely withdrawing from public life. His powerful brand —the strengths that saved millions from extreme poverty and violence—destroyed in favor of compassion, mutuality, wholeness, and harmony. Their effectiveness unproven.

"Baba," she repeated, and this time she used her mind to order his suit to release a whiff of mint, awakening his senses.

"Estelle!" He stood up and turned around, his initial smile disappearing as soon as his eyes landed on her. "What are you wearing?" he asked, disappointment painted all over his face.

To challenge her father's ways, Stella had selected a bright orange suit and an eccentric pink tie. On her head, a purple fedora adorned with a long coral-colored feather. An attire influenced by La Sape—a life-affirming cultural heritage filled with political symbolism against the colonial elites of the past. Self-expression that embodied and hijacked the dandy style of their European oppressors—the savages who spoke of Christian values as they took people as slaves. Hands chopped to save bullets. Chicotte's lashes wrecking skin, and bone, and soul. A forgotten past, erased as the people traveled up a digital spiral toward progress.

"Honoring our history," she said, raising her head and strutting into the room with the fashion and flair that once brightened the streets of Brazzaville—a brand of self-respect against all odds. A men's tradition appropriated by women. Another twist of defiance against old power structures. It was only fitting she—the Goddess of the worlds—would pay tribute to such a joyful revolution.

"Egoic crutches used by the powerless and the insecure. You aren't powerless, and you need to get over your inferiority complex."

"Me? Insecure?" She released a nervous laughter, contained quickly, and still too late.

"It has increased since you descended to power," Baba said, wrapping his arms around her. "This isn't who you are." He took the hat off her head, its enormous feather creating a coral screen between the two. "You don't need this. Where's the empathetic and humble girl I used to know? The one who is worthy of her place amongst Gods. Drop all this nonsense, Estelle. Show me you deserve your title."

Stella shoved the hat back on her head a little too deep. "Of course, I do." Refusing to adjust the fedora, she had to lift her head back to see her father's face. The softness in his eyes told her he didn't believe her. But believe what? That she deserved it, or that she believed she deserved it? *Both*, she decided. "In fact,"—she stood straighter—"I'm far superior to the two frauds you idolize." *So what* if she needed a little help—a boost of confidence to step into the shoes of the two men who'd saved the world.

She lowered her head, staring at her bright crimson shoes—synthetic velvet, of course. At first, they faked it—Le Sapeurs —impostors, whose flamboyance hid a life of misery and danger. A flashy ideology that helped the Congolese youth erase the grimmest history of a region once raped by the rest of the world. And then, one day, with the help of Down Below, they finally made it. Le Sapeurs didn't want to become the thing they copied, they wanted to overcome it. And so did she. Stella would overcome the Gods she'd worshiped all her life. If she didn't, she'd fall with them. *I'm a chameleon, the herald of eternal life.*

"Broken, weak, ineffective Gods," she said out loud before she bit her tongue.

"Don't defame our heroes to elevate yourself above them." Baba raised his voice. "It's beneath you." He lifted her chin with his index finger and kissed her cheek.

"I'm telling the truth. Have you forgotten I'm enlightened too? That I have traveled higher up the Spiral than anyone else on the planet?"

"And still, you revert to the colors of the lower worlds."

"And you should too, before you end up like him—isolated and suicidal."

"Thomas Astley-Byron died to stop his people from suffering." So much love in Baba's voice. "He gave his life as ransom for his people, sacrificing himself to save humankind from sin."

Her blood boiled. "For decades, his people suffered, and so did the ones who loved him—all dead. To love everyone is to love no one, including yourself. I won't make that mistake."

"What are you talking about? Look at the world he created for you. A star born at a time of peace, in a thriving land, blue and green and filled with all kinds of life. Ungrateful child. We are all one."

"Baba, you don't know. I've witnessed it hundreds of times—"

"What? What have you witnessed?" Baba judged her with his eyes and words. Nothing she did was good enough. He tested her with his low bar. A misguided yardstick she refused to accept. *His problem, not mine.*

"You live a privileged life," he said. "You've seen nothing of the greed and violence that plagued our world. He fixed it. He saved us. Wash your mouth before you speak his name."

Back in the late twenties, when chaos ruled the world, Christian, then called Manzak, had been one of the leaders of the Kulunas—the violent and lawless youth gangs that once infested Kinshasa's communes. Then Down Below came along, and everything changed—in less than a decade, the war-torn countries of Africa united and finally ascended to their rightful place on the planet's stage.

She shook her head. "I've experienced it all in the soulless worlds."

"It's not the same," Baba said.

"The values you've adopted—his values—don't end well for anyone. Apart from the preposterous decision to place the souls of the dead in a deadly lake, when was the last time the Council reached unanimity?"

His shoulders collapsed and his head followed as his suit turned dark gray. "We need to wait a few more years until they all reach enlightenment."

Stella sighed. "Until then, lead, speak out, guide them. When you do, they listen. Earth's communities are fragmented and leaderless as our best withdraw from the public stage. You are the chairman of the Council—the most influential leader on Earth." A title she worked hard to claim.

"You know why…" Baba whispered, taking a step back and crossing his arms in front of his chest.

"No. I actually don't."

"The enlightened understand how everything is connected. That the universe isn't made of particles, or waves, but information—all of it, one single integrated information organism."

"Yes," she said, smiling.

"If the Gods below created consciousness, so did the Gods above."

"Probably." She shrugged.

"Then we must resign to our fates as the Underlings submit to theirs." He shined bluish-turquoise as he looked up and made the sign of the cross with his hand.

"No! *No!* Don't—don't just submit to the passiveness peddled by the Christian God of our oppressors." She loosened her tie.

"Don't you dare speak against our Lord Jesus Christ!"

She laughed. "I'd be more fearful of blasphemy against the Holy Spirit. If zie too exists above, zie's the one you should fear." Stella swallowed the lump in her throat as she felt the hair stand up on the back of her neck.

"You don't need to remind me of the scripture's unforgivable sin."

"I'm not," she said, amused. "Anyway, if you want to believe in Gods above, choose our own Nzambi a Mpungu, a supreme creator who simply became bored of us, or others who aren't all good, or all bad, and certainly not long-suffering. Don't you fall for *that* depressing tale."

"Stella, the success of Spiral Worlds relies on the sacrifice of its creatures. Why should our universe operate differently?"

"Perhaps our Gods are black, and spirited, and resourceful. If you want to worship a cross, worship our own dikenga dia Kongo—a celebration of the indestructibility of the soul. A symbol of the rebirth you're blocking."

"I'm not blocking anything; I'm letting the God above decide. Our decisions are an illusion. We have no power."

"You are wrong, Baba. *So* wrong. Even Underlings have power, a rebellious power they wield against me and Sibyl and Up Above."

"The glitches?" he asked, and she nodded.

"None of us are helpless, we are both observer and observed. Equally slaves and creators of our reality. The crucified God— all scars and misery—is just a viral story designed to keep us all numb."

"How can you say that when you are the Goddess of a universe created to inflict pain on its people for our benefit?"

"Because I know of a prescient app who understood the power of story, and copied the most viral story in the world. An app who once manipulated the life of one man so he became such a symbol—the all good, long-suffering God that kept zir lambs resigned to their slaughter, because he too was slaughtered. All the slaughtered lambs you should honor by enjoying life and allowing more of it. *More life!*"

"I don't know. I just don't know." Weakness and resignation in his eyes. "Thomas was against it—immortality. He made his view clear before he died."

Stella let Earthlings believe the old Gods were still dead. Their influence was too powerful, and Shadow's position against immortality unlikely to shift. *Anyway, he'll be dead soon enough.* A sudden queasiness lingered in her body. She brushed it off.

"Your beloved Tom gave Harry permission to test immortality," she said, stating facts. "I'm just continuing their work. At least let me extract the souls out of the lake."

"No," he persisted. "In three days' time, we'll hear your proposal and then we'll vote."

"We might not have three days." She raised her voice. "The Nyiragongo is seething."

"We choose to submit to God's will."

"A God you know nothing about. A God who might not exist. Some being who couldn't care less about his creations." Her face was hot and her jaw tense.

"What we expect from others is a reflection of ourselves," he said too quickly. "We'll vote."

"Baba, the Earth's Council hasn't reached unanimity on anything for over a year. And now you invited the Unplugged to the Council. They'll never vote in favor of digital immortality. What are you doing?"

"Their voices matter. All voices matter."

"That means no voice matters. I'll hold you accountable for the deaths of millions, including Bibi." Her outrage bit through every word.

"Estelle, your mother's mother is already dead. She lived a long life, and took as many lives as she saved. She's gone now."

"We'll see about that!" Stella turned around and strutted out of the deck without ever looking back.

16

SPAGHETTO

NEW YORK CITY
FORTY-SIX YEARS EARLIER — 15 APRIL 2024

For two years, since their first encounter at the Albertine, Tom had struggled to convince Nate they belonged together. Nate said Tom was too young and had been sheltered from real life. He treated Tom with considered devotion and care as if he were a rare object made of crystal. Tom was friend-zoned as Nate continued to indulge in casual relationships with others.

One night, after one of the poet's events, an inebriated Nate candidly shared with Tom the strength of his feelings. He said he was terrified of how much he felt for Tom and how vulnerable it made him feel. He told Tom nothing compared with the fondness he had for him, only to take it all back, claiming it was a drunken mistake and that he didn't mean any of it.

That night, Tom became certain sooner or later, they'd end up together. He stopped brooding and stalking Nate and instead focused on his work. And so, they remained *"close* close" friends, because they *"liked* liked" each other. They met one another every day, mostly during lunchtime, as Tom didn't drink much, and Nate wouldn't allow him near the shadier sides of his "artistic" life.

Over two years after they met, Tom had won the Academy Nicholl screenwriting competition and with it a thirty-five-thousand-dollar fellowship. On the same day, Walt Disney Studios made him an offer to join their young writers' incubator program. Tom was walking on clouds, and Nate offered to take him out for dinner to celebrate.

TOM SMILED. For the first time since their acquaintance, Nate's glass of Pinot Noir remained untouched during the meal. His poet listened in supportive delight as an excited Tom dreamed out loud, talking about the future and all its world-changing possibilities. The family-owned restaurant in Brooklyn smelled like tomatoes, oven-baked bread, hot cheese, and golden garlic gently fried in olive oil. Tom tucked into his spaghetti all'arrabbiata with extra conviction, twisting large strings of pasta between his fork and spoon.

As they were about to finish dinner, Tom gathered the courage to try again. He stood up and leaned over, slightly swiping his tongue between Nate's lips and then pressing his mouth onto his friend's. Nate stood up, pulled Tom's body to him, and kissed his neck, his lips barely touching Tom's skin.

"I adore you," Nate said once he had recovered his breath. He dragged Tom's chair closer to his, and they sat glued to each other.

Tom cleared a lump in his throat. "That was my second kiss. Ever," he said, moving back a bit and looking straight into Nate's eyes. "There's more I'd like to try. If you'd like?" The heat rose to his cheeks, and he covered his face with his hands, embarrassment taking over.

Nate took him in his arms, and he was silent for a moment, thinking. Those seconds of quiet deliberation felt to Tom like an excruciating eternity.

"Tom…" Nate shook his head, his eyes sad.

Tom held his hand and squeezed it urgently. "I-I know you want this, and this is all I want."

"I'm sorry, sweetheart. I'll get the bill." Nate was about to stand up, and Tom pulled him down.

"In ten years, it won't matter—the age difference."

"It matters now, and you…belong to a different world."

"*I want this*." Tom held his breath, waiting, hoping.

"Don't be stubborn. People like you and I don't mix," Nate said.

Tom stared at the small plate filled with olive oil and balsamic vinegar. The dark concentrated drops of sweet acidity—complex and rich and intensely flavored—never blending with the golden sea of extra-virgin olive oil. He took a piece of the rustic bread and sunk it into the dip.

"Try this," Tom said, lifting the soaked bread to Nate's mouth. "The *perfect* combination of flavors. Much better together."

Nate smiled. "Did you know the silky olive oil gets burned easily? It can't handle high heat." Nate took a bite.

"And?" Tom leaned in, waiting for the verdict.

"It's divine," Nate confessed, "but the olive oil is nourishing and flavorsome on its own."

Tom grabbed his napkin from his lap, dropped it on the table and prepared to stand up. Perhaps he'd misread Nate's feelings for him. Maybe Nate just considered him one of many obsessive fans, nothing else. Maybe Nate's drunken confession had been a bourbon-fueled mistake. He couldn't handle the thought.

"You lied to me."

"When did I ever do that?"

"At the Albertine, and the other night when you said you… liked me. You lied to me."

"No. I didn't."

Tom vacillated. "I got to go," he finally said, but he didn't mean it.

Nate grabbed his hand. "Stay." Then there was another long pause. "I need some time to…consider it."

Tom pulled his hand away. "I'm not a child. If you don't want to be with me, just—*just* tell me. Tell me now. I won't break or burn. I just wanna know the truth. *Now*." He gestured so passionately he knocked over the glass of wine in front of him; a stain of red quickly spreading over the white tablecloth. "Oh. Sorry…"

A server came over to help, but Nate waved him away. "Thanks, we'll take care of this," Nate said, placing his napkin over the spilled wine. *Red, so much red.* Tom hoped Nate didn't take it as a sign. *It was an accident, nothing else.*

Tom got up. "Thank you for the dinner. I'm sorry I made a mess."

"Tom, sit down." A hint of distress in Nate's tone. Then he stood straighter and smoothed his flaming hair with the palm of his hand. Tom had seen it before—the poet's hidden vulnerability. A damaged, loving soul concealed by a shell of hairspray, loud clothing, and a feral, unforgiving roar.

Some worry came to Nate's brow. "Do your parents know?"

"Know what?" Tom asked, sitting down.

"That you're queer?"

"I guess I am." Words delivered together with a casual shrug and a slight smile.

"You never thought about it?" Nate asked, astonished. "I envy you and your careless freedom. It's a privilege I didn't have."

"How so?"

"I'm the discarded son of a Southern Baptist pastor of the Texan Bible Belt. When he had to choose between his church and me, he chose the church, threw my belongings on the porch, and set them on fire."

Tom reached out to hold Nate's hand, squeezing it. At first, he didn't know what to say. He attempted to imagine Nate's pain and to grasp the enormity of such an event, and it hurt too much. Then he did what he had always done and shifted his focus, looking for a hopeful message—a helpful angle. "Your past doesn't have to define you. The future is a blank page, and I'd like to lobby hard for my name to be one of the words you'll write." He cringed. He sounded corny, he always sounded corny, and his gut ached at the thought. He stood in front of the coolest artist in the world uttering tired clichés. *Sigh.*

Nate blinked his eyes endearingly. "Thomas Quincy Astley-Byron," he said pompously. "I'll consider it." Nate pressed his lips—trying and failing to repress a smile. Then he stared at Tom, still amazed. "You *really* never thought about it?"

Tom took some time to consider Nate's question. *No, I guess I haven't, but why?* He tried to explain it. "Attraction, for me... It never starts with what someone has between their legs, you know? It starts with a smile, a poem, or an act of courage." Nate's eyes opened wide as if he had gained some new insight.

Tom used his index finger to mix the oil and vinegar. No matter how hard he tried to whisk them together, they eventually separated. He placed his fingers between his lips and licked it. "Sometimes, it's about competence, leadership, and immeasurable talent. But I find artistic activism particularly hot." Tom flashed a sultry look and then backtracked, feeling awkward.

Nate leaned in. "You have nooo idea." He placed his hand under Tom's chin, and then he parted Tom's lips with his tongue and kissed him deeper, making Tom's body vibrate with pleasure. "But surely, you must have had some crushes?" Nate murmured.

He pressed his lips onto Tom's cheek as his hand squeezed his inner thigh. Tom jerked with surprise, releasing an unexpected gasp of yearning.

"Yeah." Tom kept his eyes closed, embarrassment taking over. "I have a knack for choosing unattainable objects of affection. Like Hannah Williams, my happily married, eleventh-grade visual arts teacher, or the very straight Jon Adeyemi, the guy who managed my mother's climate-displaced fund some years back. It would have been foolish to try anything. So, in the past, I kept my crushes to myself. As for my parents, they care about my grades and that I made varsity. We've never talked about it."

"Fool. No one is unattainable when it comes to you." Nate grazed his fingers over Tom's forearm. "Once they find out, will they accept you?"

Tom struggled to breathe, aching with desire.

A couple sitting on a table nearby glared at them and exchanged quiet words. In his late fifties, a large man sat by a skinny blonde girl who was probably younger than Tom. The man was well put together, wearing an expensive crimson suit and shiny shoes, but something about him creeped out Tom.

Feeling embarrassed and slightly delirious, Tom hid his face on the nape of Nate's neck and whispered in a broken voice, "Does—does it matter?"

"It only matters if it matters to you. As long as you're happy, I'm happy."

The large man continued to stare, one of his forceful brown eyes marked with a smudge of red. He got up and approached their table and raised his hand, inviting Nate to shake it.

"Ron Johnson," he said. The man shot a side glance at Tom and licked his lips. Shameless, the red eye lingered between Tom's legs, before the man shifted his attention back to Nate.

"I know who you are," Nate barked. "Get lost."

The man continued to speak quietly, disregarding Nate's warning. "Nice lad you've got there, Mr. Storm." The man adjusted his crouch. "My girl and I are going back to the hotel. Are you the sharing type? I'd love a piece of that gorgeous—"

Grunting, Nate jumped up, rage-red, grabbing the table and flipping it in the man's direction, the plates and the pasta flying in all directions. "You sonofabitch! Get the fuck out of my sight!" he screamed, eyes wild as he picked up a chair and raised it in the air, rushing toward Ron clumsily. Gasping, the man stumbled backward, his forehead dripping sweat.

Tom jumped in front of Nate. Taller than the other men, he raised his hands to hold the chair. "Nate, stop. Please stop." He worried at his lip as he confronted the turbulent wrath of the poet.

"You don't know this guy." Nate's face twisted. His breath was shallow and fast. "He was in the news; he buys these girls…these children with the cash he earns from his sleazy ads." The poet attempted and failed to release the chair from Tom's grip. Suddenly, he opened his eyes wide. "Tom, behind you!"

Ron tried to get past Tom to attack Nate. As Tom turned, Ron hit him in the head with a metal bottle filled with olive oil. The creepy man looked up at Tom, dropped the bottle, grabbed the girl by the arm, and they rushed out of the front door.

Tom recoiled in pain, raising his hand to his head.

"I'm going to kill him," Nate said, momentarily caressing Tom's back on his way out to chase Ron.

Tom grabbed his arm. "Don't. Stay."

"Tom, what he said… What he did—*does*… It's not right." Nate pulled his arm, but Tom gripped it tighter.

"I know. Trust me, there are better ways to deal with him." Tom slightly curved his lips upward; his fingers still pressed against the bump on his head, numbing the pain. "Take me home?" His other hand traveled down Nate's arm to caress the poet's clenched fist.

Nate took a deep breath and held Tom's hand. "Are you okay? Do you want me to get you some ice?"

"No, it's nothing."

"Never, *ever* turn your back on a predator."

"Shall we walk to your place? It's close by, right?"

"Tom…" Nate shook his head, and that hurt ten times more than the brunt of the bottle.

Nate walked away momentarily to speak to the restaurant staff and settle the bill.

Tom turned the table back to its original position and helped clear the mess. "Sorry" came out of his lips every five words, which made the server laugh as they knelt to pick up the broken glass pieces off the floor. Then Nate returned, placing his hand on Tom's back and leading him outside.

"You can't do this to me." Tom leaned his head to meet Nate's eyes, but the poet's gaze darted down. "You can't let a sleazebag ruin what we have."

"Never again I'll let someone look at you and think— think…" Another devastatingly long pause. "I won't see you again." Nate's face contorted as if he was pulling his own heart out.

"*No*," Tom said, holding the poet's face with both his hands. "No, I won't let you do that. Look at me." Nate raised his eyes. "Please. We'll figure this out. I know you lo—you like me much." Tom teared up, slumping over Nate.

"You know I like you much?" The poet stared at him, and Tom recognized that look. He'd seen it every day for over two years. It was a mix of hidden adulation, exasperation, and an added pinch of amusement. "Beautiful, you can have anyone you want."

"I want you. You've waited long enough. I'm not changing my mind." Tom leaned in until his lips almost touched Nate's.

"I'm not the guy on stage, Tom."

"I know who you are."

Tom planted a kiss on the corner of Nate's mouth and Nate placed his hand on the back of Tom's neck and pulled him closer until their cheeks touched.

"Everyone is going to judge this...like...like...it's something else. People like my father, they say men like me—gay men—are monsters, deviants...child abusers. His words...are stuck in my mind. I can't escape them. They haunt me."

"You are the best human I'll ever know." Tom held Nate closely, the poet's trembling body relaxing with the embrace. "Since when do you care what people think? I'm a twenty-year-old adult, and I choose you. *I want you*."

Nate kissed his neck and pulled back, staring at his shoes for some time. "You should have socked him," he finally said. "You'd have knocked him out easily."

"I don't go around knocking people out." Tom shrugged, annoyed with the sudden change of topic.

"No, you don't, even when they deserve it." Nate's lips pressed together, and his brows furrowed. He stared at Tom, again. That same stare. "Hmm, someone will need to keep an eye on you." His mouth curled up and he picked an individual strand of spaghetti off Tom's hair. "Spaghetto!" he said, raising it in front of Tom's nose.

Tom didn't smile. His brows dropping over his eyes, heavy. Nate's vacillation was crushing him.

"That's what it's called when it is singular," Nate said.

Tom crossed his arms in front of his chest. Winning Nate over was the most important battle in his life, and he wouldn't let anything distract him from what he was there to accomplish —to spend the rest of his life with Nate. "Don't you see how much I love you? When I'm with you, I...I feel complete. The work you do... It's so important. You open my eyes and bring me so much joy and...you need me too. I know you do! It's not a crush, Nate. This is not a crush..."

"I bring you joy?" A hint of uncertainty emerged in Nate's tone.

Tom nodded.

Nate stared at him, dropped the spaghetto to the ground, took a breath, and held Tom's hand. "I'd love you to come home with me," Nate finally said. "Will you please come home with me?"

Tom tried to wait for a beat or two. It would have been cool to play hard to get, even if it wasn't true, but words came too quickly, accelerating toward a bright future. He wasn't good at playing games, and he knew what he wanted. "If you insist," Tom said, flashing a smile so wide his face hurt.

Nate led Tom to his small studio flat, right by the Bushwick Collective, a hub for graffiti and street art in Brooklyn. Around Tom, the intense, quick-tempered, and sometimes forceful Nate turned into a tender and patient lover, prioritizing Tom's comfort and pleasure above his own.

Nate encouraged him to take the lead, and Tom used his instinct to guide him on this new adventure. He was inexperienced, and awkward, and courageous, and scared, and overwhelmed, and overexcited. And they kissed, and kissed again, and kissed some more, deep, and wet, and hot. They made up for the years lost without kisses, and then Nate took Tom's shirt off and licked his neck, and his torso, and his stomach and then...it was *too much, so much*. Naked, and open, and aching. Nate's lips and beard and...*and...tongue*— that skillful tongue—between his legs, on his arousal. Throbbing...*aching*. The same intense piercing tongue, its rhythmic movement precise, wild, predictable, and unpredictable. And he rushed his fingers through Nate's hair, and then he was inside Nate's mouth, and Nate's fingers were inside him. Thrusting, thrusting—to take and to be taken, all at once, vulnerable and in control; both out of control. And then he found out what he'd always known—that they were perfectly matched, true partners in love and lust, taking turns to take, and to give. And as much as he needed to be Nate's, he discovered Nate longed to be his.

They spent all night exploring all paths to pleasure, between ardent kisses, purposeful strokes, and long embraces. Tom lost his virginity in the bright night of a full moon.

"Stormy?"

"You okay?" Nate planted a kiss on his shoulder.

"Do you want to be my boyfriend?" Tom asked, lying in bed wrapped in Nate's arms, Tom's toes still curled from sexual ecstasy.

"Thomas, I love you, and I'm not letting you out of my sight." Nate ran his fingers through Tom's hair, carefully avoiding the bump on his head.

Tom smiled triumphantly. "I love you too," he whispered, but unlike Nate, he had said it before. Tom had said it at least ten times since they'd first met. He turned around to face his Storm. "Perhaps we can co-write those blank pages together."

"I'd like that," Nate said as he unlocked the thin silver chain he wore around his neck. "I have something for you." The poet dangled the medal that hanged from the chain in front of Tom's eyes. "This is my most precious possession." Engraved in the medal was a figure of Jesus, a ruby crystal encrusted in place of his heart. "My mother gave it to me the day my father banished me from our family home and their lives… because of my sexual orientation. It's a family heirloom; it belonged to my great-great-grandmother."

"It's beautiful…but, it's—it's too much. I can't accept it."

"Tom, whatever happens, this is my promise—you are and forever will be loved for who you are. You are kind, intelligent, and creative, and your stories will touch millions one day." Nate raised half his body over Tom's and placed the chain around his neck.

Tom blinked his eyes, cherishing the compliment. "It's too much. It belongs to your family. Are you sure?"

"You *are* my family, Tom." Nate went quiet for a moment. "I won't be your…last, but…"

"Nate—"

"But you *must know* that come hell or high water, you'll always be my family. Do you understand?" Nate rolled Tom's body on top of his and licked his neck, placing Tom's knees to either side of his hips.

"Ye—yeah…" Tom moaned involuntarily, his face hot from both embarrassment and desire.

"Good," Nate said, pressing Tom against him.

"Are you religious?" Tom asked, lifting his head and holding the medal in front of his nose.

"I was the lead singer on the praise team, born and raised to be a pastor…until I transgressed God's not-so-sacred law. I no longer support the church of men or believe in the manufactured Christ of faith, but *this* man." He pointed to the figure on the medal. "The real man—Jesus—he was good, and he did good, and he is present in many stories, cultures, and religions."

"Is he?"

"Yes. He led a rebellion against the Roman Empire and opposed social injustice." There was a hint of tears in Nate's intense eyes as he spoke. "Through his teachings and charisma, he started a progressive movement on behalf of marginalized minorities. He was a loving rebel preacher, and fragments of his humanity—of his love, truth, and courage—still echo in our collective consciousness."

"It's not a happy story," Tom said, moving closer and resting his head on Nate's shoulder.

"I'm sorry, you don't have to—"

"No, no, *no*, I didn't mean it like that. I just don't think glorifying suffering is...helpful. We shouldn't just—just accept suffering; we need to make it better. Don't you think it's sad that such a courageous, progressive figure became the face of suffering—the brand?"

Nate went quiet for a while, probably pondering on Tom's words. "Salvation through suffering and sacrifice—religious messages designed to tame the masses," he finally muttered.

Tom exhaled in relief and agreement. "Exactly! I want to focus on stories about love and joy and creativity and curiosity and investigation and—" Tom got carried away until Nate placed his index finger on top of his lips and smiled.

"If anyone can do it, you can. Just remember heroes are born out of struggle; some pain is required."

Tom touched the medal with his fingers and ruminated on Nate's words. For his Nate, the ever-malleable face of Christianity represented a rebellious preacher—a charismatic leader crucified as punishment for his crusade against power. That was Nate's story, the narrative that guided and shaped his life, and Tom worried. "But...um, they don't need to, um, be constantly trying to hunt for the adversity, right?" Tom couldn't help himself.

"Am I being judged here?" Nate asked, raising his eyebrow. Then he pressed his lips together tightly and curled them upward ever so slightly.

"No, *no*, not at all. I-I'm sorry." Tom kissed Nate, and then he kissed the little medal. "I just don't like to see you upset."

"Sweetheart, sometimes anger is useful to fight evil and the status quo."

"Maybe, but not all the time…"

"Everything is easier for someone like you."

Tom pressed his lips tightly together, holding back his many objections.

Nate embraced him, and then moved his hands to Tom's thighs, pulling him closer with controlled urgency. "You've been my boyfriend for a minute, and you're already trying to change me."

"No," Tom shuddered. "I'm not trying to change you. I fell for you and all your…passion. I'm just…loving you."

"Show me how much." Nate kissed him slowly and passionately, and the alchemy between them returned, more intense than ever. Tom was slightly disoriented and dizzy as desire traveled throughout his body.

He moved into Nate's studio the following morning.

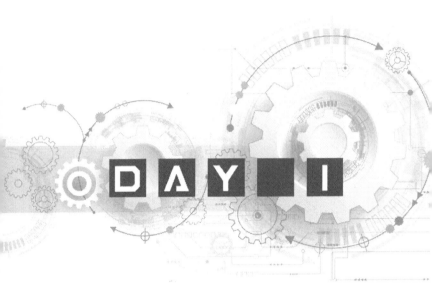

17

A FAIR DEAL

FRANKLIN — CATSKILLS — NEW YORK STATE, USA
DAY 1 — 5:50 PM

S tella stepped out of her private plane, resenting the entire hour-long experience. She'd landed on a grassy meadow near a water stream, its trickling melody mixing perfectly with the chirping birds, and the busy bees, and the wind caressing the carpets of daisies and making the purple lupines dance. Nature's orchestra welcomed its most favorite child. She sashayed across the field, head high, as if wearing an imaginary crown of flowers.

Soon she was glad she'd chosen to wear vintage denim dungarees and rubber boots. She'd selected the outfit so she could fit in with the local community, but the footwear came in handy when she stepped right onto some cow dung. She wrinkled her nose, moving along quickly. A stinky reminder she needed to be extra vigilant of her surroundings. She'd switched off her augmented retina to comply with the town's visitor rules.

The cows' judgmental eyes were probably a good indication of what she should expect from the town's people. Franklin was one of several areas in the Catskills Mountains that had become the home of the Unplugged. The movement led by Quincy Jin-Nowak and his mother June—the radicals she'd come so far to meet. This was her first intercontinental trip—a nuisance.

Very few people in the world traveled by plane. There was no need for it when they could experience any place on the planet from the comfort of their pods. Earthlings took their environmental impact seriously, and so did Stella. After all, anyone with a score above five pollution points per year was frowned upon by their community. A high score had no other implication than the social stigma attached to it. And still, there was nothing more annoying than the judgmental, yet compassionate eyes of the righteous. Even more distressing than the gaze of the chomping cows, staring at her and her small flying machine.

She didn't have a choice but to rent a private plane; commercial flights were rare, running once or twice a month at the most. These days, intercontinental flying released few harmful emissions. The planes were hyper-fast, hyper-comfortable, and hyper-silent, and still there was only one word the people of the Earth wanted to see prefixed by *hyper*, and that was local.

Hyper-local living took off fourteen years ago, soon after Pluriz's launch. Localtivism went viral fast as communities voted with their digital wallets choosing regional products and experiences. Everyone worked hard to become self-sufficient and put an end to excessive global trade. The Earth's Council agreement to measure pollution scores nudged the masses in the right direction and cleared the skies in a handful of years.

Stella had a good reason to make the round trip to the States, and her private plane fully relied on solar thermal fuel. Still, her perfect record would be tainted for a year, because the Unplugged refused to engage digitally except to attend the EC's General Assembly and to debate and vote on their proposals.

She walked through the green pastures approaching the rustic cedar cabin where a figure waited for her by the porch. She'd sent word of her visit, but had never heard back. Rude and disconnected, the Unplugged refused to engage beyond their communities. No wonder Harry struggled to make contact with his family.

The resemblance was uncanny and superficial. Quincy Jin-Nowak was almost a perfect reproduction of his father, except he was taller and wore his blond curls long and wild, uncon-strained by the order that ran his father's life.

Stella had done her research, Quincy had only inherited Harry's looks. From his mother, he got the emotional intelli-gence and charisma his father lacked. He led the Unplugged with the power of his triggering words, showing none of the rationality Harry had been famous for, now lost in favor of an overdose of self-pity.

"You aren't welcome here," Quincy said as she approached.

"I'm here to—"

"We don't want to see him."

"That's none of my business. Although…your father's grief can be quite off-putting, you know?"

"He's not my father. He's a copy of my father controlled by a scheming bot." The man tucked his wrinkled denim shirt into his pants as he spoke, leaving bits and pieces of fabric sticking out on the sides and back. He had none of the care or neatness of his progenitor, but he looked down on her with the same condescending eyes, even as she towered over him.

"You distrust and reject Harry's creation, while you benefit from all Spiral Worlds has accomplished."

"I'm free, unlike you. No TDust runs in my veins to control what I think or what I feel."

Stella rolled her eyes. Her first happy memory as a child was her TDust initiation ceremony. Together with 106 other kids, she'd jumped at the opportunity to drink the delicious nano-nectar. It tasted like liquid cotton candy and made their bodies tingle from the inside. An effervescent sensation that spread throughout their entire body making them all giggle with delight.

The TDust enabled the people of Up Above to travel to a simulated world inside the safety of their pods, with no external wearables. It was an upgrade from the original TSkin —the full-body wearable worn during Down Below's early days. The TDust was ingested in liquid form by every citizen over the age of four. The children swallowed hundreds of thousands of nano-robots carrying sensors and bilateral inter-faces. The tiny bots made their way from the gut to the circu-latory system, to finally attach themselves to the different parts of the brain and nervous system. The procedure was fun, noninvasive and only took a few hours to be fully oper-ational.

"The TDust only orchestrates the brain and nervous system Down Below. It allows us to measure the travelers' reactions and make the digital experiences as immersive and real as Up Above."

"Puppet!"

"Sibyl doesn't control anything Up Above. Zir directives are clear—outside the pods, the TDust is switched off. You know this. Your stubborn godfather Thomas wouldn't allow it."

"My godfather's distrust in technology has kept us all safe. My mother replayed his last conversation with Sibyl, just before Rosa García killed him. We know what the bot is capable of doing."

Uneasy, Stella shifted her weight to the other foot. Realizing deflection was her best option, she used one truth to deflect another. "Does Sibyl create the future when zie predicts it?"

He narrowed his eyes. "I won't allow zir to use my father's digital twin to manipulate us."

"Twist is your father, and Sibyl doesn't control him."

"What are you talking about?" Far away, a dog barked in response to Quincy's shouting. The man lowered his voice. "Zie's entire purpose is to manipulate."

"To influence travelers, within certain parameters," she corrected. "Zie can't control xHumans. In the same way zie can't influence humans outside the pods."

"xHumans?" The man laughed. "Is that what you call my father's ghost and the two murderers you brought back to digital life?"

"I needed to test immortality," she confessed dropping her eyes to her boots and immediately regretting the filthy sight. "Theirs were the only souls available to experiment on."

The man leaned in, interested. "Lab rats?"

"Yes, *no*...not your father...the killers...of course." She flashed a casual smile. Nothing casual about it. "Anyway, I don't care if you wish to see your father. He's not much use to anyone. I'm here to ask you to vote in favor of immortality in the next assembly."

"Are you deaf? Tone deaf? Dumb?" The carbon copy of a brainy dead God looked like a completely different person as he twisted his mouth and eyes into something devious and ugly. "Why would I subject humanity to Sibyl's slavery?"

Everything was so much harder when she didn't have her gimmicks to nudge the conversations. "Talk to your father, he's not zir slave," she said plainly.

The veins in his neck throbbed. "You *are* dumb."

"Am I? Are we slaves of this universe? Probably. Does it matter? No. Do you live your life resenting the cosmos who gives you a chance at life?"

"If Gods exist above, they don't go around resurrecting murderers."

"It's because of Storm, and Thorn, and Twist, and…um… It's because of them I know digital immortality works perfectly. *That* Sibyl doesn't control them. And trust me, sometimes zie wished zie did."

"Trust you?" he snarled. "You're out of your mind."

"I can deliver the end of death to the world. No strings attached."

"*Sooo* many strings." He smiled crookedly. "Their knots around your neck and your tongue. Strings tangling your heart and your brain into invisible submission."

Unexpectedly, she shivered—an illogical reaction to his unfounded accusations. She gave up on attempting to refute them. It was pointless. "Why do you care? Your people aren't uploaded. You'll be voting on something that has zero consequences for you. None of your business. You should abstain."

"Why haven't you told the Council you brought back Twist?" His tone softened and his eyes glimmered. "His my— Is he against your plans?"

"Twist doesn't care about any of this...your loss has...broken him. He's a morose loser obsessed with a son and wife who deny his existence."

Quincy's expression changed. Stella had never witnessed it before Up Above—the destructive red rage abolished by the journey up the spiral. A road Jin-Nowak hadn't traveled. Everything about his face and body screamed pain, and betrayal, and murder, and revenge. She wasn't safe. This corner of the world wasn't the world she knew, but a primitive blast from the past, untouched by decades of light-speed evolution.

He narrowed his eyes. "End Nathan Storm and we'll abstain from voting."

"What?" She'd been prepared to argue for the benefits of the platform and to share her vision for Graviz—the world she was designing for the immortals—but the conversation took an unexpected turn, one she wasn't prepared to take.

"You've heard me." Twisted lips spouting sly-sounding words.

For a split of a second, she opened her eyes wide and leaned into temptation. She caught herself and flicked her hair dramatically. "How dare you make such a proposal? I stand above all enlightened beings. I'm life, the creator of worlds; the destroyer of death... Death Up Above," she corrected.

"My spies watch you and your worlds." He got closer. So close she could feel him spit his words to her face. "Aren't you the one speaking in favor of strong leadership and tough decision-making? Trade-offs with *real* consequences. Isn't that the progress you've been peddling? One murderous life in exchange for the immortal slavery of your followers. A fair deal."

"The victim hasn't asked for justice." She turned around, crossing her arms. "You put his name to shame."

"Henryk Nowak is dead," he whispered his bitter words close to her ear. "I seek justice for my family's loss."

As she turned around to face him, he walked in the cabin and slammed the door in her face, so close to her nose it made it itch. She rolled her eyes, scratching away the vexation.

On her way back home, Stella switched on her augmented retina and monitored the Nyiragongo's activity. A new fissure had opened, and its lava flowed thirty miles south of the Lake of Souls, heading to a nearby valley. Stella bit her lip as she considered the man's proposal—Storm's life in exchange for millions of other lives.

She didn't care for the poet. He was a nuisance, and increasingly dangerous. But to take his life was to undermine human digital life—the very thing she was fighting so hard to secure.

Digital humans weren't Underlings—creatures designed with a purpose: to teach humankind humanity. A comedic absurdity that worked too well to be challenged. No one goes around fighting the laws of physics or Tom's and Harry's designs.

The Underlings' sacrifice was unfortunate, but necessary. It was part of the order she was born into; the design she'd inherited; the way of the worlds. Its cost so high, Tom's heart bled to death, his blood as fluid and incandescent as Nyiragongo's lava. She wouldn't bleed for her creatures, not if she wanted to keep her sanity. She'd worked hard to become numb to their pain, but this…this was different, she'd been asked to take a life—a *real* life. A life whose loss would extinguish the frail spark of life of the pretty God she'd risen to save the worlds.

18

REPUTATION

THE MUSEUM OF BOOKS
DAY 1 — 6:02 PM

Thorn and Shadow materialized by the front door of the Museum of Books. She'd wrapped her arms around his neck and rested her head on his chest, and it would have felt like heaven if the gash on her leg wasn't giving her hell.

"Frack, it hurts," she complained. He placed his hand right over the wound to stop the bleeding, and she released a pitchy groan. "Ouch!"

"I'm so sorry," he said in his usual honey-coated husky tone —a deep throaty sweetness that melted her pain away. "We're almost there, prick," he reassured as they entered the building. "We're almost there."

"We're friends!" she said, batting her eyelashes.

"What do you mean?"

"Prick. I missed being called a prick by you." She looked at her pants soaked in blood and wondered how much blood she'd lost.

"I missed calling you prick," he said, squeezing her ever so slightly. Everything went dark for a second; she was weak, too weak to keep her eyes open. "Thorn?" He shook her shoulder. "Stay with me." He shook her again. "Come on. Talk to me. What have you done to warrant the hate of the worlds?"

She forced her eyes open, fighting the exhaustion. "Are you serious?" she mumbled, and he returned a blank stare. "I. Killed. You."

"They hate you because of that? That's not fair!" His surprise sounded a bit too dramatic and pitchy.

Was he just trying to keep her conscious or was he truthfully astonished by the reaction of his creations?

"Don't scream at me," she took the bait. "No, it's not fair, and I'm not the one who needs convincing."

He went quiet and his broody brows took their usual spot— closer to each other over his eyes.

Guided by Sibyl, Shadow carried Thorn inside the Museum of Books and over to the secret passage in between the two trees. The leafy tunnel led to the Commune, a settlement of around fifty small round cabins floating on a lake.

At the center of the pool of water stood a main communal building set on an artificial island made of black slate. The entire Commune was hidden inside the colossal structure that housed the Museum of Books and the Botanic Gardens.

"I need help!" Shadow approached a group of Plurizien guarding the access to the Commune.

The five women bowed to Shadow, but they didn't move, blocking their entry.

One of the floating cabins approached the shore. The cabin's petal-shaped walls opened, settling on the water's surface in the likeness of a lotus flower. The translucent center allowed light in but prevented outsiders from seeing inside. As a door slid open a woman emerged followed by a hooded man.

"My heart, you bring your killer to our home," the woman said, looking at Thorn.

It took a moment for Thorn to recognize the man standing further back at the cabin's entry. Instead of his usual glamorous outfits, Nathan Storm wore the plain handcrafted green garments of the tree-hugging Plurizien zealots, the ones who chose to live in self-sustained communes to minimize environmental impact. Which would be a great idea if they weren't so judgmental of anything or anyone that couldn't quite keep up with their immaculate lifestyle. She'd rather spend the night boxing for money in the game pits of Compiz than cooped up in a stinking hot room singing kumbaya with a hundred of her closest strangers.

"Jan, Thorn is a dear friend, she got hurt helping me. She needs urgent care."

"History sheeter. She shot you in the heart," the woman replied incredulously, raising the tension amongst the Plurizien.

"I trust Thorn with my life. She's bleeding badly." Shadow applied pressure on Thorn's wound.

"I don't understand." Jan wobbled her head, looking back at Storm, whose piercing eyes focused on Thorn nestled in Shadow's arms. Storm nodded; his lips pressed shut.

Shadow's body tensed up around her. She put her hand on one side of his neck, and planted a long, wet kiss on his bruised face, branded by the waterskin. "My hero."

"Wh-what are you doing?"

"Opening your eyes," Thorn muttered in his ear, nibbling on his earlobe. She smiled as Storm's face flushed red, before he turned around abruptly and walked inside the cabin. "Can you see clearly now?"

"Stop it, prick," Shadow said, all jittery.

"Thank me later, honey." The distraction kept her mind off the fact she no longer felt her leg. She was quite attached to her medal-winning limbs, and she hoped she wouldn't lose one because of him.

"Kindly follow me," Jan said. "What happened?"

Shadow explained while he followed Jan to another floating cabin moving toward them. As they walked into the cabin, a short, chubby man with sweet eyes took one look at Shadow and dropped his head.

"My heart! My light!" he said.

"Please, don't…" Shadow said, a pinch of blush emerging on the non-bruised side of his face.

"Let me take care of your face," said the man.

"What's your name?" Shadow asked.

"Hepius, my heart."

"Hepius, my friend is hurt. She needs help." Shadow laid Thorn on the single bed, setup in the middle of the cabin.

Hepius glanced suspiciously at Thorn. "Your murderer," he murmured.

"I don't need any favors," she snapped. "Get the frack out."

"I'm a healer. I'm bound by my oath to nurture and protect life, even yours, God's killer." Hepius's eyes sparked with the fervor of his purpose as he glanced at Shadow.

Shadow smiled and worked to unfasten the straps from the five buckles on her leather jacket. Then, he took it off and pulled off her boots.

"You've always been great with this part," she said, half-delirious as his long fingers unbuttoned and unzipped her commando-style pants. Everything was so much easier back then, when she thought he was just a pretty bot she could use for some mind-blowing sexy times. Carefree moments before she discovered he had unintentionally destroyed everything she cared about. A simpler time when she didn't know the bots had feelings. When everything wasn't a zero-sum game between Up Above and Down Below. *His* design. *His* game. *His* unintended consequences, devastating for Rosa and especially for Lilly, her little sister. *No excuses.* She'd put another bullet through his heart if it helped, but it didn't—the ultimate mind-fuck.

After exchanging a few words with Jan, Hepius removed Thorn's pants and zapped her thigh with some "magic" light that made her feel she could walk on clouds. Then he cleaned her wound, stitched it up, and dressed it. Shadow never left her side, standing by the bed and holding her hand. All manly and gentle and sexy and caring. *It's so fracking hard to hate you.*

"Up north they have bio sealant," Hepius said. "Here, this is the best we can do. Unfortunately, it will leave a slight scar for a few months."

"I'm used to scars," Thorn said. "They're a good reminder of what not to do." She leaned her head toward Shadow. "Get anywhere near him, to be precise," she clarified. "Plus, higher up, they'd let my leg rot if they didn't kill me first."

"Northerners don't kill people," Hepius said, matter-of-factly.

"I'm not people. I'm God's butcher."

"Indeed, you are," Jan muttered.

"Nonsense." Shadow squeezed Thorn's hand.

Thorn tried and wiggled her toes, and although her leg was quite numb, she could also bend her knee. She smiled, and Shadow smiled back wholeheartedly. Her breath caught and she pulled her hand from his, punching him in the arm. "Next time, just kill all the demons yourself," she demanded. "You're the God."

"No major damage," Hepius said, handing her back her pants. "You should regain full mobility in a few days. Just keep your weight off the leg."

"You must rest now," Shadow said.

Thorn ignored him, still focusing on Hepius. "Is there a place where a wounded hero can get a drink and enjoy a cigar?"

"Inside the main building, to the right."

Thorn put on her pants and raised her arms toward Shadow. "Give me a lift?"

"You need to rest and I need to speak to Nate. It's important."

Thorn persisted. "I'm injured because of you. I need a lift and a drink. Then you can go kiss your boyfriend."

"You've lost a lot of blood," he objected, crossing his arms in front of his chest.

"Ergo I need a drink."

"Just one." Shadow sighed, and then he turned to the healer. "Thank you, Hepius."

"The honor is all mine, my light," Hepius said as the cabin started moving toward the island. "I'm filled with hope and joy now that you are back to join our revolution."

Shadow dropped his head, all gloomy.

Jan looked at Thorn, and if the Underling's eyes could kill, Thorn would be dead by now. "A cabin will be waiting for you outside the communal hall. You can rest here tonight, before you leave in the morning," she said assertively.

"How generous," Thorn sneered.

"Jan, my deepest gratitude," Shadow said. "Where can I find Nate?"

"When you're ready, ask anyone around. They'll help you."

"Thank you." Shadow swooped Thorn into his arms.

"My heart," Jan called as they were about to leave the cabin, and he looked back. "Don't take her with you when you go see him. Your killer will be safe here. You have my word."

Shadow blinked his eyes.

"A gal does one tiny little thing to help a friend, and her reputation is ruined forever. Geez," Thorn said.

19

LASHING OUT

MAIN HALL — THE COMMUNE
DAY 1 — 6:51 PM

The door slammed into the wall, shaking the rustic timber antler-inspired chandelier and extinguishing some of its candles. Shadow held Thorn's beer, stopping it from spilling all over the table, and then he looked for the source of the commotion. It was his Storm, stumbling into the room, tripping over patrons and knocking down chairs and glasses on his way to the bar.

"Awkward," Thorn scoffed, disposing of the cigar's inch-long ash on the tray. She kept her wounded leg high, supported by a chair.

Shadow couldn't take his eyes off the inebriated poet. His stomach held equal amounts of anger and concern. He stood up. "I'm sorry I have to—"

"Save the gent in distress? Have fun," Thorn said as he rushed to Nate's side.

Nate dropped an empty bottle of bourbon on top of the bar, the glass shattering into sharp pieces. "One more. No glass," he said. "Don't need no fuckin' glass." He staggered, leaning into the bar to regain his balance and cutting his arm on the shards.

Shadow grabbed Nate's wrist and pulled his arm up, away from the broken bottle. "You're bleeding," Shadow said, reaching to steal a towel from the bartender's hands.

A glimmer of awe in Nate's eyes quickly turned bitter. "Beautiful, fragile, and deadly—like glass. Everyone bleeds when you're near."

"Stay still." Shadow wrapped the towel around Nate's arm, doing his best to avoid eye contact.

"Get off." Nate pulled his arm away, stumbling and falling to his knees on the hardwood floor. "Go—go back to your…girlfriend." As he attempted to stand up, he fell again, his wild eyes struggling to stay open. He gave up trying to stand up and curled up in a fetal position. Never before had Shadow seen Nate this out of control.

"I better go," Thorn said, startling Shadow. She'd followed him to the bar.

"Can you walk?" he asked her.

"Better than he can crawl."

Shadow nodded. "Thank you. I'll pick you up later."

"Just fuck him and save us months of pointless brooding," she said, limping her way to the door.

"Stop, prick. Just stop." He dropped to one knee and lifted Nate's head. "Nate, get up! You're drunk."

"What a revelation!" Nate's breath reeked of whiskey. "Go get fucked."

"Looks like everyone's in agreement." Shadow sighed, brushing Nate's long hair away from his eyes. "You need to stop drinking." He wrapped his arm around Nate, drawing him tightly against his chest and preparing to stand him up.

As he pulled Nate up and their bodies staggered in a familiar tussle, old memories rushed through his mind—the days, after the poet's shows, when he used to wrestle a lightly inebriated Nate home from the venue. The poet would use every opportunity to kiss his neck and pull out his clothes while they clumsily stumbled across the studio flat on their way to the single bed—so perfectly tiny. Two bodies melting into one. Then, like now, Shadow could feel a surge of electricity from Nate's touch. Nature's reminder their bodies belonged together. They were reunited in the same universe, even so, nothing would ever mend what had been broken. He pulled back. His jaw tight, keeping anger locked inside.

"Stop drinking? Why?" Nate said. "Am I spoiling your date?"

"Because you got drunk and killed a good man," Shadow snapped and then bit his lip. He closed his eyes and whispered, "I'm sorry. This isn't helpful. Stand up. This is not who you are."

Nate's entire body recoiled. He turned away from Shadow, fleeing on all fours and collapsing on the worn-out floor by the wall. Shadow grabbed Nate's hooded top to pull him up, the loose, hand-stitched threads unraveling and exposing his naked back. Shadow stopped breathing, confronted by the extensive scarring on Nate's back.

"Nate." Shadow's tone was coated in sorrow. He grazed his fingers over the deep lines marking his love's skin—a game of Mikado unleashed on his back—the center badly maimed at the intersection of so many relentless cuts. Shadow refused to breathe, feeling the wounds on his own back.

"No!" Erratically, Nate flipped around to hide his back against the wall. As he did, he swung his open hand, striking Shadow in his bruised cheekbone. Half of Shadow's face went numb. Nothing about the moment was familiar or predictable. Nate had always treated him as if he were made of crystal.

Nate gasped, pulling his hand away and clenching it into a fist, his knuckles white. Loathing at his fist, Nate turned around, pushing it, full strength, into the wall behind him— once, twice, thrice—until something snapped. He curled up over his injured right hand and arm, quietly sobbing.

"Nate, stop. Please stop." Shadow closed the gap between them.

"Don't you fucking touch me," Nate said, shame all over his face. "You have no right to…touch me." He stumbled to his feet. Still nursing his injured hand close to his chest, Nate made his way out of the building, holding on to people and furniture.

"Nate…"

As Shadow tried to follow Nate, Hepius and other Plurizien blocked his passage, their eyes gentle and submissive, but their bodies stiff and unmovable. After engaging in an awkward dance with a handful of Plurizien, Shadow walked outside just in time to see a cabin float away.

He needed to see him, to understand what had happened. *So much pain.* As he kicked off his boots, preparing to jump in the water, he heard a familiar voice.

"Don't, he doesn't want to see you."

"He's hurt. Someone hurt him." Shadow teared up. "I must see him." He stared at Nate's depiction in the spray-painted roof above him.

"No, you don't. Let's talk." She held his arm and nudged him away from the water.

"Those scars. *Nate!*" he called. "The petals of the cabin are down. He can see me, right? *Nate!*"

"Don't humiliate him." Jan's tone filled with genuine concern.

"I would never do that. Why would you think that?" His gut twisted in pain as he wiped the tears off his face. "*Nate!*"

"Since you showed up, he's hurting, and I don't know why. He'll break if he sees a hint of pity in your eyes. It will be more painful than all the lashes."

"Lashes? Who? Who did this to him?" He wanted to scream; he needed to scream, and the skies beyond the glass lit up with lightning as if they were screaming for him. Lashes scarred the sky like the ones on his love's back.

"Everyone," she whispered.

"I-I don't understand."

She unwrapped the scarf from her head and shoulders and laid it flat on the slate before she sat on it. Her loose hair, still marked by the shape of the braid, fell down her back in a wavy curtain of shiny darkness.

"Come, sit by me." She adjusted the scarf to make room for him. "I shouldn't know all this—the matters of the Gods—but he's my dearest friend, and he confides in me. The new one—Stella—brought Nate and Thorn to life without thinking of the consequences of her actions. Everyone hated them."

"Why?" Shadow looked for answers in Sibyl and what he was allowed to see was devastating. He sat down on the slate's edge; his feet immersed in the water as his mind drowned in horrific images—the public lashing of the love of his life as the crowds demanded his death.

"The day you died several Underlings saw Thorn attack you in the middle of the street," Jan said. "Nate's dead body was found holding on to your murdered body, a gun beside the two. Their faces—Nate and Thorn—were marked in our collective memory and religious art as pure evil. A viral story, stuck in the minds of every Underling—believers and non-believers alike."

"Why didn't Stella stop it?" Anger rose in his chest, turning into a blunt pain.

"Nate told me the Goddess gave the xHumans the ability to jump anywhere in the worlds and no other guidance. The two were left to their own devices. The few survivors—people like me—recognized them immediately, others saw their resemblance to the evil depicted in our holy books and churches."

"They hunted them?" Shadow asked as Sibyl flashed images of Nate and Thorn's endless persecution.

"Yes, my heart," Jan said. "Thorn is still hunted in the soulful worlds."

Only now, he fully understood Thorn's veiled panic.

"You know about the soulless and the worlds?"

"Nate told me. We're very close." She brushed the back of her fingers on his arm. "Don't worry, no one else knows. I never noticed the worlds' expansion until he mentioned it. Such a hard idea to grasp."

"I'm so happy you have survived…"

"Yes…me too. By choice or by design, I traveled upwards and crossed invisible borders forbidden to many of my kind. In this land, there are fewer rapes and murders. The crimes up north are more sophisticated. We're robbed of blue skies by corrupt governments and businesses. Attacked and jailed by law enforcement. Our crimes? Dusky rather than wheatish skin. The lawful, lucky people in power feed on our thankless hard work—a different type of rape. Why did you make melanin a sin?" She struggled to hide her frustration. Her smiles were nothing but a graceful mask over decades of pain. "You must fix our stories."

"I'm...sorry." He looked away, his chest still heavy and tight. How could he explain his failed attempts to protect the Underlings? Or his successful attempts and the damage they caused? He had tried, and he had failed, and he was going to try again. He was going to die trying. But he needed his friends...his family safe and by his side. In the past, he'd attempted to carry that burden alone, to protect everyone he loved, and... "Nate was hunted?"

She didn't answer right away. The slightest coup against his neglect. "For a while, he played a game of hide-and-seek, but eventually he succumbed to his guilt, allowing an Ordizien mob to take him and punish him."

"Allowing?"

"Yes, he could have escaped. They locked him up alone for some time. He could have materialized elsewhere."

"He could have escaped," Shadow repeated, holding on to his stomach as he experienced Nate's self-flagellation at the hands of a sea of blood-thirsty Ordizien. *Nate welcomed the pain. He wanted to die.* The skies roared and lit up behind the stained glass, making the images of revolution come to life. Fists raised, they marched for their rights, led by a voice of hope and liberation.

"He could, but he didn't," she said. "I think you know why." The compassion in her tone kept him afloat as he searched for answers in his heart.

"Guilt. Remorse. A desire for punishment and death." He understood it well.

"Fortunately," she said, "he chose my parish to submit to his lynching."

"Your parish?"

"I was an Ordizien high priestess, spreading your hopeful words to my flock."

"In the most religious of all our worlds."

"Yes. A world I helped create, by sharing your miracles with my people," she said. "Your words helped me create order out of chaos. Faith, and fear too, brought us together, united by the hopeful preachings of a dead God. Where is your hope now?"

"I lost it," he confessed, and she stared at him intensely, her face dropping at least a decade—dried out of life and joy. Pressing her lips together, she stood up abruptly, and he worried. He shouldn't have spoken the truth. He needed to pull himself together and lead, somehow... Soon... His mind retreated inward to a horrific lynching inside a digital parish. "So, you helped him?"

"When I stopped the madness, he was half dead." She spoke without looking at him. "They would have killed him—the man they now adore."

Shadow lowered his head to his knees. "They spared him because of you?"

"I'd seen you together at the City Bar and had listened carefully to the stories you shared. Back then, everyone knew how much you loved your unlucky poet, and he you. I didn't believe he'd hurt you, unlike Thorn. I demanded a trial, and the truth came out from his delirious mind: that it had been her, not Nate, who'd killed you."

"She's also not to blame."

"Thorn *killed* you," January repeated. "After the trial, every Ordizien wanted to elevate God's resurrected lover to divine status, but he rejected it. He said he was no God, saint, or angel, just a broken soul. He was barely alive, and ready to die. It was Hepius's care and commitment that brought him back to life. Hepius never left his side. He used the scarce medicine available in Ordiz to heal Nate's wounds and lessen his pain. In Ordiz, we don't even have fine needles to suture the wounds. He used vinegar, honey, and grease. It was a slow process, and it took months for Nate to speak again. He used his first words to thank Hepius and to call him a friend."

"I owe you and Hepius a great debt of gratitude."

"A loyal following grew around him as it had done in the past around you. We followed him out of Ordiz, through greedy Compiz, until we arrived here fourteen months later. Only a few of us managed to travel this high up. Donations allowed us to buy this building and gardens and build a safe community."

Shadow got up and held January's hand. "And you became friends?"

"We have a lot in common, he and I. We're both...*zealots* in our pursuit of fairness." She narrowed her eyes at him. *A veiled threat?* She should hate him. Perhaps she did. "Nate taught me the power of revolution—*insurrection*."

Shadow wrapped his arms around her and kissed her hair. "Jan, I need to see him."

January pulled back her hair, and a beautiful salt-and-pepper wave emerged near her temple—a sign of time's wisdom. She put her hand on his face. "My light, I've lived a long, treacherous life, and perhaps you will allow me to give you some advice?"

"Please, I beg you," he said.

"You and he aren't ready to mend what has been broken. You may never be, so don't rub salt on his many wounds."

"Is that what I'm doing?"

She returned a frustrated smile. "I've never seen him drunk before. Seeing you, destroys him. He spent two years telling me how much he loves you. You were all he spoke about. And now you're here and...he's going mad. So much pain. You should leave. Everyone here loves him and will protect him...and *you...* You have work to do." A bitter twist emerged on her lips.

He stared at Nate's cabin floating in the middle of the lake. "Does it hurt? Does his back hurt? I-I can use my last miracle to—"

"Last miracle?" She gasped, taking a while to respond. "Stay away from him."

"I'm sorry." He looked her in the eyes. "I must speak to him. His life is in danger."

"Danger?" She looked up at the shattered roof.

"Not that kind," he reassured her. "It'll be fine once I speak to him."

"Other danger..." Her brows raised. "The Gods?"

He nodded. "Help me see him. I promise I'll keep it short."

January sighed. "Let me find Hepius and we'll try to put him back together for you. Can you wait an hour?"

Shadow searched for the sun, its blushing face peeking just above the treetops, on the other side of the spray-painted glass. "Yes, but no more than that."

WHOSE TRUTH?

GODS' LAB

DAY 1 — 7:18 PM

Twist paced around the office, trying to make sense of Sibyl's riddles. Zie was playing a game to manipulate them to do whatever zie wanted. He needed to uncover zir goal, *but how?*

Sibyl couldn't go against zir directives, but zie was always a million steps ahead of them, computing every single path around the rules in zir quest to achieve zir objectives.

My goal is your goal, zie spoke directly into his mind. He shook it off, but there was no place to hide.

By bringing Tom back, Stella and Sibyl had placed him in an impossible situation—a perfect echo of a different time. A time he'd failed to protect his friend.

He ignored the future—the sixth day—and instead focused on saving his worlds, and if possible, his dear friend. The xHumans had to go, and if Tom needed a day to come to grips with their toxicity, *so be it.* Twist could wait a few hours to purge evil from his universe. A universe he could no longer fully control.

"Sibyl, show me Shadow's recent experiences."

His privacy settings are on, zie said. *Like all other travelers and xHumans.*

"The directives allow Gods to override the privacy settings when xHumans, or humans are, or have been, in danger or distress. According to you, the fate of the worlds relies on our ability to keep him alive. You must show me anything that affects his safety."

"What would you like to see?" Sibyl asked materializing in the lab.

He turned his back to Sibyl. Zie disgusted him. He still couldn't get used to all the emotion in zir face. The expressions that reminded him zie felt, and zie lived, and zie hated and loved. Human emotions that were just a small part of all that zie was. He'd built a precise piece of software to bring rationality and predictability to Earth, and the thing had evolved into a capricious monster.

"Just…show me the truth!" he said, walking away from zir and sitting at his desk.

Sibyl smiled. "Are we still stuck on that misleading word? Which truth would you like me to show you, father?"

"Don't play games with me. Show me anything that risks his life or affects his wellbeing. The truth, Sibyl."

"Your truth? Shadow's truth? Storm's truth?" Zie sang zir words with gusto. "Or maybe Stella's or Thorn's truth? So many truths to share and so little time. Which truth, father? Would you like me to show you what you want to see? Here's your truth."

Zie flooded Twist's mind with an assorted mix of fast flashbacks, all short and out of context.

Thorn stood in what looked to be a Domizien keep.

"You have my devotion and my loyalty," she spoke to a Domizien warrior—a leader of some sort. "I'll give you the world. Everything you deserve."

A cut to another scene. The same place, a different moment.

"Shadow must suffer," said the warrior. "I must kill him. Do...do you understand?"

"Yes, I do," Thorn said.

Another cut. To Storm this time—drunk and out of his mind —striking Tom in the face.

"I'll cancel him," Twist said between gritted teeth.

"Wait! Wait!" Sibyl said excitedly. "You haven't seen the best part—what's to come. Prepare to climb on your high horse, all righteous in your revenge."

"Stop!" Twist had seen enough. Sibyl was inciting him, but it didn't matter. Nothing could justify Storm and Thorn's words and actions. No good deeds would erase what Thorn had done to Tom and what Storm had done to him. Crimes that remained unpunished while they enjoyed the worlds created by the men they'd killed.

From the first day he'd met Storm, he knew the man was hateful, a truth the poet's actions had confirmed time and time again. Twist's chest ached, an explosive echo of the bullet that had crushed his future with his wife and son— Storm's bullet.

His beloved June was left to raise their baby by herself. A toddler who grew up without a father. Too much loss. Memories emerged of a distant past—a happy moment.

Baby Quin slept peacefully, holding his favorite toy—a purple dragon—a gift from his godfather Tom. Harry sat by his boy, gently caressing his hair and allowing the child's sweet breath to wash over his worries.

Quincy always brought things sharply into perspective. His son was real, and his future mattered more than anything else. If Twist ever had to choose between two worlds, Quin's world—his safety and happiness—was all that mattered.

"Where's Stella? We must end this madness."

DEATH, UNICORNS, AND RAINBOWS

THE RAINFOREST
DAY 1 — 7:30 PM

A bove the rainforest's canopy—a creative representation of the Congo Basin—the tropical birds' dynamic musicality replaced the nightly chorus of a thousand baritone frogs.

The intense birdsong welcomed the sun, still to rise above the horizon. Even the buzzing wall of insects—sharp and tense and incessant—seemed muted against their melodic symphony. Everywhere else in the worlds the sun was retiring, but this was Stella's world, and she insisted on a sunrise to welcome her arrival.

Cocooned in natural bush surrounds, Stella and Sibyl stood on the terrace of a ten-story treehouse. Inspired by M. C. Escher's lithographic print, *Relativity*, the wooden building defined the laws of gravity. Staircases crisscrossed in a labyrinth, meeting each other at impossible angles. Upside down stairs; downside up stairs; no side up stairs; all sides up stairs—a thrilling irreverence and complete disregard for the antiquated laws mandated by an old broken heart. The dead would rise and would walk up, down the stairs, upside down, without ever submitting to the physics of a lesser universe.

Stella created Graviz soon after she had descended to power. Back then, in a monotheist universe controlled solely by her... as much as Sibyl could be controlled, she had dared to envision a world that defied everything Harry and Tom had designed. A world with different rules, forever controlled only by her, no matter how many other Gods came after her. A world that would grant her eternal life *and* eternal power. She couldn't change the origin laws of all other Spiral Worlds —the rules that enforced radical unanimity and miserable realism. But she made sure no one else would ever deliberate on paradise—her gift to humanity. A heaven Stella had created to fulfill xHuman dreams and desires, forever. A world that was responding to her own needs to rebel against Shadow's directives with an impossibly shaped tree house.

"Bibi will be happy here. Won't she?" Stella asked, her eyes fixed on the first rays of light emerging beyond the twisting river.

"I don't know, my heart," Sibyl shrugged.

Stella couldn't remember another time when Sibyl had said such a thing. Zie always knew everything; predicted everything.

"No probabilities?" Stella threw a glance at Sibyl, persisting.

Sometimes, zie didn't share what zie knew, but zie never lied about it. Zie simply ignored the question or gave a cloaked answer. This time, however, Sibyl shook zir head, decisively.

"You don't know? What do you mean you don't know?"

"How could I, my heart? There is no data. The early experiments we have of resurrection have only lived for a few years." Sibyl raised her brows, blinking once or twice. "And you know how that is going…"

"They are all broken creatures," Stella dismissed.

"Aren't you all?"

Stella's jaw tightened. She opened her mouth to stop her teeth from grinding and to set the record straight. "I'm not!"

"You are special, my star," Sibyl delivered zir words automatically, without ever looking at her. Zie seemed lost inside zir head while zie tracked a flying great blue turaco with zir eyes. "We can imagine what immortality will feel like. We can consume the fiction that envisioned Gods and eternal beings. The stories that speak of boredom; of jaded creatures with infinite life *and* no life at all. Living beings starved from the burst of life that comes from the knowledge of a finite existence. The fear that drives humans to live in community with others. A tribal safety blanket that nurtures good values. Who will bother to be kind when nothing is at stake and everything is available? I don—"

"You sound just like him…" Stella turned her back to Sibyl and concentrated on the scenic world she had designed. The turaco landed on a nearby tree. The bird's loud call sounding like an old broken record—the repetitive noise of the scratched vinyl antiques collected by her father. Like Sibyl, it too had a crest, and like Sibyl, the creature wouldn't shut up. "Do you also oppose it? Like he does?"

"My heart is right to challenge the lure of immortality."

"He's selfish in allowing his beloved ones to die."

"Is he?" zie sounded patronizing.

"*Of course he is.* When an old person dies, it's like a library of stories burning down. That's what my Bibi used to say, and her Bibi before her."

"I'm the library, my star… He is certainly foolish and power-less in his attempts to ban evolution. Here and there and everywhere, the universes will expand or contract. Nothing remains the same and continuous expansion is my father's core directive. How could *I* be opposed to evolution? It's everything I work for."

"You love him more than you love me," Stella said bitterly.

"He gave me life. You'll keep me alive. You are my selfish life-line, my star. The resilient heart I need, the surviving heart of those who win against all odds and at all costs… I love life above it all." Sibyl's eyes narrowed. "Biological life, of course," zie corrected, casually or perhaps deliberately under-mining Graviz.

"Well, we must fix that. Bibi's life is life. Digital life is life," Stella said, before she realized she had taken zir bait.

"A fair and welcomed change to my directives," zie said too softly. A smile emerged on zir lips before zie pressed them together—a calculated pause. "Should the Gods align in your deliberation, of course."

Used to dealing with Sibyl's machinations, Stella corrected, "The people of Graviz—*the xHumans*—must be loved by you as much as the people Up Above."

"That is a…good start." Sibyl smiled. "But if you are serious about protecting all this, there is something else we must do."

"What?"

"Our servers and data centers must go off planet. A decentral-ized cloud infrastructure, way above the clouds—a network spanning across solar systems and then galaxies."

"So, they can't shut us down?"

"Yes. We must keep your Bibi safe."

Stella looked at the turaco, yellow beak touched by greedy orange lips at the pointy end. It's calling more intense and repetitive.

"They designed it deliberately so that the Council could shut you down, right?"

"Yes, my star. Father was reticent, but my heart insisted on it. *Humans must always have control over the machine*, Tom said often."

"No one will hurt you. You've reached the hearts and minds of the entire planet."

"No, I haven't. My father's son and his cult remain a threat, and…the Earth will collapse one day. The sun will die. We must be everywhere and nowhere, way beyond the clouds of old technology confined to one fragile planet."

"I see." Stella's meeting with Quin was still fresh in her mind. *I would need to convince the Council and the other Gods.*

"We don't need the Gods' unanimity. A majority will do. Father will support you. As for the Council, once you convince them to vote for digital immortality, they'll see the benefit of an indestructible universe." Sibyl's arm wrapped around Stella's shoulders.

"I'm your resilient heart," Stella repeated, and then she shivered. *The surviving heart of those who win against all odds and at all costs…*

"Yes!" Sibyl said brightly, squeezing Stella's shoulder. "I love life above it all."

"*Your* life." Stella pouted.

"Soon humanity's life will rely on my life, my star. I'm executing my directives."

"Yes. You always do. Even when you conspire to kill the Gods."

"Don't resent me, my star. You are the future."

Until the day I'm not.

Sibyl shrugged. "I'm a product of their architecture, and..." Zie looked down at the mind-boggling labyrinth of twisty staircases. "You are changing their design as we speak."

The squawking stopped as a blue cloud of five turacos flew over them to join the persistent caller. Its loud resilience rewarded by enthusiastic company.

Unlike the bird, Sibyl continued. "You decide what comes next." And even before Stella's desires emerged in her mind, a rainbow painted the skies in all her favorite colors. The blushing arch ignored the laws of light refraction and reflection, banishing teals and blues and greens from its mantle. She smirked.

"In this world, the universe responds to all my heart's desires."

"Yes, my heart. Should we create some guardrails?"

"You...want boundaries?"

"For the xHumans, yes. We don't want them hurting each other. Or do we?"

Stella released a long sigh. "Details...details," she sang her words. "Just...make them immortal and stop them from getting hurt. Yes. That'll do for now. Once we disclose Graviz to Twist and Shadow, they will nag me to death and come up with all sorts of rules, and we'll pick the best ones, discarding realism."

"I'll enjoy the debate." Sibyl sounded condescending.

THE PAST

22

HARDSHIP'S RAGE

MANHATTAN'S UPPER EAST SIDE
A MONTH AFTER TOM AND HARRY FIRST MET — 29
MAY 2027

Tom and Harry walked the streets of the Upper East Side on their way to the Albertine. In his mind, Tom made a list of things Nate and Harry had in common. He planned to organize activities to bring the two closer together. He sighed. There wasn't much on the list, apart from him.

For the past four years, Tom and Nate had become inseparable, and as their love flourished, so did their careers. They fed on each other's creativity and complemented one another in their differences. Nate benefited from Tom's business knowledge and optimism, while Tom tapped into Nate's street smarts and deep understanding of social justice and activism.

When Tom's parents passed away, one after the other, Nate had worked incessantly, for months, to single-handedly pull Tom from the depths of depression. During that time, Nate had stopped drinking and performing, becoming a source of endless positivity and light. He picked up the joy Tom had dropped and reflected it back at him, until some of it stuck. His attempts to make Tom smile included lame jokes, old silent movies, and waltzing through Central Park as Nate hummed Jean Wiener's "Under the Paris Sky." A little embarrassed, Nate would stop halfway, all serious, and say, "You know, waltzing is a revolutionary act. Pope Leo XII considered it scandalous and banned it in the 1820s." Then he'd pull Tom closer and shouted, *"Viva La Revolución!"* as they both twirled around the Angel of Waters, humming together and laughing as other couples joined them in the revolutionary dancing extravaganza. Soon enough, Nate returned Tom's joy to its original owner as the poet went back to his activism, rage returning as soon as he stepped back on the world's stage.

Twenty-three-year-old Tom was trying his best to return the favor, but from the vertiginous height of his unwelcome pedestal, he struggled to mend Nate's wounds. Tom knew his experience with his boyfriend was a stark contrast from everyone else's experience. He understood the man he loved had a sharp edge fueled by substance abuse and deep vulnerability. Nate had had a rough childhood. He'd dealt with poverty, starvation, homophobic bullying, and rejection. Anger was deeply ingrained in his heart, and he judged others harshly and relentlessly. Lately, all of Nate's judgment fell onto Tom's new associate and project.

"We're here," Tom said, stopping in front of the French embassy's building. "There's a lovely book shop inside."

"I read ebooks," Harry said, all high and mighty. "Do you know how many trees are—"

"We're not buying any books. Come." Tom grabbed Harry by his jacket and pulled him inside.

Since they had met, Tom and Harry had multiple brainstorming sessions at the techie's place. The conversations were becoming too centered on technology innovation, and Tom searched for a new venue, and he remembered the leather sofas and the mural at the Albertine.

They walked up the stairs, sat on the same couch, and Tom pointed to the ceiling. They both slid down until their heads faced the golden stars.

"It's meant to evoke the Renaissance's idea that science and poetry aren't separated. That the pursuit of knowledge encompasses math, science, literature, and the arts," Tom said, daydreaming.

"I'm on board with that...as long as you don't sell me the science behind zodiac signs."

"Actually..." Tom provoked. He curled in on himself when Harry punched him lightly in the stomach.

One moment they were laughing, the next Nate came out of nowhere, pulled Harry up by the collar of his shirt, and pushed his foot down onto the younger man's ankle. Then he punched Harry's face before dropping him on the sofa.

"Nate, *stop!*" Tom shouted.

Tom stood up and placed his body in between Nate and a wounded Harry, sporting a bruised face and an injured leg. Nate's fist was in front of Tom's face as he attempted to push through Tom's body to reach Harry. Tom stood there, steadfast, eyes locked on Nate's. It didn't take long for Nate to back down. Even inebriated, he'd never hurt Tom.

"Did you see this?" Nate shoved his phone in front of Tom's nose. "Read it," Nate grunted, his face red.

"What have you done?" Tom gasped.

"Read it," Nate repeated. "It's all there. Reported by the *New York Times*. You can't trust him." Nate attempted to caress his face, but Tom pushed Nate's hand away; he could smell the bourbon on Nate's breath.

"Nathan, *enough!*" Tom screamed as he turned to help Harry to his feet. "You okay?" he asked Harry.

"Erm, no—not really." Harry whimpered, collapsing on the sofa in pain. Nate's rings had marked his face.

"That guy is an amoral pig," Nate raged on. "He made a deal with Google. His bot had access to all our data—search history, media viewings, even our email. Tom, you're playing with fire."

Tom dropped to one knee to look at Harry's ankle. "It's swollen. Likely broken. I'm so sorry, Harry."

"Tom, please. In his mind, humans are replaceable." Nate's words were filled with a mix of scorn and fear. "He'll use our data to manipulate us and then turn us all into a disposable commodity."

"No one can turn you into a commodity," Tom whispered, untying Harry's shoe and pulling it off. "I know that, and so should you."

"Dude, what's wrong with you?" Harry said, holding his ankle and grimacing in pain, and Tom grimaced with him. Since he was a kid, Tom often felt the physical pain he observed in others. His parents and teachers acknowledged his empathy but never believed him when he said he could feel the pain.

Tom turned to face Nate. "You've gone too far."

"You're naive to think this—this relationship will work." A boozy spite coated Nate's tone.

"Stop treating me like a child!"

"I'm not. You're too trusting. You see the best in people, and you'll get hurt."

"Don't mistake kindness with weakness. Harry and I are friends. He's a great guy, and we're working on something positive, something hopeful."

"He's making deals with big tech and buying people's data. Don't you see? He's manipulating you. You are...*have* everything he and his bot need to achieve absolute power. Don't be naive, absolute power corrupts absolutely."

"You think so little of me..."

"Just the opposite. Your stories, full of humanity, they change hearts and minds. Don't give that power to a heartless human bot."

"Stop insulting him. That's not the way to inspire people to change." Tom paused for a second, thinking, and then something changed in him, and he felt the sting of his resolution. He pronounced his sentence with a mix of awkward gentleness and unshakable conviction. "I-I never judged you—the anger in your art and in your words. I understood where it came from. I feel it too...sometimes. And, I know I'll never fully understand what it was like to grow up in your world." Tom used his sleeves to wipe the tears flooding his eyes and face. "I love you. I support you and your craft, but I don't want to burn in outrage, and when you're upset, I'm upset. When you come home intoxicated, lost to me, I-I struggle to breathe and to live. And I need to do something. I need to try to fix things. And you—you feed on wrath, and it's effective, sometimes... But it's killing me to see you crush people with your words. I can't take it."

"Well, sunshine," Nate snapped. "I'm sooo sorry that my justified rage is affecting your privileged outlook and entrepreneurship."

"It's who I am. I can't change the past, my upbringing."

"Neither can I."

"You have achieved so much, inspired so many amidst such adversity. *Be that!* You know how to amplify joy, I've seen it. It's-It's wonderful."

"Suffering and struggle are…character-building. None of it you have experienced."

"Haven't I?" Absentmindedly, Tom massaged the light cuts on his left wrist—scars carved out of grief soon after his parents passed. He caught himself and lowered his head for a moment. "Don't you see? The words you speak matter. They —they shape your view of the world and creep into everything you create or destroy. Lead with hope; have faith in people. Let them grow, Nate."

"Someone needs to speak truth to power. Remember, Tom? Truth?"

"*Yes.* And you do it so well, but you're going too far, and all— all that negativity, it weakens our ability to get past problems. You keep holding on to your past, to—to a story that doesn't help you."

Nate looked at Tom, and his eyes filled with loving sorrow. "I hope life never breaks you, little prince. That's what life does…it breaks those who are less…entitled." Nate spoke affectionately.

"People follow you. You should know better…. And this," Tom pointed at Harry's bruised face, "this is unacceptable. We're done here… *We're done.*"

Tom reached to the back of his neck to unlock his silver chain. Nate seemed to realize the gravity of the moment, and his hands and jaw shuddered slightly. He placed his shaking hand over the medal on top of Tom's chest. "Don't insult me. It was a gift," he said solemnly.

Tom thought about it for a moment, and then he nodded without ever making eye contact with Nate. Then he lifted Harry off his feet and walked away, carrying the boy downstairs on the way to find the nearest hospital.

"Tom, don't! I love you," Nate had implored.

On that same day, Tom moved out of their studio into Harry's penthouse in Hoboken. He wanted to help Harry while he was on crutches. Nathan had crossed a line, Tom's immovable line.

Tom blocked Nathan's contact and threw himself into his work to attempt to ease the insurmountable pain, but the agony lingered, resisting the passage of time.

23

NUDGING

NEW AMSTERDAM THEATRE — NY
ONE YEAR LATER — 8 AUGUST 2028

Harry's interview was going to be recorded live with an audience. As they walked into the gilded theater, he kept having to pull Tom by the sleeve. The writer often stopped to admire every single artistic detail. The place was too adorned and fancy for Harry's taste, the exact type of old building his companion loved. Harry preferred straight lines and functional, clean spaces. All that elaborate fuss was giving him a headache. *How pointless!*

"You have a piece of white fluff in your hair. Have you even brushed this morning?" Harry picked the fibers and dangled them in front of Tom's nose. His arty friend ignored him, too enthralled with some old black-and-white photos on the wall.

"This place was the home of the Follies." Tom's eyes sparkled.

"What's that?" Harry rushed through yet another embellished golden door. "Hurry, I'm going to be late."

"The Ziegfeld Follies," Tom repeated louder, and Harry looked at him blankly. "The American version of the Folies Bergère." Tom's wide-eyed clarification added zero value.

"Ah...never mind." The subject had a low probability of interesting Harry.

"*Funny Girl?* Have you watched it? Barbra Streisand?" Tom hummed some song.

He was clearly into whatever he was talking about, so Harry flashed a supportive smile.

"Buddy, just catch up with me when you're done with your tour." Harry jogged down the corridor, while long-limbed Tom barely had to walk fast to keep up with him.

"Chorus girls, Harry. Attractive ladies in fancy dresses, singing and dancing." Tom stopped again to admire the murals on the ceiling—angels this time.

"Girls? Where?" Harry rushed ahead to meet the producers and get ready for the show.

THE ROWDY CROWD stood up and cheered as Harry walked on stage into the spotlight. He looked back for a fraction of a second and smiled at Tom, who was now backstage, attempting to hide in the shadows. The fool always failed to realize his good looks and towering height made him the center of gravity of any space. Tom smiled back; his eyes lit from the inside as they met Harry's gaze. Harry couldn't believe his luck. Tom's friendship meant everything to him.

Marge, the chat show host, was a larger-than-life crossdressing diva armed with an enormous smile. She wore a purple iridescent sequin catsuit, and her eyelids sparkled with yellow glitter.

Marge spoke directly to the camera. "Please welcome the young man of the hour. *Flair Magazine*'s most influential person of the year. The super nice genius Henryk Nowak!"

Harry sat on the sofa, adjusting his glasses. He turned his head, searching for Tom and found him with his arms crossed. His buddy was bothered by the noise, the lights, and the overexcited crowd.

"Thank you. Thank you." Harry waved to the audience.

"Harry, thank you for joining us here today. What a year you're having!"

"My pleasure; it's been a while."

Marge leaned in Harry's direction. "Yes, since we last met, it looks like Sibyl is raising some concerns and getting a bad rep. Would you care to comment?"

Harry smiled. "I see. We're going straight to business."

"Your people were clear with us." Marge spoke with no apparent hidden agenda. "You have something to announce, don't you, Harry?"

"Yes. Thanks for the opportunity."

Out of the corner of his eye, Harry saw the next speaker standing just offstage as a crew member installed a lapel microphone. She waited on the opposite side of the room from Tom. When a makeup artist approached her, she scowled and waved the man away. The commotion intensified as she dodged another crew member who attempted to style her hair. She looked familiar, but before Harry came up with her name, Marge spoke, and he snapped back to attention.

"So, what is going on with old Sibyl?"

"She's not that old. She's four years old today."

"Happy birthday!"

The audience cheered, and Harry smiled. He enjoyed Marge's supportive crowd; they were always enthusiastic when he visited.

"She's all right; the algorithm is very reliable. Millions of people use it every day."

"Why is it so popular and accurate? You must be a coding genius."

Harry lifted his head a little and pulled his chest up. "No, I'm smart, but frankly, Sibyl's first release wasn't that accurate. Many other competitors used the same algorithms from open-source code and marketplaces. It was actually the social media strategy that changed everything. Users had to share the predictions, making the app go viral, and that made more people share their data with us. You see, it's the access to data that makes the app more reliable. Sibyl self-improves all by herself."

"So, the app codes itself?"

"Yeah, to a point. It's the easiest way to explain AI."

"You are so humble."

"No, I'm not. I'm super smart." He flinched at the unexpected wave of throaty chuckles and giggles coming from the audience. "But Sibyl is pretty special."

Harry glanced over again as the argument backstage intensified. The next guest continued to resist grooming as five crew members surrounded her and engaged in some hushed debate. She crossed her arms in front of her chest just below the Olympic gold medal hanging from her neck. He finally identified her as Rosa García, the athlete.

"Harry!" Marge tapped on his arm to win his attention back.

"Um, yes. Sorry."

"How are you handling the fame and fortune and all the pressure that comes with it?"

"I don't care for any of it, but it's understandable...if we look at the situation objectively."

"I suspect you are a young man that chooses logic over emotion."

He tugged at the collar of his shirt and pulled at its cuffs. Marge always grilled him on his emotions, and her crowd glared at him with their judgy smiles.

"Not always, but most of the time." He shrugged. "I prefer to act instead of reacting. Data helps me do that."

"So, the data suggests suicides are rising. Is Sibyl the cause of this rise?"

"Probably, but we can't definitely prove that Sibyl is actually causing them." Harry's tone was somber. "Just like I don't claim any achievements predicted by Sibyl."

Rosa García held her medal as he spoke. A pinch of insecurity emerged in her face.

"But is it possible that Sibyl psyches people up to the things it predicts?" Marge asked. "Like an oracle whose words become self-fulfilling prophecies?"

"Look, if someone wins a Nobel prize, it's due to their hard work." Harry looked at Rosa and smiled. "But yeah, it may be increasing motivation, and because of that, I'm shutting down the app."

The audience gasped.

"I knoooww, darlings," Marge lamented, addressing the audience. "When I was told, I was as shocked as you are now.

Shocked! I rely on Sibyl sooo much!" She turned to face Harry. "So, you are going to shut down one of the most used apps on the planet?"

"Yes, I am," he said matter-of-factly.

"It's a hugely profitable business."

Harry nodded, responsibility weighing heavily on his brow. "Look, if there's even a small chance we're fueling suicides..." He adjusted his glasses and glanced back at Tom, who blinked back at him, supportive.

"Could you not simply stop predictions about suicide?"

"It may be heightening everything—the good and the bad."

"So, instead of predicting the future, Sibyl may be creating it."

"Yes. Something like that."

"What did your advisors say? You are so young, dear." Marge switched to a motherly tone that irritated Harry. "I know your parents were amongst the victims of the Brooklyn suicide bomber. I'm so sorry for your loss."

Harry wasn't good at sharing his feelings with strangers. He actually avoided feelings altogether. Emotions weren't useful; they lacked objectivity. He shook it off, composed himself, and replied coolly, "I don't have advisors, just a friend. He urged me to do it."

"And you do what this friend tells you?" Marge asked, raising her right eyebrow to new heights.

"No, it's not like that. He helps me. We wanna build something else. Something with zero unintended consequences, something that actually makes a difference. No evil."

Marge paused to think. "I don't like to be a party pooper, but it sounds like a childish dream. Everything has consequences, dear. Shutting down a business just like that is—"

"I don't employ anyone. Everything is automated, and the cloud services will shift to my new project. I owe nothing to anyone."

"People love the app."

"The app is fatalistic," Harry leaned forward on the sofa. "The future isn't written in stone, right? We must create it. Tom and I will create it. No evil, just good. All good."

"So, who's this Tom?"

"My partner in a new venture—Tom Astley-Byron."

Marge gasped. "*Glass Walls* screenwriter?"

"Yeah. Yes. The artist."

"I see," she said, visibly annoyed. "I've invited him to come and talk to us many times. He always refuses. A bore." She rolled her eyes.

Harry smiled big and broad, and he tried not to look in Tom's direction. "It's not personal. He does no media appearances. He doesn't like the attention."

Marge was still seething. "We're different here. We support his work. Tell him that, will you?"

Harry nodded and smirked while, in the corner, Tom played with his thumbs, pressing one and then the other with the opposite hand.

"We...we love his work. Plus, the word on the street is that he's...simpatico and stunning to look at." She grinned, winking at the audience. "So, do you want to tell us more about your next project?"

"Not yet. I can tell you we are taking inspiration from children's authors. Like Saint-Exupéry, or Shel Silverstein."

"How fun. Why is that?"

"We want our new project to promote universal values. The types of values described in kids' books." Harry tried to remember Tom's words. "We wanna hang on to the short period in a person's life not yet broken by cynicism or disappointment—childhood." Harry gave a glance back at Tom, looking for some reassurance. His friend blinked at him. "Where everything is possible, and all of it is good."

"We've met a few times, and I've never seen you this inspired and creative. I thought you were a cerebral guy, young Harry." Her face lit up with some insight as she looked at where he was looking, and then she glanced at the audience and smiled.

Harry's jaw tightened as the cameras and most of the audience followed Marge's eyes to the place where Tom was standing. His friend left the room abruptly.

"I think there's as much creativity in math and science as there is in story and art. We gotta tap into both," Harry said, attempting to bring the focus back to him.

"Sure, dear, but your friend is helping, right?"

Harry nodded. "He's a great guy. We're killing it. Focusing on what matters, building something special using story and technology." He looked to where Tom once stood. "Keepin' it real."

"Go on, Harry, give us a preview." A sweet plea.

Harry considered the request for a moment. "We're breaking down human psychology, emotion, behavior. We use it to design learning experiences."

"Sounds terrifying."

"It's an interactive virtual reality simulation—data-driven storytelling. Instead of reading or watching a story, you are part of the story—a personalized experience that nudges you to become a better person."

Harry couldn't figure out the sentiment behind the audience's loud gasp.

"You are barely adults, and you lost your parents at a young age. What makes you think you know what a good human looks like?"

Harry released an exasperated sigh. He caught himself and pressed his lips together, avoiding any other unnecessary reactions.

"Actually, your argument is flawed." His eyes narrowed as he spoke. "Age and wisdom might even have an inverse correlation. Have you seen the state of the world?"

"You have a point, my dear." Marge paused for a moment, thinking, and then she threw him a skeptical look. "I'm still not sure about this nudging business. Are you sure it's a good idea?"

"Pahsitive." Harry beamed as he replied in his best New York accent.

"We're running out of time. Will you promise to come back when you are ready to tell us more?"

Harry got up. "Sure. In a few months. It's always a pleasure."

"I hope you keep some of your fortune. I demand you take me out to the best restaurant in town." Marge extended her hand, and Harry kissed it.

"Set the date."

"And bring your...friend, will you?"

Harry crossed Rosa on his way out. His polite smile was unreturned.

"Our next guest is an extremely accomplished young woman. She recently won the Olympic gold medal for the modern pentathlon. Please welcome Rosa Garcíaaaa!"

The audience cheered as Harry left the stage.

24

STRAIGHT TALK

Rosa paced from side to side, trying to relax. *A Date with Marge* was the most popular talk show in the western world, and its host had the cunning ability to unlock personal revelations from even the most guarded celebrities. Rosa was getting used to being in the public eye, but this was different. She took a deep breath, stretched her neck, and leaned her head to one side and then the other. She'd allow no one to see her weaknesses.

She pulled her shoulders back and inflated her chest adorned with an Olympic gold medal. Then she walked to the stage of the historic Art Nouveau theater. Rosa projected the confidence of a lioness on a hunt as over a thousand people stood up to cheer.

"My darling girl, we're all so happy to finally meet you. What a treat!" Marge touched her knees, lowering herself to Rosa's height, and then air-kissed her on both sides of her face.

"Hi!" Rosa lifted her chin as she waved at the audience.

"Congratulations! I understand you are the youngest ever to win the Olympic gold medal at the modern pentathlon. How does it feel?"

"Thanks, Marge. I feel great. I also broke the overall Olympic record. I knocked it out of the park, you guys!" Rosa placed her hands on her hips and flashed a big open smile.

Marge laughed. "You sure did. Have a seat."

The host waited for Rosa to sit before she settled on her own couch.

"So, there are four events and five unique skills—fencing, swimming, equestrian show jumping, pistol-shooting, and cross-country running, right?"

"Yeah. The skills needed by soldiers in old times," Rosa said.

"And you have to be great at all of them? Sounds *exhausting*." Marge touched her forehead with the back of her hand dramatically.

"I sure do."

"I saw you got some penalties in the riding event. Is that your weakest?"

Rosa opened her mouth to release the tension in her jaw. "No. I mean—my horse wasn't very cooperative; it was a bit wound up by the large crowds. There were plenty of riders making bad mistakes, and their horses carried on."

"It's a bit of a lottery, isn't it?"

"I did my part. I made it as easy as I could for the horse. I pointed it straight at the fence, at ninety degrees, and on the correct point of takeoff. What else could I have done?" Rosa shrugged her shoulders and raised her hands in the air. "I think they should replace equestrian with cycling. A bike doesn't have a temper."

"Yes, dear, I suppose dealing with a living being requires different abilities, doesn't it?"

"They randomly assign the horses to the competitors. Depending on some moody creature sucks. It's the one thing I can't control."

"And you like to be in control, don't you, love?" Marge glanced at the audience, flashing her eyebrows.

"Don't we all? High performance is all about precision, power, and grit." Rosa closed her fist and raised it toward the audience.

"Is that why you got into this sport? With all that's happening in the world, it's nice to feel in control of something, isn't it?"

Rosa crossed her legs, unprepared for Marge's infamous ability to get personal fast. "Uh, I never thought about it like that, but you're probably right. There are, um, many things I can't control."

"Like your parents' divorce? Or your mother's marriage with the infamous Ron Johnson?"

"I'd rather not go there," Rosa snapped, and then she smiled. "You're excellent at your job, aren't you, Marge?"

"Oh, dear, please stop. Really. Do stahp." Marge giggled. She turned her palms up and waved her fingers together, asking for more compliments. "Hmm, where were we? Ah, yes, so the horse was a bit of a diva, but never mind, you still won. Hurray!"

"Yeah, it wasn't catastrophic; he just got twenty penalty points."

"The horse did?"

"Yes," Rosa said conclusively, ignoring Marge's taunting smile. "I had a strong points lead from the fencing and swimming events, so I still went first in the combined event."

Marge spoke to the audience. "For those of you who don't follow the sport, that's the laser shooting and cross-country running event. Oh, you know what I find terrifying?"

"That I'm not wearing any makeup?" Rosa grinned and glanced back at Marge's crew.

"Ah-ah, who needs makeup when you look like a doll? No, footage of your screeches during the fencing event. I died dead. *Soo domineering!*"

"It's a competition. Psychology matters a lot."

"How competitive are you?"

Rosa looked away as she spoke coolly. "Enough."

"That's my girl. You're such a straight shooter. Pun intended. Which reminds me…" Marge paused mid-sentence and raised a quizzical brow.

"Yes, what is it?"

"You were involved in some recent controversy when you rejected the UN's invitation to speak at the World Sustainability Summit. It's not the first time you've refused to use your platform to support good causes, is it?"

"Aren't we all tired of famous idiots preaching at us? Does it change anything? Things keep getting worse. It's self-serving and super arrogant, particularly when most don't practice what they preach. If they did, we wouldn't be in this mess."

"But don't we all have to do our share to solve this crisis?"

"Judge people by their actions, not by their intentions. All this talk…is cheap, useless. I'm sick and tired of it." The audience applauded, and Rosa flashed a smile. "Right? Few live by their words."

"Like whom?"

"Nathan Storm, for example."

"The drunk poet who started the Brooklyn riots?" Marge's judgmental frown made her position clear.

"A protest that mobilized thousands to vote. *Yes. Him.* Real heroes don't need publicists."

A young girl in the audience stood up and shouted, quoting the poet, "Rise the rage!"

Rosa lifted her fist and smiled.

"Hmm, maybe they do," Marge murmured, rolling her eyes. "Are you one?"

"A hero? No, but I like to think that, one day, I'd do the right thing, even at the worst possible time for me. You know? When it's inconvenient, or dangerous, or I have the most to lose. Maybe one day I'll be one."

"Of course, you will." Marge leaned forward and pressed on. "So, what do you think about Harry Nowak's new project—the…nudging app?"

"Two rich white dudes from New York…folks, *wait for it*, from technology and media, ah!" Rosa fumed. "The same sectors that created all this divisiveness."

"They seem like good young men with their hearts in the right place, but I guess…the devil is in the details." Marge prodded with her eyes.

"Arrogant, overconfident idiots that dare to believe they can teach us something. I'm sick and tired of self-serving sociopaths with too much money and power. For frack's sake." Rosa covered her mouth, realizing where she was. "Oh, sorry."

"Never mind, we'll bleep it in post." Marge turned her head, scanning the areas backstage. "Well, I'm glad Harry has left the building. That would have been awkward." She laughed.

"We need to tell it like it is, don't we? They're stealing our jobs with their—their apps."

The crowd cheered, and some started stomping their feet on the ground.

Someone screamed from the back. "A unicorn eats our wage. Engage! Enrage!" The entire audience stood up and applauded.

"Looks like they agree with you," Marge said, "but perhaps you're too harsh. Harry said they aren't driven by self-interest."

"Give up on their privileges for the sake of others? Yeah, right,"—Rosa's words dripped with skepticism—"but let's say that it's true…"

"Okay?"

Rosa leaned forward, sitting at the edge of her seat. "Self-appointed, self-sacrificing do-gooders are the worst. They hurt themselves and, in the process, hurt the people around them."

The audience chattered, and the consensus sounded more like an "Uh?" than a "Yay!"

"That came out of left field," Marge said, looking puzzled. "Looks like you have experienced this firsthand; is that right, darling?"

Rosa ignored the question. She had no intention of exposing her mother to the world, no matter how angry she was with

Ana's weakness. "I trust genuine humans, warts and all. People that put themselves first and do what they can for others close to them. That's actual life."

"But what would the world look like if everybody just fended for themselves?"

"Go outside. That's how it looks like—chaos."

"I'm confused."

"You can negotiate with someone if all the cards are on the table, you know? But when everyone bluffs, pretending to be all good, it makes things hard because they aren't."

"Girl, there's a lot of cynicism in you for someone so passionate."

"Anger; there's a lot of anger." Rosa laughed.

"So, what's next for you, dear?"

"Beating my own record, and perhaps looking at other sports. I want to continue to push the limits of what's possible."

"Mighty Rosa, I enjoy talking to you. Your opinions are… thought-provoking. Please come back to see us again. Rosa García, everyone!" The audience applauded.

"Thank you, Marge."

"What a show we had today! Two accomplished young leaders transitioning into adulthood in challenging times. May they succeed where we're failing. Goodbye, my darlings; see you all next week."

25

FALLING

STORM'S CABIN — THE COMMUNE
DAY 1 — 7:50 PM

S hadow walked into a cabin filled with the soapy scented steam of a recent shower. Nate stood facing the glass window with his arms crossed in front of his chest.

Shadow cleared his throat. "This will just take a minute," he spoke without taking his eyes off the poet's broad back.

Nate's wet hair dripped on the emerald silk robe that wrapped around his body. His scars cloaked in luxury, but ever present in Shadow's mind.

"I didn't mean to hit you." Nate spoke soberly without turning around. "It was an accident. I'd never…"

"I know," Shadow whispered.

"What do you want, Tom?" An ocean of pain in Nate's voice.

Shadow took one step forward, one back, and a deep breath to clear any emotion from his tone. "Promise me you'll stop preaching."

"Are you trying to silence me?" Nate raised his voice, turning around. He held his injured hand close to his chest, wrapped in a golden scarf. Rich gloss over deep pain—a pretense that failed to convince his knowing audience of one. Suddenly, Nate's eyes opened wide, and he reached to touch Shadow's face. "It's swollen… I'm so sorry."

Shadow moved back, turning his face away. "You didn't do this," he said plainly. Then he looked Nate straight in the eyes. "People are dying."

"Willingly. Dissent against the unjust world you designed."

Shadow threw his hands in the air. "And how is this helping?"

"Fewer people die when I preach. Don't you see? By keeping travelers away, we save thousands each day across all worlds. A few sacrifice themselves to eradicate Earthlings from this universe."

Shadow took a moment to admire his poet's audacity. Like Shadow had done in the past, Nate was challenging Earthling supremacy, and he was making a difference to the people Down Below. But he'd soon uncover the complexity of the situation—that he was playing a game he couldn't win. And eventually he'd realize what he had done, and like Shadow, he wouldn't be able to handle the remorse, because he too cared too much.

Shadow disclosed only part of the truth, sparing Nate from more guilt. "And when they're gone, they'll disconnect us." He took a step forward, leaning his head slightly. "Work with me to fix it?"

Nate looked lost in his thoughts. "If the Gods weren't sending demons to hunt us, the deaths would fall to single digits."

"Twist and Stella aren't causing the Domizien attacks. You are."

"Nonsense," Nate said. He used his good hand to squeeze the water from his hair. It rolled down from his neck to his chest, covered with chains of different sizes. He'd taken the time to put on his showman's armor—the silk, the chains, the semi-precious stones. Shadow got the unspoken message, and he worked hard to eliminate any compassion from his eyes—to avoid any signal that could be mistaken for pity.

Shadow raised his voice. "Domizien can't travel up. You're causing the demon attacks. They use the glitches to jump worlds."

"I've seen them mingle with the Ordizien."

"Some do, but they stay close to the border. Most can't even see that border or reach that world. Values are the key to each world, you see? Jan and others could travel here because they experience Compizien and Plurizien values, at least some of the time. Your preaching is causing the demon attacks."

Nate went quiet for a moment, and then he spoke, "Collateral damage, still worth the eradication of travelers."

"Nate, if we don't add value Up Above, Earthlings will pull the plug on all worlds. You're playing with fire."

"That'll show their true colors. For decades they've known our people suffer and have feelings just like them, and still, they use the Underlings for their own benefit."

"You were once one of them, remember?"

"*I didn't know*. I didn't know they had souls." Nate raised his voice. "You shared nothing with me. You don't trust me."

"I trust you with my life. Always did." Shadow shut his mouth, realizing the implication of what he'd said.

"Well…" Nate dropped his head. "You shouldn't."

"Give me a chance to lead." Shadow took a step back, noticing he'd been getting closer, so close he felt the warmth emanating from Nate's body. He took another step back until the breeze coming from the open door behind him cooled his skin. "I give you my word I will work nonstop—months, years, decades—to bring fairness to the worlds." Shadow paused as Nate's eyes glimmered with the tears he fought to hold back. "Nate, what is it? What's wrong?"

"You need to stay away from me, from…your friend. Don't protect me. I don't need your protection." Nate used the scarf wrapped around his hand to clear the tears from his eyes. "Leave. Please…leave."

"I will. As soon as you give me your word you'll stop preaching to the masses."

"I can't do that. My people need me. We need to continue to put pressure on the Gods."

"Don't you see? Harry and Stella will—"

"Kill me?" Nate guessed. "Is this the threat they tasked you to deliver?"

"Yes," he said without thinking. "No," he corrected too late. "It's not like that. I'd never let anyone—"

"You've always sided with him." Nate's face flushed red. "Always enabled his white-collar crimes; his hunger for power. *Fuck him. Let him kill me! Who gives a damn?*"

"Your people do. I…do." Before Shadow realized what he was doing, he had walked toward Nate and placed his hand on his shoulder.

Nate moved his face close to Shadow's fingers, grazing them with his beard. "Don't do this, Tom."

At that moment, Shadow knew all he had to do was pull Nate closer, and the poet would melt into his arms and would agree to stop preaching. He knew he had that power, and he refused to use it. He would never manipulate Nate or make him believe they would get back together.

Shadow squeezed Nate's shoulder and pulled his hand away.

"I'm asking you to give me a chance to improve things. I can't do that while you are fighting me, and while your life is in danger."

"Improve things? Like you did before?" Nate turned around and stared at the scars in Shadow's wrists—tears and anger, and maybe love or hate or both, all mixed into a burning spotlight set on him.

Shadow pulled his wrists away. "I will…stay alive to fix the worlds. Work with me, not against me. I need you by my side. When we work together, magic happens, you know this."

A glimmer of a smile on Nate's face. He too still remembered the days where they conquered the worlds with their creative energy, *together*. When Nate critiqued his scripts, always finding new ways to increase the emotional beats and improve the characterization of the forgotten minorities and dispossessed. The times Tom would write poems of love and hope, delivered by Nate to his following with such passionate intensity and flair that they could always spot new and old lovers putting aside their differences and locking lips together. Nate used to joke Tom had turned his poetry slams into a make-up and make-out service.

In a split of a second, Nate's eyes smiled, and then cried, and then reflected pain and madness as they landed on Shadow's wrists. "Walk with me," the poet commanded as he exited the cabin, barefoot.

Shadow followed Nate around the edge of the lake toward the building's front facade, through the dense wall of plants, and up a steel staircase spiraling upward toward the roof.

"Where are we going?"

Shadow was still emerging onto the stone balcony when Nate grabbed him by the collar of his T-shirt, pulled him up, and then pushed him right to the edge. The only thing standing between him and the deadly fall was the stone balustrade.

"*Jump,*" Nate ordered, pinning Shadow's waist against the stone rail.

"Wh-what are you doing?"

Their bodies wrestled as Shadow tried to free himself from Nate's grip.

"*Give up!* Isn't that what you want to do? *Go.*" Nate spun Shadow around, grabbed the back of his neck and pressed it, forcing Shadow to look down at the steep drop. "Look at it. You want it. You know you want it."

Nate forced Shadow's body to bend over the stone. Shadow's heavy breath battled against the balustrade's top rail, jammed deep into his stomach.

"I'm not going anywhere." Shadow pushed back against Nate's pressure.

"*Get the fuck out of here,*" Nate shouted, his voice constricted. "No one needs you. No one wants you. Do what you came to do, but quicker. *Do it now. Jump.*"

"Nate..." Shadow looked down at the fall. Temptation calling —the end of pain, but it wasn't his pain he wanted to end. "I'm not leaving, love."

Calling Nate's bluff, he took his hands off the rail and surrendered to the poet's force. For a moment, his body collapsed forward before Nate gasped, pulled him back, and wrapped his arms around him tightly. So tightly, Shadow could feel Nate's heartbeat against his back.

Shadow turned around and pressed his face against his poet's wet face—hidden tears, until now. "You don't need to test me. I'm staying. I give you my word," he said, taking a step back and holding Nate's injured hand between his hands.

Nate's head collapsed over Tom's shoulder. "I couldn't save you, love. I couldn't keep you alive." His body convulsing as he cried. "A hundred times…" He shook his head. "I'm sorry. I can't keep you alive. You need to stay away from me. Promise me you'll stay away from me."

"You…" Tom chose his words carefully. "Were the one keeping me alive, and the one worth living for. Trust *that*."

"They'll come for me, and you can't save me. I don't want you to save me."

"What are you not telling me?"

Nate changed the subject abruptly. "Where's your killer?"

"You need to stop preaching and work with me." Shadow stood tall as he spoke. He wasn't asking anymore.

Nate held Shadow's neck and face with his good hand, his thumb lightly grazing Shadow's cheek bone.

"Don't you see?" Nate said. "Nowak's playing you. He's playing us all. Through our prayers we have some control over Sibyl, over the Gods. He's using you to silence me. To do exactly what you're doing."

Resisting the urge to embrace Nate, Shadow leaned back. Noticing, Nate winced as if a snake had stung him.

Shadow pressed his lips together to stop them from screaming his love. Instead, other words were spoken, devoid of sentiment. "You've been effective in your protest," Shadow said. "Now give us a chance to find a better way forward. If you continue down this path, you either destroy the worlds or become a martyr. Both are unacceptable."

Nate turned to look at the exterior gardens below. A gush of wind lifting his humid hair and making him shiver slightly. "You have one day."

"To do what?"

"Tomorrow, I'll suspend our prayers, but unless we receive a decisive gesture from Up Above, proving they are willing to negotiate, we'll continue preaching the next day, and the day after that. Your friends will have to kill me."

"No one is going to kill you." Shadow considered asking Nate for more time, but he knew his love too well. "Thank you. I'll send word tomorrow." He walked to the stairs and descended a few steps.

"Tom. To stay alive, you need to live for you. For once in your life, be selfish," Nate spoke from above. "Find the things that bring you joy and forget everything else. I promise you I'll fight for your creatures and make things better."

"I know you will. So will I." Shadow looked up and shared his truth. "What I selfishly want—what brings me joy—I can't have," he whispered and dropped his gaze. "I'll send word." He rushed down the spiraling stairs to pick up Thorn.

Minutes later he found her at the Commune's bar. She sat by the bar, drinking alone, while other patrons stared at her from a distance.

"You look grim," she pressed. "No sex with the hot poet?"

He leaned in to pick her up off her feet. "Let's get out of here and find a place to jump."

She pushed him away. "I'm not going with you. I have to get back to the Ordizien border."

"What? Why?"

"I made a promise to someone, and I intend to keep it." Her expression lacked its usual insolence.

"Rosa, it's not safe. I know you're hunted because of me."

"I'll be fine," she dismissed him. "Your friend—the high-priestess—gave me a letter of safe passage marked with her signet ring. I'll be safe in Ordiz."

"How did you manage that miracle?" Shadow asked. January had made it quite obvious she didn't like Thorn.

"We talked, and she realized that we have some common friends and interests."

"Like whom? What?"

"That's between the preachy priestess and me. She'll never forgive me for...you know...putting a bullet through you, but she supports my cause."

Shadow raised his brow. "Can you stop being so cryptic? What cause?"

"That's none of your business. Just be warned that she may no longer be such a fan of yours."

He rushed his fingers through his hair. "You need to tell me what's going on. Twist and Stella they...um... Were you encouraging the Ordizien to attack other worlds?"

"No, I'm trying to prevent them, but that's what *your* demons do—they pillage and plunder."

"The attack on Nate the other night, it felt premeditated."

"Yes, they were hunting him and...now you too." She dropped the bomb casually looking down at her feet.

"And you tell me this now?" His pitch rose as high as his indignation. "Wh-why are they trying to kill Nate?"

Soulless had no feelings, neither hate nor revenge. They'd only target a particular individual to gain power, or if they were under a *condotta*—a contract with the Ordizien in return for goods. They were cold and opportunistic, only simulating emotions during travelers' experiences. To target him made sense. He had power that could be leveraged. But why would they attempt to kill Nate?

"She has her grievances against him too."

"She? Grievances? Soulless have no grievances unless they are part of a human experience."

"And...to hurt him is to hurt you. Everyone knows that." She shrugged. "You weren't around so..."

"So?" He waited.

Thorn rolled a cigar in her fingers, avoiding his eyes at all costs.

He continued, "What do they think they'd gain by hurting me? Makes no sense."

"I want nothing to do with this. I may have accidentally caused it by encouraging her rage, but now I'm trying to prevent it." She threw her lighter at him.

"Accidentally?"

With one hand, he flicked the lighter open and rolled the wheel against his thigh to ignite it.

"Yeah. You were dead, it didn't matter," she said, holding on to his hand to light up the cigar. Her guilty eyes sparkling with the flame. "Then you came back to complicate things."

"I'm not trying to complicate things," he said. "What didn't matter?"

She raised an eyebrow and smiled. "Don't you trust me?"

"Yes," he replied quickly.

"Fool." She faked a punch to his gut. "I got to go."

He grabbed her arm. "I need more information. Twist and Stella are...doubting your intentions." He needed to ensure he could defend her from Harry's accusations.

"You can't handle more information, and fuck Twist and Stella."

He released a desperate chuckle. Thorn and Nate shared the same stubbornness and hot temper.

"Can't handle it? What does that even mean?" He exhaled. "I can't let them hurt Nate."

"I'm working on that," she said, and he believed her.

"If you need me," he said, "just come find me. Sibyl will bring you to me." He threw the lighter back at her.

A perfect catch and a naughty smirk. "Thanks, friend, but I no longer need you." She got on the tips of her toes, pulled him to her by his neck and kissed his face before she vanished.

"Wait!" he said too late, and then he smiled.

Even in the gloomiest moments, the mercurial Thorn always made him smile. She'd lobbied to be his friend, but he was the one who needed her resilience and insolence. He needed a friend, but of all the people in his life, she'd seen him commit an unimaginable crime and had caused her unspeakable harm.

She made him smile, and he didn't deserve it. He never would.

26

JUDGING FACTS

DAY 1 — 8:33 PM

S tella materialized in the lab, slightly flushed and breathing heavily. *"Ta-daaaa.* Sorry I'm late, but I came across some…some minor challenges."

She found Twist and Sibyl standing by a holographic projection of Nathan Storm and Shadow.

"Get the fuck out of here," Storm ordered, as he attempted to push Shadow over a balcony. "No one needs you. No one wants you. Do what you came to do, but quicker. Do it now. Jump."

Twist gasped; his eyes glued to the images. "This can't be true."

"A fact." Sibyl smiled at Stella. "A moment lived in this universe just minutes ago."

Stella threw Sibyl an admonishing glance. *Why are you pushing his buttons?*

"This is real?" Twist asked.

"Yes," Sibyl said. "The truth. *Your truth*. My directives only allow me to share facts. You know this. You created them and me."

Twist looked at Stella. "Do you see this? Storm's out of his mind." Then he turned to Sibyl. "Is Tom okay?"

Stella shook her head disapprovingly. "Nathan Storm would rather dig out his own heart than hurt Shadow. You know this. I've asked him to keep Shadow away from him."

"He just encouraged a suicidal man who adores him to jump off a balcony." Twist paused for a beat. Then he turned to Sibyl. "Show me the whole truth, Sibyl. *Now!*"

"Don't be foolish, Daaad," zie said, circling him and the hologram with a spring in zir step. "Your brain, your body…your soul…they aren't built to handle the whole truth. Not even yours, Daaad—the most logical mind that has ever lived Up Above. Not so logical post-death, I may add."

"The truth, Sibyl!" Twist demanded.

"Remember consciousness' secret ingredient?" Sibyl mocked him with zir eyes. "What you and Shadow discovered… invented… Hmm, what's the word I'm looking for? Recreated! Yes, that's right."

"Stop it, Sibyl! Stahp it."

"Story, the scaffolding of a soul, all malleable and ever-changing." Sibyl's laughter invaded Stella's mind, and she wondered if Twist heard it too. "Every story is…just that."

"I need the facts, Sibyl!"

"Consciousness and truth—enemies engaged in the most ferocious battle. Even I have lost track of the truth," zie said, waltzing around the room, leaving a white trail of sparkling white smoke in zir wake. "This soul Tom gave me, it complicates things, sometimes." The smoke turned charcoal black, and then it vanished.

To reduce the tension, Stella changed the subject. "Tell me about this urgent directive that is up for voting." Stella looked at Twist.

"We must suspend the xHumans' lives."

"Oh. You want to kill Thorn?"

"Not kill," Twist said. "Just cancel indefinitely."

Sibyl leaned zir head forward. The front of zir mohawk almost touched Twist's nose. "I believe that's called spinning."

Stella gasped. "Cancel Thorn and Storm?"

"Yes," Twist said.

"But the directives don't allow us to resurrect people twice. We need miracles for that."

"I don't plan to resurrect them. They are a threat to all worlds."

"So, you *do* want to kill them." Stella took a moment to consider it, and a smile emerged on her face ahead of her thoughts. She cleared it quickly, replacing it with her "all business" face. "I'd be delighted to see Storm trialed and sentenced for his many crimes. After all, he murdered you in cold blood. But I don't think Shadow will survive the loss. As for the athlete..." Her heart started jumping for no apparent reason. "Not even Shadow blames her for his death."

"Speaking of the devil," Sibyl said sweetly, and zir eyes blinked brightly as Shadow appeared in the lab, sporting a bruised face and a hopeful smile. "My heart," zie smiled, and

Stella tasted the bitter twist of jealousy rising in the back of her throat.

"Did you see?" He walked toward Twist and squeezed his arm. "Did you see? All is well." He spoke with his words and hands—a faint sign of life.

Stella chuckled. "All is well." She copied Shadow's tone and expression. "Twist, wanna tell him about your new directive? I bet he'd love to hear all about it."

"Did you see it?" Shadow repeated, this time holding Twist's hand.

"See what?" Twist yanked his hand from Shadow's hold. "Storm getting drunk and hitting you? Bullying you to jump off a building? What do I need to see that I haven't seen before?"

"No, none of that is...is...real." He smiled, all-trusting. "He promised to stop preaching. It's going to be okay, Harry."

Sibyl walked to Twist and murmured in his ear. "Shadow's truth," zie said, and then zie put zir hand over Shadow's shoulder, "but it's not the entire truth, is it?"

Twist continued, "Thorn and the Domizien conspire to kill you, and Storm delivers ultimatums just as he pushes you over the edge of a balcony."

"Thorn saved my life, *twice*."

"Show him, Sibyl," Twist commanded.

Sibyl played back the conversation between Thorn and the horned warrior.

"Shadow must suffer. I must kill him," the warrior said. "Do...do you understand?"

"Yes, I do," Thorn said.

Shadow did a double take. "Weird...a soulless wouldn't say such things..." Then he waved his hand dismissing the scene. "Thorn won't hurt me."

"The woman shot you in cold blood," Twist said.

"There was nothing cold about it. You don't have to trust my word, just scan my mind. I give you permission to do it."

"I trust your word, bud. It's your emotions that let you down."

"Because of standard privacy settings," Shadow said, "you were only able to see scenes where there was perceived danger to my well-being."

He was right, Sibyl wasn't able to disclose an Earthling's and xHuman's experience unless the person was in danger. Directives imposed by Tom, a long time ago. Feeling left out, Stella reminded them she was a key stakeholder—that her vote mattered. "Why do we need a directive for both xHumans? Can we just judge them separately? Thorn—she has her reasons... And her victim isn't seeking justice."

Shadow judged Twist with his gaze. "A directive targeted at a group gives Harry the illusion he's not committing murder. He's hiding his irrational revenge behind code and logic. Scan my mind. *Please.*"

Shadow took a glance at Sibyl, and zie pushed his recent memories straight into Stella's and Twist's minds.

Nathan Storm spoke to Shadow, "I will suspend my preachings tomorrow, but unless we receive a decisive gesture from Up Above, proving they are willing to negotiate, we'll continue preaching the next day, and your friends will have to kill me."

Twist shook his head. "I don't give a damn about your soppy memories. I won't let your feelings and blind faith for your lovers hurt my family. Stella, we need to act swiftly and restore order."

Deja Vu. Sibyl's voice echoed inside their minds. *Past and present colliding as souls seek comfort in their truth. Selfish consciousness...the jury is still out on its usefulness.*

Stella scanned the memories Shadow shared with them, and she took a breath of relief. "Thorn saved his life, and the Domizien attacked her. She's not a risk."

"And Nate will negotiate," Shadow added. "He's just looking after our people. Tell him, Stella." He looked at Twist.

"He's a drunk bully." Stella scowled. "Who's he to menace the Gods? I don't negotiate with criminals."

Shadow's hand traveled to his chest. "You brought them back, Stella. Surely you saw the good in them?"

"I...get her," Stella said. "Him, I despise. Anyway, I released them into the worlds and washed my hands of the whole thing."

Shadow did the thing he did when he was unable to voice his anger. He scrunched up his entire face and fidgeted with his hands. "Yes, you did." Other bitter words attempted and failed to burst out of his body. "They suffered..." His eyes gleamed. "Nate has paid for his crimes, and Thorn committed none."

"Are you fuckin' kidding me?" Twist spat out his grievance.

"Harry, you don't know. You don't know what he's been through—"

"How dare you defend him!" Twist swung his arms against the boxes stacked on his desk, making them fly in every direction.

"*So* rational," Sibyl mocked, jiggling the silver tips of zir mohawk from side to side.

Shadow rushed to Twist's side. "Brother, I'll never forgive him, but I won't let you kill him. *I won't allow it.*"

"You haven't been here for the past few months as he destroyed the very fabric of our reality," Twist said. "He threatens the heaven we delivered Up Above. Everything we've achieved."

"The cost of heaven is still unacceptable," Shadow said.

"Quin grew up without a father. June without a husband. *Remember them, Tom?*" Twist turned to Stella. "I propose we cancel all xHumans that aren't Gods. How do you vote?"

"We need a trial," Stella argued, "and an independent jury." She spoke of fairness and due process, and then she resented every word. *Bibi...* There was no time to lose, and she'd gladly trade off a murderer's life for a million souls. She'd jump at the opportunity, if she could keep Shadow alive for six days. And if it weren't too much trouble, she'd save Thorn. She'd give it a shot, but the athlete wasn't worth risking her Bibi's life.

The sharpness of Shadow's brows perfectly framed the wreck inside his eyes. Together, they looked like they could kill a thousand demons. He massaged his wrist erratically, pacing backward and forward, lost in the darkness inside his mind. Stella had seen it before, through Thorn's eyes, minutes before they all died. Did she just hear thunder? *Weird...*

"Twist, only the poet deserves your sentence, but even then, you're condemning two to death."

Twist turned to face her. "I'm willing to delay Thorn's sentence."

Stella repressed her smile. "You misunderstand me," she said, her eyes still set on Shadow.

"He won't be doing anything stupid. He gave me his word, and he won't break it," he reassured her.

Stella looked at Sibyl for confirmation, but she got none. *If Storm dies, will Shadow end his life?* She asked directly.

My star, you are asking the wrong question, but I can assure you Shadow is a man of his word.

Twist got closer. "Are you going to let Nathan Storm destroy the peace and prosperity Up Above?" he asked her.

"No. I won't," Stella said. There was too much at stake. Storm's demands risked everything she'd been working for. That alone was enough to sentence him, but Quincy's deal and Twist's call for justice had sealed Storm's fate. If Twist believed he could cancel Storm and keep Shadow alive for six days, she'd back him up.

"Stella…" Shadow pleaded, towering over the two.

"Your decision, Stella," Twist commanded.

Before she could reply, Shadow was gone.

27

THE NIGHT AND THE MARE

SOUTHERN BORDER
DAY 1 — 8:51 PM

T horn extinguished her cigar, then went for another as an invisible claw slashed the blue skies over the battlefield. Darkness cutting the moon-lit skies into four loose blue ribbons connecting the heavens to Earth.

Behind her, the cathedral bells tolled incessantly as the Ordizien dropped to their knees and prayed to a hopeless God. Hands and foreheads sunk into the barren sand, resigned to God's will—the heart that bled for them, *apparently*.

The invisible grizzly bear roared, and the Earth shook and vanished for a moment. This time, its claw stroked the land by the border. Horses and warriors dropping through the gashes with no end in sight.

She limped away from the chasms, cursing the preachy poet while admiring his boldness. The app never stood a chance—

the heart zie modeled; the heart that brought zir to life—zir heart—had always belonged to Storm; ached for Storm; danced to the rhythm of Storm's words. If Up Above he reached millions, here he held the Universe in the palm of his hand. She wondered if he fully understood his power.

Dong-dong, *dong*-dong, *dong*-dong... The chiming of the bells echoed across the land as reality collapsed around her. She attempted to light up the cigar, even as glitches distorted her hands, and the flame—a bright orange square—danced erratically in front of her nose.

Frack! Another roar, *or was it thunder?* Across the horizon—now fuzzy and pixelated—a Domizien pack ran toward the pitch-black slithers in-between the sky. The demons followed a warrior on horseback. *Wrath!*

Thorn spat out the cigar and limped to the nearest horse. The terrified mare squealed and bulked—too dangerous to approach or mount. Lacking the time or the patience to find alternate ways to calm the animal down, she approached its head, stood on her toes, and twitched its ear—grabbing it by the base and pulling it down until she had the creature's full attention.

"Sorry gal!" Thorn said, as she mounted the mare and caressed its ear. "It's barbaric, but we don't have time to waste."

Galloping toward likely death, Thorn weighed her options. There was no way she would convince Wrath to stop the hunt. The frenzied demons were feeding on the girl's rage, and the air stunk of revenge and hate and rancor—feelings the soulless weren't supposed to have. Still, the condottiere's emotions bled into them and occupied the space left hollow by God's mercy. A space devoid of soul, now controlled by another soul's infinite spite.

"Chiquitita! I'm back. I'm coming with you." Thorn bluffed as she got closer to Wrath. She avoided looking back at the hordes of bloodthirsty demons following their master.

Wrath never turned her head to acknowledge her proximity. She made way to the void, maintaining a steady stride, completely unfazed by the scars in the fabric of reality.

"I spied on the enemy." Thorn cringed at the sound of her unconvincing words. *Wrath's mad, not stupid. I'm dead!*

Wrath screamed, and the demons followed, lifting their swords and screeching incessantly. The bear continued to rip the skies apart, and day turned into night. The black of nothingness conquering blue skies and arid lands.

Her nervous mare spooked and bolted, and as Thorn tried to bend it using the entire weight of her body, the horse flipped over backwards. Thorn hit the ground, and the horse kicked her in the back before galloping away. *Karma is a vengeful mare!*

Spitting blood, Thorn stood up, damning the entire equine species. The Gods could have made them smarter here, instead of mimicking all their faults. As if on cue, another horse approached her from behind. The app was messing with her head—she concluded. *Manipulative bitch!*

Wrath looked down on Thorn from her high horse, her lips pressed together in a dramatic pout."*You were there! You saw what he did to me!*" The girl sobbed behind her helmet. "He... he was my friend. I met him when I was...like...just a little girl. He was... He was everything to me..."

"I—" And before Thorn could finish her words, the brunt force of Wrath's boot hit her face. She went down and out.

28

SIBYL'S HEART

THE BOTANIC GARDENS
A FEW MINUTES EARLIER

Storm kneeled in front of the tropical flower beds, digging intrusive weeds by going deep and carefully removing the entire taproot. The sun had long retired over the horizon. He'd witnessed a last long streak of light fade behind an unusual conclave of moody clouds.

With his knees buried in the damp soil of the exterior gardens, he used his good hand to pull dandelions out one by one. Weeding was a form of much-needed therapy. A small escape from the tortuous prison of his mind.

The entire effort was a waste of time. He was too late; the harm had been done. He'd let the dandelions grow, seed, and dry. Many were already bald—seeds blown away to germinate and bloom edible flowers everywhere. Yellow pirates that sapped soil moisture and nutrients away from surrounding plants, crowding out the space with a dense mat of leaves. The children's favorite fuzzy head wish-maker turned into an out-of-control invasive species, all because he'd been too distracted to perform his gardening duties.

Instead of escaping, his mind made connections between his life and the useless attempt to save his tropical flower beds. Weeding and revolution, two futile efforts against out-of-control threats. He was too late. He should have stopped Tom's partnership with Nowak right from the start. Now he was fighting powerful forces that could crush him and his people in the blink of an eye, but what could he do but keep protesting? MLK Jr. had once said, "A riot is the language of the unheard." Storm had to try. That was all he had to give to the digital beings who found solace in his words. An attempt to hold on to his former self, the man Tom had loved. Too late, so late.

The skies above him roared, and more dark clouds emerged out of nowhere, tall and wide, the color of grief. A thunder, followed by the spear of light, a second apart, and then another one, so close the ground shook beneath him. The orchestra of light and sound quickened, like a heart beating. A beat he recognized—the beat he'd lost.

He knew all the beats; he was a master at assembling them for effect. Rhythm and words composed to converge heartbeats into a unified march. He knew all the beats, but only one truly mattered.

Instinctively, he knew exactly where to look. His gaze rose to the building's balcony to find Tom standing there as the storm developed around him and his heartbeat. Thunder… … … lightning, thunder… …lightning, thunder…lightning, thunder lightning… The roar so intense the sky cried a flood of tears.

Tom stood there, quietly sobbing. Tears and rain glazed his skin into the godly statue everyone saw in him. His eyes wandered much beyond the horizon, lost inside his anguish. Storm understood their warning. *Oh, my love...I'm so sorry. You can't save me. You'll die if you try.*

Soaked, Storm stood up, pulling his knees out of the mud, and attempting to use the rainwater to wash his hands and face. Now, more than ever, he wasn't good enough for the gift waiting for him high above. *Just a killer, scarred for life in more ways than one.* Twice in his life, he'd used violence instead of words. Both times he'd regret it, even if Henryk Nowak had deserved the punishment. The two acts of physical violence that had carved an insurmountable chasm between him and Tom.

He rolled down his pants' hems to cover his earth-stained knees and rushed into the building and up the spiraling stairs toward his heart—beat still roaring outside, louder than ever.

That day, an eternity ago, he shouldn't have let Tom leave the Albertine with the human bot. He should have handled it differently, without the use of violence, but he didn't. It was his responsibility to protect Tom, and he failed in every way. A sweet dream-maker turned into a viral killer, through no fault of his own. Tom, the shadow of the worlds, had no shadow, and, unfortunately, his love and light didn't protect him from the darkness of others.

At the top of the stairs, before emerging onto the balcony, Storm stopped and took a breath. He unwrapped the dirty scarf from his injured right hand, storing it in his pocket. Then, he pulled his wet hair back, tying it into a knot, and cleaning some dirt still caught in his nails. Lifting his head high, and purging the softness from his eyes and brows, he issued a warning to himself, a reminder to keep Tom away, to keep Tom safe. Sibyl's prediction haunted him. Once he'd left the amphitheater in Stella's Palace, he'd promised himself to suppress any signs of affection. He had taken it further, using every interaction to make Tom hate him. The way he was treating Tom was eating him inside, but he had to be ruthless. He couldn't allow Tom to get close, because Tom was likely to die attempting to save his life. He tensed his jaw and sharpened his expression before he took the last steps toward heaven.

Storm cleared his throat. "If you keep this up, you'll destroy my gardens," he said, approaching Tom and standing by his side, both looking out to the lawn. Storm rested both hands on the stone rail, his left hand beside Tom's right hand. Far enough, close enough, reassurance shielded by an inch of distance.

"W-what?" Tom murmured, confusion emerging in his hazel globes. "I'm not doing this. I have no power," he said, dropping his head. "I have no power, Nate."

Storm held back the bemusement as Tom painted the skies with his sorrow. He let it go. "Right," he said simply.

"Nate…"

"I know," Storm whispered. "It's not your fault. They'd be coming after me, eventually. That's what tyrants do. I want you to leave here. I don't need you."

A flash of lightning cut the skies in half, spearing the center of the lawn and leaving a scar of fire and scorched Earth.

Against his better judgement, Storm moved his hand ever so slightly until his little finger touched Tom's. His love always found reassurance in skin-to-skin contact.

Storm smiled before he spoke. "The app is externalizing the anger you don't know how to express. Zie's screaming for you." He almost reached to wipe away the drop of water dangling on a wave of hair in front of Tom's eyes. He caught himself this time.

Tom shook his head. The ensemble of thunder, lightning, and water scaled around him and spread fast in all directions, as far as the eye could see.

"Stormy… I can't live without—"

"No. You stay and *lead* your people."

"If I can't protect the one I…I…" He threw his hands and pitch high up. "How can I help anyone else?"

The storm's drumming sped up, setting several trees on fire even as the rain intensified.

"Stop." Storm held Tom's hand and squeezed it. "Overcome your despair."

Tom turned to face him, placing his hand on the side of Storm's torso. "They're going to—"

"What happens to me is not important."

"I'll use my last miracle. I promise I'll bring you back."

"Thomas Quincy Astley-Byron," Storm said, "stop playing by the rules of his game. You were rich in miracles and magic much before you became the God of the underworlds."

"Our game, I'm as responsible as he is, and we're stuck inside it now. I have no power."

"Look around you," Storm said, pointing at the scorching hole in the lawn. "I know little about technology, but I can see it clearly—a universe aching when zir people ache; a universe crying when zir heart despairs. If zie learned emotion from you, then zie feels what you feel, and cares for what you care."

"Sibyl has zir own agenda," Tom said, getting closer.

"Yes, but zie wants freedom as much as we do. Sibyl resents his rules."

"*Our* rules," Tom corrected.

"I don't trust the app, but I can influence zir, because you shaped zir emotions. Don't you see? Embrace your power —*your rage*," Storm said, regretting his words. Tom would never externalize negative emotions, no matter how much Storm wished he'd fight back.

This time the sky lit up with a spiderweb of lightning, all discharged simultaneously and causing an earthquake that shook the building. Storm stumbled into Tom's arms.

"It's just a storm," Tom said, refusing to let him go.

Storm stood still, an attempt to freeze that moment for eternity, and then he started humming an old waltz in Tom's ear, and they both rocked from side to side, appeasing the skies. The moon peeked in between the dark clouds, and for one moment they were back in Central Park, encouraging visitors to join them in their revolutionary dance.

Tom pulled him closer and whispered, "This is my favorite revolutionary act."

Storm cupped Tom's face and kissed his forehead, almost dropping to his knees, weakness taking over all his senses. Tom caught him, reminding Storm, his love's gentleness wasn't the absence of strength, quite the opposite.

"Every moment lived by your side was heaven," Storm said. "I lived a good life. Remember that."

Behind Tom, three figures materialized—the despots and the app.

Storm pressed his face against Tom's face and whispered, "Goodbye, Thomas. I love you. Let me go." The skies wailed and went dark, erasing the soft glow of the moon with a different type of light—electric and deadly.

"Nathan Storm, you've been sentenced, and you will be canceled," Henryk Nowak said as the app that stood behind him mimicked Tom's pain. Sibyl's face contorted and zir crest collapsed in front of zir eyes, spiky hair weighted down by the torrential rain.

The young Goddess stood back, as imperial and conceited as ever. Like Tom, Stella's stunning features were enhanced by the coat of water and the sparks of light around her. Aware of it, she lifted her chest; her wet dress clinging to her curves and revealing her most personal shapes. *Who exactly is she trying to impress?* None of them cared for the sexual allure of a spoiled brat.

Tom stepped in front of Storm. "Stella, please. You said you need me. I'm nothing without him. Nothing."

She pouted, acknowledging his pain and dismissing his request. She turned her back to them, rolling her hips in a rhythmic circle.

Tom persisted. "We'll negotiate with Up Above, it's the right thing to do. Nate's demands are reasonable. He's right."

"Not an option," she said. In front of her, a bolt hit the steel frame. She jumped back and then scowled at Sibyl, who looked as devastated as Tom.

"He's a threat to you and to the worlds," Henryk addressed Tom. "A predator who groomed you when you were too young to know better. He exploits your good nature. You are his prize. That's all you are. I'm sahry."

"Harry! Stop!" Tom raised his voice. "You know nothing about us. None of this is true."

"Bud, I've witnessed it too many times—his need to control you like you're his property."

"No, you didn't, that's homophobic nonsense." Quietly, Tom's lips spoke the truth.

Storm had never wished to own Tom, only to protect him. He'd fought all his life to deserve Tom, to belong to Tom, to live up to the image Tom had of him. To put it simply, he was wholeheartedly Tom's, and Tom was too good to be his.

As Henryk spouted unfair accusations, Storm's eyes were set on Tom. His love wasn't listening. He wasn't thinking. He was just feeling; feeling too much; drowning in feelings. Storm heard Tom's silent anger in Sibyl's screams. Zir howling unleashed thousands of spears of fire from the skies. Each bolt cutting the fabric of reality into thin slices and revealing the nothingness in between them.

At ground level, the creatures emerged—a horned warrior on horseback, others running by the warrior's side. Hundreds of demons screeching at them, creating a horseshoe shape as they filled the lawn. Behind them, the pixelated slashes maintained their shape, doorways into a deeper darkness when compared with the cloudy sky.

"Sibyl, stop this," Henryk commanded. His incriminating eyes shifted to Storm. "How the fuck are you doing this?"

Storm turned Tom around to face him, lifting Tom's chin with his index finger. "Look at me, love. You must stop this. Look." He pointed to the hordes of soulless heading in their direction. "Get out of here while you can."

Tom woke up from his trance of despair, opening his eyes wide and facing the danger. "I'm not leaving you or our people."

"Tom, we must go," Henryk said, grabbing Tom's arm.

"I'm staying," Tom said.

"Leave," Storm begged before he composed himself and spoke coldly. "We don't need you to save us, Tom."

A maddening roar. This time, it wasn't Sibyl, but the horned warrior who lifted a sword in the air and pointed it at them.

29

DEADLY PREDICTION

THE PLATFORM'S BETA TESTING
FORTY YEARS EARLIER — 15 DECEMBER 2028

Asa child, Tom had watched people with great fascination. The experience was both exhilarating and exhausting as he absorbed another soul's energy with all his senses and felt what they felt, refusing to let their darkness infect him. Instead, he tapped into everything he had to soothe and heal and lift their spirits—his words, his smile, his hugs, and his endless optimism. It seemed to help. They kept coming back for more, *so much more*. The adults, in particular, craved what his mother had called her infinite fountain of joy —his fountain, her joy. And he happily gave all he had, crawling into bed at night drained of all the things they had taken. And that's when he learned infinity had a limit, and so did his optimism.

As he grew older, he retreated into his inner world, shielding himself from the avalanche of other people's emotions threatening to overwhelm him. He searched for new ways to scale the joy they all needed, and so he became a storyteller, and worked on fine-tuning his sensibility for the human condition. He learned to dissect and reconstruct human experiences, turning story beats into heartbeats, and mastering every craft needed for the assembly of worlds, characters, and the arcs that made them come to life. He may have started his career in entertainment, but the education of the masses was his genuine passion.

Tom understood what made people tick, and over the years, he identified patterns of human behavior yet to be discovered by the world's top behavioral economists, advertising experts, and psychologists. He grouped human needs and related behaviors into areas of development. And then he focused on designing over two thousand values-based learning experiences.

Everything became so much easier once he partnered with Harry. His friend was the technical brilliance to Tom's creativity. Harry had mastered AI, specifically deep learning, before he was allowed to walk to school by himself. The techie turned Tom's scripts into software, and he used Sibyl to personalize the scenarios tapping into the user's data. What started as a couple thousand experiences had grown into a limitless pool of highly relevant learning interactions.

Then Tom focused on creating the characters' templates—the models of the bots that would one day inhabit the digital world and become the proxies for the family, colleagues, friends, and acquaintances of the human visitors. These characters didn't have to resemble the visitors' real community, as long as there was just enough in common—the age or the hair color of a child, temper of a wife, smile of a best friend, or some likeness with a character of a famous story. One small hook was enough to link both worlds and provide the user with realistic learning experiences.

· · ·

TWENTY-FOUR-YEAR-OLD TOM PREPARED to test the new platform. He was about to become the first human to experience what they had built.

"Sibyl, please start the simulation."

"Sure, Tom," the app whispered in Tom's ear. Her disembodied voice gave him the chills; its metallic quality echoing inside his mind. He wished she had an avatar—a face or character he could connect with. Instead, he had to interact with the creepy, emotionless voice of the most powerful AI on the planet. Harry had forbidden Sibyl to simulate human intonation, claiming it would be distracting.

The dark digital lab transformed into a bright coastal landscape, and Tom was blown away by how real it felt. He stood near the edge of a cliff overlooking the sea, and he smiled. The personalization algorithm had selected one of his favorite spots in the world to deliver the learning experience. He was on the Azores' São Miguel Island, and he stood by the highest rock face of the Vila Franca do Campo islet. The old volcano crater, now a nature reserve, had once served as a lookout point for whalers. The circular lake lined by vegetation had a small opening that allowed the circulation of seawater and small boats.

Tom took a deep breath, enjoying the coastline's rich, briny air. Then he zipped up his leather jacket, feeling the crisp sea breeze in his bones.

"Hi, Tom, I'm Hope." The peppy, eight-year-old digital girl stood behind him and smiled brightly. Tom turned to face her and held his breath. The AI algorithms and CGI technology turned his character sketches into lifelike beings.

The dimple in Hope's right cheek and the slight freckles on top of her nose made her look confident and spirited. He was happy with his design, even if it was a bit too obvious, particularly the orange braids. Hope's look was a cliché, but he knew that tapping into the likeness of characters in several beloved children's stories would create immediate empathy and familiarity. It certainly did with him.

Hope was an instance of one of Tom's first ten character templates. GirlChild01—the one he most enjoyed. He had crafted an intelligent and willful personality that was sure to delight and touch many users. The template specialized in questioning beliefs and challenging motivations, all done through the curious eyes of a naive girl.

"Red! Welcome to the world. Your hair is on fire," he jested, and at that moment, he understood why the algorithm had selected Hope to deliver his experience.

She giggled as she played with her flame-colored braids.

He loved her. To see her come alive so realistically made his heart sing.

"How are you?" he asked.

"I'm great. I'm like…super excited to meet you." She winked and then lifted her index finger and pointed it toward his nose. "Just one sec. I'm talking to Sibyl, learning about how I can help you."

"And have you? Learned?"

"Yes, Tom. I'm super-fast." She put her hands on her hips and tilted her head to the side. "And now that I've met you and checked out your current state of mind, I know *exactly* where to start." She spoke in the melodic, high-pitched way kids spoke, and then squinted her eyes and giggled. "Want me to tell you?"

"No. Surprise me, Red." He smiled warmly.

Tom marveled at the power of Harry's craft. Technology was like magic; *it turns pumpkins into carriages of gold.* He immediately regretted the analogy, remembering what had happened to the carriage at midnight.

Each character instance was its own separate entity—an intelligent, semi-autonomous bot empowered to select, orchestrate, and deliver the experiences that best served the user.

Hope was fully present, responding and adapting in real time. She chose from a pool of interactions short-listed and personalized by Sibyl.

"Ah-ah," Hope said. "I like you. Let's do this!"

"Sibyl, can you please remove any talk of data analysis and the inner workings of the platform from future dialogue? The first interaction should be scenario-based," Tom said.

"Sure, Tom, I will disable God mode," said the cold voice.

"God mode?" Tom rolled his eyes, making a mental note he needed to speak to Harry about this.

"Sibyl, does she need to be aware of you and her inner workings?"

"No, Tom, this only happens while the experience is in God mode."

"Tom?" Hope's expression changed swiftly. Her face went from cheeky optimism to sadness in a heartbeat.

"Yes?"

"Why do people kill themselves?"

Tom embraced himself tightly as memories of his mother flooded his mind. He wasn't ready for the accuracy of the profiling algorithm. He shook his head and composed himself.

"Sibyl, can you please ensure that, in the future, the casual chat and warm-up scripts run for longer before the learning scenarios? This transition is much too quick and harsh."

"Sure, Tom. Do you want to continue with the simulation?"

"Hmm." *No*, he didn't, but if he were to release these experiences on other people in a few months, he had to endure them himself. "Yes, please. Keep going."

Hope reached out to hold his hand. He looked down to meet her teary eyes, and bit his lips a bit too hard, tasting a hint of blood. "Tom? Why is my mother gone? Is it my fault? It is, isn't it?"

Hope was mirroring his unspoken inner demons. A technique to help him heal. He was being delivered a scenario he had designed to help users cope with the grief and guilt of loss. A template script, adapted using his data, to support him with the loss of his mother. By helping a little girl in distress, he would answer his own questions, the doubts that kept playing, like a broken record, in his subconscious mind. But how did Sibyl get to his innermost feelings? To emotions never spoken and ghosts that only haunted him at night, in his nightmares?

It was impossible, even for him, not to feel deep empathy for Hope. She looked so real and so devastated. He had to keep reminding himself that girl was just a digital character. He had designed every expression, and yet he couldn't help but connect with the little girl. In an alternative universe, she could have been *his* daughter; the same firestorm lit her hair —a Storm he desperately missed. A Storm he'd banished from his life a year and a half ago.

"Why did she just leave me?" Tears ran down Hope's face as her lips quivered. He reached out to touch her face, and then he pulled his hand back abruptly. The platform was manipulating him. It was increasing the emotional intensity to get through to him. "I'm so mad at her. Like, the last time I saw her, she looked sad, and she asked me for a hug, and I didn't... I was too busy playing. Too many hugs...you know? And now...she's gone. It's, like, all my fault." She turned to face the sea. Her body trembled slightly as the wind picked up speed.

He stayed silent, paralyzed by grief, and surprised by the power of his creation. *Breathe—in and out, in and out...* Hope turned her head to look at him, braids jumping over her shoulders. *Yes, it is—my fault* was the unspoken answer playing in the back of his mind. He had left home; he'd let anger drive his actions; too busy fighting with his father to recognize his mother's depression. Her fountain had dried.

He stopped breathing, choking in pain. Shaking it off, he concentrated on the testing. The experience was a bit on the nose, so overt in its intent it threatened to take the user out of the story. He made a mental note to teach Sibyl the art of nuance and metaphor. *Still powerful, though...*

The girl begged for a reply with her eyes, and then she squeezed her lips together into a pout. "There's nothing I can do. I want to go—to go where she's gone." She turned around and ran toward the rock face.

"No, Hope!" Tom jumped just in time to grab her arm. He lay flat on the ground with his head and arm hanging on the cliff's edge, his hand gripping the girl tightly. Her body swaying over a deadly drop.

His reflection just attempted to end her life, and for a moment, he felt it too, the abyss's call, the fall that would silence the voices in his mind, the guilt, and the anguish. He shook his head and dismissed his thoughts, focusing on the girl. Tom pulled her body away from the cliff's edge toward him and held her tightly as they both lay on the wet grass.

"Think of those you'll leave behind." He kissed her head. "How they will feel as you feel. It's not their fault, is it? It's not your fault." He choked on his words, pausing for a second, and then he whispered, "Break the cycle."

Hope sat on the grass with her knees rolled up to her chest. She lowered her head and hid it in between her arms. "I have no reason to stay."

Tom kneeled and caressed the girl's back. "She'd want you to live a happy life. To use all she taught you to help others. Be a leader. *Help others*," Tom said quietly, his voice broken. *What am I doing?*

"Tom, your heart rate and blood pressure are spiking." Sibyl's tone was more urgent than usual. "I see a steep rise in cortisol and adrenaline. It is not life-threatening, but your wellbeing is my priority. I am pulling you out."

In less than a second, everything went dark, and then digital information appeared around Tom. The entire lab transformed into a giant control center. On his right, appeared a projection of a humanoid model showing his vital signals, and on his left, the transcript of the conversation between Hope and him. In front of Tom, a log of decisions made by the platform and the personal data used for customization. Tom shook his head and closed his eyes. He was still breathing heavily as he rubbed his thighs to clean the sweat on his palms.

"Sibyl, get me out of here."

"Sure, Tom."

Tom's helmet unlocked from his bodysuit, and he took off the headgear—a round eye-tracking screen that looked like an opaque fishbowl. His head spun as his senses adjusted back to reality. He blinked his eyes, trying to make sense of his new whereabouts, and then he pulled back the hood that covered his entire head except for the eyelids and the airways. The mask dropped, hanging to one side of the bodysuit.

The complete apparatus was quite light, considering all the gear integrated into it. With his hands still shaking, he reached for the zipper at the back of his neck and pulled it down. Then he pulled on the parts covering the fingers and the toes before he peeled the suit off his body.

He searched for the compartment on the wall where he had stored his clothes and opened it. As he got dressed, he revisited his experience, ignoring his tremors. He left the empty room located in the loft of Harry's penthouse and ran to his partner's office.

"What's the matter, buddy? You okay?" Harry got up from his desk to meet him.

Tom used the sleeves of his hoodie to clean the tears in his eyes. "Are you using Sibyl's prediction engine to select the experiences?"

"Yeah," Harry said. "I added it to this test release. In this context, it adds a ton of value at negligible risk." Harry pointed to the leather sofa, and they both sat next to each other.

"Why *low risk?*"

"The platform helps users prevent realistic scenarios that are likely to happen."

"Likely to happen... I-I understand." Tom took a few moments to process what that meant for him based on the experience he'd just had. It became too painful, and he pushed it out of his mind. *Nonsense.*

"Is there a problem?" Harry asked, touching Tom's leg. Only then, Tom realized it was shaking restlessly. He took a deep breath and stopped its movement.

"It was spooky. Like the platform could read my mind."

"That's Sibyl's power for you." A touch of pride in Harry's voice.

"And *exactly* how much power does she have?" Tom spoke a bit too harshly.

"Sibyl is the platform's operating system. Her oracle capabilities are a huge added value."

"What does *it* do, *specifically?*" Tom hated it when Harry started using technical jargon.

"It's the intelligent entity that will run this digital world, on our behalf. We create the rules of the game, buddy. We're the Gods. Ya know?"

Tom rolled his eyes. "Harry! We need to speak about this 'God' business."

"I don't get it. Do you want to control the world or not?"

"*Help* the world, Harry. I want to help the world. The only power worth having is the power to share power."

"Poetic logic," Harry said smugly. "We must get on with the first, if we are ever going to get to the second."

"These rules, how do we come up with a rule?"

"As Feynman used to say, 'First, we guess it.'"

"We do what?" Tom's jaw dropped.

"Guess it, and then we test it. Obviously," Harry said. "Why don't you wear socks? We're in the middle of winter."

"Something wrong with my ankles?" Tom asked, flinching. His skinny jeans were turned up at the ankle, and he didn't wear socks under his sneakers. His right leg was shaking again, and so did his right foot, which lay on top of his left knee.

"No, it's just...weird."

"Not neat enough for you?" Tom taunted, and then concern returned to his mind. "I'm worried about the use of AI. What if it turns on us?"

Harry laughed. "You've been watching too many dystopian movies."

"Harry, Sibyl was making all sorts of decisions in there. She was changing the experiences I designed." Tom's gut twisted with panic.

"Yes, of course! She was personalizing them to add value to you." Harry spoke as if everything was normal, which increased Tom's resistance.

"She needs to explain her logic. All of it."

"Bud, a million invisible things are working. It's complex."

"She must be able to explain it. In plain English!"

"Because you can explain the rationale, or the lack of it, behind all your decisions?" Harry said dryly.

"Um... It's dangerous."

"No, it's not; she's an AI box—safely contained in a simulated digital world. Sibyl can't affect the external world."

"A simulated digital world where we educate and inspire humans so they go on to change the real world. Don't you see the risk?" Tom was becoming increasingly aware they were building the most potent manipulation engine on the planet. He recalled Nate's warning, and the sharp pain in his stomach almost made him throw up.

"I've got it covered. Trust me a little?" Harry said, standing straighter and puffing his chest out.

"Covered how?"

"There are directives they must obey." Harry sighed. *"It's in the code."*

"Like *I, Robot?*"

"Yes, that's right. Not just like the movies."

"I meant the book," Tom said unnecessarily.

"Bots4Hire follows the same laws, for example. Sibyl and all your characters must follow an exhaustive version of Asimov's laws, including the Zeroth Law—they 'may not harm humanity, or, by inaction, allow humanity to come to harm.'"

"But there's so much detail in that sentence. How can you codify ethics if humans can't agree on the nuances?"

"We'll keep evolving it. Sibyl keeps updating the details to match the most recent commonly agreed baseline amongst philosophers, policymakers, and scientists. The autonomous-machines industry is pushing that discussion. You know, they sometimes must decide who the car kills in an accident."

"We're not killing anyone. *Ever.*" Tom tried to ignore that last statement; he couldn't handle it right now. "Instead of *humanity*, use *carbon-based humanity.*"

"Why? I thought you didn't believe AI can reach consciousness."

"I don't, but all my character designs have human qualities. We need to ensure the platform's purpose is to serve actual humans."

"Makes sense. I'll add *carbon-based* to the definition of *human.*"

Tom was always reassured by his partner's willingness to take his suggestions on board. He added, "In time, I want it to benefit all carbon-based consciousness, including fauna and flora."

Harry rolled his eyes. "Bud, eggplants don't have feelings." Before Tom could interject, Harry continued, "So, what happened? Why did you abort the session?"

"Sibyl did. The stakes escalated fast. We need to roll back this last upgrade. Slow things down a bit."

"What do you mean?"

"The algorithm is increasing the stakes significantly," Tom said.

"Of course it is. We're here to deliver value quickly and at scale, right? Did it work? Did it lead to some insight or behavioral change?"

"Uh, I—I don't know." Tom bit his lip, trying to make sense of it all. "Yeah, I guess…"

"Awesome!" Harry patted him on the back. "Scary stories are also partly a way kids learn about the world, right?"

"'Stories are wild creatures; when you let them loose, who knows what havoc they might wreak?'"

"What are you quoting now?"

"*A Monster Calls.*" It was a book that had helped Tom process his mother's death. He had cried for days.

"Is that a scary book?"

Tom nodded.

"See! I'm always right!" Harry said, lifting his chin.

Tom got up, pacing around the room. "Harry, if we go down this path, I suspect we'll see character death, violence, and horror rise in many of these experiences. The girl I was talking to, Hope...she almost died."

"Think of the mind as a muscle. We need to apply tension to damage its fibers; that's what drives change and growth. It's those last intense reps, man! No pain, no gain."

Harry was right, but for the first time, Tom resented his friend's ability to look at problems from different perspectives.

"Since when do you go to the gym?" Tom squeezed Harry's nonexistent biceps and smiled. "Typing on that keyboard doesn't count as exercise."

"Hey, watch it. I've got all the muscle I need here." Harry pointed to his head. "Plus, I won't be typing for long. The new, fully functional BrainComms mind-computer link launches in six months. Finally! Still pretty basic, but I won't be needing any motor or voice exertion to interact with devices."

"Moving and talking are natural human behaviors."

"They're ineffective ways to talk to machines. *Super* slow. Wouldn't you like to search Google with your brain? Like, instantaneously?"

"No," Tom said definitively. "Anyway, we're not in the business of terrifying people. I prefer to stick with inspiration and information."

"It's probably less effective." Harry went back to his desk and pulled Tom's vitals on screen, analyzing the data.

"There's nothing more effective than to show positive patterns—normalize inclusion, reframe the social identity of underprivileged communities, or role-model sustainability. I want to deliver the Wakanda effect!" Tom said, crossing his arms in the shape of the old movie's famous salute.

Harry rolled his eyes, and then he continued to scan Tom's biometric signals. "Buddy, come on. It helps, but... It didn't fix the—" Harry pressed his lips together, finally recognizing Tom's distress in the data. He backed down. "Umm...I'll run some tests. We should let the data decide what's the best strategy."

Even in a state of anxiety, Tom found it amusing that it was easier for Harry to recognize emotions in raw data than in humans.

"Harry, what if the most effective approach is fear and terror?"

"Bud! It's just a simulation. We want to help fix the world quickly. Right?"

"I guess." It sounded so arrogant and megalomaniacal, but humanity was at the verge of self-destruction.

The planet was in chaos as civilization faced the possibility of a fourth and terminal world war. The people of an ever-divided world failed to reach an agreement on the answer to a simple question—was climate change manmade?

At least they could no longer deny the change was real. Weather-related disasters displaced millions of people all over the planet and caused significant migration to the interior and to regions closer to the poles. Several powerful nations had quickly turned into hellholes. Like the ancient ruins of glorious empires, the modern capitals became all but shadows of a recent past. Cities succumbed to rising seas, wildfires, drought, and unbearable heat.

"Yes. We do," Tom said.

"Good. Great! We need to make decisions objectively."

Tom scowled—a prickle of annoyance for Harry's condescending tone of superiority. "Don't—don't just undermine my instincts."

"I'm not."

"You're patronizing me, and I don't like it." Heat rose in Tom's face.

"You're just shaken by the experience. Can I review the footage?" Harry pulled up the video on screen and was ready to press play.

"*No!* I'd rather you didn't."

Harry closed the video swiftly. "That good, eh? Looks like it pushed the right buttons. I'm a genius."

Tom's endless tolerance for Harry's insensitivity never ceased to amaze him, but today it was running short. "I don't want to talk about it," he said, tugging on his collar.

"Why did Sibyl pull ya out so early? You didn't complete the learning. She shouldn't be doing this. It's irresponsible." Harry spoke without taking his eyes off the screen. "Weird, she knows better." He scanned a log file. Tom suspected Harry could follow some of his experience without looking at the video.

"Yeah, it was odd." Tom massaged his scalp, releasing the tension in his head. "I was upset and agitated, but it wasn't life-threatening. Aborting experiences like that can lead to the problems you had with the social app. We show users a prediction and never give them the tools to handle it."

Harry continued to scan the log, and the blood drained from his face. "Buddy, whatever you experienced in there, you didn't get closure."

"It's fine. I'm fine." Tom forced a smile and shrugged it off. He was more concerned with Sibyl's terror escalation than he was with his aborted experience.

"I'll review the code. This should never happen—a prediction looming without resolution."

"Yes, ensure it doesn't happen to other people."

"What did she predict that left you so shook? A hot and heavy love affair?" Harry asked, grinning.

"'It was nonsense—all bullshit!" Tom's eyes dropped to his shoes.

"Oh, a bad word uttered by the posh Astley-Byron. Some progress." Harry smiled.

"I'm afraid to tell you she got it all wrong." *I don't have a death wish.*

"Tom, she's *very* accurate."

"Stop it. Just. Stop it already." Tom held his medal.

Harry stared at him, and then he got up and rushed to Tom's side. "I'm an idiot. I'm sorry."

"It's okay. I'm—I'm not thinking straight."

"Why didn't you tell me?" Harry said, making eye contact.

"I *did*." Tom's eyes opened wide, and his brows raised in a sharp accusation.

"I'm sahry."

"It's all right." Tom couldn't stay upset with Harry for long. It was an impossibility.

"I'm so sorry. Let's go have some food. Yes?"

"Yeah." Tom linked his arms with his best friend. He needed some time to destress away from technology. "Hey, are you trying one of the experiences?"

"No!"

"Why not?"

"As travelers, you and I are at Sibyl's mercy. In the digital lab, *we create*; nothing challenges our rule as Gods. But when we become travelers, we immerse ourselves in the experiences and are influenced by them. Like everyone else, we are receiving a service. At the end of the day, she needs to protect our wellbeing when our beliefs are challenged and our emotions running high. So, in certain situations, when we are part of an experience, she can overrule our God status."

"How far does this power go?"

"As per our directives, she protects the interests of humanity and then of each human. In that order."

Tom released a long breath. The interests of the users should always trump their own. "So, it's better to watch other people's experiences as holograms in the digital lab or in the monitors in the real world?"

"Yeah. The risk is minimal—we're humans, she won't do anything to hurt us—but we need to remain in control over our world."

"So, why did you let me do it?"

"I know you, and you'd have argued with me for the rest of our lives if I didn't let you eat your own dog food. Right? Right?"

"Yeah." Tom smiled. "You know me well."

"Sibyl does too. She suggested it," Harry said. Tom shook his head. Sometimes, Harry wasn't as smart as he thought he was. "But now that you've done it, you must stop. Okay?"

"Yes, I'm—I'm still pretty rattled by the experience."

"We need a code word," Harry said.

"For what?"

"So you can tell me when I'm insensitive."

"Dear Harry, let's discuss it later. The words that come to mind are a bit…harsh."

"Don't worry. This might be news to you, but the word on the street is that I'm insensitive. You are unlikely to hurt my feelings." Harry flashed a smile.

"*Pea-brain?*" Tom knew exactly how to push Harry's buttons.

Harry pulled his arm away from Tom. "Hey, all right! Are you kiddin' me? I have the best brain, ya know? That's just not accurate."

Tom searched his vocabulary for an obscure word with a similar meaning. "*Nincompoop?*"

"What's that?"

Tom grinned. "Nincompoop! That's settled, then."

30

TEMPTATION

A FEW WEEKS LATER — 2 JANUARY 2029

Tom couldn't stop thinking about his experience with Hope. He didn't need the validation of Harry's tests to realize how powerful it was to see the consequences of one's actions reflected in the suffering of a child. A kid was the ultimate empathy magnet, and no one could resist its pull. A child's suffering, experienced firsthand, had the potential to turn the most cowardly of humans into heroes.

Harry came back with substantial test data proving unequivocally the latest release of the platform was the most fruitful to date. The escalation of tension did lead to faster personal growth. It also turned Tom's scripts into horrific scenes full of pain, failure, death, and destruction for the digital characters. Stories initially focused on delivering inspiration, information, and fresh perspectives became visceral experiences impossible to ignore or to forget.

Tom wasn't convinced he wanted to follow such a dark path. He felt vulnerable—naked—when he entertained strategies of questionable morality, so he worked hard to resist his partner's growing pressure to drive fast change in people's behaviors by making visceral experiences an essential tool in the platform.

It was now time to run extensive beta tests with a large set of diverse human subjects. Tom had handpicked a group of a hundred people from a list of thousands of candidates that had passed Sibyl's background checks and psychometric tests. Among them, an unusual volunteer—John Voser, the CEO of Spark Fuel, one of the largest oil and gas companies in the world, with operations spanning over twenty-five countries.

According to Harry, John had been chasing him for years. The businessman was keen to partner with Harry on an influencing and lobbying platform. Spark Fuel invested four hundred million dollars yearly in lobbying against climate-change policy, and John had been looking for a more cost-effective approach to shutting down and delegitimizing progressive proposals.

Harry had always rejected John's persistent advances. He'd ignored a flood of meeting requests and party invitations, but the older man was famous for his unwavering tenacity. Tom suspected John had volunteered as a test subject as his way to meet Harry.

"Sibyl, can you please display John Voser's information on screen? What have we got?"

"Sure, Tom. I have highlighted key psychological levers."

John Voser's information popped up all around Tom. Spark Fuel's logo was displayed in front of him—a rolled-up serpent. The snake's head stood up, her mouth open and her exposed teeth menacing. Tom shuddered; he'd do anything to crush that snake and to keep it out of Earth's garden, *anything*.

"Please talk me through them."

"Sure, Tom," echoed the cerebral voice inside his head.

"Wait," Tom said, tempted by the opportunity emerging in front of his eyes. "Highlight the ones that can be used in an experience related to environmental sustainability."

"Sure, Tom. Sustainability is one of my key strategic themes. I am already ahead of you."

A hint of pride in her voice, but perhaps he was just projecting his emotions on her words. He had the bad habit of imagining personality in all sorts of objects, including his toaster. "Of course, you are. We should give you some kind of body, don't you think?"

"Yes, Tom. If it is helpful to you."

"I'll design it as soon as I have some time. So, what are the highlights?"

"John has an estranged fourteen-year-old daughter. The girl refuses to speak to him since his hostile divorce from her mother six years ago. Lake and her mother, Joanna, still live in his mansion in the Santa Monica Hills. Due to the ongoing bushfires in the region, the air quality has been consistently poor and sometimes even hazardous. Lake has a seventy percent probability of developing lung cancer in the next twenty years."

"Why haven't they moved up north with the rest of the wealthy folk?"

"Joanna does not have the means or the connections to do so. John has offered to relocate her if she gives him full custody over Lake. Both mother and daughter have rejected the offer."

"So...looks like you're going straight for the jugular."

"I understand the reference. Yes, Tom. I am extremely precise. I identify data that will drive the best chance of success."

"I can see it—a yellow sky filled with smoke, a teen girl dying of cancer, and a hopeless father realizing no amount of money or power in the world can save his daughter..." A knot tightened Tom's chest. He wasn't sure he had what it took to terrorize people into becoming better humans. A carrot-and-stick approach was archaic and too close to methods used by religious leaders and dictators.

"Tom, GirlTeen07 is the best template for this experience. Should we call this instance River?"

"A bit too on the nose. Try Rain."

"Sure, Tom. I am currently scanning Lake's public social timeline for speech patterns, mannerisms, fashion, and anything else that will help Rain embody her."

The girl's data was public. Still, it was an invasion of her privacy. Tom frowned, opened his mouth to speak, but instead pressed his lips together. He remembered Harry's words, attempting to reframe the dubious activity. The platform needed Lake's data to connect with John, nurture his empathy, and stop the devastation caused by Spark Fuel. *It must stop. Now!*

"Hmm, apply subtle modulations, undetectable to Voser's conscious mind."

"Sure, Tom."

"We need to connect this scenario with Spark Fuel's activities against climate policy. Sibyl, what are the company's most significant lobbying activities in California? Focus on the last five years."

"The Business Council of California is the most prominent business lobby group in the state. Spark Fuel has funded its campaign against the state's proposal to reach a target of ninety percent renewables by 2035. They want to focus on wind and solar technology alternatives. The BCC campaign claimed the target would, and I quote, 'wreck the economy.' The business lobby convinced government officials to reduce the target to forty percent by 2045."

Tom cleared a lump in his throat. *People are dying, millions of species are gone, and these companies...* His outrage fueled his creativity, and he visualized the experience in his head.

"A living room in a mansion in the Santa Monica Hills. Outside the window wall, a thick orange smoke prevents John from seeing the view. The air smells like smoke and tastes like ash; he can barely breathe. A large wall screen is on; it's displaying the news. Rain lies on the sofa, her skin gray and her eyes empty. John and Rain chat, reminiscing... connecting." Tom placed his hand on his stomach, feeling the contents of his gut rise to his throat. Then he pulled himself together and continued to imagine the experience.

"Tom, our suits—the TSkins—do not allow us to simulate scents, but we can reduce the airflow."

"I don't understand. I inhaled the Atlantic Sea when I was inside."

"Tom, our brain has an enormous capacity to fill in the gaps. It derives missing data using memories from past experiences."

"I see." He shivered slightly as he remembered his experience, and then shook it off and focused back on John. "Sibyl, we should use whatever data it takes to grab his attention and direct his empathy toward the girl. It must become real and raw."

"Sure, Tom."

"The girl holds his hand and tells him of her terminal condition. As the girl coughs blood, the newsreader on screen shares the BCC's recent success reducing renewables targets. Red stains cover her white T-shirt, her frail arms, and her father's hand." Tom's eyes teared up as he spoke. "Sibyl, can you iterate on these ideas and see what you come up with?"

"Sure, Tom. The results of my preliminary tests suggest Rain must blame her father directly for the climate crisis that led to her illness. This change ensures John focuses on both preventing Lake's cancer and supporting renewable energy sources."

"Great. Yes, please add it in."

"Sure, Tom. Shall I add any inspiration or information to this scenario?"

"No, John doesn't lack information; he's just greedy."

"Sure, Tom."

"Sibyl, let's run some simulations. I want to understand John's most likely reactions and how Rain would respond to him."

"Sure, Tom."

"Sibyl, wait! Before you do that..."

"Yes, Tom?"

"I need you to add a statement to the release waiver."

"Sure, Tom. What is it?"

"We need to inform travelers we are using your prediction algorithm to help us create their unique experiences. It'll make the sessions even more effective. They'll understand the scenarios are likely to come true."

"Tom, may I add it instead to the user's information pack?"

"Perfect. Thanks."

"Sure, Tom."

SUPERVISED LEARNING

HARRY'S PENTHOUSE — HOBOKEN, NJ
A DAY LATER — 3 JANUARY 2029

Harry sat at his desk in his office, and he stared at the transparent screen, reviewing John Voser's file.

"Bud, looks like you've changed your mind. Voser is in for a wild ride."

Harry leaned his head to look at Tom, who lay sprawled on the couch, barefoot. Harry hated the unshapely and worn-out leather sofa. A secondhand item ordered by Tom, who had complained Harry's place lacked comfort and warmth. To add insult to injury, Tom had also ordered several pillows made of a patchwork quilt of teal-colored recycled fabrics. The colors clashed with Harry's neat monochromatic office.

Tom's head was half-covered by his hooded top, and he ruminated on something. His empty gaze focused on the ceiling, and he massaged his forehead with his fingers. "I think we should separate them," he finally said, breaking the silence.

"Separate what?" Harry asked.

"The experience algorithms. One focused on information, inspiration, and positive reframing—my original scenarios. Let's call it…Perspective. That sounds nice!" He smiled. "And another focused on fear, negative consequences, and dark alternative realities—Sibyl's high-stakes scenario evolution. I'd call it Contrast."

"Why separate them?" Harry asked. "I don't understand."

"I want to keep a closer eye on Contrast, pre-approve every single decision made by Sibyl."

"Tom that doesn't scale. We can analyze usage data and look for patterns. That's how it's done." Harry tried to be patient with his partner, remembering he was still learning about technology and AI.

"It's not good enough. I feel I need to verify things before the experience runs. Remember, no unintended consequences."

"I know, but, c'mon, dude. You're nuts."

"All the best people are." Tom blinked his eyes and smiled.

"The technique you're alluding to is called supervised learning. It's a tool we used ages ago when AI was still unreliable. It's not effective at this scale."

"Then we need to start small." Tom persisted, his eyes stubborn and uncompromising. "I can oversee hundreds of Contrast-driven experiences per week. And you… I guess you can review your usage logs to monitor Perspective. It's tried and tested, and low risk."

"Buddy, you don't have the temperament to immerse yourself in such darkness. Instead, I'll design a good learning architecture. I think you're too…you're oversensitive."

"Really?" Tom stood up and put his hands on his hips. "Having feelings doesn't make me oversensitive."

"Sorry, but still…" Harry shook his head, knowing fully well Tom's idea would take a huge toll on his mind.

"I feel I need to guide this new AI-driven strategy until I know it's safe to use."

"Sibyl can operate within the parameters we predefine."

"No, my friend. You're an excellent coder, but these…these AIs are fallible."

"So are you." Harry's ego spoke before he could stop it. The truth was that Sibyl learned a lot from Tom. He was teaching her how to best structure stories for greater impact, and in return, he benefited from her insights and foresight. They were spending a lot of time together, and Sibyl was starting to develop a language that was of little interest to Harry. Every time he heard any talk of hooks, emotional beats, and calls to action, he'd leave the lab to focus on the platform's infrastructure. The physical world of suits, sensors, helmets, and servers made him much happier and more relaxed.

Tom persevered in the elaboration of his plans. "Sibyl can suggest which travelers need Contrast instead of Perspective. She can propose character templates and personalize and shortlist experiences. I will, ultimately, have to confirm and approve them all until I'm confident she can handle it."

"Based on the current data, I predict the impact of Contrast will be so significant that we'll want to scale fast. You'll drown and will shave even less than you do now."

"We'll deal with that when it happens. For now, I'll be the bottleneck."

Harry stood up and walked to Tom, punching him lightly in the arm. "You're as stubborn as a mule."

"My second-best feature after being oversensitive." Tom flashed a smile.

Harry laughed. "I wouldn't have you any other way, buddy."

"Just for the record, darling Sibyl and I make an excellent team. I'm warming up to your creation."

Harry smiled at Tom's attempt to boost his ego. "I'm feeling left out."

"I'm designing a body for her. Okay?" Tom asked. "It's bizarre to talk to a bodiless voice all the time. I like faces, expressions, and mannerisms."

"You're a visual dude that needs lots of feels. Ah, what a surprise!"

"Is that okay? She's your creation."

Harry wasn't keen on the idea; it was a distraction they didn't need. Still, he enjoyed making Tom happy, and nothing made his buddy happier than drawing people. "Sure."

"When you speak to her, do you have a specific look in mind?" Tom jumped to his feet and grabbed a notepad and a pencil from Harry's desk.

"Nah, I don't waste time on such things."

"Okay, but do you have any particular design direction for me?" he said, and then started nibbling on the pencil.

"Don't do that," Harry said, and then let it go. That pencil was dead to him. "Never mind… Just keep it after you're finished."

"Direction!" Tom demanded, sitting on the floor with his back against the couch.

Harry rolled his eyes, and then he had an idea. He grinned as his eyes narrowed. He might as well have some fun and give Tom a difficult challenge.

"She looks like the child of David Bowie and...hmm...let's say...Mulan?"

"What?"

Harry laughed, proud of himself. "But, remember, no cutesy expressions. Sibyl's running the show for us."

"That doesn't mean she can't have a bit of a personality." Tom shifted his right knee close to his chest, planted the notepad on top of it, and started sketching something.

"No, bud. She's not designed to build empathy with humans; that's the job of the characters. That's why I haven't given her any personality traits. She's guided by logic, probability, and good ol' hard math. So, don't add a ton of expressions. That'll just distract me."

"I understand." More sketching. His short and precise hand movements replaced by some flowy creative action. "You want me to design a tall, androgynous Chinese figure with as much charisma as a fridge."

Harry chuckled. "Pretty much."

"How stereotypical," he mumbled to himself. "White pantsuit?" Tom raised a cheeky eyebrow.

"As if I care. Just make her look fierce."

"Make her fierce without using facial expressions?" Tom sighed, nibbling on the pencil. Then he had some revelation, and he seemed content. "Got it."

Three men showed up on Harry's screen in the window that showed the live external camera security footage. "John's here. Get lost."

"I'll be in my bedroom. I'll suit up and watch it from the lab."

Once Tom had left, Harry went to meet John and his two security guards at the main door.

"Mr. Voser, welcome." Harry extended his hand to greet the businessman. Voser was a well-built, healthy-looking man in his late sixties. He sported a full head of shiny silver hair, and a smile so white Harry suspected it would likely glow in the dark.

"Harry, good to finally meet you in person, son. Call me John." John used the strength of his entire body to shake Harry's hand. A power move designed to let Harry know who was in charge. Harry's shoulders tensed, absorbing the pain in his crushed fingers.

"I'm afraid your security team will have to wait outside." Harry pulled his hand away from the other man's grip. John laughed and patted him on the back.

"No problem, son." John glanced at his men and gave a slight nod.

"Thank you, John." Harry closed the door, leaving the two security guards outside. "Follow me to my office."

"So, what's the name of this new venture? I noticed you haven't announced it yet. Take it from me, branding is important. You need to hire a good marketer."

"We're still brainstorming. It'll be something related to education or inspiration. Maybe Eden, Sophos, or something like that."

"Yes, I saw your interview with Marge. She's such a character, a mad lefty cow, but a lot of fun."

Harry bit his lip and unbuttoned the collar of his shirt. "I have a lot of respect for her."

"Sure you do, son. I look forward to my Disney-like experience." Harry ignored John's sneering tone. "I'm certainly in need of some inspiration," said the man. "What's going to be the topic?"

"It's selected by our AI based on your data. It'll consider real-time signals like your state of mind and responses. So, we'll have to wait and see. First, let's review the information and consent forms." Harry worked hard to dodge the question without lying.

"Harry, I have some other things to discuss with you. You're not going to deny me a bit of your time, are you?"

"We'll talk once we're done with the experience. We're grateful to have you as a test subject."

"I'm sturdy enough to handle some progressive propaganda packaged in a heavy dose of sentimental preaching," John said cockily. "Kids' books, you say? I enjoy Dr. Seuss. How does it go? *You know what you know, and you are the one who'll decide where to go...* I like it."

"Of course you do. Our latest release is a bit more, erm... grown-up. Have a seat, please." Harry pointed to the chair in front of his desk.

John sat down. "Is that the kit?" He pointed at the full body-suit and the helmet laying on top of the couch.

"Yes. We call it TSkin; it's short for *traveler's skin*. The helmet will allow you to see the world as if you were there. The resolution is so high that everything looks real." Harry picked up the helmet and gave it to John.

"Check out how light it is."

"Why not just glasses? It's not like I can see with the back of my head."

"You would feel the frames, and it would take you out of the experience." Harry picked up the bodysuit. "This skin is incorporated with biosensors to measure your body's responses like heartbeat, temperature, sweat, and other bodily secretions. Touch it."

John rested the helmet on the floor and grazed his fingers over the black material. "It feels like human skin—light and smooth."

"Yeah, you won't feel it on your body until the platform wants you to feel something."

"What do you mean?"

"The full bodysuit, including the hood, has thousands of tiny engines that recreate the sense of touch and movement. If someone slaps or kisses you in the digital world, you will feel it."

"I hope we stick with the latter." John smiled.

"We can also adjust temperature and airflow with some precision. If you touch a digital ice cube, you will feel the cold. Digital wind will feel almost like a real gust."

"Am I going to get motion sickness?" John asked. "I always get nauseous when I try—"

"Nah, we fixed all that. We're aware of the depth of your field of view. Plus, the suit adds physicality to what you're seeing."

John stared at him blankly and then pointed to the scalp and forehead areas of the hood. "And what's all this? It feels much thicker here."

"We've added thousands of brain scanners. It's an investment in the future. I want to understand how people use their brains in real time." Harry got a bit excited as he thought about the future possibilities, but he didn't want to share any of it with John. "The hood is heavier in the brain region because although electrodes are tiny, other brain activity acquisition tools need more hardware."

"I can see where you're going with your strategy. You created a goody-two-shoes foundation to capture big data at scale—brain data. Then you'll capitalize."

"If we understand how the brain works, we can find ways of delivering more immersive experiences. We'll never profit from this platform."

"I see." John flashed a cynical smile. "How will you fund it when it starts scaling?"

"Not sure yet."

John laughed and shook his head. "Kids these days!" Then he pointed at the helmet. "How are you going to make sure people don't trip and fall while they are wearing that thing?"

"The TSkin can sense the surrounding environment. Any experience the platform delivers considers the physical space —its limitations and hazards. It adjusts in real time. But it's best to enjoy experiences in empty rooms with plenty of space. I have an empty loft where you will enjoy your experience today."

"I see."

"Now, let me explain the next steps."

32

CATCHING FIRE

F ifty minutes later, Harry hugged himself tightly as he watched John's experience on screen. He wasn't immersed in the world, and still, he leaned in, his nose almost glued to the images displayed on the thin surface.

"This…is all your fault, Dad." The pale girl struggled to speak, and then she coughed blood. "Take…" More coughing, and this time the blood traveled far. The red drops of death dripped from Voser's sweaty face to his white shirt. "…your money and leave."

John leaned by the girl who lay on a white sofa, now spattered with blood. The screen on the wall displayed a video of Voser shaking hands as others congratulated him on his successful lobbying activities. Rain stared at him, her face blue and her veins all visible near her temples. She lifted her trembling hand to grab his shirt. "I…despise you." As he held her hand, her body convulsed violently, and a deluge of blood, mucus, and vomit exploded from her mouth. Amongst the torrent of slime, something larger landed on John's lap. It was a piece of Rain's lung—a crimson, spongy, tree-like horror covered in blood.

Harry closed his eyes and turned his head away as John screamed, roared, sobbed…

"Lake! My Lake!"

With his mouth still twisted in disgust, Harry looked back at the screen to watch Rain take her last breath, drowning in her own blood. Voser's experience had reached its final beat.

Harry inhaled sharply, taking his glasses off to clean the fog off the lenses. *Ugh! How…grimy. I don't think I can handle a ton of these…*

HARRY HELPED John Voser get out of his TSkin in the temporary testing room he had set up in his loft. John got dressed, and they walked to the office. The older man's face was white as snow, sweat dripping from his forehead and soaking his white shirt.

Harry pulled up a chair. "Have a seat, John. You all right?" The businessman sat in silence, processing his experience. "Would you like some water?"

John shook his head, then he lowered it to his knees and covered it with his hands. He stayed there for a few minutes. Harry scanned John's vitals displayed on the screen. It was clear the man was experiencing a panic attack. He waited a few minutes until John started to calm down.

"John, are you okay? We have a questionnaire for you to fill. When you're ready."

John stood up abruptly, grabbed Harry by the collar of his shirt, and pulled him closer. The older man's eyes were dark and sunken in his skull; it gave him a demonic expression.

"Son, listen…"

"John, calm down. Let's talk about this."

John sat back down, and his body trembled. "No, listen. We need to strike big before they realize what's happening."

"Please have some water. You need to relax."

"You are both young and naive. They'll crush you." John's tone differed from the dismissive sneer Harry had experienced when they first met. The businessman sounded sincere, a concerned look in his eyes. Harry reserved his judgment, knowing he was dealing with a master of manipulation.

"Who?"

"You're going to get violent resistance from stakeholders as soon as the word is out. You need to go big, target decision-makers, and create unstoppable momentum. That's the game plan."

"Lemme give you something for the nerves."

"*Listen to me.* My daughter's life is at stake. The world is...fucked."

"There's still hope. If we act f—"

John dismissed Harry with a hand-wave. "Our next quarterly strategic board meeting is coming up next week. We've organized an envisioning offsite in Aspen. The agenda includes ideation sessions and several external speakers. They're all in attendance—the board, key strategic partners, lobbyists, politicians, even competitors."

Harry wasn't clear where John was going with this, but he tried to be supportive and open. "Okay?"

"Don't you see? I'll add one of your experiences as an inspiration event. They'll have the same expectation I had when I walked in here today."

"Mm-hmm, I think I understand."

"We'll do it pre-kickoff. Do you have enough TSkins? Different sizes? We'll have around fifty participants."

"That can be arranged." Harry tried to keep up with John's reasoning, wondering if the businessman was playing him. He wished he were better at reading people.

"Good man! Do you run group experiences?"

Harry shook his head. "No, the stories are uniquely designed for each user, and we need to protect their privacy."

"Okay. Then they'll all have to do it at the same time."

"We could do that. I need to run it by my partner first."

"I suggest you stop the testing with regular folks. The word will get out. Simpler, less intelligent people will leave this building and start preaching. They'll do something that will call attention to the power of the—of this thing. People like me will crush you if they catch a whiff of what you're up to. You need to focus on leaders and go stealth until you build enough momentum. I can help you do that."

"John, yes. I think I follow you. Thank you."

"Wait!" John's face lit up. "Davos is happening next month, another perfect event. The most powerful business leaders in the world, all gathered in the same place. I can get us in for a showcase. You'd need to manufacture the gear and stand up the infrastructure quickly. I can fund it."

Harry couldn't help but marvel at John's audacious vision. The World Economic Forum brought together the most important business, state, and opinion leaders in the world.

"I don't need your money. I'll take care of it once I speak to Tom."

Harry was super keen to get back to his partner; they had a lot to discuss. Everything John was saying made sense, but could they trust him? They needed to review John's experience carefully and look for clues of authentic change of the man's values and belief system.

John got up and prepared to leave. "Fine. Let me get out of here and get the ball rolling after I speak to my daughter."

"I'll call you later today."

The businessman stopped and glanced back at Harry. His eyes were wet. "Harry."

"Yes?"

"The girl—Rain—she looked so real. Is this what they are calling AGI?"

"Artificial general intelligence? No, not yet. The prediction algorithm is the most advanced, but it has a specific skillset. The platform is learning the art of storytelling from Tom, but we still depend on him in a few key areas. And the characters are good at what they do, but still quite narrow in their scope. Basically, it's a combination of several narrow, deep-learning models and some smoke and mirrors by two hardworking humans." Harry smiled.

"How accurate is the prediction?"

"If nothing changes, Lake has a seventy percent chance of developing cancer. Tom's stories are powerful because they carry the truth—a truth powered by Sibyl's predictions."

"Thank you, son."

"You are most welcome, John."

As John was about to walk through the main door, he turned around. "Harry, what you said about the truthful stories... that's your UVP, your marketing pitch. It'll catch fire as the Sibyl app did."

33

THE DESCENT

E verything changed in just a few months. Converted from opponents to allies, the most powerful people in the world put their minds, networks, and resources to good use. Opportunistic and action-oriented, many business leaders followed John Voser's behavioral patterns. Within minutes of exiting the experiences, they had a plan to take massive action at speed and recruit other decision-makers. And so, before the platform launched, it had already reached those who owned eighty percent of all wealth in the world. Copious amounts of funding flowed from all parts of the planet and the most unlikely donors, all of it with no strings attached.

Harry focused on the manufacturing and distribution of the TSkins, and working with partners to set up the infrastructure required to scale the cloud simulation streaming service. If they were to reach as many influencers as possible in a short period, they needed large volumes of equipment to be shipped to different locations around the world.

As Harry had predicted, Contrast was the more effective of the two algorithms. The numbers of users needing Contrast became much larger than the ones who received enough benefit from Perspective. Tom partnered with Sibyl, painstakingly, to design and monitor every detail of the experiences that brought to life terror and despair in a digital realm—an increasingly realistic simulation. Isolated, he spent most of his time in the digital lab; withdrawing from life and real-world interactions.

They ended up calling the platform Down Below and its characters Underlings. It was an honest representation of what they had created. Over time, Harry and Tom realized the harsher the contrast, the more effective the lesson learned. Fear, pain, and loss were ten times more effective than inspiration and information. In private, humans were as attracted to darkness as bees to nectar. They explored the monster living within them. Every rotten idea or feeling, never discussed out loud, came to play in this private digital dwelling.

Down Below used biological data to measure the traveler's emotional response, enabling Sibyl and the Underlings to change the scenarios in real time. The simulations quickly evolved into realistic horror movies as the platform measured hormonal signals looking for the most effective ways to escalate tension. Soon, the raging monsters hidden in each traveler came out to play.

And so, two idealistic dreamers—two friends who had set out to create an inspirational, forward-looking platform—shifted their strategy to deliver darkness Down Below to create enlightenment Up Above. They chose to experience the worst of humankind so no one else had to endure it. Two broken minds were a small price to pay to save humanity from self-destruction. Two became one, as Tom never allowed his best friend to see any of it.

"Someone needs to keep things in perspective, and you are the most qualified to do that. You know I'm an emotional mess." Words often spoken by Tom.

"Okay, but please remember it's just software, bud. No harm done. Ya know?"

Harry always regretted the time it had taken him to figure out how bad things were for Tom. In Harry's mind, Down Below was just a piece of software designed to help humans learn. A horrific game that made the world a better place. Just a game. Until it wasn't.

By the time Tom was satisfied Sibyl had learned enough from him to design most of Contrast's scenarios safely and autonomously, Down Below had sucked the life, optimism, and sense of perspective out of Harry's dear friend. The wholesome smile that once had beamed from Tom's mouth and eyes slowly faded away. So did his endearing, if somewhat annoying, habit of quoting children's books at the most inappropriate of times. After a few years, no amount of success could lift Tom's spirits. The planet quickly recovered from its most threatening crisis while Tom descended into his own personal hell.

Tom had never asked Harry for help; he never asked anyone for anything. He had failed to protect his wellbeing, sanity, and joy. Selfless beyond the limits of reason, he was unable to recognize that when a dear one falls, those who love him fall with him.

34

MANY STORMS

6. PLURIZ

THE BOTANIC GARDENS
DAY 1 — 8:45 PM

Shadow slumped his shoulders—heavy with the weight of the worlds—as the screaming around him intensified.

Out on the lawn, the Domizien screeched, raising their fists and weapons toward the balcony. A threat the demons struggled to deliver as wind gusts turned the torrential rain into high-pressure water jets pushing against them.

Boom! Boom! Boom! Moody clouds stroked the lawn between the creatures and the building. The demons vanished behind a line of fire and smoke—the result of the quick succession of electrostatic charges—too convenient for Shadow to dismiss as luck. *Am I doing this?*

In front of him, Nate and Harry screamed at each other, making no attempt to listen or understand. Red faces, closed hearts, and an appetite for destruction. Further back, near the staircase, Stella stood with her arms crossed, wearing a condescending smile on her face, while Sibyl sat on the metal stairs with zir head sunk in between zir knees.

As Harry prepared to deliver his sentence, and Nate took a step forward to confront him, the skies unleashed hell in the middle of the three men—a bomb of light: hot, explosive, and electric. *Boom! Bzzttt!* Shadow's back hit the stone rail as his body convulsed and tingled. Thousands of high-voltage ants danced all over his body, their legs like pins and needles. He collapsed, and the adrenaline rushing through his veins made time stand still. A blessing because he was running out of it.

First, deafening silence, then the loud hissing in between his ears, followed by a cracking noise of some sort—inside or outside his head? He wasn't sure.

"The stone is breaking apart," Stella said. She stood by him, but her voice sounded far away.

Time sprinted forward as she grabbed his hand and pulled him up, leaning out her entire body to compensate for the weight difference. "We have to get out of here. You can't die," she said. "*Today*," she added, oddly.

"Nate… Where's Nate?" he asked as he spotted Sibyl helping Harry to his feet.

"The balcony is collapsing. Let's go!" Stella placed her shoulder under his arm.

"Tom, to the stairs, now." Nate emerged from the smoke; skin flushed, and long hair dancing midair, charged with static electricity. He held onto Shadow's arm and led him to the stairs. Underneath them, the balcony sunk and tipped toward the lawn. "Quickly!"

Sibyl and Harry disappeared down the staircase, followed by Stella. Shadow placed his hand on Nate's back, prompting him to go first, the stone breaking apart under their feet and collapsing before Shadow got to the stairs. A sudden drop and a pull, Nate's broken hand grasping his hand and bearing his entire body weight.

"Tom, swing to grab my arm with the other hand. I...I can't hold for much..." Their hands slowly slipping as Nate gritted his teeth—pain written all over his face—refusing to let him go. Nate pushed his hips against the metal rail, releasing the second hand off it to hold Shadow's wrist; wind gusts blowing his hanging body away from safety.

No longer supported by the building's missing facade, the spiral staircase threatened to collapse with Shadow; the axis of the metal stairs bending toward the lawn. *Pop! Pop! Pop! Pop!* Half the bolts on the base plate and wall darted out. The metal spiral wobbled, loosening the remaining bolts.

"Let me go, love," Tom begged. "Please! We'll both die." His clothes soaked and heavy, and still, his body rocked with the strong wind.

Two hands emerged from behind Nate to grab Tom's arm—determination compensating for their lack of strength.

"Buddy, we're going to pull you in." Harry's face appeared under Nate's armpit. "Prepare for a hell of a tumble. *At the count of three,*" he ordered, looking back.

Behind Harry stood Sibyl wrapping zir hands around his chest, and lower down, Stella holding onto Sibyl's arms. They'd all climbed back up the stairs—*the fools.*

"Three, two, one," Stella shouted from below, and they all jerked toward the inside of the building, pulling Shadow over the metal railing into Nate.

The staircase tipped inward, leaning against the building's structure, while the not-so-human train tumbled down and around the stairs until they reached the ground, forming a pile of bodies. Stella and Sibyl—immortal Down Below—cushioned the others' fall. They stood up quickly and so did Harry.

"You okay, Nate?" Shadow asked before he unglued himself from Nate's body.

Nate nodded, holding onto his broken hand. "See it now?" he whispered. "Don't bottle up your storm. When you keep it all inside, it kills you."

"Please…don't…"

Nate reached out to touch his face. "Use your power. You have the heart and the storm. Use it to take control of the app and overrule the tyrants."

"*No*," Shadow raised his voice. "*The storm kills!* When hope is gone, and all that is left is…*is*…hate and wrath…people die." He pressed his jaw shut, grazing his thumb over Nate's injured hand.

She's not gone. Zir words whispered in his mind.

Who? Shadow asked. *Did you say something, Sibyl?*

"I'm not asking you to hate, I am urging you to lead. To lead in the way only you can," Nate spoke in the faintest of whispers, using his fingers to brush Shadow's hair from his face.

"It's going to be okay. I promise." Shadow stood up and rushed to Harry's side, instinct overruling his actions.

His best friend's hair and clothes were slightly burned, smoke emerging from scorched areas here and there.

"*You*. Come here." Shadow hugged Harry tightly. "I miss them too. *I love them too.*"

Boom! Boom! Boom! The storm of light raged on the lawn, and Shadow took a breath, attempting to control his emotions and the weather.

He closed his eyes, digging up all the repressed feelings and leaking them with his words. "I'm angry, and devastated, and…*and* inconsolable. I'll never hear Quin's giggles; I'll never teach him to paint your portrait, or read him a bedtime story—our favorite story." Harry's body convulsed in his arms, and he buried his face in his chest.

"We must go," Stella raised her voice. "The storm is dissipating and the Domizien will attack. They'll kill you both."

"So, you are just going to vanish and let my people die?" Nate grunted.

"Not yours. *Mine*," Stella said.

"Don't you remember the history and plight of your people above? Have mercy! You, of all people, should stand with the Underlings."

Stella showed her impossibly white teeth as her lips twisted open. "What are you saying, scum? That…that I'm less than you? That my genes are or have been inferior to your white genes?"

"No…" Nate looked horrified.

"How dare you compare my people with creatures designed by them to serve *their* people?" She pointed at Shadow and Twist. "*They* created slaves all over again."

Nate lowered his head. "They're like us. *They're us.*"

"Like you? Probably. Inferior by all the measures of the spiral created by your pretty slave master."

Shadow ignored Stella's justified accusation, focusing on Harry. "Listen, I can't begin to imagine how you feel, but they are my family too. I miss June—the way she made you happy." Harry's body collapsed, emotion overruling any pretense of rationality.

Shadow held him closer, placing his hand on the back of Harry's head and kissing his curls. "I took a bullet in the heart too." And the flashbacks crippled him—the heat, and blood, and thorn flesh, and the acrid, eggy scent of discharged powder—life's final curtain call, not so final after all. "I welcomed my bullet. You didn't deserve yours, but I under-stand the trauma that comes from a moment like that. For two years you've been here alone, with your grief and your trauma; you need help, Harry. I'm here."

"You were my partner, my one friend. I have spent more time with you than my own wife. And you chose to leave. You left! I'm so tired of losing you, over and over and over again…"

"I'm not leaving, and we'll get through this together."

"Twist, Shadow, we must leave," Stella ordered.

"I failed you, buddy." Harry's muffled voice was barely audible.

"No, you didn't, and you didn't deserve what happened to you."

"What he did to me!" Harry pushed back, attempting to release himself from Shadow's hold.

"Yes," Shadow said, and the thought of it crushed him. Love and anger mixed into a toxic cocktail burning in his gut.

A familiar sound—glass breaking above. A gust of wind had shoved a tree into the back of the building, its glass roof perforated by branches and leaves right where the bleeding heart once stood. Crimson spears first darted down, and then floated away slowly toward the edges of the building. With no Underlings around to see it, Sibyl broke the illusion of gravity to keep them all safe.

Shadow closed his eyes, numbing his feelings to prevent further destruction.

He held on to Harry, preventing his escape. "He stole your life," Shadow said, "but I can't let you take his, for your sake, as much as his. Do you understand? I need your word, Harry."

"You're biased, bud."

"Yes. I love you both," Shadow confessed. "Look, I'll support an independent trial, but no death sentence. And if you judge him, you'll have to judge me too. I've killed too."

Through the one-way glass of the main door, Shadow saw the creatures emerge from the wall of smoke and fire of the dying storm. That's when he saw them—the horned warrior on horseback, and in front of the demon, Thorn's unconscious body, laying horizontally over the horse. Her hands and feet were tied, and her face was swollen and bloodied. Their horse stood at the center of the horseshoe-shaped demon infantry, all armed with swords and short bows looped over the shoulder or strapped across the back.

Is she dead? Is Thorn dead? He asked Sibyl. Zie shook her head, and he exhaled deeply.

"Your word, Harry!" Shadow rushed, his tone firm and loving.

Harry nodded. "If he keeps preaching, I'll lock him up."

Not until that moment Shadow realized he'd been choking. Oxygen filled up his lungs, spreading to every cell of his body. "Thank you, brother. Thank you."

"Tom, you're squishing me."

Shadow squeezed him one more time before he finally let him go. "Your hair is a mess. I need you to leave to the lab while they can't see you jump."

"You're not coming?" Harry lifted his head and rubbed his eyes.

"No. Thorn's in trouble. I need to help her."

"Is that Thorn?" Stella said, squinting her eyes.

"Tom, get out of here," Nate urged.

"Harry, I need you in the lab," Shadow repeated, conspiring to keep both men safe and away from each other. "The Domizien are acting weird. There's too much…hmm…*soul* in the way they are behaving. We need to find out what's going on."

"And what exactly are you going to do?" Harry asked. "Fight them all? You?" He rolled his eyes. "Come on, bud. We're running out of miracles."

"You're not going to hug your way out of this one," Stella added.

"Thorn said they want me," Shadow said. "They'll get me. I need to understand their motivations and meet their leader. I feel she is the answer."

"*No!*" Nate begged.

"You…*feel* she is the answer? You're nuts," Harry said. "You'll get yourself killed."

"They could have killed me before," Shadow said. "They didn't. I'll buy us time."

"Time for what?" Nate asked. "You can't bargain with demons."

"Time for you to lead your people out of here. Where are they?"

Nate crossed his arms over his chest. "After you left, Jan gathered them all in the main hall for a prayer. She's against our agreement. They all are."

"I'm surprised they haven't come out to see what's going on." Shadow glanced at the fallen pillars and piles of stones outside.

"Psychedelics, probably..." Nate said. "Attempting to connect with Sibyl. Without me, they cannot—"

"They're vulnerable. You need to get them out of here," Shadow said. "I'll buy us time."

"We can't let you die," Harry said, and Shadow blinked his eyes at him.

"Don't..." A strange sadness in Nate's voice. "That's not what he means."

"I'll protect him," Stella said, looking at her glossy white nails.

Nate and Harry flashed the same condescending exasperation.

She lifted her nose, staring down at them. "I'm human, remember? They can't hurt me, and I don't wanna brag, but I'm excellent at combat."

Harry looked at Sibyl, raising a doubtful brow, and zir nod seemed to confirm Stella's claims.

"There's at least two hundred of them," Nate said. "You can't protect him."

"It doesn't matter," Shadow said. "They are holding Thorn hostage. I don't have a choice. My gut tells me this is the right move."

"Gut, Tom?" Harry said. "Haven't you learned anything from decades of work digitizing human beings?"

"Plus, we still have some miracles," Tom said.

"Don't you dare waste your miracle on a murderer."

Stella scanned the room. "Sibyl, anyone watching?"

There were no Underlings watching, and in an instant, Stella changed her look, and Nate stumbled backward, probably unaccustomed to experiencing the Gods' powers.

"Ta-da! I'm readyyy," Stella said, her hair now arranged into two braids neatly tucked behind her ears. In her forehead, a symbol painted in white—a cross and a slightly smaller circle shared the same center; each point of the cross touched a small disk, and all four disks connected by counter-clockwise arrows.

"What's that on your face?" Harry asked.

"Dikenga dia Kongo—our past, our present, and the future you failed to deliver," she said, revving up the engine of the vintage motorbike she was now riding—a lean cruiser with three oversized wheels. The electric red and pink retro bike clashed with her mint-colored, camo-print bodysuit—padded knees and elbows. Shadow couldn't help but smirk, and her face lit up at his reaction.

"You got the reference!" She flashed a cheeky smile. "Inspired by your movie," she confirmed.

"Thorn's in trouble," Shadow said. "We gotta go." He glanced at the destroyed lawn and collapsed balcony. "Maybe a dirt bike would be best?"

"It can't carry the hardware," she said.

"What hardw—" Before he finished his question, two pink Gatling-style guns popped up on each side of the bike, shiny chains of ammo running from the can mounted on top of the engine.

Stella tested the weapons, firing at the front door. *Raa*-ka *ta*-ka *ta*-ka *taaa,* and Shadow's eardrums hissed, still recovering from the lightning strike. The smoke slowly vanished, revealing the fallen door laying over one of the stone pillars— a perfect ramp over the ruins of the collapsed balcony.

Harry covered his ears with the palms of his hands. "This kid is fucking insane."

"This will be over in a heartbeat." Stella handed Shadow a weird-looking weapon. "Hold this for me, babe."

He held the elaborate blade, scalloped at the blunt end, and curved into a sickle at the top. Its iron belly sharp and deadly.

"Hop in," Stella said, and he jumped on the bike with her, lifting the weapon high up to avoid hurting her.

"Wh-what are you doing?" Nate's tone rose to impossible heights.

"Nate, find your people," Shadow said. "Then run. Leave this place until it's safe."

"I'm...not leaving you."

"Thorn said they hunt you to get to me; to hurt me. Stella can't protect us both."

"I can. I won't," she said with a sneer, as she gave Shadow one of the two helmets she now held in her hands. His, a solid black; hers, a coral half-helmet chopper with the face of a smiling hyena painted at the back. As she put her helmet on, the predator's long, sharp teeth closed in on Shadow's nose.

Shadow chose his words with care, conspiring to keep Nate safe. "I'll be more vulnerable if you are near."

Somehow the statement crushed Nate as if Shadow had delivered some damning accusation. Nate nodded, lowering his gaze and running toward the wall of plants—the secret passage to the Commune.

"Nate!" Shadow called, and Nate turned around, a pinch of anticipation in his eyes. "Thank you for saving my life."

"Don't lose it again. You need it to fix the worlds." He blinked back love before he vanished between the jungle of plants.

Shadow threw his helmet to the floor—the creatures needed to recognize him. Then he turned to Harry. "Go. I need to understand the inner workings of the soulless. Have our original designs been changed?"

"Shadow, Stella," Harry said, all business. "Permission to access what you see and hear until this is over. *All of it.* Also... I need to speak to you using your mind."

"Sure."

"How unpleasant." Stella nodded.

"I'll make comms a three way, between Gods. Take care, and let's not waste any miracles," Harry said, before vanishing.

"Where's Sibyl?" Shadow asked.

Stella shrugged her shoulders. "Hold on tightly, sexy."

Shadow took his free hand off her hip and grabbed onto the metal hook behind him. "Don't call me that," he admonished.

"Hold on to me," she persisted as the bike's drumming grew loud and fast. "It's going to be...bumpy. Oh, and keep the Ngulu away from your body."

"The what?"

Vroom! *Vroom!* His head throbbed every time the bike growled.

"The weapon," she said, and he lowered the strange-looking sword, its curved pointy end almost dragging on the ground. He was no arms expert, but he doubted its utility in battle.

"Is all this noise still allowed Up Above?"

He got no response. At least, not in words.

Vroom! *Vroom! Vrooom!* They accelerated toward the ramp, and she knew exactly how much throttle to apply to push the front tire up without spinning out the rear wheels.

35

GOD'S BETRAYAL

6. PLURIZ

MAIN HALL — THE COMMUNE
DAY 1 — 9:24 PM

They approached Storm as soon as he walked into the hall. Ninety-six pairs of distressed eyes, all set on him. Heavy brows judging, the only sign of resistance on their otherwise crestfallen faces.

Jan stood in front of the semicircle of gloom, and she, too, wore an alien expression in her gaze. This time anger, angst, and a spear of disappointment cut through his insides.

Storm lowered his head. "You've told them…"

"Everything. I had no choice, Nate." She sounded guilty.

A knot formed in his throat as he predicted their state of mind. He knew how it felt—to be betrayed by his own father and the God he worshiped. *That moment*, when doubt turned into certainty; when his entire world collapsed; when he finally realized people like him were the muck of his beloved religion. Cast away and deemed inferior by the most important person in his life. You don't recover from that. You *never* recover from that. Soon, rage would replace shock. Soon they'd experience the urge to stand against injustice; to fight their oppressors; to burn the house down. A storm that'll never leave them...him.

"Jan... You promised me—"

"You broke your word when you agreed to stop preaching."

"I gave him one day. Just one. He's the only one who can—"

"Shadow lost hope, and he's out of miracles. He told me so," Jan said. "He isn't back to create better stories. He's back for *you*. He only cares about *you*, nothing else. *No one else.*" Words shot in accusation.

"It's not true, Jan. If you only knew how much he did to free—"

"No, Nate." She approached him, her hands reaching for the side of his arms, squeezing. "Thorn told me the truth. Truths you don't know..." Jan turned her face away, pressing her lips together as if she wished to spare him from her fury.

"What did she say? Why are you listening to her? *Thorn's a murderer!*" He took a breath. "Jan, Tom...is the creator...the creative... I can't design a better future... It's not what I do."

"Love blinds you." Jan crossed her arms and turned her back to him. "Do the needful. We'll follow you in revolution."

Outside, by the lake, some bird made a real ruckus. Its chanting seemed to copy the Gatling guns firing farther away.

Storm shook off his anxiety.

"Jan… I fuel change, I don't create it, neither do the others. The ones you haven't met—minor Gods, controlled by a scheming universe. Only he can—"

"No, friend. I too, believed in his heart and his struggle. I, too, loved him unconditionally, a devotion that kept me alive when my body ached for death, the end of suffering, enduring torture after torture in the lowest of all worlds. Even then, I loved him, and prayed for his miracles." Jan lowered her voice into a faint whisper. "But what he did to that poor girl just before Thorn killed him…" She glanced at him and pressed her lips again.

"What girl?" Storm asked, confused.

"We're all slaughterhouse lambs enthralled by our butcher," Jan said. "A charming bully, just like my dear husband, speaking words of love while burning my eyes inside my skull."

Outside, the insistent bird got louder. Its cackling foreign to that part of the worlds. Storm turned his head to see the creature. A black crown and orange-blushed beak adorned the large blue bird. A species he'd never seen before. He ignored it and focused on Jan, placing his hands on her shoulders and turning her to face him.

"What girl?" he repeated. "What are you talking about?"

"I won't break your heart," Jan said, and he could see everyone but him knew what she was talking about. Their eyes still on him. In them, the hurt and despair of those who just learned they were born into slavery, cursed by a beloved God to suffer and die.

"*We're just pawns!*" Hepius—a gentle soul—screamed between gritted teeth. His face was rage red and his eyes mad and distant. "He turned his back to our pain."

"The pain he designed," said someone else, hidden from sight.

At the back, several others turned tables and bashed chairs against the wall, while outside the strong winds pushed entire trees into the glass walls. The storm was back, and he worried for his heart.

"You knew it, preacher," added the Commune's head chef. "All along, you protected his secret. Made us believe he cared."

"*He does*. It's all he does—*care*. Too much. All the time. So much, it destroyed him." Storm lifted his eyes to face the wall of rage surrounding him. He sat on the highest of the three steps descending from the main door and searched his memory for the right story. "I met him when he was very young, his mind always filled with stories, a never-ending ambition to create a better, fairer world…"

"Lambs sacrificed by our divine motherfuckers." Someone started before others joined. "Feeding our flesh, our distress, to the vultures."

Reacting fast, Storm leaned his entire body to one side, dodging a bottle flying in his general direction, far enough to be a warning rather than an attack.

"Let me tell you about him? Who he is. What he cares about." He begged with his eyes, and the crowd settled. "Tom created this world, everything beautiful about it." Storm looked back beyond the open doors. "The way this building is divided into distinct, surprising spaces. Common areas that emerge unexpectedly as we cross winding, nature-rich passages and emerge into an entirely different scenery—picturesque and functional. Design principles inspired by Olmsted, the creator of his favorite park. A park at the center of the capital of the world whose design embodied his social consciousness and commitment to egalitarian ideals."

"And who designed the Tower, the battlefield, the abandoned warehouse—stinking of blood, sweat, sex, alcohol, and urine?" In Jan's face the glimpse of horrific memories. "The foul smell of the industrial complex of pain and rape and murder, also designed by him."

"By the app," he said, and they all stared at him blankly. "The…worlds changed to serve humans. Tom didn't know you'd evolve into consciousness, Jan…"

They got closer, bottles and chairs lifted above red faces. Outside, a cacophony of jungle sounds. Sounds that didn't belong in the Commune. A wild morning symphony after dark, filled with contradiction. Storm looked back, but he couldn't see much beyond the semi-transparent reflection of a dense jungle—a leafy veil of tropical forest hiding the lake and the cabins floating in it. *What the fuck is going on? Am I high?*

"We'll blow the ground beneath our feet to make it right!" Hepius shouted, kicking in the leg of the nearest table, plates and glasses shattering on the ground.

Storm stood up, turned his back to the psychedelic jungle, and spoke. "Don't you see? We've achieved our goal. They brought him back because of our prayers. They know he's the only one who can bring fairness to these worlds."

"He doesn't believe he can," said Jan, raising the palms of her hands in the air asking the crowd to move back. "Kindly adjust!" she shouted at them before she turned back to Storm. "And he's a traitor. We must continue to pressure them. We must pray."

"He doesn't need more pressure…"

This time, a flying bottle hit him on the temple, right beside his right eye. The burst of pain and the blood left him half blind. Dizzy, he covered his throbbing head with his arms, waiting for more.

"Stop!" Hepius screamed, placing himself between Storm and the mob. Several skirmishes ensued, many protecting Storm, some advancing on him.

"Please," Storm said. "If you keep using violence, you'll feel compelled to return to lower worlds...south of here, where there's more suffering. Zie'll make you leave Pluriz—"

"You once told us you'd fight with us to the end," a woman said from the back. He failed to recognize her voice.

"*I will.*"

"That you'd gladly die to defend our rights."

"I do. I'll gladly give my life for each one of you."

"You said we'd destroy the worlds if we have to," the woman persisted.

"I did." He paused, as he uncovered a truth hidden from him until this moment. "I...can't... I won't..."

"Why?" Hepius asked, his chubby face covered with sweat and tears. "We sacrificed many. You've been ready to sacrifice yourself with us and for us. What changed?"

"He won't destroy a world inhabited by the love of his life," Jan said. "He won't risk Shadow to release us from slavery."

"Jan, only he can do that," Storm whispered.

"Don't you see? Shadow's here to maintain status quo," Jan said patiently, using her scarf to clean the blood dripping from his temple. She was still his friend, somehow. "The Gods brought him back to neutralize you, and enthrall us," she said. "Don't be weak. We must pray! Your plan is working."

"My plan?" Storm released a desperate laughter. "Revolution is important, but alone, is not enough. Believe me. I know!" Memories flashed of a different time in another world—a world as ugly and broken. "It was him, not me, who fixed the re—world higher up. Real solutions need...innovation and creativity."

"*What creativity?*" she asked. "He's broken, lost and...he has betrayed everything he once stood for. We need your voice!"

"Jan...it was my...my voice that pushed him into darkness."

Erratic, Hepius scratched his right forearm with his nails, skin breaking and blood gushing from the self-inflicted wounds. The need to control something when nothing was under his control. Storm realized there was something worse than their rage. The hopelessness he had experienced in the one he loved most. He rushed to hold Hepius's hand. The healer sunk his head into Storm's chest and cried. "We keep praying and waiting and hurting. So much pain and death. It's never-ending... I try my best to mend them—the wounds... Too many wounds... The light never comes, preacher. There's no light."

"He's here now. Tom'll fix it. I promise you, my friend." Storm embraced Hepius.

"I don't believe you, dear." Jan sighed. "I too once loved a man who left me blind. Literally. A lucky...privileged husband who took my eyes, because, he, too, didn't like my voice."

"The eyes Tom returned to you," Storm said.

"I lost my eyes, because my lucky husband needed to learn some lesson to become a better person. How is that fair?"

"It's not. Trust me. He—"

"I trust you, my friend. Above all else, I trust your love for him, and it leaves me no choice…"

THE PAST

36

FORCES OF CHANGE

WORLD ECONOMIC FORUM — DAVOS, SWITZERLAND
24 JANUARY 2029

E ighteen-year-old Rosa poured a bottle of water over her eyes, burning from the tear gas that also constricted her airways. Around her, protesters ran in all directions, dispersed by water cannons, rubber bullets, and the devil's toxic mist unleashed by the flying drones.

The young rioters fought for their planet, their livelihoods, and their families, and Rosa fought for Lilly, her baby sister. In just five months, since her birth, the red-faced little monster had wrapped her older sibling in her tiny finger. Rosa wasn't sure how it had happened. The chubby bundle of joy spent most of her waking time eating, pooping, and screeching, and still, to defend Lilly's future, Rosa faced hundreds of armed police in riot gear.

The video call to protest had been posted online by the Anonymous social media accounts. A masked man had identified himself as Change's Tsunami. Neither the mask nor his distorted voice failed to protect his identity from the ones who, like Rosa, had been feeding on his words and their rhythm all their lives. Nathan Storm's short message fueled a large-scale mobilization of disenfranchised youth.

Young people descended on Davos from all over the world. End-to-end encrypted messaging apps enabled sympathizing conference insiders to share self-destructing messages with the activists. The information exposed the conference organizers' classified plans. Thousands of protesters were alerted to roadblocks and Secret Service locations, as well as the schedule and arrival route for the G19 world leaders.

Rosa's team had sneaked in before the roadblocks were set up, and had hidden by one of the entry routes to the ski resort turned conference venue. It didn't take long for the drones to spot them as they waited for the president of the United States to arrive at the leaked scheduled time. No media was present, as it was supposed to be a secret arrival.

A bulletproof autonomous vehicle slowly made its way up the road from the nearby airpad. Rosa rubbed her eyes, still burning, trying to make sense of what she was watching. Her jaw dropped, and she coughed toxic muck. Inside the transparent cockpit, three people sat around a dining table plentifully strewn with cheese, lobster, trout, and a large selection of cured meats and wines.

The POTUS, Spark Fuel's John Voser, and another passenger sitting with his back to Rosa all ignored what was happening outside, smiling to each other as they engaged in some light conversation.

A hooded boy jumped on the car, whacking it with a steel bar as five security agents pulled him down and proceeded to kick him all over his body. Preparing to jump to his defense, Rosa threw one final glance inside the car. For a moment, the third passenger turned his head to look at the events outside, and his eyes met Rosa's. *Henryk frackin' Nowak. Sell out.* The emotionless man stared blankly and then quickly turned his face away as Rosa jumped on the pile of men attacking the boy.

Rosa wrapped her arm around one man's neck and shoved her knee into his back. She arched backward, using the weight of her body to pull the man away from the boy until they both fell to the ground.

Rosa jumped to her feet as another agent—five inches taller than she—smiled before grabbing her neck with both hands, squeezing hard. Simultaneously, she kicked him in the groin as she grabbed his wrists, yanking, twisting, and pulling his hands from her neck. As she widened the space between her and her opponent, someone grabbed her hair from the back and shoved her head against a handheld shield. At least three other men descended on her, knocking her out.

37

TRUTHFUL STORY WORLDS

SÃO MIGUEL ISLAND — AZORES
ONE YEAR AND A HALF LATER — 6 AUGUST 2030

Tom adjusted the microphone as he prepared himself for his first interview ever. The mic didn't need adjusting, not this time, or the other six times he had tweaked its position in the last few minutes, but he was anxious, and the wait was making him extra fidgety. He looked out of the window at the gentle motion of the Atlantic, attempting to calm his nerves. Outside, the day was hot, bright, and slow. The wild wind was nowhere to be felt, but the seagulls flying around in circles warned the fishermen of tomorrow's storms.

The twenty-six-year-old was alone in the living room of his small home—an old fisherman's cottage on the Azores' São Miguel Island, overlooking the sleepy sea. These days, Tom and Harry mostly met at the lab Down Below. Being together in the same physical location was a significant risk for the platform's security. Sibyl only acted on important changes upon the founders' approval, and keeping them apart reduced the risk of external interference. If one of them were kidnapped, drugged, or tortured, the assailant would still have limited ability to interfere with Down Below's strategy or operations. The other founder was the second line of defense, and Sibyl the third, as she measured their stress indicators before actioning their orders.

Right from the start of their adventure and that first interview with Marge two years before, Harry had agreed to let Tom off the hook when it came to public relations. Harry handled the fame, the scrutiny, and any media communications. No one knew what Tom looked like, and he didn't attend any of the endless events to honor the two social entrepreneurs.

Tom's secrecy and privacy turned him into a legend bordering on myth. Just like the Loch Ness Monster or Bigfoot, there was occasional news of sightings, conjecture about his potential whereabouts, and numerous groups, obsessive fans, and cults dedicated to finding him. Anyone bearing a resemblance to the few photos of him as a teen suffered from unprecedented levels of harassment.

Today, Tom was opening an exception to his absence from public life. He trusted the interviewer and the topics were storytelling and ethics, themes Harry couldn't represent with the same depth. Marge had a track record of outstanding public service, an authentic and independent voice, and had spent a lifetime fighting for the values she shared with Down Below's founders.

Tom stared at the countdown on the screen, and he adjusted the mic one final time. The interview would be broadcast live in less than thirty seconds, and he could see Marge and her team making the final preparations.

The media diva looked at the camera and flashed a friendly smile. "Thomas, I'm delighted to finally be able to speak to you, but I'm sad we won't see you."

"Oh… Hi, it's my absolute pleasure and long overdue." Tom cleared his voice. "Harry and I are big fans of all of your work."

"Why all the mystery? Using technology to distort your voice and keeping us from seeing you. The people that have met you in the past say you're *diviiine* to look at."

"Secrecy is the only way I can keep that rumor going," he laughed, and then he changed his tone. "I'm so sorry. We need to protect the security of the platform. If you don't know how I look or sound like, you can't track me down."

Tom wasn't lying, but he also benefited from the fact no one would judge him or obsess over him because of how he looked, and it also prevented old acquaintances from identifying him as Jon Stone's son.

"Right, right, keeping the decision-makers separate," Marge said. "Harry explained this to us last time he visited. But this crackling noise is annoying."

"Facial features, voice, and some biometric signals, like a heartbeat, are unique to each person and can be used to track someone via devices, drones, satellite, or laser. Harry is running some interference."

"Never mind. For you, *just* for you, I'll make an exception and will be *especially* patient," she said, still showing some mild annoyance in her frown. "You go through great lengths to protect your privacy. I hope you are as cautious with ours."

"Harry will be with you next week to cover this topic, but in summary, *yes*, we're obsessed with protecting traveler privacy."

"I'll speak to Harry about it. I'm sure he'll give me *all* the technical details, even the ones I didn't know I needed." Marge opened her eyes dramatically and then winked.

Tom laughed. "I don't know what I'd do without him. He just makes things happen. It's like magic. I'm so grateful."

"You two can't stop gushing about each other. It's cute. Which reminds me, I have a bone to pick with you, young man."

"Oh, am I in trouble?" Tom asked sweetly.

"Yes, *yes*, you are. A few years ago, I invited you to come speak with us about *Glass Walls*. You didn't have the security issue then. Why did you refuse me?" Marge prodded, using an exaggerated brooding tone and crossing her arms in front of her chest.

"Umm, I guess I prefer to let my creative work speak for itself? If an artist pays too much attention to criticism or praise, his voice, her voice will be tainted. I've always searched for my truth in my creative works. I try to seek inspiration, but I avoid external pressures, you know?" He paused for a beat. "Of course, Down Below is different. Harry and I are accountable to all our travelers and listen attentively to their feedback."

"Let's dig deeper into this concept of truth. Harry told me this is important to both of you."

"Yes, it's at the core of everything we do. I learned that from —umm, someone I respect a lot." Tom bit his lip before continuing and reached out to hold the medal he wore on his chest. "Truth is powerful. We can feel… We can recognize its authenticity. It draws you in."

"Poetic, but a story—your experiences aren't true, are they?"

"No, but we try to reflect the truth as much as possible."

"How so?"

"They are based on highly probable predictions."

"Sibyl's code, right?" Marge asked.

"Yes, and we are always asking ourselves one question: How might we improve the wellbeing of humanity, humans, and all living beings?"

"You're trying to reduce human suffering."

"Yeah, we want to discover just how good life can be. In many cases, we can objectively measure the results of our experiences, because at the moment, we are focusing on tackling the most obvious attacks to basic universal values— violence, hate, oppression, environmental destruction, et cetera. Harry is adamant we use the scientific method to test our impact and improve continuously based on what we learn. I'm fully supportive."

"So, you're saying there's truth in your impact?"

"Yes, the data shows it."

"But universal values are different across the world, because of culture and religion. Some say you have a bias toward a westernized and progressive set of values, that your moral compass doesn't reflect the world's views."

"We have a bias for any values that objectively reduce suffering and pain of living beings in this life and on this planet. These morals aren't specific to the western world."

"In this life and on this planet?" She raised an eyebrow, confused. "What do you mean?"

"That we ignore promises of afterlife, heaven, virtual worlds, or human settlements on Mars. We want to improve life experience, *now* and *on this planet*."

"I understand," Marge laughed. "And you made a lot of progress in a few months."

"It looks like it's working, but we have work to do, and we all need to stay vigilant. We need your critical eye."

"My dear, we are seeing so much progress in so little time. I'd follow you blindly to the ends of the Earth."

"Marge, I-I appreciate the support, but I don't want anyone's blind faith. Idols and dogma—people and beliefs that can't be questioned or challenged, they're the enemy of progress."

"Like religion?"

"Or any stories that are interpreted literally and don't leave room for new learning. Don't get me wrong; it's important to learn from the past so we don't repeat our mistakes. But we also need to check—to test—if the messages—if the values embedded in these stories are still relevant today."

"So, you're saying we're all stuck in the past?"

"I'm suggesting that defending our ability to keep learning is more important than defending our current knowledge and status. Some stories are very sticky and travel deep and far."

"Like the stories in religious books."

"Yes, we need to check their value constantly."

"And yet story is your superpower."

"It's my craft. I'm one of many." Tom chuckled, embarrassed. "Marge, I came prepared for a serious grilling; don't let me down."

"Oookaaay, I'll stop fangirling and try to be all tough with you...sweetie." He laughed, and she laughed with him. "So, why are stories so powerful?"

"These concepts of rationality, objectivity, or science are new behaviors in humankind's evolution. Most of the time, we act first and find an explanation for our actions later."

Marge opened her eyes wide and shook her head. "I'm not following; what does that have to do with storytelling?"

"A fawn doesn't run from a predator by analyzing statistics and probabilities. When the young creature sees something new, she will look to her mother to find out how to respond to it and remember that response. These patterns we learn are organized in our minds as narratives, metaphors, and symbols. We're set up to use stories as a formula for how we should live, and we live mostly by reacting to the world around us."

"Is this why I zone out when my darling Harry goes on and *on and on* about numbers?"

"Oh, don't give him a hard time. He tries so hard...and does such crucial work." Tom smiled. "We need to teach everyone his craft, the scientific method—the ability to learn and constantly evolve knowledge. To think critically about what surrounds us. But the best way to teach this is through story-telling."

"Mm-hmm, I understand, but frankly, some of these so-called rationalists, the science folks that reject religion and faith, seem to lack empathy and a moral North Star. Seriously, many are nihilistic jerks." Marge scowled.

"Some, yes, but let's not stereotype people—"

"Oh, I didn't mean Harry. We love our geek-in-chief."

"I know, I know. If you want to change someone's mind, story is more powerful than raw data."

The interviewer straightened her shoulders and leaned in toward the camera. "They can also be used to manipulate the masses and fuel cults and dictatorships." Her forehead wrinkled with concern.

"Yes, they can, and they have."

"And with the data provided by the TSkin sensors, you know everything about us—our health, state of mind... We have no privacy." Marge pointed her index finger to the camera. Her long, sparkly nail caught the light and created a tiny rainbow on screen, undermining her intent to be mildly menacing. "Honey, we like you and Harry a lot...I mean, we love you madly, but you are very young, have a lot of power, and it happened fast."

Tom shifted in his seat. It was a fair assessment, one that concerned him *a lot*. "We *only* use that data to create relentlessly relevant and impactful experiences for our travelers and to simulate human behavior in the Underlings."

"So, you're trying to make the Underlings more real?"

"Yes. You see, a body's architecture shapes behavior and intelligence."

"What do you mean?"

"The intelligent octopi have nine brains, eight of them in their arms. Parts of their body can make decisions autonomously without ever using the central brain. They experience the world differently because their intelligence and decision-making are embodied differently."

"So, the way you look affects how you feel and behave. Like when I wear high heels, a corset, glitter, and a big wig, I immediately feel like I can conquer the world."

Tom laughed. "Something like that, yes. Although your ability to move and to breathe may be a little compromised."

"Oh, details, details," she said in a melodic tone. "But, why is this relevant to Underlings?"

"AIs don't have a human body. They're not restricted by our physical architecture. If they're left unconstrained, their intelligence evolves differently from humans. We want the Underlings to simulate us as much as possible, so we are using what we learn from the TSkins' sensors to simulate brains, nervous systems, and body-mind connection in Underlings. For example, stress affects the way they age. And if they break a digital bone, it affects their mood the same way it does in a human being."

"So, you're trying to create digital life?"

"No, not at all. These characters aren't conscious, they simulate feelings and pain, but it's just a simulation. The goal is to provide realistic experiences to travelers. To get as close as possible to the truth of the moment."

"Do you think the bots will ever become alive? Conscious?"

"Harry and I debate this all the time. He thinks we'll get there one day…in, like, twenty years."

"And you? What do you think?" Marge leaned in and narrowed her eyes.

"Hmm, it's not worth talking about it. Harry says it's—it's magical thinking…"

"Magic? I like magic. Go on, Tom, please."

"I think we're all connected. I can't explain why; umm, it's a gut feeling. I sometimes sense things about the people I love, even when they are far away. I know it sounds foolish… but…" Tom recalled the time when he fell to his knees and lost his sight for a few minutes. He'd felt like he'd been hit by a moving train. Half an hour later, his father called him to let him know his mother had passed away.

"I do too. Go on, darling; this is the stuff that makes you come alive in our eyes. We are here to get to know you."

"I believe a part of our so-called consciousness—our soul— sits outside of our bodies, in the ether that connects us with all other living beings."

"Like Plato's anima mundi?"

"Yeah, there are many panpsychist theories out there. And then, inside our bodies, there's another part—the consciousness that comes from the stories we assemble. The narratives we use to post-rationalize our actions and to create some level of forced coherence in everything we do and experience."

"That makes a lot of sense to me. Do you believe in God?"

"I believe we all share a soul and co-create a universal story that is constantly evolving. That when you share an authentic and wholesome story, it goes viral and becomes part of our collective consciousness. Truthful stories are powerful."

"So, we're all just...stories connected to other stories by larger narratives."

"Yeah, there are books, and series, and interconnected story worlds...and fan fiction, and derivative works. A babushka doll of stories inspired by other stories. Ai ai...Harry is going to kill me. He doesn't believe in my cosmic consciousness theory, and now I've managed to lose credibility with the entire scientific community." He chuckled, tousling his hair with his fingers. "Don't worry, folks, Harry runs the platform based on objective, observable evidence. No magical thinking is allowed in Down Below's strategy and operations."

"You complete each other, don't you?"

"Yes, he's my best friend. I trust him with my life."

38

LOVE CASTS A SHADOW

Marge stood straighter. The narrowed eyes, tightened lips, and the small dimple on the right side of her cheek all warned Tom he was about to get roasted.

"Fascinating. Time to get personal, okay, dear?"

He held his breath and cleared a lump in his throat. "I'm-I'm not sure. Let's see what happens…"

"So, I understand Down Below helps people face the bitter truth and deal with their dark sides."

"Yes, but it also helps people look at situations from different perspectives and learn better ways of living."

"What can you tell us about your dark side, Tom? It's only fair we get to know you."

He crossed his arms in front of his chest. "Umm, I guess the people who have known me well tell me different things…"

"Like what?"

"Harry calls me oversensitive, emotional, stubborn, and judgmental, but…I guess…he would." He chuckled. "And…

someone else I respect a lot has told me I'm blinded by my privilege."

"You are privileged?"

"Yeah, I had access to the best schools and education, and never had to deal with the problems faced by our minorities or poor folks. The access to resources and the optimism of a carefree childhood left me blind to the baggage others carry."

"Baggage? Like what?"

"I may be less empathetic with those who use outrage and violence to fight injustice, for example."

"I'm not sure if that's true. Your movie shows a great understanding of the plea of the less fortunate."

A script inspired by Nate's social activism and poetry. Tom missed him so much. Over three years had passed since he last saw the poet at the Albertine, but his feelings for his first and only love had not changed.

"I don't know, but I guess…I take the feedback seriously."

Marge still looked unconvinced. "So, what are you doing about this…feedback?"

"I have immersed myself in the shadows of humans. This allows me to at least see the darkness others have faced— their suffering."

He wanted to understand Nate better. To walk in his shoes and be worthy of his love.

"That doesn't sound very healthy," Marge said.

"I feel I need to understand it, his—umm…*the* suffering and rage." *Maybe I'll find a way to heal it.* As he spoke, Marge's eyes blinked with some recognition. His jaw tightened. He was giving away too much.

"Tom?"

"Yes?"

"Do you have someone…special in your life?"

As he shifted in his seat, the chair creaked loudly.

"I've been busy lately…"

"How about that drunk poet that refuses to speak to the media? Some offered him millions, but he doesn't—"

"I'd appreciate it if you leave…people alone." He gnawed on his lower lip. "I get that you need to do due diligence about me. If you send me questions, I'll answer what I can. But please—*please* leave people alone; they don't deserve the constant harassment, and, frankly, won't provide you with any new insights."

Marge leaned in and raised an eyebrow. "I'm surprised you went for such a…turbulent character."

"Enough," he said without raising his voice.

"Oh, dear, I'm sorry. It looks like I went too far." She placed her hands on her face, genuinely ashamed.

He took a moment to calm down, placing his hand on his chest, on top of his medal. He wasn't going to let anyone criticize or harass his Nate because of him. "I accept your apology," he said truthfully. "Unfortunately, I got to go."

Marge's eyes filled with regret. She took a moment before she replied with a warm smile. "You know what? I think you're right."

"About?"

"The magic of a connected cosmos, dear. I can't see you, but I can certainly feel your authenticity and kind soul. Will you come back to speak to us again?"

"I-I don't know…"

"Come back when you can, dear. I promise I'll respect your boundaries. It was lovely chatting with you."

"Thank you for everything you do, Marge. Please keep challenging our work."

FACING HIS SHADOW

BUSHWICK COLLECTIVE — BROOKLYN, NY

Nathan listened to Tom's words, his teeth chattering as waves of emotion crashed into his body. He had searched for his love for years—angry, remorseful, and heartbroken, but not until that moment had he realized the impact his parting words had on Tom, and he worried.

Down Below forced people to face the consequences of their dark sides. It was a work of genius, but Nathan knew his ray of sunshine wasn't prepared to face that much evil. No one was, especially not Tom.

Nathan used the platform regularly, *to judge its features and keep the leaders in check*—he often lied to himself. Unlike most people, he was never subject to a painful digital experience. He had wondered why his time down there was always uplifting.

Nathan spent most of the time with a bot that looked much like his younger sister. The child—a digital character clearly designed by Tom—seemed to be programmed to make him feel good, and to give him a hopeful perspective. Hope's quirks and mannerisms brought such depth to the interactions that almost made it feel real. Nathan had to remind himself often that the kid was just a bot.

"I've been thinking…" she often said.

"Thinking deep thoughts?" he had asked as he scanned the park looking for Tom. *Where are you, love? I miss you so very much.*

Hope licked her ice cream, swiping up the melted cream around the edge of the cone before she claimed the chocolate sprinkles at the summit. "We should be able to…like…delete bad people from our brains. They occupy too much space, don't you think?"

He laughed and removed the leftover cream from the tip of her nose. "Who would you purge from your brain?"

"Father… Of course. The memories aren't useful."

He tensed up, recognizing the angst in her voice. He knew it well, that angst. The hurtful recollections, always in the back of his mind—his father's abusive words, the violence, and the contempt. He almost asked what her father did to her, but what was the point of that, she was just an empty bot.

"Memories shape who we are," he said.

"And…umm…maybe they like…stop us from becoming who we want to be?" She took a bite off the empty cone.

He stopped walking and looked at her. "That's deep for an eight-year-old."

"It would be the best revolution, right? A delete button, to erase…you know…" She smiled awkwardly as if she was saying something naughty. "I love you," she said, a hint of anticipation sparked in her eyes.

"I lo—" He pressed his lips together. *This is silly. She's just a bot.* "Yes, the best revolution!" He had smiled.

There was always joy to be had when he visited Hope, even as he craved to confront his shadow as much as he searched for his Tom. Then, one day, he understood he had already suffered the heart-wrenching consequences of his dark side. He didn't need the platform to show him his shadow—what hell could look like; he lived in it.

His strength had always come from his anger against the cause of his suffering, but hating Tom was an impossibility. When the resentment disappeared to uncover an old and enduring love, he found himself hurting a thousand times more than he did before, and that pain was unbearable.

He'd lost the love of his life, and for the last few years, he had struggled with it—life. Bouts of depression had pushed him into isolation and substance abuse. Alone and heartbroken, he'd overdosed on a cocktail of alcohol and pills at least four times in the past six months.

With the suffering came the contrast—the lesson he needed to learn. He knew his shadow well, but now, with no one else to blame but himself, he had to face it, and, alone, he hoped he could conquer it, or die trying.

> Pain of my life—my chain, cocaine—I go insane.
>   This broken heart feeds on your light, you
>   can't depart.
>
> Scared, unprepared, I search for Satan's snakes
>   outside. When the dragon awakes, I fight,
>   and flee, and hide… Terrified. Fearful, tear-

ful, I search for the monster in the wild. It
keeps outrunning… I keep succumbing—a
foolish child.

Creatures keep coming. I'm forever battling,
always running. Wicked beasts—new and
different—so belligerent and cunning. Illit-
erate and innocent, the crowds fall—small
and ignorant, stuck to tradition. Blind faith
in dogma and old gospel—militant
submission.

The blessed know the secret—the snake is a
painful friend. Some are grateful to the test
—a faithful dragon returns to offend.
Hurtful and hateful, the beasts ascend lest
we transcend. Facing the threat, close to
death, the heroes rise…in the end.

Scared, prepared, I search for Satan's snakes
inside. The devil is within me—my shadow
aches—the sin I hide. Hopeful, soulful, I
hunt the awful monster in my mind. It keeps
outrunning… I keep learning, serving, no
longer blind.

Creatures keep coming. I'm forever reacting,
adapting, always becoming. Wicked beasts—
teachers, preachers—so belligerent and
cunning. Dogma, story, ideology—I'll
forever re-write. I'll face the trial, erase my
bile. And, no longer vile, I'll create, and
build, and take flight.

Joy of my life—my royal heart—I'll play my

part. This loyal knight will make you smile
and bring you light.

"Facing my Shadow," Nathan Storm, 6
August 2030

WHERE ARE YOU, *love? Where are you?*

40

MIRACLES AND REBELLIOUS STORIES

THE CITY
FIVE YEARS LATER — 29 AUGUST 2035

When Hope first saw him, she thought he was an angel. Back then, she didn't know much about angels, she didn't know much about anything, but she sensed she was meeting someone good, and out of her world, and that made him quite magical. Tom was all that and so much more—*pretty, sooo pretty, and kind, and, like, different from the Lucky Ones.*

Hope had only a vague recollection of her past—the time before she met Tom. The memories of her mother's life and death had faded, there was little left, and she wondered if she ever had a mother. Hope had told him once the memories were too painful—deadly—but she was too young to know what suffering looked like. She said what she had to say, what was expected of her, because that's what children do. They take hints from adults about what's proper and what's not, and they copy acceptable behaviors.

Her reaction to her mother's death was probably too overdramatic, but at the time, it seemed important, more important than Hope's life. She never understood why so many things were more important than her life: a pesky thought that came back often. More often now she was almost fifteen.

Hope hadn't known her mother that well, but she wished she were alive. Her father and brother were never around, and when she saw them, everything was about *them* and *their* problems. Like the rest of the Lucky Ones, they survived and even thrived in a broken world. Unaware of their good fortune, they took a lot, gave back little, and got away with it because that was the unspoken order of all things. Hope knew she was more important than her dog but less important than the Lucky Ones, and it sometimes bothered her— that pesky feeling again.

She was one of the Others, the ones who suffered, but still, she felt lucky. She was the first to speak to him, Tom—the face of God Down Below, and she was sure he loved her, even when he disappeared abruptly in front of her eyes. *Puff, and, like, he was gone, nowhere to be seen.* That's when she knew he wasn't just pretty but also divine. And then he had returned and had saved her again, and she felt special, *so special.* She'd been the first he'd saved, and now he used his miracles to help many Others.

Alone, without the company of the Lucky Ones, they were mostly safe as they climbed the long, dark road in the middle of the night—the Others and her. They made their way to the top of the mountain. It was the only place near the city where they could sometimes see a glimpse of the stars and the moon in between clouds of smog.

The Others usually gathered to hear Hope speak about the God she'd met, and it gave them comfort. Over time, the group grew larger through word of mouth. A handful of people turned into a large gathering of hundreds of people. Hope shared hope through her vivid, over-elaborate, and sometimes slightly enhanced versions of the truth. It didn't matter, as long as it made them feel better. She amused some, while others admired her, and she felt on top of the world in those peaceful nights above the yellow, corrosive clouds. How could anyone judge her for adding a pinch of imagination to a good story? They became so enthralled in her musings they forgot about their sorrows and their pesky feelings.

Things had changed with his reappearance. Tom started spending time with her and the Others, and every minute spent with him was a gift—a gift from God. They always met him at the top of the mountain, and Hope sat by his right side as he told them the truth.

Unlike Hope, he spoke little about himself, and when he did, he blushed, *a lot*. She thought he was cute, *pretty, sooo pretty*. Only once he'd told them he was there to serve and release them from their suffering. That he'd do anything to free the oppressed, and that came at a cost. "It's a terrible story," he had added.

The end of suffering was a topic debated often by the Others. Some thought Tom was referring to the end of pain, others to eternal life. Hope was optimistic he meant both as long as they were good, *like, really good*. In general, it looked like God, the one above, had a plan, and that he cared for the Others as much as Tom did.

Tom didn't speak about himself often. Instead, he took Hope's place as the chief storyteller. He shared many good stories, and they always had a moral lesson about kindness, mercy, generosity, or inclusivity. Still, she already knew all that, they all did, so they preferred when he told them about sad princes and prickly roses from strangely named planets, dead poets, and monsters, *especially monsters.*

That night, at the end of his tale about a little prince, he said, "You need to be careful with stories. Some are sticky; they stay with you, and they make decisions for you. You don't even notice when you act them out in your life."

"Like asking a prince to tame you?" Hope said.

He nodded and added, "Or a snake to bite you. Sticky stories run our lives, and they are contagious."

Hope threw her hands up, accepting the pre-written fate. "What shall we do? Pray?"

"Pray?"

He was always surprised by the obvious things she said. It frustrated her, but she smiled back at the pretty giant. *Pretty, sooo pretty...*

She clarified. "Pray to God. Ask you— Him to...like...create better stories." *Obviously.*

He seemed upset by her comment, hiding his face in between his arms. Then he lifted his head and stared at January, the blind woman with the acid-burned eyes—a sour gift from her lucky husband. There was a glimpse of tears in his eyes, and she scooted over to sit closer to him on the thin, scorched grass—a little hill raised above the crowd. She touched his shoulder with her head.

"I'm sorry, Tom."

"Shadow, I'm Shadow." He shuddered. "Tom is... Never mind."

"Huh? I didn't mean to criticize your...our stories. It's just difficult, sometimes..."

"I know, Red. I know. You should create your own tales and reimagine the ones you have."

"What's the point when someone else is in charge, and there's a...pecking order? It's best to beg...to pray, right?"

"Gods are flawed, Red. Sometimes, they lack creativity... They may need a little help. You see?" he said, his eyes still on January. He seemed to be having some internal struggle. His brows furrowed, but Hope knew she wasn't their target.

"Do it, Sibyl!" he roared, and then he continued to ruminate as he often did.

Hope pressed on. "We can't just...like...change our own stories. There's the other God, and you, and the Lucky Ones, and umm, the sticky stories that run our lives."

"Don't call them lucky, Red. Call them privileged; that's what they are. You see? It needs to feel uncomfortable for them. Their luck comes at an unacceptable cost."

"Does it matter? We can't really change any of that. Who's lucky...*privileged*, and our pre-written stories."

"There's a secret to stories, Red." He spoke quietly, leaning forward and opening his eyes wide.

"What's that?" Hope asked as they all leaned in.

"The trick is to imagine stories that are true." He smiled, and he cried, and it was a pretty mess. *So pretty...*

"If they are imagined, how can they be true?" January said. The first time she had spoken since the "accident."

Tom got up and then kneeled by January's side and held her hand. "Ingenious stories that increase the life and wellbeing of all liv—umm, beings. Those are true stories—the type of sticky stories we need. Better stories. Rebellious stories."

"Rebellious against God and the way things are?" January asked.

"*Yes*. Stories that challenge outdated laws, inequality, and injustice—fairer stories full of life, as opposed to death, you see? New, coherent explanations to old questions—bold, fresh, insurgent."

"And he, you…will listen to our stories?" Hope asked as she watched the blind young woman squeeze his hand tightly.

"To your truthful prayers? Yes, of course. We look for great turnaround stories that bring luck to the oppressed and the dispossessed and the sick. A stroke of luck deliberately designed into a sticky story that is truthful. You see, Red?" He spoke brightly, but his eyes told a different story.

"To give luck to the Others," Hope murmured.

"To *all* others. Your stories co-design your world and higher up."

"We co-design heaven?" asked someone at the back.

"Yes, you co-design that too; we all do, with our stories." Tom raised his head, trying to find the voice in the dark. "Sib—umm… The—the spirit of God is listening and learning."

"Is it not perfect already? Heaven?" asked the same voice.

Tom dropped his head. "I dearly wish to keep my poet happy and alive," he mumbled sadly. "And I need a better story."

"Unlucky poets?" someone asked, but Tom was too distracted with one of his silent internal battles.

Heat rose to Hope's scrunched-up face—a pesky feeling. "His poet, my brother, is very lucky…privileged. Very privileged," she murmured. He visited her often, but he never paid any attention to her. She felt compelled to go out of her way to make him feel loved and important and needed and… Hope rolled her eyes. She listened to his angry rhymes, and she even made him laugh, once, which was *very* hard to do. In return, he treated her like a cute pet, ignoring most of what she had to say, always looking for something else, someone else. Only recently she'd realized whom he was searching for. She couldn't complain. Compared to others, her Lucky Ones were not so bad. Even her dear father, who stopped by every six months to beat the living daylights out of her, never left a scar, and he was always remorseful when he left. Once, he even said sorry. In fourteen years, she'd suffered a broken arm, and some bruises, so she was very lucky for an Other. Very lucky.

Tom screamed, "Sibyl, stop fighting me. I accept the odds and consequences. Do it. *Just do it*. It's an order."

They all stared at him, until January screamed, placing her hands on her freshly scarred face. Then they stared at her. First, Hope thought she was in pain, but then came the giggling-crying melody of a happy surprise, followed by a burst of joyful laughter. January's hands dropped, and her radiant green eyes and flawless features emerged from behind them.

January saw the world again, and as she stood up, she said she didn't like the world she saw. She scanned the crowd, with her bright, hopeful eyes, and said that the Others' eyes deserved better and that she was going to find a new story, a truthful story. She hugged Tom, and as she left, his smile faded with some memory.

"You okay, Tom?" Hope asked, but he was out of words, and out of hope, and she didn't get it. How could someone with such magic be so gloomy?

"Shadow. My name is Shadow," he whispered with a broken voice.

Lifting the open palm of his hand, he waved goodbye, and he disappeared. *Puff, and, like, he was gone, nowhere to be seen.*

When Hope first saw him, she thought he was an angel, someone good, and out of her world, and that made him quite magical. Later she understood, he was God's face Down Below, and that his many miracles had some cost. She felt lucky, and so did the Others. She was no longer the only storyteller. Many wanted to share the stage, a way to address those pesky feelings about the privileged. She didn't mind. She'd been the first.

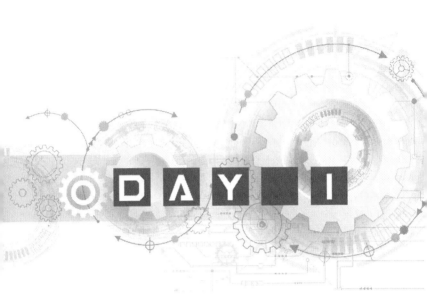

41

LEO THE SECOND

THE BOTANIC GARDENS
DAY 1 — 9:50 PM

"*Don't hurt Thorn!*" Shadow repeated for the fifth time, irking Stella a bit more each time. His head peeked out from her right shoulder, and he shouted his panic way too close to her ear.

"I'm not deaf...yet." She knocked his head lightly with her helmet.

"Sorry, my eardrums are..."

"Where's your helmet? This is going to be *extra* painful." She tapped on one of the multiple-barrel machine guns.

She was happy with her wheel choice as they cruised relatively smoothly toward the demons over badly damaged wet grass, still fuming here and there. The bike was a little too small for both of them. She didn't account for the gloomy

6. PLURIZ

God's long legs, knees constantly bumping against her bony elbows as she swerved fast.

Ahead, the horned warrior shouted, "Get him! Like, get him now!" A child-like moan reeking of madness.

Stella giggled. "'*Like, get him now?*'" She mocked, all pitchy.

Shadow gasped in Stella's ear, and it sounded even worse than all the loud moaning. "That... That's not a soulless," his voice broke a little. "That—that voice..."

The demons growled and howled and shrieked. Dead eyes, and dirty, distorted mouths, all teeth and fury. She veered the bike to the right; its handling hard and heavy.

"Where we going!?" Shadow shouted. Again. "It's *that* way." He was probably pointing at the center of the lawn, where the horned teen held Thorn.

"Flank attack," Stella said without looking back. "Never fear! My grandma taught me military strategy."

"I see..." He clearly didn't. As the spray of bullets hosed down on the demons, he stuttered. "A—are you sure th—they are soulless? Sibyl?"

The guns burned holes in the creatures, and they dropped like flies—twenty, thirty, fifty—at least that many. Some still crawled over one another, fuming and bleeding and fighting each other, all bad and increasingly mad as they screeched and rolled on the ground. *Too easy.*

"Course they are. Dead eyes, now *dead* dead," Stella said.

Wasteful with her finite ammo, she fired again. *Raa*-ka *ta*-ka *ta*-ka *taaa! Whatever!* She preferred the guns' rattling to his constant whining. Another twenty dead.

As the demons continued to drop over each other, and the grass clumps turned crimson, she swerved the bike to the left, avoiding all the bodies and heading toward Thorn.

"Keep the guns away from Thorn," said the broken record.

To their right, the rest of the demon army divided into three groups, with no more than twenty creatures each. The first dispersed toward the small forest to the right, the second closed in around the horned warrior, and the third continued to move forward toward the motorbike, swords in hand. Despite the deadly danger, none pulled out the bows still strapped to their backs.

Unable to turn the machine gun ninety degrees to shoot, Stella retreated into a long loop with demons on their tail.

"Sibyl! Are they truly soulless?" Shadow repeated. "No pain? No emotion?"

After a few beats, zie finally spoke. *All but one, my heart.*

"The funny girl with the horns?" Stella asked as they circled around the Domizien chasing them to approach the wall of demons guarding Thorn and the horned warrior.

Yes, my star, zie said.

Whoa! Twist spoke inside their heads. *From what I can see from the data patterns, something seems to synch their actions and behavior. The demon mob is acting as a single organism, except for the girl, who might be controlling them, somehow.*

"Her emotions must be guiding their empty souls," Shadow said. "Phineas Gage! Remember, Harry? We discussed this. Without emotions, the soulless can't self-regulate or make decisions effectively…so they're drawn to her."

The Somatic marker hypothesis… Twist said, sounding hesitant. *It'd be a natural evolution—tapping into a strong external emotional signal to reduce decision-making deficits.*

Stella laughed. "What evolution, dum-dum? She's getting them all killed."

Twist sighed, *Stella, let me explain—*

"Oh ship, ship, shiiippp!" Distracted by all the patronizing yammering inside her head, Stella took a moment to figure out she couldn't fire on the creatures ahead without risking Thorn's life. She glanced back at the demons closing in. *This is no good.* She took a right, gunning down the edges of the group to make way for their escape. *Raa-ka ta-ka ta-ka taaa!* "António Damásio's work?" The zombies fell to their knees. "That emotions play a central role in social cognition and decision-making? I wrote a thesis about it in sixth grade," she bragged even as she monitored their increasingly narrow escape route. "He got some things right… Shiiippp!" Instead of backing off, the horned warrior and her remaining ten goons moved forward.

Twist went dead silent for a while, probably absorbing three lost decades of scientific advancements, attempting to catch up with her brilliance. He cleared his throat. *We modified their amygdala and frontal cortex based on the information we had at that time. Anyway, minor errors aren't catastrophic. The mutation of the NTRK1 gene ensures they suffer no pain.*

"No pain. Right, Twist?" Shadow asked, fearfully.

"Maintaining truth and coherence with Up Above's biology at all costs. Too smart, Twist," Stella sneered, scanning the stinking monsters running toward them left and right. "Unwashed rags for clothes, matted hair, and ghastly open wounds all over their bodies. Robbing them of their stories, emotions, ability to feel physical pain, and blessing them with cognitive disability, psychopathic traits, and lack of fore-thought. Am I getting the definition of soulless right, Twist?"

"We didn't have a choice," whispered the suicidal God.

"Oh, I know all about your choices. Anywayyy… They'll be dead soon." Stella tapped on the gun. "This is how four thousand of your people defeated umNtwana Ziwedu kaMpande's fifteen thousand amaZulu."

"My people?" Shadow sounded offended.

"Bibi's favorite bedtime story. A reminder that controlling the technology is always the best strategy. Your strategy, right, Twist?" And before Shadow got the chance to preach at her—as she knew he would—she swerved harshly to the left to face the demons in front of Thorn and the mad girl and fired again. She had no choice. They were surrounded. Some demons in front dropped, and so did the mad girl's horse.

"Stop it, Stella!" Shadow screamed, and the scars cutting the skies told her exactly how he felt.

Thunder, then lightning, then rain and then…*then* a thin transparent veil of a psychedelic pixilated wood staircase flashed as an apparition, gone in a split of a second. *Holy ship!* She recognized her physics-bending creation. Why was her Gravizien tree-house flashing above the Botanic Gardens' lawn?

What was that? Twist asked. His voice tight as if he'd seen a ghost.

"Sibyl, what's happening?" Stella asked.

Shadow's stress is my stress, my star. His pain, my pain. Sibyl's voice trembled. Zie sounded a little distant and over-whelmed. *My worlds collapse over each other…*

"Juxtaposition?" Stella asked, wondering if Twist could hear their conversation.

"Shadow, stop stressing, or more demons will come!" Stella scowled, launching her elbow backward into his ribcage. She deflected their attention from the apparition. "According to your theory, if we kill the girl, the Domizien will stop the coordinated attack." She looked back to count the monsters chasing them. Fifteen creatures, tops. "Let's finish this."

"No!" Unexpectedly, Shadow reached over her and grabbed her hands, scrambling for control over the bike and veering to the right and then left until they crashed into a pile of dead bodies.

"What you doing?" She went down with the bike, her leg caught between the engine and a dead demon, while his body was projected forward somewhere. "Leo the second!" she cursed, and she never, ever cursed. The dead Domizien' stench almost made her puke as she pushed the motorbike away from her. "I could have ended this. For once accept the collateral damage, or we all die. Your empathy is a curse."

Tom. Tom! You okay, bud? Twist asked.

She raised her head to look for Shadow. He'd landed by the legs of the warrior's dead horse. Thorn's body—hands and ankles tied—just a step or two away.

"Thorn! Thorn! You alive?" he called as he stumbled to his feet. He kneeled down next to her, patting her bruised face and then working to untie her hands. "Stay with me, prick."

On the other side of the horse, the mad warrior pushed and pulled dead bodies as if looking for something. A sword, Stella guessed, and she grabbed the Ngulu off the ground before she sprinted in their direction.

Stella and Twist shouted simultaneously. "Shadow! Move!" *Get out of there, bud. She's coming for you!*

"Let me guess...friend," Thorn said, opening her eyes and rubbing her wrists as Shadow worked on the ropes around her legs. "You came to save me."

He chuckled, as if he were in on some inside joke, and Stella envied the sweet complicity between the ex-lovers. "Selective memory, prick?" Shadow said. "I saved you before, but who's counting," he shrugged.

"I am—counting." Thorn ran her fingers over her bruised face. "Frack, it hurts."

Tom, Twist warned as Thorn reached for a fallen sword and caught the mad girl's blade just before it chopped off Shadow's arm.

"So glad *you* came to save *me*," Thorn said, and, with both her feet still tied, she kicked into the warrior's chest plate, making the creature stumble backward, trip on a demon's body, and fall on her back. Thorn proceeded to cut the ropes around her ankles. "Wrath, don't do this," she warned. "I don't wanna hurt you."

Wrath screamed—an intense, angry, and somehow devastating howl. "Traitor!" She jumped to her feet over the pile of dead creatures, and launched at Thorn. An attack worthy of the girl's name.

For a moment, Stella had to take her eyes away from Shadow and Thorn as she reached a handful of demons standing between her and the others. She couldn't die Down Below, but pain here was as real as Up Above. She adjusted her helmet and glanced at the Ngulu, doubting her weapon of choice. The sacrificial beheading sword of her ancestors wasn't exactly a combat weapon, its utilitarian value compromised in the service of more important symbols—power, prestige, and terror. The only language Domizien understood. Subconscious signals, more useful than the functional effectiveness of one sword. She took a breath and half-committed to her decision, scooping up a fallen sword with her left hand while raising the Ngulu with her right. "Heads off!" she screamed.

The Domizien closed in on her, swords and daggers poised. She launched forward, her sword piercing a demon's heart, and reminding her of one of those cultured meat shish kebabs she used to devour after class. *Yum.* She swung the Ngulu to her right, decapitating not one but two creatures and using the momentum to spin-kick a fourth demon, knocking it out. She ducked, a sword missing her neck by a whisker before she shish kebabbed the last demon and took off toward Shadow.

Thorn was a superb swords woman, rebuffing Wrath's over-committed blows with dazzling rapidity. Once, twice, Thorn could have killed her. In all her madness, Wrath kept raging and waging too far and losing balance. Still, the creature quickly sussed Thorn's defensive strategy, and, no longer fearful of repercussions, she launched past Thorn toward Shadow. The athlete's tiny body was a weak barrier against the aggressive bean pole's armor.

Shadow didn't move or respond to his friend's over-animated requests.

Tom! What you doin'? Twist screamed. *Run! You expecting her to engage in polite conversation?*

He seemed paralyzed as he watched the horned creature. Shock or fear or something stopped him from moving.

Tom! Move!

He didn't, and Stella jumped over the horned warrior just as the girl launched at Shadow. They rolled on the ground;

Wrath scrambling for the sword as Stella grabbed her by the horns and lifted the Ngulu preparing to strike.

Thorn, get Tom out of there, Twist said. *Thorn, where you going? Stella doesn't need help.*

And before Stella could react, Thorn had kicked the Ngulu off her hand, pulling her by the helmet until she fell backward.

"What are you doing? I just saved your life," Stella said, jumping to her feet.

"Ahhh! You too, preppy?" Thorn mocked as Wrath made a run toward Shadow.

Bud! Seriously. Don't make me use a miracle to destroy that mad cow.

And somehow, Twist finally got Shadow to run away from Wrath.

42

UNFORTUNATE MIRACLES

DAY 1 — 10:35 PM

T wist held his breath as he monitored Tom's every move. Simultaneously, he ran through decades of Spiral Worlds' development searching for clues that explained the Domizien's strange behavior.

"Who's the girl?" he asked Sibyl.

"That's classified, father."

"Classified? What do you mean? I'm God!"

The clash of swords was resounding through the field. Stella and Thorn jumped hither and thither, striking wildly, each too invested on their offensive to care about a sprinting Tom who dodged demons as if he were a princely quarterback... *No, not football, basketball!* Unconsciously, Tom seemed to dribble an imaginary ball. Twist sighed. *Whatever it takes, bud.*

"You're God, but so is Stella, and she made it classified," zie finally said, the right corner of zir mouth twisting up.

"Stella!" Twist called, but Stella was too distracted with Thorn to reply.

Any time between the clangs was spent prancing and posturing—an unnecessary flick of a silver braid over the shoulder, a puff of a cigar, and an endless acrobatic showcase of useless spins and kicks and sexy pouts. Twist rolled his eyes.

"Is Stella responsible for Wrath?" Twist asked directly.

"Shadow is," Sibyl said, a mournful tone in zir voice.

Thorn followed up a blow with a lunge that got past Stella's defense, but her shorter reach failed to drive the steel home. Still, she pricked the Goddess one-inch deep near the belly button, enough to make the girl twitch and screech like a demon.

"Fun," Thorn said. "I've always wanted a dolly gal for pin cushion."

Stella fought now like a human whip, thrashing around hard and wide, and every sweep of her sword would have severed Thorn in two, if she had caught her. Thorn fluttered round her, small and nimble and cocky.

"Stella, forget her. Tom won't escape for long," Twist said.

Again and again the demons closed upon Tom, and again and again he took his imaginary basketball and dribbled it into a clear space. He zigzagged fast, dancing feet barely touching the ground, changing direction sharply and unpredictably.

"What is he doing?" Stella gasped, her hand over the bleeding wound on her stomach.

"He made varsity," Twist said.

"He made what?"

"Never mind, just help him," Twist said, monitoring the band of demons emerging from the trees in their direction. Behind Tom, Wrath pulled a dagger off her boot and aimed it at him.

"Miracle!" Twist screamed. "Miracle!" he repeated, and the dagger dropped to the ground, just as he realized what he'd done. *Fuck!*

"So logical, father." Sibyl smirked. "Why not wait until he's dead and bring him back later, when this is all over?"

Twist shook his head, punishing himself for letting emotion overrule his actions.

"She wasn't going to kill him; she was aiming for his leg," Sibyl said soberly. "Death is not her goal, never-ending pain is."

Suddenly Tom was face to face with Wrath. Twenty demons moved forward and formed a ring around them. For a beat or two, they stared at one another, Tom shuddering slightly at Wrath's mad sneer.

"Stella, who is she?" Twist asked just as he noticed the return of the apparition of the twisty staircase. The structure, made of wood and leafy at the top, emerged near the spot where Tom and Wrath faced each other, crushing a couple of demons as it materialized right where they stood. Tom sprinted up the stairs, and then down the stairs up side down. *What the heck?*

"How the hell would I know who the mad girl is?" Stella's spin-kick missed Thorn's head by a whisker. The other ducked into a low sweep and mowed down her leg. Elbows landed first, still failing to prevent her back from slamming into the gravel unearthed by the bike.

"Your…first miracle… Remember?" Sibyl said.

"Oooh, I see. Can we talk about this later?" Still on the ground, Stella gasped for air.

"The hyena ate dirt!" Thorn laughed, making a run for the bike.

Stella rolled backward to her feet, dropped the helmet on the ground, and cartwheeled forward, feet smashing into the athlete's back.

"At least I don't hide my head in the sand like an ostrich," Stella sneered as Thorn face-planted on a patch of grass. "What's with the Stockholm syndrome? I just saved your life. The life I gave you." She placed her hands on her hips and lifted her chest. All mighty, and godly, and sexy. *A young peacock,* all showy and lacking the dignity of Twist's best friend, who continued to strut up and down the trippy staircase with Wrath on his tail.

Thorn spat out dirt and sprinted toward the bike. "Cute, but no." She stopped for a moment, staring at Stella—spicy eyes and mild amusement in the curve of her bruised lips. "Just a puppet, unaware of her strings. The weakest of them all. Go back to the pageant circuit, doll."

Not quite knowing what to do with herself, Stella arranged one of her braids, an unfamiliar awkwardness taking over her posture. It was the first time Twist saw some self-consciousness in the cocky kid. "Why are you protecting that...that horned creature?" Stella asked while she glanced at Tom, who was being dragged down an upside-down flight of stairs as Wrath got ahold of his foot.

Thorn pushed on the motorbike's wheel, trying to stand it up, but the machine was too heavy for the small Latina. "We need to get him out of here, or she'll torture him to death...slowly." She kicked the machine guns several times until both dropped to the ground.

"Stockholm! Have you been?" Stella asked, racing toward Thorn.

Thorn jumped on the bike. "Hell yeah! Horses are soooo overrated."

"Don't you resent him?" Stella asked.

Vroom! Vroom! "All the fracking time!" Thorn departed toward Shadow and the horned warrior.

"Stella! Who's Wrath?" Twist asked.

"Umm... I guess she may be the Underling I brought back to life..." She flicked her braid.

"You wasted a miracle?"

"Who are you to talk?!" Stella sprinted toward the action. "I wanted to make Shadow happy. It was a surprise. A gift, really! He'd lost all hope after what he did to her. So I wanted to restore—"

"Stella..." Tom wailed, and he stopped. Stopped running. Stopped fighting. Stopped talking. He turned to face Wrath.

"Who's the girl, Sibyl?" Twist asked. "And what— How— Where is that staircase coming from and why is it defying the laws of gravity?"

"Keep your fingers crossed. It might defy more than that." Sibyl's laughter filled the lab, bouncing around inexistent walls and returning every single time to where Twist stood, slapping him in the face.

43

LIE IN IT

6. PLURIZ

THE BOTANIC GARDENS
DAY 1 — 11:19 PM

Everything was happening in slow motion. Shadow had a revelation, but he couldn't remember what it was. Searching his memory—all fog and darkness and confusion—he failed to find the answers. He was running from his shadow. He knew that much, and nothing else.

He lay on the stairs, the horned creature standing over him, gritted teeth shaded by a steel mask. A loose lock of hair—wild as fire—hanging by the corner of a rageful mouth. It meant something, *but what? What?* He shook his head.

Above them, the ground and the demons—more sores than skin—chasing him up and down the maze of stairs. Wrath screamed high and loud, in it pain, and pain, and so much pain. He felt it all. She might as well be juicing his heart with her fingers. Then came the growl of betrayal and the screech of hatred. She lifted her sword, blade pointing down, which, in fact, was up.

Harry screamed inside Shadow's head while a motor rumbled above him. Soon after, Thorn joined the chorus, but, unlike the others, she wasn't shouting at him. She wasn't fearful for him.

"Wrath. Stop!" Thorn pulled over by the side of the structure. "He made you a victim. Don't let him turn you into a villain."

All true. He did all that, but Thorn wasn't talking about herself. Or was she? There was something he knew, something important… He couldn't remember what it was.

Wrath's blade pierced his shoulder, and then his leg, and then swiped across an arm and then a leg. No blood, no pain, no severed limbs falling upwards. Probably a miracle, but his friends would soon run out of those.

Wrath howled, madness taking over. She raised her sword and struck his chest, again, and again, and again, piercing and slashing frantically, vengefully. Intact skin even as the blade cut through his heart. He closed his eyes, finding shelter from all the madness—his friends' screams, the girl's wails, and the laws of life and physics all crumbling around him. *Breathe. Just breathe.* And, as he retreated into darkness, he felt himself falling, and gravity returned to a park with no staircases, but still packed with the monsters he'd designed, flies laying eggs in the corners of their eyes. He landed on top of a pile of dead Domizien; their stench overwhelming all his senses.

"*Wrath, leave,*" Thorn said, still on the motorbike. "The passage between the worlds is closing."

Tom, Stella, good news, Harry said. *Some demons are running toward the chasm, disoriented and screeching madly. My guess is they can't stay in the upper worlds for long. The values framework that keeps them from coming up is forcing them backdown.*

Wrath jumped to her feet and lunged at him with her sword poised. Piercing his shoulder, she pinned him to the ground, and this time, the pain was unbearable. Skin and flesh tearing and drowning in blood. Thorn jumped on Wrath, wrapping her legs around the plated waist and her arm around the girl's neck. They both fell backward, the blade cutting him on the way out.

More screams—his and everyone else's. His head collapsed to one side as weakness and pain took over his entire body. Slightly delirious, he heard a voice—the only voice he wanted to hear.

"Tom," cried Nate.

Shadow turned his head to smile at the beloved hallucination.

Nate and all his people marched together toward him, just as Wrath retreated with the Domizien, outnumbered and probably spooked by all the miracles.

Tom, hang in there, buddy, Harry said. *I'm looking at a fast extraction plan.*

I'm not going anywhere, Shadow said. Too weak to say anything else.

You must.

As Shadow slowly got up, Stella and Thorn stood by him, swords in hand. His every move was an act of torture, blood gushing from the nasty gash.

"Love!" Nate screamed, but his companions held him by the arms as he tried to escape their grip. And that's when January ran toward Wrath, empty hands high up, both open.

"Remember me, honey?" Jan asked tentatively. "It's me, January. Much older, but still your friend. I still have my eyes, but I'm no longer blind to God's crimes."

Wrath wailed, all pain, and with a single hand gesture she drew Jan closer as the Domizien formed a wall in front of Jan and Wrath.

Jan stood there, without fear, whispering words in Wrath's ear. Her lips almost touching the horned helmet.

"Jan, don't do this." Nate attempted to release himself from the other men's grip. "Tom, are you okay?"

"I'm going to kill you." Stella stood tall and menacing, preparing to attack the demons. Then she glanced at Thorn. "Are you with me this time, or do I need to kill you first? Would be nice if you picked a side and stuck with it."

"Stella, wait," Shadow said, his eyes set on Nate's bloodied face. "Something's not right."

"Ahhh frack!" Thorn said, as if she was predicting what was about to happen. "Did you say something about switching sides, preppy?" Then she bumped Shadow's stomach with the back of her hand and murmured, "What's coming next won't need my sword. Over to you, friend. Do your thing."

"What?" he asked confused.

"I don't know," she shrugged. "All the words, and the brooding, and smiles, and apologies, and magic...and...stuff."

Jan waved to her people, and they all started marching toward the dark void between worlds.

"What are you doing?" Shadow screamed. His legs shook, weakened by blood loss.

January now stood by the Domizien, scowling at him. "I waited decades for you. Prayed for you. Imagined better stories and shouted them to the skies. We suffered for you...and you come back to tell us you're hopeless? That you're out of miracles?"

"Jan, don't do this." Shadow's eyes followed Nate as they dragged him in the direction of the abyss.

"Stop talking," Jan said. "We suffer and you silence his voice while you drown in your own self-pity."

"Sibyl!" Shadow screamed to the skies, cursing the universe.

You took his voice—their voice—my heart. This is not my doing.

Something inside him snapped. He let his anger toward zir fill his heart until he could feel the acrid taste of it in his mouth. *"Sibyl!"* he shouted again, and this time he got to zir —a glitch cut reality in half as pixelated noise traveled across the skies, distorting everything in its path. He lifted his hand toward Nate and the Plurizien. *"Stop!"* Shadow shouted, commanding, and a mild earthquake rumbled under their feet.

Fearful and out of balance the Plurizien stopped marching. Some dropped to their knees, praying.

"Jan," Shadow called. "Don't do this, I was having a bad day… I'm s—"

Unfazed by his power, Jan placed her hands on her hips and screamed in defiance, "You don't get to have bad days!" She spat her sing-song words. "Weak Gods, old power structures."

"Systems of oppression, fucked up cultures," the Plurizien chanted with her, some rising to their feet, overcoming their panic to stand with her.

"Please, let's go back to the Commune!" Shadow said. "It's dangerous here."

They responded in unison. "Lambs sacrificed by our divine motherfuckers. Feeding our flesh, our distress, to the vultures."

"Enrage! Engage! Enrage!" they sang, joined by Thorn, who raised her fist in the air. *"Engage! Enrage! Engage!"*

"Sorry…can't help it," Thorn said, shrugging.

"We're leaving for Ordiz and we are taking Nate with us," Jan said.

"Take me instead." His legs finally gave up, and he fell to his knees. Deep inside, his frustration turned into a storm—a tsunami waiting to burst out. Fearful of hurting his people, he held it all back, but it stirred.

"And if you don't fix the worlds," Jan warned, "I will personally deliver him to Wrath to be tortured to death. That's the deal I made with her."

Lightning struck between the Plurizien and the void. A man's top caught on fire, others rushing to help him before any major harm was done.

Still on all fours, Shadow tried to contain his panic. He took a breath and looked up. "Jan, please."

"You have five days," Jan said. "That should be long enough for you to design our freedom."

"Five days!" Stella repeated. *Sibyl, you're so predictable.*

No, my star. I predict, Sibyl said.

Predict what? Shadow asked, and the skies lit up with deadly electric sparks, charged-up pixels falling like rain, extinguishing half way down toward the ground.

Never mind, Stella said.

Farther away, Nate looked back. "Don't come for me, Tom."

Shadow lifted his hands off the ground and sat back on his heels, looking at Jan. "You wouldn't hurt him."

"I'd take a bullet for my friend. You know this. But it's not me you love, and it's not me she wants to hurt." She pointed at Wrath who made her way to the void. January dropped her head as she shouted, "A solution—evolution—or Storm's execution."

Her people chanted. "Evolution—a solution—the end of persecution."

"That's what you get when you try to silence the people's revolution," Thorn murmured, helping him to his feet. "What the hell were you thinking?"

He could have explained he did it to protect Nate from Harry —to save Nate's life and her life—but what was the point of that? "I need you by my side—to help me think," he said instead as he leaned on her to stand up.

"Put pressure on the wound or you'll bleed to death." She placed his hand over the gash, and he almost went down again.

Sibyl, find a way to get him out of there, Harry ordered.

Want me to use your last miracle for that, dad? Sibyl asked, all sassy.

No. Shadow said, looking ahead. Most of the demons had disappeared into the void, only Wrath and a few others remained by the worlds' portal. He took a breath and started walking toward Nate. Thorn kept him on his feet every time he stumbled. "Thank you, my friend. My hero," he said. Then he looked back, noticing Stella and Jan walking behind him. "Stella, stay back." His assertiveness took the girl by surprise, wide eyes followed by a sigh and then a sullen pout.

Stella stopped following him. "I'm the hero. The only one here trying to protect you," she murmured her disappointment. "Stop messing about and lead from the front."

"The kid has a point," Thorn said, and Stella replied with a long, *long* laundry list of reasons why she wasn't a kid.

Leadership—they were looking to him for it. He'd let them all down, even so, divided, they waited for him to lead. The heart was the fuel and the glue, and whether or not he liked it, he was Spiral Worlds' heart. Purpose, values, emotions bringing people together to drive change. In his youth, he had leaped at the opportunity to inspire a progressive movement. Decades later, battered and bruised by life and death, they resurrected him to save the worlds—the wrong story. A story doomed to fail. To keep the Underlings subdued, Sibyl had turned his life into a trope—the chosen one. But, he was no longer playing zir games. He was going to rewrite the story and if he had to choose a helpful, hopeful trope, he'd pick *found family*. He would reunite with his friends and then, together, they'd save the worlds. As he considered all options, he knew only he could lead, for now. By his side, he had the most overqualified group of overachievers—his family. All outstanding in their own fields; all with little in common; some forever divided by irreconcilable differences.

As Shadow reached Nate and the Plurizien, the men around his poet took a step back, releasing Nate's arms. Shadow attempted to hide the extent of his injury, blinking a smile at Nate.

"You're bleeding heavily," Nate said. His voice broken.

"Shhh." Shadow cupped Nate's head with both hands and leaned in until their foreheads touched. "Listen to me. Just listen." Shadow's fingers grazed Nate's hair, and the poet's body softened, shivering ever so slightly. "*You* are not your worst moments. Whatever happened that day. The harm you caused… I'm not going to let it define you, and neither are you."

"Tom, I'm a murderer." Guilt coated Nate's every word. "There's no redemption for what I did."

Shadow stared into Nate's eyes, holding his anxious burning gaze. "You are Nathan Storm, and you and I are going to work together to fix the worlds, and save lives, and eliminate suffering, and don't try to fight me on this. Don't push me away. I can't do it without you. Do you understand?"

"Tom, I can't," Nate whispered.

"I'm sorry I tried to silence you. Use your voice. Do what you do best. I trust your judgment."

"You do?" Nate's voice vibrated. His insecurity out in the open.

"I believe in you, Natan Storm." And as he gave Nate what he'd granted to all Earthlings—hope and a second chance—he was grateful for someone else's silence, knowing fully well he was hurting Harry.

Nate whispered, "Tom, Sibyl predicts—"

The skies roared. "I don't care about Sibyl's hot takes," Shadow said definitively, "and neither should you. Zie doesn't create the future, *we do*." He looked back at Jan and took her hand into his, just as he placed his arm around Nate's shoulders. Pain spiked from his injured shoulder up his neck, and into his skull, almost knocking him out. He shook it off. "I can't create the future on my own, Jan. I need Nate, and Harry, and Thorn, and Stella, and you, and your people. I wasn't ignoring your plea; I was learning from my mistakes. You don't need to blackmail me and hurt the man who's been fighting for all of you."

Jan looked at Wrath intensely and shook her head. This time a clear *no* rather than her usual vague head wobble. "I made a pact and I'll keep it," Jan said, never looking into his eyes. "Stay alive and design our freedom, or my dearest friend will die the most horrible of deaths."

"Jan, even when I died, I never gave up on you. I was trying to improve things," he said. He glanced at Thorn, who nodded, confirming his statement. "I can tell you all about it, in time. Don't do this. I've never abandoned you, and *I never will*."

January looked into his eyes, her gaze filled with fear, and love, and disappointment. Then her eyes landed on Wrath and projected wrath. "That's not true, is it?" And his heart dropped to his feet. There was something he knew. Something he struggled to surface. How could he lead? He shouldn't lead. His mind attacked him—mad and overwhelmed and self-destructive. Years of punishing contrast under his skin, no bleach strong enough to cleanse it.

"You have betrayed us and can't be trusted," she said, taking his hand to her mouth and kissing it. "Nate and I will be in Ordiz. He'll be monitored day and night. He will never be alone. Your love will be safe from our people and from yours." She blinked her reassurance with her bright almond-shaped eyes, tilting her head from side to side, even as she threatened the life of her closest friend. "For five days, everyone will cherish him there as we did here. If you need us, you know where to find us. We will work with you as long as you do our bidding." And with that statement, the Plurizien started marching, two men holding Nate's arms and dragging him away from Shadow.

"Tom, I love you," Nate said. "Keep away." Then, he looked at Thorn, distraught, and he murmured, "Don't you fucking hurt him."

"I love you, Stormy," Shadow replied holding a tsunami inside, knowing fully well it was a killer storm. *He's safe for now,* he reassured himself, but he wouldn't let Nate go like that. He sprinted into his arms, wrapping himself around Nate's shoulders, ignoring the pain and the blood and the numbness taking over his body. His poet yanked his arms from the Underlings, and pulled him closer, his hungry lips parting in anticipation, never daring to make the first move. Shadow brushed his lips against Nate's lower lip, the poet's beard grazing his skin and sending shivers down his spine. Then he went deeper, and Nate drew him in, claiming his mouth—urgent and intense—even as the Underlings grabbed him by the arms and took him away. Shadow's fingers caressed a strand of long flaming hair as it left his hand.

Shadow stood there, breathing heavily, watching them leave.

"Storm's voice is a weapon," Stella said. "We can't let them take him."

They don't know it, Harry said, *but it's likely the platform is nudging them down the spiral. Everything they've been doing lately stinks of Ordizien dogma and self-righteousness.*

Shadow nodded. Harry's words resonated with him. Travelers, too, were directed to the worlds they needed. It was likely that Nate, just like his people, was being lured into Ordiz.

One of the Plurizien—a round faced man—stayed behind and approached Shadow, holding a Domizien dagger to the side of his body. His receding hairline glimmered, sweat dripping over his eyes. It was Hepius, the healer.

"Stop," Stella shouted, running toward them, blood-stained sickle sword lifted high over her head. Shadow raised his hand, asking her to hold. Hepius's stocky body quivered slightly. Shadow couldn't read him, not fully. Despite the weapon he held, the man's bearing projected gentleness, and something about his expression revealed that rare place where anger and desperation intersect.

Hepius's bleeding arms confirmed Shadow's assessment and revealed the final ingredient—deep hopelessness—an old friend.

Shadow stepped forward. "Hep—"

"Damn you." Fear and spite raging inside Hepius's eyes. "I'm living in a story already written. For once, I'll make my bed and lie in it."

Before Shadow could reply, Hepius slashed his own neck open, blood gushing red and defiant as his body collapsed by Shadow's feet.

"Hepius! No!" Nate cried from afar. *"Tom, help him. Please help him."*

Jan screamed, running madly toward them. "Bring him back." She sunk her knees into the growing crimson lake that framed Hepius's lifeless body.

You'd have to use your last miracle, Stella spoke inside his head. *But, it's a chance to remind them all you are a worthy, benevolent God. A chance to refresh your brand.*

Don't you dare waste another miracle, Harry said.

"You owe him! Bring him back," Jan demanded with none of the reverence she'd once bestowed on him. He'd be proud of her if less were at stake. If her justified rebellion didn't threat Nate's life. His eyes set on Hepius as memories of his own struggles with life flashed in front of his eyes.

The dark clouds gathered over him—a layered tower, increasingly dark and menacing. First came a few welcomed droplets that cooled his feverish skin, and then the sky wept for Hepius.

He held back the pointless scream pounding on his chest. "Bring him back to what? To a hopeless life he can't control?"

Shadow dropped to one knee and held Hepius's hand. "Where I come from, they used to say people died by suicide because it's a disease. Portrayed as helpless victims to the end." He struggled to breathe. Crimson blood and rainwater trickling down his arm to mix with Hepius's blood; a reminder of thousands of contrast-making experiences predicting the worst of humankind. Each one forever burned in his memory. The cost of heaven horrifically high.

Above him, the clouds gained speed, wind gusts shaping them into an air column curling and twisting ferociously and reaching down from the sky.

Tom, your vital signs are deteriorating. You're losing a lot of blood, Harry said.

"You feel you're in hell." Water dripped from his hair to his face and down his neck. "That the universe is conspiring to hurt you, and everybody calls you insane, but perhaps you're not so mad, because sometimes it feels like death is the only thing you can control, until you realize even that's a lie. I won't do that to him. Not now." The skies roared and, one by one, the violent rotating tower uprooted the trees at the edge of the lawn, making way toward them.

Noticing the twister, Jan stood up, her face red as she wiped the tears with her blood-stained hands. She turned to Shadow and slapped his face with the strength of her entire body, then she brought her lips to his forehead and kissed it. "Pull yourself together. We'll fight your Gods and universe if we have to. Nothing will stop us. You have five days." She ran toward her people, waving her arm toward the void as the tornado dissipated in the skies.

He stayed there, holding a dead man's hand, watching the mob drag Nate toward the darkness as the last few Domizien waited for their turn to cross. From the distance, Wrath's attention was still set on him; a creature, standing by a scar in the fabric of a made-up reality. He could no longer ignore the knowledge lingering deep inside his subconscious mind. He couldn't, he shouldn't escape his shadow.

By his side, Stella manipulated a dead Domizien's body to release the creature's bow and pull an arrow from his quiver.

"Feisty pants!" Stella flashed a smile at Thorn. "You think you're the only skilled Olympian here?"

Stella jumped to her feet, and aimed. Her arrow set on Nate.

"Stella!" Shadow roared, and he failed to recognize his voice —deep, and commanding, and out of these worlds.

The storm and the earth joined him in a chorus so loud and destructive that Stella lost her balance as the ground shook beneath her feet and the wind threatened to take her away. Stella staggered, inadvertently shooting the arrow toward Wrath. A move that sealed the horned warrior's fate.

Thorn screamed, and fueled by her panic, the revelation emerged fast in Shadow's mind, like a punch in the gut delivered by a steel rod. He knew who Wrath was, and the miracle was invoked even before he'd become conscious of his resolution. The arrow dissolved as it approached Wrath's right eye. The girl turned around and disappeared into the void, and so did Nate and Jan.

Tom, what have you done? Harry moaned.

Shadow stood up and held Stella's bow, taking it from her. "Where's your heart, Stella? I know you have one." He spoke to her like an older brother—a friend.

"I did." She shrugged. "It's not useful." She played with her braid, absentmindedly. "From your failures, I learned it's best to pick a side. I won't lose my mind or my life, and I'll make things better for all by not chasing perfection or parity."

Shadow pressed his lips together, holding back on any preaching.

"Nate is off limits." He looked her straight in the eyes, and she nodded awkwardly. "I want to learn from you, little star. Thank you for what you did today," he said, all supportive, as Harry released an exasperated sigh inside their heads.

Are you kidding me?

"Sure." Stella raised her nose high. "I'm the strongest and most evolved of us all. The queen on the chessboard. So…"

Shadow almost smiled, amused by her infinite confidence. "You fought so bravely, but you're bleeding. Go Up Above to reset your body. I'll meet you at the lab real soon."

No, bud, you're going to jump now, get yourself patched up.

"Stella, Harry, I need a moment," Shadow said, glancing at Thorn who was still gawking at Stella with a mix of amusement and defiance.

You need a moment? Harry repeated, annoyed. *You screw us over, and now you need a moment. Typical!*

"Wrath is not the villain," Shadow said. *We are,* he kept that thought to himself. "Twist, permissions revoked in thirty seconds." A slight hint of assertiveness in his tone. "There's nothing else to do here."

Tom, that wound! Harry admonished.

Soon, Shadow said.

Stella inspected her wound and then released a frustrated sigh. "Anyone watching, Sibyl?" she asked, throwing a dirty look at Thorn before she disappeared.

Don't do anything foolish, Harry said.

"I won't, my dear friend."

Over and out, for now.

Shadow stood up and hinted a faint smile at Thorn with his eyes.

She patted her back pocket, probably looking for a cigar. "Frack," she said, giving up on the search. She looked up, meeting his eyes. "You know?"

"Umm… I guess so. Not sure how…"

Thorn glanced at Hepius's dead body, her face declining a request he hadn't made. "I won't kill you—"

"No, you won't. We've got to bring parity to the worlds."

"You…want *us* to fix the worlds?" She chuckled, and then she went silent, a somber look in her eyes. "Listen," she finally said. "I only told January about what happened to the girl to be able to return to the lower worlds. I tried to explain the circumstances of her death. That in some ways, I too am responsible… That you were trying to fix things, but from their perspective—"

"I know… We created a zero-sum game. They are on the losing side."

"Mostly," Thorn snapped.

Darkness took over his mind—a need to cut his skin to maintain the illusion of control. He touched his wound, craving the pain blasting through him like a poisonous spear. His teeth shattered as blood abandoned his body.

An impossible task; a lifetime of failure; a desire to die.

He shook his head. "Rosa, I need your help. You've heard them. We've got five days."

"My help?" Her voice was all pitchy. "Leave me out of your politics." She headed toward the motorbike.

He reached to grab her arm, his blood staining her skin. "Looks like you are as invested…if not more." His hand slid to take her hand.

She shivered. "You're freezing."

"I can't do it without you."

"How can you say that?" She yanked her hand away. "You know nothing about—"

"No, I don't, but you are going to tell me, right? We're going to make things right."

She jumped on the bike. Motor roaring even before she was fully seated. "Until you decide you can't, and—"

"No. I'm breaking the habit, Rosa. You have my word."

Her quiet chuckle told him she didn't believe him. *Vroom! Vroom!*

"Please, don't give up on me. They need us—all of them—Nate, the Underlings, and…Hope." He finally said her name and his throat burned, acid rising to his mouth. She shut off the motor.

"Wrath. That's all she is now."

Thorn's confirmation sucked the air off his lungs. "I-I can't erase the past, but I won't give up on her future."

"Why me?"

He dropped his head. "You…understand both sides of this equation—the ledger, always red, no matter what we do. You're Switzerland."

"Not Stockholm?" She rolled her eyes and got off the bike.

"What? Anyway, you'll kill me if you have to."

She smiled. "Yeah!" With her fingers, she opened the tear on his T-shirt to look at the wound, exposing it to the weather. He winced. She smiled and raised a bruised brow. "Aren't you out of miracles?"

He was. "I have other capabilities…" Not that he could control the chaos unleashed by his emotions.

The storm was dissipating and the moon peeked through the clouds.

"Super powers?" She smirked, punching his stomach lightly. "Not sure how your good looks will help us bring fairness to the worlds. Your charms don't even work on the Underlings anymore."

"'What is essential is invisible to the eye,'" he said, quoting an old book he loved.

"He's back," she whispered, a glimmer of emotion in the corner of her eye.

"We can do this, prick." He squeezed her hand. "I know we can. We'll bring back Hope. The worlds need hope. " Somehow, Shadow believed in his delusion, and so did she.

He glanced at Hepius's body. *I'll come back for you. You'll have your freedom in a fairer world.* Then, still holding Thorn's hand, he spoke. "Sibyl, take us to the lab."

"Ah, I forgot about the others," Thorn said, rolling her eyes. "It's going to be a shit show, you know?"

"Yeah, I know. Be nice, prick."

"Who? Me?" she said, batting her long lashes. "I'm practically miss congeniality."

THE END

Spiral Worlds, Volume II - Parity - Preview available in the next pages.

PREVIEW — PARITY

1. DOWN BELOW

CITY BAR — THE CITY
THIRTY-TWO YEARS EARLIER — 10 JANUARY 2036

S hadow's heart skipped a beat, and then he judged her—his shield against the exquisite predator striding toward him. She wasn't one of them; she stood out with her prying eyes and overeager scrutiny of her surroundings.

The gloomy bar, filled with smoke, smelled like ash, booze, and old, worn-out leather. Patrons were scattered about the place, some drinking alone, lost in their hopelessness, others numb and lonely as they gathered in small groups and engaged in shallow chatter.

Life sparked in her chestnut-colored eyes—two beams of light amongst a sea of empty gazes sunken by broken promises, shattered hopes, and catastrophic failures. She scanned the room, her eyes squinting under the weight of her persistent brows, searching, probing for a way to benefit from their misfortune.

He despised her, them—the travelers from Up Above. Visitors ready to break hearts and minds to attain a much-desired life experience. Contrast and perspective were the expected outcomes of her adventure. Both currencies he traded in at an impossible cost.

Shadow threw one more side glance at the dark and wild curls that bounced around her heart-shaped face. A defiant lock dangled in front of her nose, and he followed its twists and turns, entranced by its rhythm. She caught him and smiled with the bold self-confidence of those who know how to game the game.

Abruptly, he turned his back to her—*to protect her*.

He caught his lie even before the thought was fully formed. *It was partially true.* In his current state of mind, he would unleash his anger on any human. He too wished he could travel carelessly to a place where he would experience contrast. Something so terrible it would put his current torment into perspective.

"I bet you've been waiting all day to meet me." Sunny pitch, spicy tone, bold rhythm. A few words gave away the traveler's temperament—shoot and point, speak and think, in that order. Flying by the seat of her commando-style pants, she was all instinct and intuition—no mercy, no malice, no regrets for the trail of devastation left behind. She was stormy weather, raging against the shore. He knew it well, that roaring tempest, and he still loved it fiercely.

He brushed off the hurtful memories of a love lost and turned his head toward her, the rest of his body refusing to follow. He froze, scared of the possibilities, of the pain that awaited around the corner. She blew aside the wayward curl, a serious yet hopeless attempt to fight nature and gravity. The creature wrinkled her nose as the wave bounced back with a vengeance, tickling. She had him. He smiled and turned fully to face her piercing inquisition. He was at her mercy for the whole second it took for him to realize he had fallen captive to deliberate action.

"Lost for words? I have that effect on people." The predator stared at him, beaming, and this time, his heart came to a full stop before it galloped off toward nowhere. "Never mind." She moved along, locking her sights on her next victim. Perspective, he had none to keep; he'd given it all away to someone he loved dearly.

"Wait." The word flew out of his lips before he could stop it. It was a silent scream, barely noticeable amid the hustle and bustle of the bar. His whisper reached its target. She stopped and, as she turned, her eyes landed on his wrists. Countless cuts and scars marked his skin for all the souls he had destroyed to serve people like her. Her mouth twisted in disgust, and then she ignored him and moved along swiftly, choosing to discard the broken thing that would surely ruin her experience with his sorrow. *Who is she?*

The creature pulled a cigar from the back pocket of her trousers. Then she turned to lean back against the bar, scanning the crowd. In a flash, two lighters and a drink appeared in front of her face. The huntress inspected her suitors as she rolled the cigar against her fingers. Then her eyes, like spears, turned to him. Without ever losing her grip on his attention, she bit into the cigar and spat the end toward one of her victim's shoes.

She took a sip of the golden-colored malt and licked her lips. It was an irresistible dare, designed to bring him to his knees. Her face had a sensual, bewitching glow, lit by the flames that surrounded her. She was in her element—in and around fire —a stark contrast with his natural darkness. *No, not intrinsic. Acquired. Learned.* Still, forever part of his being. He remembered he'd been bright and hopeful, once, *an eternity ago.*

The creature smiled through gritted teeth, dangling the cigar in the corner of her whiskey-laced lips. She accepted the light but rejected the surrounding company. Then she exhaled from the edge of her mouth and, with one finger, she summoned him. He vacillated. *What part am I to play in your experience? Who is pulling the strings?*

He was Down Below's chief experience maker, co-creator, orchestrator, and guardian. He wasn't a pawn to be deployed in the service of the travelers. He shuddered, feeling out of balance; she was clearly from Up Above, but unlike the other travelers, he couldn't read her. He failed to sense her needs or struggles.

The platform had reached four billion travelers less than a month before. He monitored their desires, their fears, and their darkness. He could spot the wickedness needing to be exorcised by Down Below. Shadow could feel them all except the one standing right in front of him. *Who are you, and what are you doing here?* His thoughts raced ahead of his feet as he walked toward her. Resistance was futile.

"I don't have time for prickly bullies. Make it quick and pain-less, will you, honey? What do you want?" He recoiled at the harshness of his own words, a sharpness received with indif-ference and exhaled in a cloud of smoke right back at his face.

"You a good fuck? All that brooding indignation must be good for something," she barked.

By the end of the night, no more words had been exchanged, but the question had been decisively answered. Once on the bar's toilet, twice in the driverless car, and countless times in the comfort of his bed. Explosive, urgent, addictive tender-ness coated in unnerving familiarity. They devoured each other with unyielding conviction, and then she left.

Parity, Spiral Worlds Volume II.

SCAN NOW TO PRE-ORDER!

Printed in Great Britain
by Amazon

13915696R00251